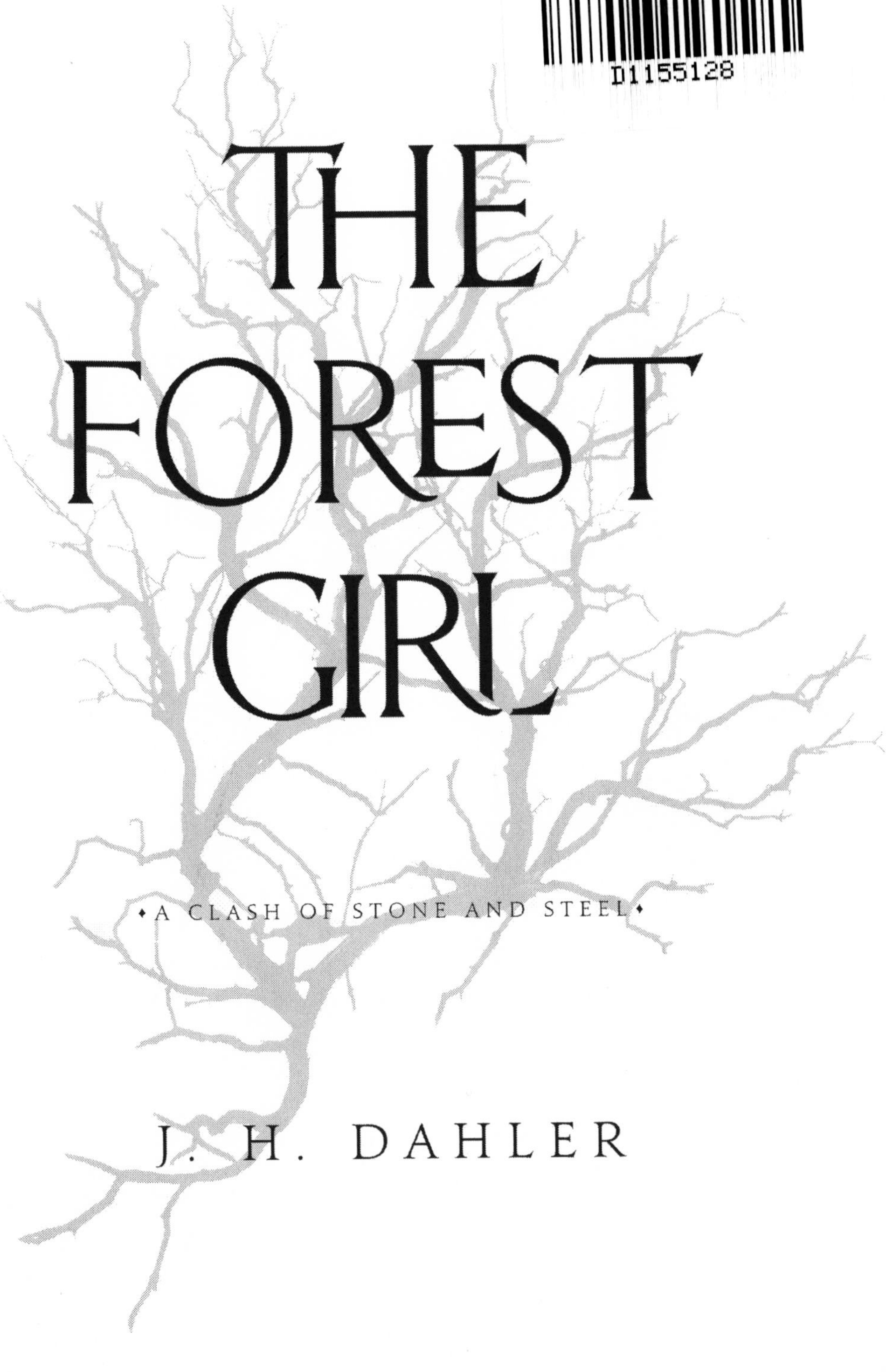

THE FOREST GIRL

A CLASH OF STONE AND STEEL

J. H. DAHLER

The Forest Girl
First edition, September 2022

Cliff Dancer Publishing LLC
Nottingham, MD
jhdahler.com

Proofreading: Shayla Raquel, shaylaraquel.com
Cover Design & Interior Formatting: Miblart, miblart.com
Map Design: Moor Books Design, moorbooksdesign.com

ISBN: 978-1-7371683-0-0 (paperback)

This book is dedicated to my family.
Thank you for believing in me
from the very beginning.

Sandamedan Empire
and Surrounding Territories
Desert
YAYIDAN LANDS
ABTUZO
SARPASKA
ULMENTU
Eastern Sea
Western Sea
SANDAMEDA
Tarven River
VALDERN
ISHTIA
CYBELON
TELETMOORA
Silver Sea
GALEED
FOREST LANDS
Raleah Lake
FORT OVANDIS
Charpan Wastelands
CHARPA
ZURPESH

Nations/Provinces

Charpa	Kingdom south of Galeed
Cybelon	Town on the border of Galeed and Sandameda
Forest people	Hunter gatherers whose lands border the Sandamedan Empire
Fort Ovandis	Imperial army fort on border of Charpan wastelands
Fort Renvivis	Imperial army fort in Sarpaska
Galeed	Southern province of Sandamedan Empire
Ishtia	Capital city of Sandameda
Mar Dun	Forest village
Sandamedan Empire	Consists of Sandameda, Galeedan, and Sarpaskan provinces
Sarpaska	Northern province of Sandamedan Empire
Teletmoora	Kingdom across the Silver Sea
Valdern	Sandamedan city on coast of Silver Sea; Mattos's home city
Wanderers	Nomadic merchants
Yayida	People who live in the desert north of Sandameda
Zurpesh	Capital city of Charpa

Characters

Achi	Merchant that Mattos's father has traded with for years
Alanna	Elmaturis's wife
Alentor	Officer serving in imperial army (Falcon rank)
Alistes	Sandamedan soldier serving in imperial army (Owl rank)
Anwyn	Galeedan woman
Anundi	Sarpaskan soldier serving in imperial army
Balen	Sandamedan soldier serving in imperial army
Barsis	Officer serving in imperial army (Falcon rank)
Beldos	Officer serving in imperial army (Osprey rank); second-in-command of Hawk
Borus	Sandamedan soldier serving in imperial army
Brense	Ulek's dog
Cylin	Lucen's wife
Daneen	Derk's younger sister
Darius	Officer serving in imperial army (Falcon rank); Beldos's nephew
Derk	Galeedan boy
Diakiris	Officer serving in imperial army (Harrier rank); commanding officer to Mattos
Edar	Lucen's horse

Ekil	Desert fox; Sarpaskan folk hero
Elgust	Leader of Charpan band; son of Amelger of the Moon clan
Elmaturis	Officer serving in imperial army (Falcon rank)
Esnin	Merciful Galeedan goddess
Evendos	Sandamedan soldier serving in imperial army
Imari	Sandamedan goddess of women and fertility
Isandor	Eagle; commander of the imperial army
Jefton	Galeedan soldier serving in imperial army
Kiri	Forest girl
Kordrick	Galeedan soldier serving in imperial army
Ladius	Sandamedan soldier serving in imperial army
Layna	Servant girl; Mattos's first love
Lentavus	Renowned Sandamedan artist
Lido	Forest man; Kiri's first mate
Livius	Sandamedan god of industry
Lucen	Officer serving in imperial army (Falcon rank); son of Haventar and Vian
Marenda	Wife of Mattos (deceased)
Matron Calla	Derk's mother
Mattos	Officer serving in imperial army (Falcon rank)
Meadow	Forest Woman

Mekindu	Sarpaskan soldier serving in imperial army (Owl rank)
Nevtu	Sarpaskan soldier serving in imperial army
Nika	Mattos's horse
Nuendos	Sandamedan soldier serving in imperial army
Odern	Sandamedan god of war
Oistin	Officer serving in imperial army (Falcon rank)
Omeldor	Sandamedan physician serving in imperial army
Orrik	Galeedan who once served in the imperial army; Ulek's father
Orston	Galeedan soldier serving in imperial army
Ortid	Sandamedan blacksmith
Ozias	Sandamedan soldier serving in imperial army
Ria	Diakiris's wife
Wren	Friend of Kiri; her second mate
Stavis	Sandamedan soldier serving in imperial army
Tengish	Horde
Thais	Officer serving in imperial army (Hawk rank)
Thulu the Revered	Sarpaskan mystic
Ulek	Orphaned Galeedan boy

Table of Contents

Chapter 1

KIRI

The crowd gathered in rows around the bonfire, the scent of woodsmoke seeping into hair and clothing. Elders perched on logs in the front while the rest of the villagers sat on the ground behind them. Kiri walked along a row as she searched for an open spot. She would have preferred to remain with her family farther back, but the elders had insisted she sit near the front should they need her to speak. She pulled her fur cloak higher, as much to block stares as to shield herself from the early spring chill. As one of the few adults to survive the attack on Mar Dun, she attracted curious gazes from the new arrivals. An older woman caught her eye and scooted to the right as she patted the ground beside her. With a grateful nod, Kiri settled next to her.

People repositioned themselves, coughed, shushed crying babies, but none spoke. Over fifty years had passed since the elders of every village had gathered. It had taken months of messages and planning to get them to Wolf Village. They'd begun to arrive after the last snow melted. Once assembled, the elders had deliberated in private for days. A few times, they'd summoned survivors, Kiri among them, to give their personal accounts. Now they had reached a consensus and called for an audience. Anticipation rose off the crowd like heat.

Cida, an elder of Wolf Village, stood, her diminutive size belied by her commanding presence. Her white hair brushed her shoulders. Like many her age, she still wore her full winter furs, a long necklace of blue and green beads her only adornment. She gazed over the crowd, most of them from her own village, many her kin and direct descendants. Finally, she spoke.

"Two years ago, the Sandamedans came to us with gifts. They wanted passage through our lands so they could wage war on Charpa. They used the sea, but the Charpans build better ships and fight better on water. The Sandamedans wanted to send armed soldiers through our forest, where we hunt, fish, and live so they could reach their enemy by land. Countless soldiers. What if the Charpans sent their own warriors? How long until war broke out between them in our lands? We could not allow it, yet they came into our lands anyway. Since then, we have been at war. One year ago, they attacked Mar Dun." The wrinkles on her forehead deepened as her eyebrows drew together and up. Cida bowed her head, her lips parting in a silent scream.

The sight of the old woman's naked grief brought the sting of unshed tears to Kiri's eyes. Memories of the attack assailed her. The blood and screams. The people killed. Wren, standing so tall and defiant. And then… Kiri touched the left side of her face, her fingers sliding over the deep scar that ran from the outer corner of her eye to the corner of her mouth. A soldier had nearly half blinded her that day. In her mind's eye, Kiri saw Wren's mischievous smile when they played together as children. She saw him as they lay together in the forest, two days before the attack. Wren, who had been so full of life, now dwelt in the spirit world. A painful sob lodged in her throat. She clenched her teeth against it. Not here. She'd given in to grief for over a year. Now was the time for vengeance.

Cida drew a shaky breath and seemed to recover herself. "They attacked and spared no one. All in the village that day who still live survived because they escaped." Her gaze shifted to where Meadow sat holding her sleeping baby, and all eyes followed. Meadow's round face, once full of mirth, appeared expressionless. She looked ahead with blank eyes, as if unaware hundreds of people stared at her. She'd lost so much that day: her mate, siblings, mother, aunts, uncles, and friends. With Kiri's help and protection, she'd saved her children and her siblings' children. Pregnant and close to her time, she had managed to reach Wolf Village. She and the babe survived the birth soon after, but it became apparent her spirit was damaged. She never laughed or smiled and seldom spoke. Instead, she focused her diminished will to live on caring for her baby.

A friend in Wolf Village and her siblings had adopted Meadow as a sister and taken her and the children in. Meadow nursed her baby, kept the children clean, and sometimes sewed and mended clothes but could do little else. Kiri had heard from Meadow's new siblings that she didn't hunt, fish, gather plants, or prepare food. She showed affection for the children and comforted them but never guided or instructed them. The siblings were even hesitant to leave Meadow alone with the baby. They feared she might ignore a cry or fail to notice an injury or illness.

Lost in thought, it took Kiri a few moments to realize Cida and everyone else were staring at her.

"We owe our thanks to Kiri for protecting the other survivors and leading them here," Cida said.

Kiri bowed her head, unsure if or how she should respond.

"We are grateful for those who survived," Cida said, "and mourn the dead. But now we must act." Her voice rose, rage superseding grief. "They entered our lands even after we refused them. They burned down our trees and attacked us without mercy or provocation." She paused, making eye contact with those close enough. "Our main concern is, and always has been, the protection of our people." She gestured at the group of elders sitting nearby. "The Council of Elders knows the non-Forest, especially the Sandamedans, are dangerous. We have deliberated on what we must do to protect our people. If we don't respond, they will think us weak, and it will only encourage them to attack further. We fight them when they come into our lands. We have killed many, but more come. It is time for us to attack them in their own lands."

Murmurs broke out.

"When the Sandamedans know we can attack them where they live, that there are consequences to their actions, they'll fear us. The cost of waging war against us will be too high. They'll find another route to Charpa." Cida turned toward the council and held out a hand, beckoning someone.

A middle-aged man rose and came to stand beside Cida, towering over her. He wore his long black hair half pulled back, revealing shell earrings dangling from his ears. He'd donned his best clothing for the occasion, leather tunic and trousers dyed a brownish red and decorated with wood beads along the hem. Having been declared an elder only a few years ago, he still possessed the vigor of his prime. He was Ash, Kiri's sire.

"This is Ash's plan," Cida said. "He is the one to explain it." She made her way back to her place on a log by the fire.

Ash waited for Cida to get settled before he spoke. "You know we tracked and killed most of the soldiers who attacked Mar Dun, but you don't know what one of them told us before he died. We tortured him for information and gave him the ulnu root to make it harder to think of a lie. He gave the names of the two men who escaped and told us where we could find them. Orrik and Kordrick. Both are Galeedan and don't live far from the border. We will send an assassin to kill these men. Their crimes are worthy of death."

Several in the crowd murmured their assent, nodding.

Expression grim, Ash reached behind him and withdrew a knife from under his belt. He held it aloft. "Steel," he said. "We traded with the Wanderers for it. The assassin will use this blade to kill Orrik and Kordrick. And when they are dead, the assassin will find Isandor, commander of the imperial army, and kill him too."

Gasps rang out. A low hum of hushed voices spread through the gathering.

"Isandor wasn't in Mar Dun," Ash continued. "He didn't commit the soldiers' crimes, but he *is* responsible. He is their army's leader. He sent the soldiers here. He knows they've set fire to our forest, that they've attacked us. When we kill Isandor, their army will be leaderless. There will be confusion. But they must know it was the Forest people who killed him, so they realize crimes against us will not go unpunished. That is why the assassin must use this knife. They will take personal items from Orrik's and Kordrick's bodies. They will leave the knife embedded in Isandor's body and place the personal items taken from Orrik and Kordrick on him. When the Sandamedans see the Forest-styled knife handle and the items from Orrik and Kordrick, they'll know the Forest people were responsible for all three deaths."

Kiri's heart pounded as an energy that had long lain dormant surged through her. After over a year of shock, grief, and anger, her people would finally respond to the horrors committed in Mar Dun. They would bring the fight to the Sandamedans. A fluttering sensation filled her stomach.

"The time has come," Ash said as he tucked the knife in his belt, "to choose the assassin. Whoever goes must be a proven warrior, someone who has shown courage, endurance, cunning, and a strong will." He walked along the open space between the fire and the crowd, his eyes searching faces. "Many of you are warriors who have traveled a great distance to be here today. Perhaps you suspected the Council of Elders would make a decision that would require warriors. Know that there is little chance of returning home. To find and kill Isandor will be difficult, but to kill him and survive, avoid pursuit, and travel home safely…" Ash shook his head. "There is great honor in carrying out the will of our people, in protecting Forest lands, but also great sacrifice. Knowing this, who among us will volunteer?"

Necks craned as the villagers looked around. People shifted and cleared their throats. Then a voice rose from the center of the crowd. "I!"

A tall man Kiri didn't recognize stood with his broad shoulders back, eyes intent. His hair fell in a thick braid down his back. His large, muscular arms negated any question of his strength.

"Who is he?" Kiri whispered to the older woman beside her.

"A great warrior from Salamander Village far to the north. He has killed many soldiers."

Before Kiri could reply, another voice rang out, "I will go!"

All eyes turned to the middle-aged woman who now stood. Kiri gasped when she recognized Jaya, a hunter and warrior of Wolf Village and mother of one of Kiri's best friends. More warriors volunteered, most of them from distant villages. Kiri studied them, wondering who the elders would choose, when her gaze fell on Meadow.

Meadow's usual blank stare had transformed into one of rapt attention. Lips parted, she clutched her baby close. She looked from one volunteer to another, her eyes conveying an almost frantic concern. Did she disapprove of the council's decision? Or did the choice of volunteers not satisfy her?

The memory of Meadow struggling through the forest, her pregnant belly protruding before her, came to Kiri. Meadow had been overcome with grief, shock, and terror, yet had made the long, arduous journey to Wolf Village. She'd gritted her teeth and continued on, determination to save her children and her nieces and nephews driving her. Despite all she had lost, she'd made Kiri stop so she could bandage her face. She had been the one to urge the children forward, saying what they needed to hear to keep them moving. At times she carried the youngest ones on her back or in her arms. Kiri had forged ahead unburdened, keeping her bow at the ready, lest more soldiers attacked them. So many villagers perceived Meadow as weak, as a victim. They only knew her in the aftermath of loss and trauma. They hadn't witnessed her strength.

At that moment, Kiri realized the assassin had to be someone from Mar Dun, or who had survived the attack. The outsiders and Jaya hadn't seen the atrocities. They didn't truly understand. But who was there? Most of the survivors were children who'd escaped into the forest while the adults stayed behind to defend the village. There was an old woman who'd fled, carrying her infant grandchildren, and three children a few years from adulthood who'd guided younger children into the trees. And Meadow and Kiri.

Kiri rose without thinking, as if her body decided for her. Her furs slipped from her shoulders, letting the crisp air penetrate her tunic and trousers.

Ash frowned. "Kiri? Do you wish to speak? You were there, after all."

Kiri swallowed and lifted her chin. "I will go. I will kill those men, as I have the most right. It must be someone linked to Mar Dun."

Ash's lips formed a straight line as he strode toward her. "Your courage and desire to protect your people are admirable, but you are younger than every other volunteer. We need proven warriors."

"I *am* proven," Kiri said. "I fought the soldiers the day they attacked. I killed one. How many warriors here can say they fought a soldier face-to-face, instead of sneaking up on them or killing them in their sleep?"

The warrior from Salamander Village glowered at her as those who'd accompanied him on his journey spoke in hushed voices.

"Kiri," Jaya said in the motherly tone she used with her son's longtime friends, "you must consider the sacrifice the assassin might have to make. You have already done so much for our people. Let someone older carry this out. You haven't even had a chance to take a life mate or have children."

"Isn't it better that I will leave no mate or child behind? No one depends on me."

"You are too young," Ash said, his voice firm. "We are grateful for your willingness to do even more than you have already, but leave this to an older and more seasoned warrior."

He turned from her then, and Kiri sensed the crowd accepting his words. They wouldn't consider her, but she had to be the one to go. Whatever stirred in her knew this to be true.

"Do not dismiss her!"

All eyes turned to the young, round-faced woman standing by the fire. Meadow, who usually behaved as if she didn't notice what went on around her, had not only spoken, but had called out in anger. Even the elders appeared stunned.

Meadow approached Ash with a fierce expression, the baby in her arms now awake and chewing on a fist. "If it weren't for Kiri, everyone who escaped would not have survived," Meadow said. "The soldiers took us by surprise, but she reacted quickly. She saw her childhood friend, who had recently become her mate, die. A soldier cut her face open. But she didn't panic or give in to grief or despair. She protected us and guided us here."

Only the crackling of the fire and her baby's babbling answered her. Meadow gazed back at hundreds of pairs of eyes. No one spoke. No one moved.

An elder from a distant village recovered first. Rising, she came to stand beside Meadow. She appeared to be about Ash's age, and her loose hair cascaded down her back. Her smile reached her eyes as she said, "Kiri, your account of that day helped us to come to our decision. Your courage and composure during an attack are indeed commendable. I've asked about you. I understand you are a celebrated distance runner and have won many races."

Kiri nodded.

"And a good hunter and tracker?"

"A better tracker than hunter, but I won't starve."

The woman nodded. "And if chosen, how would you travel beyond our lands to find these men? We know about where two of them live, but we don't know where to find Isandor. How will you travel through lands you've never been to without being caught and killed?"

Kiri swallowed. She'd thought the council would have pondered that and had suggestions. She closed her eyes, picturing herself in lands without tall trees. She walked in the open, with nowhere to hide. She could travel at night or… When the answer came to her, she opened her eyes. "I will disguise myself as a Wanderer. We can trade for their clothing. They are secretive about their ways, so the Galeedans and Sandamedans won't know much about them either."

"The Wanderers never travel alone," the loose-haired elder said. "The whole clan travels together."

"I-I'll say I am running away from a cruel husband, that I'm looking for my birth clan. If an area seems dangerous, I'll travel at night. I can avoid being seen. The non-Forest make a great deal of noise when they walk. I'll hear them long before they get close."

The elder raised her eyebrows. "A good plan." She turned to Ash. "The girl is an athlete and shows cunning. She's proven her courage, ability to act decisively when threatened, and devotion to protecting her people. And I agree that as a survivor of Mar Dun, she has more claim than most to go. We should consider her." Several people called out their approval.

The loose-haired elder reached into a small leather sack that hung from her belt and withdrew a handful of yellow powder. She tossed the powder into the fire, causing blue flames to leap and twist in a mesmerizing dance. As Kiri stared into the flames, her surroundings faded. Voices became muffled, and moving figures transformed into blurry shapes. Somewhere far away people talked excitedly. Then horrid screams engulfed her. Kiri couldn't move, couldn't feel her body. She didn't know if she stood or floated. Soldiers appeared, their swords and armor bloodied. She was in Mar Dun. Wren sprinted past her and drew his bow. Kiri watched, helpless, as soldiers bore down on him. "Run, Kiri," he said. A soldier with bright green eyes came into view. Kiri tried to scream a warning when she recognized him, but her lips wouldn't move. She saw, for the second time in her life, the green-eyed soldier cut Wren down. Anguish overwhelmed her; still, she could not move. The attack continued. An elderly woman fled before an advancing soldier. When she tripped and fell, she held up a hand as if to protect herself, begging for mercy. The soldier didn't hesitate. He raised his sword and—

Kiri watched in horror, unable to even cry out. She saw a little boy she'd played with three days before, lying on the ground, unmoving. Villagers died within arm's reach.

"Kiri!"

Kiri gasped and flailed her arms as she stumbled backward. She was in Wolf Village, still standing in the crowd gathered around the fire. All around her, people called her name. Some sounded celebratory, others mournful.

They surrounded her, making it difficult to breathe, as they ushered her closer to the bonfire. Kiri caught a glimpse of Meadow, who stared into the flames, transfixed. Then she stood before the Council of Elders.

Expression solemn, Ash withdrew the knife in his belt. "For the one who has been chosen," he said, holding it out to Kiri.

Had they chosen her? Kiri struggled to make sense of what she'd just experienced. Somehow, the fire had taken her to Mar Dun on the day of the attack. It had been more than a vision or memory, for she'd had enough of those to know the difference. How had she seen deaths she'd never witnessed? How long had she been there? How long had the elders deliberated?

Kiri accepted the knife. The sharp blade was the length of her hand, and thick leather, dyed brownish red, covered the wooden handle. The image of a snake had been burned onto one side of the handle, and an angular tree, the symbol of the Forest lands, onto the other. The snake symbolized Mar Dun, as it was often called the Snake Village. Kiri admired the handiwork, running her fingers over the symbols. Then she returned Ash's gaze. Despite his stoic expression, a glint in his eye betrayed emotion. Foreboding?

"A good knife," Kiri said. As she turned, the crowd made way, and Kiri saw several of her friends huddled together. They stared at her, eyes wide and mouths turned down. Guilt stabbed at her. She might leave her loved ones behind forever. She dreaded facing her family, gathered farther back.

A sudden grip on her shoulder caused Kiri to whirl around. Meadow stood close, her face streaked with tears. "Did it happen to you too? Did you see Mar Dun?"

"Yes," Kiri whispered. She cleared her throat, took a breath. "Yes," she said, more firmly.

"It had to be you, Kiri. You can do this."

"If not for you, I wouldn't have been chosen."

"If not for you, I wouldn't be here," Meadow replied.

"Then if I succeed, perhaps it will heal us both," Kiri whispered.

Cida approached and laid a hand on Kiri's arm. "Come," she said. "We have much to plan."

Chapter 2

KIRI

The small cottage sat atop a grassy hill, its outline pronounced in the moonlight. The long grass swayed in the gentle breeze. Kiri kept low to the ground as she approached, careful to avoid making noise. The animals had been led into their shelter for the night, but Kiri wouldn't risk their detecting her and bellowing an alarm.

When she reached the cottage, Kiri crept along the side until she found an open window. She peered inside, noting with relief that the moonlight illuminated the room. Earlier that day, when she had observed the cottage as she lay hidden in the tall grass, she'd seen a boy of about twelve years. He'd stayed close to Orrik, and Kiri assumed him to be Orrik's son. But the large figure sleeping on a straw bed in the corner couldn't be the boy.

With a deep breath, Kiri climbed through the window. She drew her knife and approached the sleeping figure. He had broad shoulders, with hands almost twice the size of her own. His receding hairline made his rounded forehead appear even larger. He bore the pale skin of his people, and curly brown chest hair jutted from the low collar of his tunic. The thin blanket covering his body undulated with each breath. A breeze swept into the room, and Kiri tensed as the man shifted. She advanced when he resumed his even breathing. Her heart pounded.

She had traveled so far to find the man before her. The last time Kiri had seen him, he'd charged her people, wearing bloodied armor. She lifted her free hand to her face, tracing her scar.

It had taken a month of planning, preparations, and ceremonies before Kiri could set out from her village. It had taken another month to reach Galeed and find Orrik's home. Every village she'd traveled through on the way to Galeed had wanted her to speak with their elders and feast with them. And now, she finally stood over the first man she'd been commanded to kill. It felt abrupt, as if the preparations and journey were fragments of a dream, and she had just awakened.

A place on Orrik's throat visibly throbbed with his lifeblood, exposing his vulnerability. Kiri hadn't expected guilt or pity. She'd thought her grief and rage would sustain her, that her people's strength would flow through her veins. But now, with him helpless before her on a quiet night, she faced his humanity. He had a spirit and drew breath, same as anyone. Worst of all, his child slept in the next room. Orrik had to love his child, and if he could love …

Doubt seized Kiri. For the first time, she considered she might not be able to complete her task. Before, when she'd taken human life, she'd been defending herself and others amid screams and confusion. The attacking soldiers had been faceless. Orrik's death would be the coldhearted slaying of an unarmed man.

Let me be strong.

Kiri willed herself to think of the evil Orrik and his companions had done. They'd killed children and elderly people. The skin around her scar ached with remembered pain. She let the rage fill her, its fire licking her insides.

Kiri knelt on the edge of the bed, causing the bedding to shift.

Orrik stirred and opened his eyes. He looked about the room, blinking. He appeared not to see Kiri, as his eyes probably hadn't adjusted to the darkness.

It was foolish not to have stabbed Orrik in his sleep. Waking him almost ensured he would fight back, but Kiri realized she needed to confront him, needed him to witness her people's vengeance. "Do you know me?" She struggled to twist her tongue around the syllables of the common language.

Orrik gasped as he propped himself up on an elbow. He looked to the room's entrance, eyes wild, before his gaze settled on Kiri. He murmured in what must have been Galeedan.

"Do you know me? Do you remember?" Kiri said again, this time louder. The moonlight glinted off her knife.

"I-I know your people," Orrik rasped. He didn't move. "You're not real. This is another dream."

Kiri hadn't expected him to fear her. How could anyone who'd done what he had be capable of fear? Pity again stirred inside her. *Remember Mar Dun. Remember.* She clung to the rage, pulling on it for strength.

Kiri's voice rose as she leaned forward to give him a closer look. The light slanted across her. "Tell me! Do you remember Mar Dun?"

Orrik's stare moved to the left side of Kiri's face. His terrified expression transformed into realization.

He knows why I've come. Fierce resolve settled over her.

Orrik shifted to make his move.

Kiri sprang forward, plunging her knife into his throat. As his body jerked against hers, Kiri whispered, "Those you killed in Mar Dun await you in the spirit world."

Kiri fell back on the bed, shaking. She could still feel his breath on her face and the terrible intimacy that had existed between them as their bodies had pressed together.

The room spun as bile rose in her throat. Kiri gripped the blanket and gritted her teeth, willing the room still. All the apprehension, rage, and doubt that had surged through her dissipated. Disgust and horror took their place. It had been so much harder than fighting in battle, and she had two more men to kill. She didn't feel avenged or triumphant. Instead, she fought nausea as the trembling continued. Kiri took deep breaths as she gradually regained control of her faculties. The spinning abated, and then stopped. She noticed the warm, spattered blood on her hand and wiped it on the blanket.

The knife remained embedded in Orrik's throat. Kiri pulled it free and wiped it on the bedding. She pressed her lips to the handle in gratitude and climbed off the bed.

Kiri noticed a braided leather cord around Orrik's neck. She lifted it to find a small wooden ring dangling from it. Even with the moonlight illuminating the room, she couldn't make out the details. She knew from touch that the delicate band had been crafted for someone with slender fingers. It was the kind of personal possession she needed. She removed the leather cord from around the dead man's neck. Remembering the boy would discover the body, Kiri pulled the sheets to Orrik's chin and closed his eyes, unable to suppress a shudder when her fingers brushed his skin. She turned away as she fought a second wave of nausea.

Crossing the room, Kiri knelt by her pack. She dropped the ring inside and withdrew a bundle of clothes. The elders had approved of Kiri's plan to disguise herself as a Wanderer and had obtained appropriate clothing through trade. They'd presented Kiri with a full-skirted indigo dress that fell to just below her knees, a matching scarf, and a pair of soft leather boots that laced up to her knees. To honor her people, Kiri had worn her Forest garb to kill Orrik. Now she changed into the Wanderer clothes. After lacing up her boots, she slipped her knife inside one. She wrapped the scarf around her head in the Wanderer fashion, letting her hair fall loose over her shoulders.

Someone stirred in the next room, and she froze. *The boy.* Muscles tense, Kiri waited for another sound but heard only silence. She exhaled in relief and lifted her pack. She needed to leave before the boy woke and found her.

Just as Kiri pulled her pack loops over her shoulders, she heard distant rumbling. She climbed through the window, straining to listen as her feet touched the grass. She'd never heard this sound before; too rhythmic to be thunder and too strong to be anything else. Kiri crouched, pressing her hands to the soil. A faint vibration shook the ground. Had Orrik summoned spirits of the dead to attack her before she'd killed him? Fear bumps rose on Kiri's skin. She had no idea what could happen in these open places devoid of protection of tall trees.

The sound grew louder. Kiri broke into a sprint, heading east for the distant tree line. She ran blindly, without knowing what she ran from. She only knew something in the darkness headed for her. She focused all her strength on one thought: *Let me reach the trees in time.*

A high-pitched animal cry emanated from the south. Tall, fast-moving forms took shape in the moonlight. They traveled on four legs, and the thundering came from the impact of their feet. There were many of them, far too many to count in a glance. They were too close; they would overtake her before she reached the tree line. Crying out in desperation, Kiri lost her footing. She hit the ground hard, and then scrambled into a crouch.

The creatures approached, and in the moonlight, Kiri saw them clearly. They looked like the shaggy ponies that pulled Wanderer wagons, but these animals were tall and elegant. Horses? Kiri had heard of the beasts but had only glimpsed them from a distance during her journey. She would have been relieved at her discovery had it not been for what rode them.

Men. Or were they spirits of the dead? People said Galeedans rode on horses. Perhaps Orrik *had* summoned dead Galeedans and they'd materialized in the wind. Still crouched, Kiri squeezed her eyes shut and waited for the attack. One could not fight spirits.

The thundering engulfed her. The ground shook. When the expected attack didn't come, Kiri opened her eyes to see a horse sailing over her, its back hooves half an arm's length from her face. The mounted horses sped past her in the moonlight. Then the men started yelling.

Horses circled Kiri. They loomed over her, breath rising from their nostrils into the night air. The men had short hair, closely trimmed beards, and their coloring matched her own. They spoke in a guttural language, their voices rumbling. They weren't Galeedan. If the riders weren't Galeedan, they couldn't be spirits of the dead summoned by Orrik.

One of the riders unsheathed his sword.

Kiri gripped her boot. If she reached her knife, she might be able to catch an assailant off guard and escape into the night. Her fingers twitched.

Her resolution must have shown because the man with the sword called out to his companions.

Thudding boots hit the ground, and she spun to face the men.

Two rushed at her, not bothering to draw their weapons.

Someone caught her from behind, and then she was lifted, her arms pinned to her sides. The starry sky spun. Where had the third man come from? Then someone tied her hands behind her. Kiri screamed with rage as the men dragged her to one of the mounted riders. The rider hauled Kiri up so she sat before him, her legs dangling on either side of the horse. Before Kiri could think of what to do, the group rode into the night.

Chapter 3

ULEK

Rough hands jerked Ulek upright. "Get up," a voice said in heavily accented Galeedan.

Ulek blinked and looked around. A burning candle in his room revealed three strange men. Charpans. "Father!" Ulek screamed. "Father!"

A hand slapped Ulek's face with such force that his head snapped backward. He stared, dumbfounded, at the imposing man looming over him. The man's dark eyes glowered over a straight nose that ended in a point. His brown cloak almost reached the floor, and red squares sewn together made up his knee-length tunic. He wore boiled leather armor over his tunic.

The Charpan grabbed Ulek's arm. "Get up," he snapped in the common language as he hauled Ulek to his feet.

The two other men turned and headed for his father's room.

"Father!" Ulek yelled. "Charpans!"

This time, the tall Charpan struck him with the back of his hand. Orange light flashed behind Ulek's eyes as he fell across the bed.

The Charpan picked Ulek's boots off the floor and flung them at him.

Ulek obeyed the implicit command and pulled his boots on with shaking hands. His head spun and he strained his ears, listening for the sound of his father waking with a yell and fighting back. It didn't come. Perhaps he had warned his father in time, and he'd escaped? This hope swelled when Ulek heard the two other intruders speaking rapidly. He couldn't understand them, but he recognized shock in their voices.

The two men reentered Ulek's room. One spoke in an urgent tone to the tall man in red as he gestured to the other room.

Ulek exhaled in relief. His father was safe.

The man who had been speaking turned toward Ulek. He drew a dagger from his belt as he strode forward. He held the dagger to Ulek's throat and pressed, drawing blood. Ulek's heart, which had been beating as if he were running, seemed to stop.

The tall man, who appeared to be the leader, barked what must have been an order, because the dagger's pressure against Ulek's skin eased.

The Charpan who held the dagger looked over his shoulder and spoke, his tone harsh.

The leader raised his voice, and the dagger disappeared from Ulek's throat.

As he was dragged from his house, Ulek wrenched away and ran to his father's room. He wanted to see the empty bed for himself and know his father had escaped. He would go straight to Fort Ovandis and bring the imperial soldiers after them.

The blanket had fallen to the floor. His father lay there, eyes closed, arms at his sides. For a moment, Ulek thought he'd only been knocked unconscious. Then he saw the gaping wound across his father's throat and the dark stain on his tunic.

Ulek knelt by the bed. His father's skin bore an unnatural pallor. The blood, thicker than any liquid he'd touched, had started to congeal around the wound. *They killed Father.* The low whimper that rose in Ulek's throat grew into a wail as one of the men dragged him outside.

Ulek choked back his tears when he saw the mounted Charpans gathered outside his home. *I won't cry in front of them*, he promised himself as he clenched his teeth. Someone produced a strip of leather and bound Ulek's wrists behind him. Did they mean to enslave him? Ulek's grief, fear, and rage retreated to a place deep inside, where they remained on the periphery of his awareness. Voices became distant. He barely felt the fingers digging into his arm as someone hauled him onto a horse. He turned and met the stare of a wide-eyed girl with bound wrists who sat before a rider. The moonlight revealed her black hair and olive skin; she was no Galeedan. Then he noticed her Wanderer clothes. The girl held his gaze as if trying to reassure him, or perhaps discern what had happened in the cottage. Ulek looked away from her as the Charpans urged their horses forward.

Chapter 4

MATTOS

The guests were well-fed, and several had drunk enough wine to behave with boisterous conviviality. Children, excited to be up at such a late hour, played under tables while youths and maidens sat in groups on cushions on the floor. Mothers with small children gathered in a circle in one corner of the hall while their young ones rolled about inside the circle. The older men stood together, talking and laughing louder than they would have without the effects of the wine.

Mattos slipped past them, searching for a place he could relax and sit unnoticed. In a dim corner of the hall, he spotted a lean man drinking from a wine bottle. Mattos strode over and sat on the empty chair next to him.

"Enjoying the celebration?" the man asked as he wiped wine from his lips.

"Not as much as you appear to be, Lucen," Mattos said. "How'd you get a whole bottle?"

Lucen grinned. "A drunk old man gave it to me. The bride's uncle, I think." He took another swig. "She's pretty. Elmaturis is lucky."

"Pretty and rich," Mattos said. "His parents went to a lot of trouble to arrange his marriage and escort his bride here."

"A Sandamedan officer who wants an important position in Ishtia would fare better with a woman from a well-connected family," Lucen observed. "An ambitious man like Elmaturis understands that. What surprises me is the girl's family agreed to the match and escorted her all the way here without ever meeting the groom. His family must be as rich and influential as he claims."

Mattos chuckled. No one doubted the wealth or influence of Elmaturis's senatorial family. Lucen's family held even more wealth and power than Elmaturis's, but Lucen never mentioned it. His open disregard of pedigree made him Mattos's only real friend among the officers.

"Relieved to be finally getting rid of these people?" Lucen asked.

"I won't be sad when I see them riding off," Mattos replied with a wry smile.

The two men sat in relative privacy, ignored by most of the guests. Their close-cropped hair marked them as soldiers. The military of the Sandamedan Empire had learned the disadvantage of having long hair in close combat many years ago.

Excited voices rose at the edge of the crowd, and the bridal couple came into view. Silver disks cinched the bride's gown at her shoulders, leaving her arms bare. A silver sash tied under her breast line accentuated her slender frame. The rest of the blue gown fell loosely to the floor. She wore her long curls piled high on her head, giving prominence to the silver earrings dangling halfway to her shoulders.

Elmaturis stood grinning beside her, wearing his green officer's cloak fastened at his right shoulder with a copper medallion bearing a falcon's image. Both were tall and, like most Sandamedans, had olive skin and black hair and eyes. But the similarities ended there. The bride's features appeared delicate, while Elmaturis had an aquiline nose and a cleft in his prominent chin.

The couple's grins lit their faces. Mattos marveled at how joyful they seemed, considering they'd only met a few days ago. His own wedding to a pretty, kindhearted woman had not been a joyous occasion. At the thought of Marenda, guilt and grief assailed him. He pushed her from his mind.

Mattos stood. "I'm going to offer my good wishes. Might as well get it over with."

"I'll come too," Lucen said, rising from his chair.

They pushed through the onslaught of well-wishers until they stood in front of Elmaturis and his bride.

"Congratulations to you both," Mattos said.

Elmaturis's jovial expression stiffened. He had always scorned Mattos's common birth. Though usually civil, due to them having the same commanding officer, he was condescending and antagonistic on occasion. "My dear, this is Mattos. He also serves as a Falcon under Diakiris. Mattos, this is my wife, Alanna."

Alanna gave a formal bow, never losing her friendly smile.

"Mattos is the son of a wealthy merchant," Elmaturis said, smiling, though his eyes remained cold. "Despite his low birth, he built a successful fabric trade. His family is now quite respectable, and he bought his son a posting in the army. Isn't that impressive?"

Mattos kept his expression neutral as he stared at Elmaturis, who met his gaze with a smirk. Elmaturis hadn't bought his posting; the sons of the senatorial class paid only with their bloodlines.

Alanna appeared not to notice her groom's mocking tone. "Oh, yes, very impressive."

Elmaturis gestured toward Lucen. "Diakiris's third Falcon, Lucen, son of Haventar and Vian. You've heard of his family, of course."

Lucen bowed. "I hope you are happy here. You'll find the Galeedans are friendly people. My wife is a local woman."

Alanna's eyes widened. "I know soldiers sent to the provinces often marry women of those lands. But an officer ..."

Lucen chuckled. "It *is* rare. I'm the only officer stationed here married to a Galeedan girl, but there's no law against it."

"Is she here? I'd like to meet her."

"Allow me to find her for you," Lucen said before walking off.

Mattos noticed Alanna looking at him expectantly, and he realized she waited for him to mention or introduce his own wife. At twenty-three, he was too old to be unmarried. Mattos met her gaze, keeping his mouth shut. No need to spoil a happy occasion by talking about a dead wife. Alanna turned to her husband before the moment became awkward.

"Come, dear," Elmaturis said, taking his bride's arm. "I have *friends* I'd like to introduce you to." As they walked away, Mattos heard Elmaturis tell her, "You shouldn't speak with him. He's a commoner. And you shouldn't get too friendly with a Galeedan woman. I'll be grand counselor to the emperor someday, and we have to choose our companions wisely."

Mattos watched them go, feeling only mildly annoyed. He'd grown accustomed to Elmaturis's petty insults. Having fulfilled his social obligation, he headed for the exit, eager for his room's solitude.

Chapter 5

KIRI

The moon had slipped behind clouds by the time the riders stopped to make camp. They lit no cook fires; instead, they ate food right out of their saddlebags. The unfettered horses stayed close to the men, some wandering through the camp to nudge their riders.

Kiri kept still as she focused on possible methods of escape. If she could run into the darkness, the riders would never find her; she knew how to move soundlessly and avoid detection. Somehow, she had to reach her knife and cut herself free. A nearby grunt caught her attention. She turned to see the boy scooting toward her, his progress slow and awkward. When the horsemen pulled Kiri and the boy from the horses, they'd bound their ankles with rope before tossing them on the ground. They hadn't even bothered to search or remove Kiri's pack.

When the boy finally reached Kiri, he sagged against her so that they huddled back-to-back. Orrik's son had to believe the Charpans had killed his father. He wouldn't have approached, seeking comfort, if he suspected she'd done it.

Guilt gnawed at Kiri. She had expected to be far away when the boy woke and discovered his father dead. Instead, she'd heard his anguished cry when he must have seen the body. She'd seen his stricken face as a Charpan dragged him from the cottage. "What are you called?" she whispered in the common language.

"Ulek," he replied. "And you?"

"Kiri." She'd decided to go by her real name lest she fail to respond to a fake one. She doubted non-Forest people would recognize a Forest name anyway. She leaned against the boy. "Ulek, I have a knife in my boot."

Ulek started to turn toward her, but Kiri gripped his hands.

"Wait." She turned and curved her body around him, hoping it would appear she only comforted him. "Here," Kiri murmured as she pressed her left foot against his back. She felt Ulek's hands move awkwardly along her boot. At last, he reached the top and slid two fingers inside. The knife slid up her leg, then it stopped. Again, Kiri felt Ulek tug the knife, and this time it slipped from her boot.

Ulek's arms jerked against Kiri as he cut himself free. Then he cut Kiri's ankle bindings.

With the chance of escape so close, Kiri shook with anxiety. She glanced over her shoulder at the men, who talked as they ate. She counted twenty-eight of them. How much longer would she and Ulek be ignored? They still hadn't been fed. Kiri twisted to position her back to Ulek. She silently urged him to hurry as he sliced through the leather around her wrists.

When her bindings fell away, Kiri took the knife from Ulek, careful to keep her arms behind her.

Ulek leaned toward her ear. "We need to get to the horses."

"No," Kiri whispered. She had no idea how to ride a horse or make it go where she wanted. Besides, these men had a connection with their horses. The beasts changed direction and pace at the men's will without a spoken command, as if the horses knew their riders' minds. Surely any horse she and Ulek took would betray them.

"Kiri, we have to." Ulek's whisper sounded angry. "We can't outrun horses."

No, they couldn't, but if they got far enough away in the darkness, they'd be able to hide. If they rode away on a horse, their captors would follow and eventually catch them. Their only hope was slipping away without being noticed. Before Kiri could explain this to Ulek, a black horse wandered near them.

"Now," Ulek said, leaping to his feet and hauling Kiri to his side. Without letting go of her, Ulek sprang toward the horse and caught hold of its saddle. The horse sidestepped in surprise as Ulek climbed onto its back and tugged Kiri's arm. "Hurry!" he ordered.

It all happened in a few moments. The men flung aside their food and jumped to their feet.

Resisting the temptation to hit Ulek for ruining their chance of sneaking away, Kiri clambered up.

Ulek slammed his heels into their mount's sides.

The horse bolted forward, breaking into a gallop only moments after standing still. Kiri gasped, her head flung backward at the sudden speed, and she wrapped her arms around Ulek's waist to keep from falling off.

Behind them, the men mounted their horses. When Kiri looked over her shoulder, she saw only long grass covering the hill. Their pursuers were still some distance away. She had to act now. Tightening her arms around Ulek, Kiri threw them from the horse.

They landed with a painful thud in the tall grass. The horse continued its flight as Kiri gasped for breath to replace the air knocked out of her. They scrambled backward so they wouldn't be in the riders' path. The thundering grew louder, and the horsemen charged by in pursuit of the riderless horse.

Once the pounding of the hooves faded, Ulek stumbled to his feet. "Why did you do that?" he cried out. "That horse will slow down, and they'll know we jumped. They'll come back looking for us."

Kiri stared at him. Didn't he realize the horsemen would have caught up to them anyway? "Of course they'll come back," she snapped. "But unless they can track in the dark, they'll never find us hiding in the tall grass." Kiri stood. "I have to go," she said, eager to put as much distance as possible between herself and the horsemen before they realized their mistake. She took off at a gait she could maintain all night. She was the best long-distance runner in her village and had often taken part in races. She'd only run about ten paces when she heard Ulek huffing behind her.

"Wait," he called.

Kiri stopped and turned to look at him in exasperation. Did he *want* to be recaptured?

Ulek stopped too. "This isn't the right way." He brushed his curls out of his eyes. "We need to go south to the fort."

We. Why did this Galeedan boy assume they would stay together? "I'm not going to the fort," Kiri said, anxious to continue before the riders returned.

"N-Not going?" Ulek stammered. "But we have to tell them about the Charpans. We have to tell them about my—" His voice faltered. "My … father. The soldiers will take you back to your caravan. Your family probably went to the fort when you were taken. They might still be there."

Kiri gritted her teeth. They had no time to argue. She could start running again, but Ulek would probably follow and call after her and give them both away. Perhaps if someone else were there to look after him … Because of her, Ulek had no protector. If this boy died because of her actions while she fulfilled her people's will, then his innocent blood would be on them all. It would displease the spirits protecting her, and she needed their favor now. She had to stay with Ulek until he rejoined his people. Kiri sighed. "We will go to the fort."

Chapter 6

MATTOS

In his three years at Fort Ovandis, Mattos had never been inside the Hawk's cramped war room. Several open windows provided the only light. A small desk stood in the corner covered with rolled-up scrolls, and a map of the known world hung on the wall. Six wooden chairs were pushed aside to make room for the officers gathered. Like Mattos, the other officers had been pulled from their duties or training. The odors of sweat and dirt permeated the room.

Hawk Thais stood before a long rectangular table, looking grimmer than he had in the past weeks. Dark circles stained the skin around his eyes. The wrinkles on his leathery face appeared to have deepened, and his short hair was now more gray than black. Beside him stood Osprey Beldos, the tall, thin-faced second-in-command. Hawk Thais cleared his throat. "We are evacuating," he said. "We have orders from Eagle Isandor to abandon the fort and head north to Ishtia."

No one moved or spoke, but Mattos felt the collective shock. He stared at Thais in disbelief. No military commander had ever ordered the abandonment of a fort.

"Weeks ago, my scouts brought me information that the Charpan horde showed signs of preparing to invade." The men shifted and glanced at each other. "Horsemen are arriving from all over the wastelands of western Charpa and are gathering at the border."

Mattos lowered his gaze, taking a deep breath. It had been a risk when the empire had declared war on Charpa four years ago to gain another province to pay tribute and taxes. The dense Forest lands to the east and the wastelands to the west separated the empire from Charpan cities. That left the sea. The Sandamedan Empire was renowned for its mighty army, not its navy. Thousands of imperial soldiers and sailors had died at sea. The few thousand who had reached Charpan shores held off the Charpan Army, but they had no chance of taking cities. They languished in the hills outside the Charpan capitol. Intent on securing a land route for their invasion, the army tried to force its way through the Forest lands. The Forest people proved tougher than expected, and little progress had been made.

The Sandamedan Army could never invade Charpa by crossing the vast wastelands. They contained a sea of grass, but no plants fit for humans to eat. Thirst and hunger would take them before they reached a Charpan stronghold. The Charpan riders had no such disadvantages. They thrived in the wastelands and knew where to find water. With their many horses, they could cross much faster. They could dry meat, the bulk of their diet, and carry it long distances. They could ride all day and even eat in the saddle. Only the garrison's worthlessness had spared it from attack. But after four years of war, and the western horsemen eager for a fight …

"Let us stand and fight them!" one of the younger officers said.

Thais didn't reprimand the man for speaking out of turn. Instead, he responded in a booming voice, "If we did, every last one of us would die."

Silence.

Thais continued. "They outnumber us sixteen to one and have three to four horses to a rider. We could hold them off for a time, but eventually, the fort will fall. Most of the empire's soldiers have sailed for Charpa or are fighting the Forest people to the east. They're too far to come to our aid. This fort is a relic of the war with Galeed; the army didn't build it to withstand a Charpan siege. We'd be cut off from our food and supply sources. We're stationed here only to support the governor and *observe* the Charpans. Eagle Isandor has ordered us to abandon the fort and escort the Galeedans to Ishtia. Our task is to get there before the Charpans do. We will evacuate these lands within two days. The governor and the northern magistrates sent their people north already. The town of Cybelon sits empty."

Osprey Beldos unrolled a scroll, placed it on the table behind Thais, and beckoned the men to gather around. Mattos spotted his commanding officer, Harrier Diakiris, as he maneuvered close to the table, his close-set eyes revealing nothing. Mattos hung back with the Falcons, the most junior of officers. He could just make out a map of the empire.

When Mattos had first come to the outpost, he'd felt like he'd been sent to the world's edge. The Galeedans caused little trouble, and the mountain bandits avoided the soldiers. Beyond the lonely border, wastelands stretched as far as the eye could see. Mattos had wondered how he, a young officer commended by his superiors, had been stationed in such a remote location during wartime. He'd wanted adventure, a challenge, and the opportunity to prove himself. Instead, he'd been ordered to an outpost where bored, off-duty soldiers drank too much and pursued local girls. Now the 318 soldiers in the safest of garrisons faced five thousand men on horseback. Mattos suppressed a laugh of bitter irony.

"We can't take the main road," Thais said. "It'll be too easy for the Charpans to reach us and too hard for us to bring enough water. We'll have to follow the Tarven River and cut through the mountains. It'll be hard traveling. Luckily, the mountains will be harder on the Charpan horses than it will be for us on foot."

As they studied the map, Mattos could only think of the near impossible task laid upon them. It would be difficult for their company to escort roughly four thousand people through the mountains. Not to mention, the horde of five thousand Charpans thundering in pursuit. The company could be ready to march within hours, but he didn't see how the local villagers could be ready in two days.

Elmaturis stepped toward the senior officers. It was his first day back on duty after his wedding two days before. He rapped his fist against his breastplate to request permission to speak.

"Speak, Falcon," Thais said.

"Hawk," Elmaturis began, "why not tell the locals to flee to the hills? We can't possibly outrun the horde if we're escorting thousands of people through the mountains. The Charpans aren't after *them.*"

Several officers muttered their assent.

Thais held up his hand. "We are escorting the southern Galeedans to Ishtia because that is what the Eagle commanded us to do. We don't question our superiors' orders." He fixed his eyes on Elmaturis. "And we *will* reach Ishtia with the local people before the Charpans do. The Sandamedan Empire's army is the greatest the world has ever seen. I don't want to hear another word about failure!" His right eye twitched as he stopped for a breath. "You all have your orders. Dismissed."

As the men filed into the courtyard in small groups, Mattos sought out Lucen. Elmaturis joined them a moment later.

"Instead of finally getting to fight, we have to abandon the fort we're supposed to protect," Lucen grumbled. "We'll be the first company to lose a fort."

"Don't be callow," Elmaturis said. "The fort's lost anyway. Better to lose it and live than lose it and die. What doesn't make sense is the order to lead the Galeedans all the way to Ishtia."

"They're citizens of the empire," Mattos said. "We can't just abandon them."

"Citizens?" Elmaturis snorted. "They can't even speak Sandamedan. We're no help to them anyway. You heard the Hawk. A horde of five thousand will be chasing us. We can do the honorable thing and die, or we can do the smart thing and flee with our families to Ishtia. Leave the Galeedans to their fate."

Lucen, perhaps thinking of his wife's family, narrowed his eyes. "What about all the relatives Alanna brought to celebrate your wedding? They're bound to slow us down. Maybe we should leave them behind too?"

"They have horses," Elmaturis said. "They'll keep up."

"Don't you have men to address?" Harrier Diakiris asked as he walked toward them, his tone not as reproachful as his words. Diakiris, who had a reputation for being a quiet man who always measured his words, didn't appear alarmed or excited.

Nobody responded. Surely, he would have more to say about the invasion.

Diakiris turned around to gaze at the distant Tarven Mountains. His three Falcons stood staring at his back before he said, "I've always wanted to travel through those mountains. What an adventure we will have." When he turned back to his Falcons, he wore a thoughtful expression. "Still here? I thought I told you to go back to your men."

Mattos, Lucen, and Elmaturis glanced at each other before going to their separate units. Lucen headed toward the drilling fields, and Elmaturis returned to where his men chopped firewood.

Mattos's unit had been on a six-league march when he'd been called away. They'd be headed back to the fort by now. The sun shone in his eyes as he hiked up a nearby hill. Once at the top, he set off in a different direction from the route he and his men had taken that morning. By cutting through the wooded area, he'd be able to intercept them.

He welcomed the rare solitude as he jogged along the wide dirt trail through the trees. He vacillated between the humiliation of running and the cold reality of facing a bloodthirsty enemy of superior numbers. Something else caused his stomach to twist and tighten.

Thais had seemed certain the horde would pursue the retreating company rather than take the abandoned fort. Did he have reason to believe the Charpans didn't want the fort? What did they want then? Even a cavalry five thousand strong couldn't take Ishtia, the capital of Sandameda, or maintain control of Galeed. Yet Cybelon, a significant trading town on the border of Sandameda and Galeed, had been abandoned. Mattos came to a halt. If the Eagle had given the order to evacuate Galeed, the Charpans could only want one thing. They loosed the horde to slaughter as many as possible in their path, forcing the imperial army to defend its own people and abandon the invasion of Charpa.

Chapter 7

ULEK

Ulek ran toward his cottage. They couldn't reach the fort without passing close to Ulek's farm, and he'd been unable to resist heading for it. Last night's events didn't seem real, as if Kiri and the Charpans had materialized in a horrid dream. Even as a strange energy coursed through Ulek, giving him strength to keep moving despite fatigue and lack of sleep, fog enveloped his awareness. If he could reach the house, the fog would dissipate and his mind would clear. Perhaps he'd wake and find all had indeed been a nightmare.

"No," Kiri called, sounding angry. "We can't stop."

Ulek ignored her. The sun rose over the horizon in a burst of orange and pink. Mist lingered over the low hills, and dew moistened Ulek's boots and trousers. The barn doors and the gate to the attached fenced-in area stood open. The Charpans had taken Wind, his father's old mare. Snowflake bellowed behind the fence, waiting to be milked. Her weaned calf, Wildflower, started toward Ulek at a leisurely gait.

Upon reaching the open cottage door, Ulek gripped it with both hands for support, the wood rough against his skin. Morning rays lit the interior, revealing little amiss. The table and chairs stood where they always had. Nothing appeared to have been touched, the faint footprints on the hard-packed dirt floor the only evidence the Charpans had been inside.

Ulek shook even though his feet felt like they would turn to stone at any moment. He couldn't go inside. Entering would mean seeing his father's body and facing the truth of his death.

He glanced over his shoulder at Kiri, who strode toward him, her expression livid. Ulek pressed his forehead against the door, taking deep, steadying breaths. It had to be done.

Still clinging to the door, Ulek slid one foot forward. He took another breath before moving his other foot. He let go of the door and continued into the room. It seemed to take a long time to reach his father's bed. He lay as Ulek had last seen him: arms at his sides and eyes closed. His blue lips were drawn in an expressionless line, and the dark stubble on his chin stood out against his ghostly pallor. The wound on his throat had dried, leaving a brown stain on his tunic.

Hands shaking, Ulek knelt by the bed. He touched a cold arm and buried his face in the blanket-covered bed straw. The white ships had borne his father's soul to the Hills of Idenya. For the first time since seeing his father's corpse and being kidnapped, Ulek gave way to sobs.

The man who'd returned from the war a little over a year ago had been very different from the father Ulek had remembered. His temper would erupt over slight annoyances, and he often struck Ulek during his rages. Once or twice, he'd hit Ulek's mother, who had succumbed to fever shortly after his return. After her death, his father's disposition worsened, and at night, he woke screaming from nightmares.

Despite the fear Ulek had had of his father, there'd been happy times too. When in a good mood, his father would whistle as he cared for the livestock and joke with Ulek. Sometimes, he wrapped an arm around Ulek's shoulders or tousled his curly hair. They had each been, after all, the only person in the other's life.

"Ulek?"

He sniffed and wiped his eyes before turning toward Kiri. She stood three paces away, staring at him with brows drawn. She shuddered when her gaze shifted to the body.

Ulek cleared his throat as he stood. Even now, he felt embarrassed to be seen crying. "Please. Let me bury him."

The Wanderer girl's eyes widened. "No! We don't have time. We're going to the fort *now.*" She walked out of the house without a backward glance.

She was right. If the Charpans still searched for them, they'd come to the farm. Ulek could almost feel Kiri's rage at him for putting them in such danger. But he'd had to come, to see his father's body in daylight, to absorb the death. Grasping the blanket, Ulek drew it over the body. "Father," he murmured, "I'll come back. I'll bring imperial soldiers, and we'll give you a proper burial." Then he reached for the leather strip his father had worn around his neck since his wife's death. It wasn't there. Years ago, his father had carved a wooden ring for his mother. She'd used barberry dye to paint yellow flowers on it. After her death, his father had slipped it on a leather cord and worn it around his neck every day. Ulek had been sure his father had even worn it to bed. He searched the bed but found nothing.

A small trunk sat in the corner of the room. Ulek hastened toward it, lifted the lid, and dug through the contents. He drew out a leather coat. It would keep him warm during the chilly nights they traveled to the fort. Despite his careful search, he couldn't find the ring. His father would never have been careless with such a valued possession. Had the Charpans stolen it? The ring's only value had been sentimental. Ulek emptied the trunk's contents in desperation.

"Ulek!" Kiri's angry shout sounded from just beyond the door.

With or without the ring, they had to go. Ulek hurriedly bundled the coat in his arms. He retrieved his straw hat and filled a sack with what little food he had in the cottage before rushing outside. He cast one final glance at his home.

As they headed away from the farm, Kiri broke into a run, Ulek following suit.

When they'd put some distance between themselves and the farm, Kiri slowed her pace. Grateful, Ulek panted beside her, tasting bile in his throat. Kiri breathed easily, as if accustomed to running. Since their inauspicious meeting, he'd been too preoccupied to be curious about her. Now her strangeness intrigued him. She showed no fear, could run like a doe, and bore a scar across her face only a battle veteran should have.

"How old are you?" Ulek asked.

"Twenty."

"How …" Ulek hesitated, afraid of her reaction. "How did you get that scar?"

"My husband," Kiri replied, keeping her eyes forward.

Ulek gaped at her. He'd expected a childhood fight gone terribly wrong or an accident, not something as common as a cruel husband. He recalled the way his father had sometimes struck his mother. So many times, he'd longed to protect her, and had failed to do so. Kiri must not have had a protector either. "How did the Charpans take you?"

"The way they took you." She still didn't look at him.

"Yes, but … I mean, did they attack your clan?"

This time, Kiri turned her large eyes on him, her irises so dark Ulek couldn't distinguish them from her pupils. "No. I was alone."

"Oh." When Kiri looked away, Ulek studied her. Her accent differed from that of the few Wanderers he'd spoken with. But he knew little of the nomadic traders. They spoke a dialect of Charpan, but perhaps each clan had a variation of that dialect.

"Do you think your clan realized what happened? Do you think they went to the soldiers for help?"

"No."

Ulek waited for her to elaborate, but she said nothing else. She certainly didn't like talking.

After a moment, Kiri turned her gaze on him. "Where is the rest of your family?"

He was ill-prepared for that question. The shock and pain of his father's murder were still fresh. Ulek's throat ached. "There's no one else."

Kiri cocked her head as if she didn't understand or believe him.

"It's true," Ulek said. "I don't have any brothers or sisters, and I never met any of my grandparents. My father had four brothers and sisters, but they all died when they were real young. My mother had a brother and sister. My uncle fell off his horse and broke his leg, then the leg got infected, and he died. My aunt died trying to have her baby. The baby died later, and then her husband married someone else. My mother never saw him after that. My mother died about a year ago, and then it was just my father and me. Now it's just me." His voice shook with his last words, and he clamped his mouth shut. He was twelve years old, owner of his own small farm, a man grown.

His mother had always mourned the absence of relatives beyond her husband and son. It wasn't until this moment that Ulek truly understood the misfortune of not having a family. He'd grieved his mother almost a year. Now his father—who had survived illness, injury, and war, and should have lived to be an old man—had been murdered in his bed. Tears Ulek didn't want to admit to burned in his eyes. He was alone, utterly alone.

Chapter 8

MATTOS

The column traveled along the Tarven River, leaving behind a trail of trampled grass, extinguished cook fires, and excrement—human and animal. Hawk Thais, his aides, senior officers, and one Falcon unit led the column, followed by six hundred fort dependents. The visiting Sandamedans who'd come for Elmaturis's wedding, plus their officers' wives and children, rode on horseback. The families of regular soldiers walked beside the pack ponies laden with provisions and belongings. Behind them came four thousand Galeedans. Some drove or dragged carts; others carried possessions on their backs. Sheep and goats bellowed as children prodded them into a steady gait. Cows were left behind, as they could never make the journey through the mountains. Barking dogs chased each other before being called back by weary owners, and infants wailed at being roused from sleep. The eight other Falcon units were interspersed throughout to keep the villagers from slowing their pace. Three or four horse-drawn wagons carrying the fort's grain and food supplies, as well as any food the locals had brought, accompanied each unit. The chatter of people, animal cries, and impact of so many feet against the ground made such a racket the blind could have followed the column with ease.

A large sheep plodded by, carrying two laughing children who kept calling to their mother, demanding she look at them. Mattos smiled ruefully. *At least some people are enjoying themselves*, he thought. Most looked tired and anxious.

Mattos was grateful he rode his warhorse, Nica. She'd been a gift from his parents upon his receiving orders to report to Fort Ovandis. Only officers could afford horses, and few among them had mounts as fine as Nica with her shiny chestnut coat, white blaze, and imposing stature. She tugged at the reins, anxious for a run.

Mattos's unit marched beside him, showing no signs of fatigue. Imperial soldiers regularly marched as if on campaign, so they'd be used to the weight if war did come. They wore metal breast and back plates, connected by leather shoulder guards. Leather cingula cut into strips and studded with metal disks protected the groin. Metal greaves extended over the knee, and leather vambraces shielded the lower arm and hand. Swords the length of a man's lower leg were sheathed in wood and leather scabbards that hung from the cingulum belt. Each man had a quiver of twenty-four arrows and a leather bow case containing an unstrung bow slung across his back. Beneath their armor, they wore woolen tunics, trousers, and heavy boots. Their wooden shields covered them from chin to shin. Green-dyed leather had been glued to the outside of the shields. Each bore the Eagle emblem painted in gold.

Mattos commanded thirty-three men as all Falcons did: three Owls, two Sparrows under each, with four soldiers under each Sparrow. Despite the identical uniforms, one could easily identify the provincial soldiers. The Sarpaskans had deep brown skin with black eyes and coiled black hair. The fair-skinned Galeedans burned easily in the sun, and many had blue eyes and blond or red hair. About half of provincial soldiers served in their own lands, and half were sent elsewhere. Sending men to different provinces reinforced their loyalty to the Sandamedan Army, as they had no connection with the local people. Also, too many provincial soldiers serving in their own lands could lead to rebellion. The locals might realize their own soldiers outnumbered those of foreign birth and try to retake their lands.

The clear day made it possible to see a great distance across the hills. When Mattos looked east, he spotted two figures approaching. Since beginning the exodus two days ago, the column periodically gained locals and would continue to acquire them as it traveled north. These newcomers, however, held Mattos's attention. They moved quickly, carried no burdens, and drove no livestock. The column had picked up most Galeedans from villages along the river, yet these two came from the hills. Most unusual of all, they had no one else with them.

It took some time for them to near the column, as Mattos had seen them a long way off. When he could make out their clothing, he realized they were Wanderers. The clans usually kept to the lowlands, and he couldn't imagine why they would travel through the hills, but there was no mistaking the woman's short dress. It stopped just below her knees, something Galeedans and Sandamedans considered scandalous. Her smooth black hair fell to her waist. Mattos surmised a clan had seen them and wanted news.

Mattos, now abreast of them, urged Nica from the column and rode to meet them.

The boy stumbled forward, grasped Mattos's boot, and fired questions in rapid Galeedan. "What is this? Why are you leaving? Do you already know about the Charpans?"

Mattos started at hearing a Wanderer speak Galeedan. Then he studied the boy more closely. His fair skin, gray eyes, and style of clothing were Galeedan. Mattos had been too focused on the woman's appearance to scrutinize the boy's. What in the name of Odern were they doing together? He turned his gaze on the woman, managing not to flinch when he saw the horrid scar on her face. She'd been too far away for him to see it until then.

The boy tugged at Mattos's boot. "Do you know about the Charpans?"

"Of course we know about them, boy. We're escorting these people to Ishtia before they arrive. Where's your family? Why are you with a Wanderer?"

The boy ignored the questions. "But the Charpans are already here."

Something twisted in the pit of Mattos's stomach. "What are you talking about?"

"The Charpans," the boy cried, his eyes wild. "They're here. They killed my father. He was a soldier in your army and fought the Forest people. The Charpans came into our home four nights ago and killed him. They took me and

Kiri, but we escaped, and we came—" He stopped, gasping for breath. "We came to warn the fort."

Mattos turned to the young woman, who had stared at him wide-eyed throughout the exchange. She looked no older than eighteen. "The Charpans attacked your clan and took you?"

The girl narrowed her eyes as she backed away.

Realizing he'd spoken to her in Galeedan, Mattos repeated the question in the common language.

The girl hesitated before answering. "I was alone when the riders took me. Then they took Ulek. We escaped and headed for the fort."

Mattos turned back to the boy. "Ulek, is it? How do you know those men were Charpans and not mountain bandits?" He listened with growing horror as Ulek described boiled leather armor over jewel-colored tunics, uncooked food, and small but sturdy horses so well trained they could be left unfettered at night.

"Stay here," Mattos ordered before urging Nica into a gallop toward where Diakiris rode with the senior officers.

Reining in Nica near the front of the column, Mattos called out to Diakiris.

Diakiris turned his head and, catching sight of one of his Falcons, rode toward him. He listened, grim-faced, as Mattos repeated everything Ulek had told him. When Mattos finished, Diakiris stared out toward the distant mountains, his brown eyes thoughtful. "It's smart of the Charpans to send riders ahead of the main force. They can watch our movements and communicate them to their leaders."

"Communicate them?" Mattos repeated in surprise. "How?"

"I think we should know by now not to underestimate the Charpans," Diakiris replied, his gaze still turned inward. "I've heard stories of them using pigeons to carry messages back and forth." His eyes flicked to Mattos. "The Hawk needs to hear this. Come."

Soon after, Hawk Thais, the senior officers, and Mattos listened attentively as Ulek told the story of his father's murder, his capture, and subsequent escape with Kiri, the Wanderer girl. Thais wanted to know how many men there had been, the location of Ulek's farm, and the direction the horsemen had ridden.

"They must be headed for the mountains," Osprey Beldos said in Sandamedan. "They can spy on all of southern Galeed from there without risking discovery."

"Except they *have* been discovered, and they know it," Thais said, nodding toward Ulek and Kiri.

"All the more reason to head toward the mountains," Beldos replied. "Even with us knowing they're there, they'd be almost impossible to find."

Thais sighed. "It doesn't make a difference. We don't have enough time or men to look for them. This has been a race to Ishtia since leaving the fort. The Charpans were bound to realize what we're doing and where we're going. We can't stop now." His fierce gaze settled on Ulek and Kiri, and he switched to the common language. "Neither of you will speak of this to the other travelers. Ulek, since your father was an imperial soldier, I think you understand the importance of keeping this information within the army."

Ulek nodded.

The stern expression on Thais's face softened. "I'm sorry to hear of your loss. Your father would be very proud of you for warning us about the Charpans."

Ulek blinked before squaring his shoulders and lifting his chin.

Thais then turned to Kiri, studying her.

Mattos wondered if Thais's thoughts aligned with his own. It didn't make sense for the girl to have been alone, and it was a strange coincidence that the Charpans had come across a lone figure in the hills. The Wanderers originated in Charpa. She could be a spy, and yet … Wanderers weren't considered true Charpans. They didn't worship the Charpan Sky God. Their refusal to denounce their religion meant they couldn't own land or join the ruling class. Mattos's tutors had taught him that the first Wanderers had turned to trade due to their status. As their caravans traveled ever longer distances, they started taking their families with them. Eventually, the road became their home. It seemed unlikely a Wanderer would spy for Charpans, and they didn't need a spy. They knew where the column headed.

"You say you were alone when the Charpans took you," Thais said. "What were you doing alone in the hills?"

"My husband beat me, so I ran away. I'm looking for my birth clan."

The scar on Kiri's face took on new meaning. Mattos stared at it, wondering if her husband had given it to her. Plenty of men beat their wives, but what kind of man would deliberately disfigure the woman he had to look at every day? The only time Mattos had heard of such a thing, the wife had been unfaithful. That was probably it. The girl had been rolling in the grass with another man, and her husband had scarred her for it. It explained her desperate flight across the hills. She must have been disgraced and friendless within the clan and forced to strike out on her own.

Thais studied Kiri a moment before he said, "You can come with us, or you can go back to your clan and the husband you ran away from, but you must know by now you can't travel north by yourself. I'm shocked a woman would even attempt such a thing, with or without roaming bands of Charpans." He didn't wait for the girl to respond. Instead, he focused on Mattos. "Falcon," he said in Sandamedan. "I want you to keep an eye on these two. Ensure they travel in your section of the column."

Mattos turned to Kiri and Ulek. He didn't welcome the burden of watching over an orphan and a runaway wife. Yet these newcomers piqued his interest. Of the thousands in the column, only they had faced the Charpans, and as helpless as they seemed, they'd escaped. No wonder Thais had ordered him to observe them.

Chapter 9

KIRI

The morning sun peeked over the horizon, offering dim light. Kiri rolled out of the blanket the soldiers had given her and stood, stretching her arms over her head. People went about their morning routines: striking tents, preparing food, and wrangling children. Nearby, two soldiers stood by a food wagon and handed out rations to villagers. Ulek lay wrapped in his blanket, which rose and fell evenly. Kiri didn't see how he could sleep amid such commotion.

Looking around for a place to relieve herself, Kiri noted the absence of trees and foliage for privacy. People simply wandered a distance from the camp before crouching in the open. By an unspoken agreement, women kept to one side while men kept to the other. Kiri slipped her pack over her shoulders; she didn't dare let it out of her sight. A curious child might rummage through it, find her Forest clothing, and expose her. She headed for the women's side.

She'd expected she and Ulek would part ways once they reached the column. Instead, Ulek had stayed by her side.

Last night, he'd shared the last of the food taken from his cottage with her. When she'd curled up in her blanket to sleep, he'd lain next to her.

Had she been able to leave Ulek with his people and go off on her own, this wouldn't have been a problem. As it was, Kiri had no choice but to travel with the column. She didn't know the way to Ishtia, and she might run into the Charpans again. The imperial soldiers would escort her to Ishtia, protecting her from the Charpans and providing her with food the entire way. But she had another reason to stay with the column: Kordrick, the second man she needed to kill. Almost all southern Galeedans had joined the column, and as a southern Galeedan, Kordrick probably traveled within it.

Kiri gazed out over the mass of people stretching off into the distance. Somehow, she knew she and Kordrick would meet. Their life threads were already entangled. *I have only to pull your thread, Kordrick, and I will find you.*

Her thoughts drifted to the day that had led her to this moment. Kiri had traveled to Mar Dun during the spring celebrations. There, she'd visited with friends, Wren among them. He and Kiri had known each other since they were small children, exploring the forest and catching tadpoles together. One summer, they wandered so deep into the forest they lost their way. As dusk fell, they huddled together in the hollow of a mighty oak. They were still asleep, stars twinkling above the trees, when Kiri's uncles found them. During the long, silent walk home, Kiri could think only of the thrashing she'd receive. But Wren had pleaded, "Don't punish Kiri. It's my fault. I'm the one who wanted to go farther." In the last few years, a potent tension developed between them, and Kiri couldn't ignore the rumble of Wren's deep voice, or the way his eyes crinkled when he grinned.

Soon after Kiri's arrival, Wren asked her to hunt with him. Kiri soon gave up on shooting a deer when she realized her companion was far more interested in speaking with her than in providing food for his family. Abandoning the hunt, they fished in the shallow river not far from the village. Afterward, they lounged on the riverbank tossing stones into the water. Wren studied Kiri's face as they talked, waiting for a signal. When at last she fell silent, meeting his eyes with a smile playing on her lips, he reached for her. Two days later, an imperial soldier cut him down.

There had been a moment when they'd stood side by side, between those who fled and the wall of steel sprinting toward them. With growing horror, Kiri watched as her arrows glanced off the soldiers' armor.

As still as a bobcat before attacking his prey, Wren stood with his bow drawn, waiting for a definite kill. "Run, Kiri," he said, keeping his eyes on the enemy.

Kiri had turned toward him in bewilderment. She wouldn't abandon him or the other warriors scrambling to grab weapons.

"Run."

She would have died beside him if she hadn't seen Meadow struggling with her children. Meadow clasped her two-year-old to her chest while dragging her shrieking four-year-old behind her. She tried to run, hampered by her protruding belly. Her siblings had joined the fight, and those who fled ran past her. She looked around, expression panicked, when her eyes met Kiri's. "Help us!"

With a final glance at the advancing soldiers, Kiri sped toward Meadow, snatched the little boy off the ground, and grasped his mother's arm. She guided them from the village, looking over her shoulder only once. It was enough. She saw Wren fall, the soldier before him wielding a bloody sword. Even at that distance, Kiri saw the soldier's bright green eyes. She let out an anguished cry. Then a soldier charged them. Kiri dropped the child and relinquished Meadow's arm to grab her bow. She brought the soldier down only a few paces from them, the arrow protruding through his throat. But he still lived. He stumbled to his feet, his rage and- pain-filled eyes fixed on Kiri. His short sword cut across her face as she sprang backward. He fell again, coughing up blood, and didn't rise. Kiri had only a moment to clamp a hand over her face. If she hadn't jumped back, she'd have lost an eye. Then another soldier appeared, and Kiri shot an arrow at him. She missed, but the time he took to throw himself to the ground gave Meadow's siblings time to reach them. They fell upon the soldier. Meadow's sister, club in hand, looked over her shoulder, her eyes lingering on the children. To Kiri she cried, "Get them out of here!" then turned back to the fight. Kiri kept her bow handy, leaving Meadow to carry her children herself. In this way, they traveled through the forest, Meadow half carrying, half dragging her children, and Kiri guiding and protecting them. The others who escaped the slaughter eventually found them. Kiri led them all to her village. Only when she fell into her mother's arms did she let herself cry.

When the elders had chosen her to carry out their plan, Kiri had been full of purpose. She would end the war, perhaps even ease the suffering of those who'd lost loved ones.

Now, having joined the column, Kiri realized her mission was more complicated than she'd anticipated. The invading horde made an already difficult task seem impossible. Then there was Ulek … After she relieved herself, Kiri reentered the camp area, vowing that she'd wake before dawn for such needs. Squatting in the open before innumerable strangers was too much exposure for one accustomed to dense forests. She maneuvered through tents, campfires, and bustling people.

As she neared the location where she and Ulek had slept, something hard hit her shoulder. Biting back a cry of pain, she whirled around, searching for her assailant. A rock the size of her fist rolled at her feet.

No other rocks were thrown, and no one faced Kiri ready to attack. She caught sight of a yellow-haired boy of about fifteen running in the opposite direction. A large hand grabbed the boy's arm, stopping him in his tracks. Kiri couldn't see the man's face, but he wore a green-crested helmet. Soldiers of rank wore crests on their helmets to display their importance. Of course, this also meant the enemy knew who to kill. Imperial soldiers were stupid that way.

Too stunned to move, Kiri watched the soldier drag the struggling boy toward her.

"Tell me why you threw a rock at this girl," he said, his voice rough with anger.

Kiri recognized the voice of the soldier who'd ridden to meet her and Ulek when they'd joined the column.

Two boys ran up, leading a man and a woman carrying a baby in her arms. A girl of about seven trailed behind them. The man spoke to the soldier in what Kiri assumed to be Galeedan.

"I saw your son throw a rock at this girl," the soldier responded in the common language. "We have four thousand villagers here who are behaving, and I'd like to know why your son decided to cause trouble and attack people."

"She's a spy!" the boy burst out. "Why isn't she with her clan? How could she escape Charpan riders? They let her go so she could come to us." The boy's eyes filled with hate as he bared his teeth in a snarl.

The people nearby went about their business, as if indifferent or oblivious to the confrontation.

The soldier turned to Kiri. "Are you Charpan? Are you a spy?"

"No," Kiri answered, too bewildered to say anything else.

"You heard her," the soldier said. "She's not a spy. What could she tell the Charpans that anyone couldn't see for themselves? If I see you attack anyone else or cause more trouble, I'll whip you myself." He thrust the boy to his mother. "Watch him."

The woman clutched her son as the family moved away, the boy's friends lagging behind. One shouted, "Scar Face!" then sped away.

The soldier hissed something under his breath.

"Thank you," Kiri said, turning away.

"Wait."

Kiri glanced back at the soldier.

He reached up, undid the clasp under his square jaw, and removed his helmet. His prominent nose looked like it had once been broken. His hazel eyes had flecks of gold. They lingered on her scar, his expression inquisitive. "I am Falcon Mattos."

To humor him, Kiri repeated his name: "Mattos." She doubted she'd need to remember it. She didn't intend to speak to him again.

Mattos took a step closer. "If you or Ulek have any trouble, you can come to me, and I will help you."

Why would he take an interest in her and Ulek? They'd already told him all they knew about the Charpans. Kiri's heart quickened. Did he suspect she wasn't what she claimed to be? "Thank you," Kiri said. Then she hurried away.

A small fire burned next to Ulek, who sat eating mush from a bowl. Another mush-filled bowl had been placed across from him. "I got us some food," Ulek said, nodding toward the bowl.

Crouching, Kiri lifted the bowl and sniffed. She managed not to wrinkle her nose. It wasn't meat or any plant she recognized. Didn't these people know how to hunt? She used her fingers to scoop up the mush and stuck it in her mouth. It was tasteless, but hot and filled the stomach. "I spoke with the soldier called Mattos. He says to come to him if we have trouble." She hoped Ulek would have some insight as to why he'd shown an interest in them.

"*Falcon* Mattos?" Ulek looked over his shoulder. "He hasn't been helpful so far." He turned back to Kiri. "They won't take me back to bury my father."

Yesterday, Ulek had argued with the soldiers in Galeedan. Though Kiri hadn't understood them, she'd guessed the meaning of their argument.

"He served in their army, and they won't give him a decent burial," Ulek continued bitterly. "They expect me to let him rot." His eyes filled with a look of resentment. "You should have let me bury him when I had the chance."

Holding back a retort, Kiri fixed him with a level stare.

Finally, Ulek dropped his eyes. "I know we couldn't stay—the Charpans were looking for us. But imperial soldiers wouldn't have to worry about that."

Kiri kept silent. What could she say to an angry and grieving boy?

Ulek focused on the hills from which they'd come. "I hope Snowflake and Wildflower are all right. I wonder if I'll ever be able to find them when I go back." He sighed. "Whenever that will be."

Kiri studied Ulek as he returned his gaze to his morning meal. Like all Galeedans, he had pale skin, though the sun had turned his face and hands darker than his arms. She'd glimpsed the difference when his sleeves rode up. Ulek resembled his father: light brown hair, gray eyes, a long, straight nose. Traveling with him proved difficult. Kiri had to witness his grief, knowing she'd caused it. Every time she looked at Ulek, she was reminded of Orrik and what he had done to the Forest people, and what she'd done to him. Yet Kiri had started to like Ulek. He'd stayed calm throughout their ordeal with the Charpans and shown concern for her, even amid his own suffering.

Ulek's lack of family troubled her. She'd known no woman lived in the cottage and hadn't given much thought to this absence. It wasn't her fault the boy's mother had passed into the spirit world. Hearing Ulek speak about having no other relatives, however, had shocked her. Kiri couldn't imagine life without family; counting all her relatives would be difficult. Forest children were raised by their mothers and their mothers' siblings. If a child lost their family, everyone in the village would be willing to adopt them. Ulek had spoken as if nobody would want him. Did Galeedans allow children to remain alone and uncared for?

It didn't make a difference. Kiri pushed aside her nagging regrets. Orrik had deserved to die, and so did the other men she sought. She had to kill them, not just for herself, but for the future of her people. The soldiers had to learn the danger of attacking the Forest people. There would be no mercy.

Chapter 10

KIRI

Kiri stood on the bank of the Tarven River, which seemed to mirror her inner turmoil. She watched the raging current pass by, carrying debris and fallen tree branches from the storm the night before.

Travelers ventured out of their tents to find supplies soaked and the ground covered in mud. Boots and dress hems were soon mud-spattered, and carts slid on the wet grass. The overcast sky promised a gloomy day.

Crouching, Kiri thrust her hands into the turbulent water. She let it gush between her fingers, eventually turning them numb from the cold. It was a relief to focus on the sensation instead of her thoughts.

I have to do something about Ulek. It had pressed on Kiri's mind since they'd joined the column, but now she needed to act. Ulek was too attached to her, treating her like an elder sister and taking it for granted they'd look after each other during the journey. Ulek's father had attacked a Forest village. In turn, she had killed his father. Their life threads had been entwined by violence even before they'd met. They would both be better off parting ways before their lives became more enmeshed. He needed to build a new life, and she needed to focus on ending the lives of two men—something she couldn't do with a child in tow. Also, she'd been unable to find Kordrick in their portion of the column. She needed to search the rest of it, and Ulek had already gotten in the way of that. Besides, she traveled to her death. Ulek had already lost his parents. It wasn't fair to let him get close to someone who would die soon.

Finally, Kiri cupped her hands and brought the water to her lips, the cold stinging her mouth as she drank. She gasped, then buried her hands in her skirt to dry and warm them.

Standing, Kiri headed back to the camp. If she tarried too long, Ulek might come looking for her. She studied the families she passed, wondering if any would be willing to take Ulek in. They were unlikely to do so as long as he traveled with her. The Galeedans mistrusted and avoided Kiri. If Ulek distanced himself from her, a family might be more likely to adopt him.

Kiri had learned about marriage from Wanderers. The Forest people had life mates they loved and had children with; but save for a few taboos, they could mate with whomever they wanted, even after they found life mates. The idea someone could be satisfied mating with only one person in life baffled Kiri.

Kiri had also learned that non-Forest people left their childhood homes to live with their mates and raise the children they made. Kiri had observed these families since joining the column, eager to understand their peculiar living arrangements.

Among the Forest people, a mother raised her children with the help of her siblings. If a woman had one child or only children of the same sex, cousins or friends acted as siblings. Because children grew up alongside their cousins, little difference existed between siblings and cousins anyway. This was the value of siblings, the only true life companions. Mothers, aunts, and uncles were supposed to die first. Life mates and children came after reaching adulthood, and one made friends throughout life. Siblings were there from the beginning to the end.

Because Galeedans didn't share their offspring with their siblings, families were limited to the children the wife gave birth to. This gave Kiri hope that a family lacking a son might want Ulek.

Ulek sat on his blanket, digging his fingers into his bowl of mush. He'd set Kiri's bowl on her folded blanket. Since they'd joined the column, Ulek had been the one to fetch their meals. Kiri wondered if he did this because he sensed her fear of the soldiers.

Kiri lifted her bowl and sat on a blanket, tucking the folds of her dress between her legs so the fabric wouldn't fall into the mud or wet grass. She scooped up some mush and ate it off her fingers. She ate slowly. She still found the mush unappetizing. Finally, she set her empty bowl aside. "Ulek?" she began. When Ulek glanced up, she drew a deep breath. "Would you join a Galeedan family?"

The boy's brows furrowed. "What do you mean?"

Kiri swept her arms out in a gesture meant to include the entire camp. "Galeedans don't like Wanderers—they don't like me. If you travel with me, the Galeedans eventually won't like you either."

For a moment, Ulek looked concerned, then he snorted. "Don't worry about them. They won't bother us. Besides, I think they've gotten used to you."

"They don't *like* me."

Ulek grinned as if trying to assuage hurt feelings. "*I* like you."

"Ulek, you are Galeedan. You need Galeedan people, a Galeedan family."

Leaning forward, Ulek met Kiri's stare. "My father's dead. I'll get another family when I marry and have children. Until then, I'm on my own."

Kiri stared in amazement. How could he possibly bear to be alone so long? "You are a child."

Indignation flashed in Ulek's eyes. "I'm almost a man. Now that my father's dead, the farm belongs to me. If we can't ever come back, I'm no worse off than anyone else." He turned away, gazing in the direction from which they'd come. "At least you can go to your birth clan. Your people take your homes and possessions with you, but my people are farmers. The land is everything, and we're running away from it. When we get to Ishtia, we'll have nothing. No family's going to take in another mouth to feed—not now."

Dropping her gaze, Kiri studied her entwined fingers. Not only did Ulek lack a family, but he lacked a home—a fate she couldn't comprehend. Ulek's bitterness and defeat reminded her of the few children who'd survived Mar Dun. A dangerous thought came to her, twisting over her skull, forcing itself into her mind. Did Ulek suffer more than she had? She would never see her village again, but only because she'd volunteered to carry out her people's will. It was her decision. No one had driven her from her home. She knew of several villages full of people who loved and cared for her. Even now, in a foreign land surrounded by strangers, she felt their love. Every day they thought of her, spoke of her, grieved for her. Ulek had no one who loved or cared for him. The Charpans drove Ulek from his home, but she had killed the last of his kin. Kiri shook her head, trying to dismiss the thought. When she looked at the curly-haired boy across from her, she willed herself to remember the way his father had attacked her people. "We can't travel together."

Ulek only stared as Kiri stood and gathered her bowl and blanket. She half expected him to plead with her or call after her as she walked away, but he said nothing.

Chapter 11

MATTOS

Mattos walked through his camp on his way to share the evening meal with Lucen. The nine Falcon camps surrounded the civilian camp, allowing the soldiers to spend their evenings away from the villagers. Mattos was grateful for this. The villagers were friendly enough, but also needy and demanding, and he valued his time away from them. His soldiers seemed to share his attitude. Many took advantage of the lingering light to shave. As Mattos entered the clearing between Lucen's camp and his own, he heard a shout.

"Sir! Falcon Mattos!"

Mattos turned to find one of his Owls, a tall Sarpaskan, striding toward him.

"What is it, Mekindu?"

"Ozias, sir. He ..." Mekindu paused and looked at his feet.

"Out with it," Mattos snapped.

"Ozias can't be found."

"Can't be found?" Mattos repeated. "I saw him not that long ago."

"Yes, he volunteered to water Nica at the river, and he'd been so quiet lately we thought he wanted some time alone. That was hours ago, and he hasn't been seen since then, and Nica …" Mekindu faltered and cleared his throat. "Nica is missing also."

It took Mattos a moment to grasp Mekindu's meaning. "Ozias has deserted and taken *my horse*?"

Mekindu nodded.

"Are you sure he has deserted? How far have you searched?"

"We found horse tracks at the river that lead northwest to the main road. We didn't follow them far, but there's no doubt where he's headed."

Mattos ran his fingers through his short hair. "He never said anything to any of you?" he shouted without any effort to control himself. "After leaving the fort, he never hinted at deserting? He just left without any suspicious behavior?"

"He never said anything," Mekindu insisted. "He was no more scared than anyone else. He talked about the horde and the rumors, but then so did … We didn't suspect he'd desert."

Mattos struggled to maintain his self-control. Fear plagued the column. Hope, and perhaps denial, sustained order and kept everyone going. Word of a soldier's flight would cripple that hope, and one successful desertion would lead to more attempts. Ozias had to be caught and made an example of. "Go back to camp, Mekindu. Tell the men I said to keep this in the unit."

Mekindu hurried away.

Mattos quickened his pace to Lucen's camp. He needed to act quickly, while Ozias only had a few hours' head start.

Having a soldier desert was shameful enough, but for that deserter to steal one's own horse … Mattos would never outlast the disgrace if Ozias escaped. He dreaded explaining the situation to Diakiris before leaving.

Boulders and rock formations dotted the steep hills. Mattos rode Lucen's stallion, Edar. It didn't matter that the hoofprints he followed disappeared once they reached the tall grass; he knew Ozias's destination. One couldn't cross the mountains alone. With their hidden valleys and deep caverns, the Tarven Mountains were a haven to bandits. To avoid the dangers, Ozias would have to reach the main road.

Diakiris had agreed that Mattos should go alone after Ozias. They could spare no more horses. Mattos had stopped to make camp last night because it would have been too dangerous for Edar to continue in the dark. The horse could break his leg in a rabbit burrow. Plus, he needed rest. Ignoring the danger to Nica, Ozias had probably ridden during the night to put as much distance between him and the company as possible. Mattos hoped Ozias would be exhausted from traveling and, therefore, careless. He planned to make up lost ground and find the deserter by nightfall.

Not only did he have to bring Ozias back, but he faced losing Nica, a good warhorse worth at least fifty gold pieces. More importantly, she was his companion. He'd grown attached to her since the day his parents gifted her to him. He hoped she'd come to no harm.

Ozias's lack of riding experience put him at a disadvantage. As someone who'd only sat a horse a few times in his life, Ozias couldn't be a fast rider. He'd already traveled farther than Mattos had expected. Desperation must have made him a quick learner.

Mattos tugged Edar's reins to slow him as they descended a precipitous hill.

As they reached the bottom, a strained voice called out, "Falcon Mattos, stop!"

Mattos twisted in his saddle to see Ozias astride Nica. Boulders near the base of the hill partially hid them. Nica looked well, as if she had only trotted the whole way. Ozias, however, looked worn out and terrified. He wore no helmet, revealing bloodshot eyes and a dirty, sweat-streaked face. Mattos noted this with a small portion of his mind while the rest focused on the spear Ozias held aloft, aimed at Mattos's chest.

"Get off the horse, Falcon," Ozias commanded.

Ozias was only a few paces away. Despite Mattos's armor, the spear could kill him at that distance. "Don't disgrace yourself more than you already have," he replied, his eyes never leaving the spear.

"I will kill you if you don't get off the horse."

"Ozias, you can still come back." Mattos made his voice low and calm as he dismounted. When both feet reached the ground, he stood with his palms facing out, away from his sword. "You'll be publicly whipped and lose a month's pay, but if you come back with me now, you can return to the unit. Throw down your spear."

For a moment, Ozias seemed to waver, then he must have read the lie in his Falcon's eyes. "I'm not stupid," he spat. "They'll kill me if I come back with you. Gather your food and water, and leave. Sorry to take your mount, but it's better than killing you. If you have to walk all the way back to the company to get another horse, I'll be too far away for anyone to catch."

Mattos stepped back toward Edar's saddle. As he raised his hand to the saddlebag, he yelled, "Nica, up!"

Nica reared in the air, her hooves thrashing at the chest of an invisible enemy soldier, just as she had been trained to do.

Ozias fell from the saddle, dropping his spear as he hit the ground.

Mattos sprinted toward Ozias.

Struggling to rise, Ozias unsheathed his sword just as Mattos landed on top of him. Ozias gasped for air at the impact, even as he drove the hilt of his sword at Mattos's face.

Mattos caught Ozias's wrist, preventing the hilt from reaching his nose. The pair rolled on the ground, grappling for the sword. In the struggle, Mattos found himself on top and, still holding Ozias's wrist with his left hand, pummeled Ozias's face with his right. Blood from Ozias's nose and mouth spattered onto Mattos's hand.

Younger and smaller than Mattos, Ozias could try only to block the blows. As a punch drove Ozias's head into the ground, the sword slipped from his grasp.

Mattos let go of Ozias's wrist and wrapped his hands around Ozias's throat, his fingernails digging into the skin.

Ozias clawed at Mattos's fingers and struck his face.

Mattos squeezed Ozias's throat as he twisted his head to avoid the blows. It became a battle of timing and endurance—

Mattos's ability to endure the punches against Ozias's ability to withstand the choking. Ozias's eyes bulged as he ceased hitting Mattos's face and attacked the fingers digging into his throat. Blood from Mattos's mouth dripped onto Ozias's face as Ozias bent the little finger of Mattos's left hand backward.

Tears streaming down his face, Mattos maintained his grip as a scream ripped from his throat. He threw his head forward and slammed his helmet into Ozias's forehead. Stunned, Ozias released Mattos's finger. Again, Ozias clawed at Mattos's hands, with less strength than before. When an empty stare replaced Ozias's dazed expression, Mattos let go.

Mattos sat up, wiping the blood from his face and poking his lips. No loose teeth. He examined his little finger, relieved it wasn't broken. He tried not to think of the way Ozias had looked the moment life left his eyes. Mattos feared he'd remember that image for the rest of his days. After staggering to his feet, he approached Nica. She snorted as he rubbed the white blaze that ran down her face. "Good girl," he whispered, pressing his face against her head. Then he lifted Ozias's waterskin from Nica's saddle and, after removing his helmet, poured the waterskin's contents into it. He offered the helmet to Nica, who drank greedily. "Didn't share much with you, did he?" he asked.

Although Ozias's body lay on the ground, the worst was not over. The Hawk would want proof of his death.

Blood vessels in Ozias's eyes had burst, adding a ghastly element to his death grimace. Mattos tried not to look at Ozias's face as he pulled the armor off the body. The Sandamedan Army didn't tolerate wastefulness; he would bring back Ozias's armor and weapons. After tying the armor to Edar's saddle, Mattos drew his sword. He gazed down at the young man who had served in his own company. He couldn't have been more than nineteen.

Sandamedan short swords were stabbing weapons, not slicing ones, so the head wouldn't come off with one swipe. Mattos placed a hand on Ozias's forehead and hacked at the neck. It felt horrible, like cutting meat. Finally, the blade cut through Ozias's neck bones and, with one last sawing motion, severed the head.

Mattos pulled a sack from Edar's saddlebag and took a few steps toward the head before falling to his hands and knees and emptying his stomach. His body heaved in a foul rhythm as he gripped handfuls of grass. When the retching subsided, he wiped his mouth on the long grass.

After all his yearning to learn how he would perform in the act of killing, the first person Mattos killed was one of his own soldiers. He almost laughed at the bitter irony. Officers were expected to take care of their men, earn their trust, and lead them into battle. Instead, he'd killed one with his bare hands. Of all the ways an officer could lose a soldier, he had never imagined this.

Once again, Mattos walked toward Ozias's head, threw the sack over it, and scooped it up. He tied the sack to Edar's saddle before giving him a final pat. He then gathered Edar's reins and mounted Nica. Mattos kicked Nica's flanks and rode away without looking back at the headless body left to rot in the sun.

Chapter 12

KIRI

Most Galeedans preferred to eat where they camped for the night, so Kiri easily found a private place along the riverbank. Bowl of mush in hand, Kiri walked toward an area that looked comfortable when she spotted a soldier with dark brown skin resting his large frame on a boulder. In the fading light, Kiri saw he used a small knife to carve a piece of wood.

Before Kiri could change direction, the soldier looked up, called out, "Kiri the Wanderer," and waved her over.

Afraid of angering him if she didn't go, Kiri walked toward the soldier as he blew dust from his carving. Although he sat and she stood, the difference in their statures and the height of the rock made them almost face-to-face.

"I'm Mekindu," the soldier said. "I was surprised to hear a Wanderer was traveling with us. I've never heard of one traveling alone—certainly not a woman." He spoke casually, as if commenting on the weather.

Kiri forced a smile but didn't respond. The less she said, the less chance she had of giving herself away.

Mekindu studied her face, his black eyes darting back and forth. He leaned forward, resting his arms on his knees. "It's hard being away from home, isn't it? I'm from Sarpaska, and it's been years since I've been there."

Unsure how to respond, Kiri let her eyes linger on the scar that wrapped around Mekindu's neck.

He noticed. "A cord around my neck did that when I was ten," he said, running a hand along the scar. "I was four when the empire conquered Sarpaska. By the time the war ended, our leaders and many of our warriors were dead. Our people were weakened. Yayidan raiders attacked remote villages in the desert to steal women, children, and livestock. Sometimes the women and children were absorbed into the village, and sometimes they were little more than slaves. I was one of the unlucky ones." He sighed. "My people sailed here from Teletmoora hundreds of years ago after a failed rebellion. Maybe someday I'll travel there to see the civilization we came from."

"How did you become a soldier?" Kiri asked to change the subject. She'd never heard of Yayidan raiders but didn't dare admit it. There seemed to be frequent contact between the non-Forest peoples, and they knew much about each other's customs and lands because of it. Kiri's unfamiliarity with such topics would make her suspect.

Mekindu stared into the distance as he spoke. "There's a man in Sarpaska who believes all people have worth and that cruelty to other humans is a crime against the divine. People call him Thulu the Revered. His followers helped me escape. I would have joined them, but I wanted to go back to my village. I hadn't seen my family since the day raiders attacked our village. I didn't know what had happened to them. When I went back, I learned my parents were dead, but my sister was overjoyed to see me. She has a husband and children now. She wanted me to stay, but I traveled to Fort Renvivis. The Sandamedan Army had started to allow Sarpaskans to join if they were too young to have fought in the war. Some older men called me a traitor for joining the very army they'd fought years ago. But the Yayidans took me, not the Sandamedans, and a man with no money and no craft can find a place in the army. They sent me to Ishtia and eventually here." He shook his head and smiled wryly. "I don't even speak much Galeedan; it was hard enough learning Sandamedan."

The back of Kiri's throat ached. This man's village had been attacked just as Mar Dun had. As a child, he'd been torn from loved ones and all he knew. Kiri clenched her teeth, trying not to think of Mar Dun. Mekindu's candid divulgement of such pain surprised Kiri. When Forest people met, they never volunteered personal information until they had established how they were related, however distantly. Every village linked in some small way to every other, so usually a connection could be made between strangers. However, Mekindu seemed comfortable telling Kiri about himself despite having no familial or cultural connection.

Gesturing toward the scar that ran down Kiri's face, Mekindu said, "I see you have a scar of your own. People say you ran away from a cruel husband. Did he do that?"

Kiri nodded.

"It's a mean man who would do that to a pretty face."

"Very mean," Kiri said.

The soldier seemed to pick up on Kiri's discomfort with the subject and held out his carving. "My people honor the desert fox. This is Ekil."

Kiri took the carving, a fox with erect ears and tail, and ran her fingers over it. Tiny cuts in the wood indicated fur. The fox's eyes, nose, and mouth had been chiseled so it appeared to be almost smiling. It reminded Kiri of the toy animals she'd played with as a child. This fox had been carved in a different style, but as detailed as Forest work.

"He is one of your gods?" Kiri asked.

Mekindu chuckled. "There is only one god. Ekil is just a cunning fox we tell stories about. He will bring me luck."

As Kiri handed the carving back, Mekindu tugged on a cord around his neck. A small pouch attached to the cord slipped from beneath the armor on his chest. Sticklike designs had been burned into the leather. Mekindu must have noticed her staring because he said, "That's my name in Sandamedan. We all have our names burned into our coin purses." He dropped the carving into the pouch, which he tucked back under his armor.

The sound of hooves striking ground interrupted their conversation. Kiri turned to see a soldier riding toward her and Mekindu. She recognized the brown horse with a white stripe down its face as Mattos's mount. The mighty horse was the largest creature she had ever seen, its shoulders high above her head. It snorted through large nostrils and a rich, not unpleasant odor emanated from its coat. Bruises covered the visible parts of Mattos's face as if he'd had an accident. Dirt clung to his armor, and his swollen mouth bore a grim expression. Behind them trailed another great horse carrying armor and supplies.

Mekindu's friendly expression transformed into one of alarm. Kiri followed his gaze to a sack caked in dried blood that hung from the second horse's saddle. Guessing Mattos had gone hunting, Kiri eyed the sack. He must have made a messy job of it for the animal to bleed so.

Mattos reined in his horse in front of Mekindu and Kiri. He said Mekindu's name, then spoke Sandamedan in a weary voice.

Mekindu replied as he rose to his feet.

As they talked, Mattos's tone became harsh.

Kiri watched the two men, the language barrier making it impossible for her to understand the situation.

Mekindu gave Kiri a quick nod before he hurried away, leaving Kiri alone with Mattos. Neither spoke as they faced each other. Dried blood stained the corner of Mattos's mouth. Though shadows hid his eyes, Kiri knew he stared at her.

Mattos dismounted and led the horses to the riverbank. "What were you and Mekindu talking about?"

"Sarpaska and Ekil."

As the horses drank, Mattos removed his helmet, revealing an eye swollen purple. He hadn't had an accident; he'd been attacked. Crouching beside his horse, he splashed water on his face. "And what did Mekindu have to say about his homeland?"

"He misses it."

Mattos gazed across the river. "Do you miss your home, Kiri? I suppose your caravan is your home." His questions were like Mekindu's, but he had an edge in his tone.

Kiri heard anger, and something she couldn't identify. "What happened?"

Mattos stood and faced her. "I killed a man. I killed one of my own soldiers for desertion." He sounded shocked, as if he couldn't believe his own words.

Kiri didn't move. Mattos had killed one of his own people. She understood the man had broken non-Forest rules, but what could warrant death? Even if the man had needed to die, how could Mattos have borne killing him? Killing Orrik had been horrifying enough. What kind of person could bring himself to kill one of his own people just for fleeing the enemy?

They stared at each other for what seemed like a long time. Mattos appeared to be waiting for her response, but Kiri didn't know what to say.

Finally, Mattos turned away. "I have to speak with the Hawk." He gathered the reins of the horse that carried armor and mounted his own horse. "Good day, Kiri," he said before riding off.

Kiri stared after him in horror. Mattos hadn't wanted to kill that soldier and had obviously been shaken by the deed. Yet he'd done it. How cruel the non-Forest people were, to have customs that forced a man to kill another, when neither had done any wrong.

Chapter 13

ULEK

The mouth hung open in a silent scream. The eyes bulged, and dried blood and mucus spattered the skin. The face had been beaten, and the nose broken before the head had been removed from the body. The skewered head was on display near the front of the column. Vultures, circling overhead, were kept at bay by the thousands of people trudging past.

Parents tried to shield their children from the sight, though none shielded Ulek's gaze. He found it almost impossible to believe it was a human head, for there was nothing human about it. It seemed more like a hunk of meat, or a slaughtered animal, than a face that might have smiled not long ago.

The head hadn't been there when the column had made camp the night before, but it had been present and ready to greet them when they woke.

Turning toward a gray-bearded man, Ulek asked, "Who was that man?"

"Not much of a man anymore."

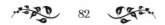

Ulek waited for the old man to continue, but he volunteered no more information. "Who was he?" he asked again.

"*That,*" said the old man nodding back toward the head, "belonged to a soldier who stole Falcon Mattos's horse and deserted."

"But how did they … ?"

"The Falcon went after him. Brought back his horse and the head."

Ulek turned to look back at the head. It didn't make sense for a soldier to desert now. They were fleeing the enemy, not headed for a battle. They had food and safety in numbers. By striking off one of his own, the soldier had risked danger from mountain bandits *and* the Charpans. The soldier had lost his mind or been a fool, unless … Could the Charpans be much closer than the soldiers let on? If so, the deserter had run away because he didn't believe the column would make it to Ishtia before they were attacked. Ulek had been so grief-stricken by his father's murder and having to leave the only home he'd ever known that he hadn't had a chance to fear the Charpans. Until that moment, he'd assumed the column would reach Ishtia before the Charpans caught up with them. But with soldiers deserting … Ulek shuddered before he resumed walking.

A snicker interrupted Ulek's troubled thoughts.

"What's wrong? The head scare you?" A tall, lanky boy a few years older than Ulek fell in step beside him. His shaggy blond hair fell across his heavily blemished face. Two brown-haired boys, one covered in freckles, followed close behind.

"No," Ulek answered, staring straight ahead. His father had told him that if he didn't show fear when threatened by bullies, they would lose interest.

"I think it does," insisted the blond boy. "I saw you shiver. I think you're afraid of dead bodies."

"I'm afraid of the Charpans," Ulek said, meeting the blond boy's stare. "I'm the one who told the soldiers a band of Charpans is already in Galeed. Maybe you heard. While your mother tucked you in bed, I escaped the Charpans who murdered my father."

The two other boys looked impressed, but the blond boy's eyes flashed with anger. "Where's your scar-faced sweetheart?"

"The Wanderer girl is traveling on her own," Ulek said, careful to keep his tone indifferent. Kiri's abandonment pained him more than he wanted to admit.

"What happened?" the blond boy taunted him. "Did you have an argument, or did you just get tired of looking at her ugly face?"

"No, but I'm getting tired of looking at yours."

The blond boy shoved Ulek so hard he stumbled back several paces. "What did you say to me?"

A fight was now inevitable. Ulek charged, slamming into the older boy with such force they both fell. Ulek managed to get in two good punches before the other boy rolled on top. The two dark-haired boys gathered around, encouraging their friend.

The blond boy's fists crashed into Ulek's face and stomach.

Ulek held his arms over his face, trying to protect himself against the older boy's superior strength and speed. The blows to his stomach knocked the air from his lungs. The beating seemed to go on forever, then the punches stopped, and the other boy's weight lifted.

"What were you trying to do? Kill him?" A red-bearded villager stood beside Ulek with his hands on his hips. The blond boy lay nearby where the man had tossed him. The two other boys hung back, watching the man with wary eyes.

Ulek propped up on his elbows, gasping for breath. Blood trickled over his lips. His head spun, and everything ached from the waist up.

Grasping the front of the blond boy's tunic, the villager yanked him to his feet. "What's the matter with you, picking on a smaller boy? He must be three years younger than you." He turned to Ulek. "Are you all right, boy?"

"Yes."

"He started it," the blond boy argued. "He punched me first."

"It's true," the freckled-faced boy said. "We were just talking to him, and he went after Derk."

The villager dragged Derk toward Ulek. "Is that true? Did you start this fight?"

"I punched him first," Ulek said, wiping the blood from his face, "after he shoved me."

The villager snorted. "Now I see." He glanced toward a woman and two children who stood alongside the moving column. Ulek guessed them to be the man's family, waiting for him to rejoin them. The children clutched their mother's hands as they stared wide-eyed at the scene. "Where are your people?" the man asked Derk.

"They're back a ways," the boy answered, scowling.

The man started to drag Derk in the opposite direction of the moving column. "I'm taking you to see your father so you can explain to *him* what you've done."

"What is this? Keep moving."

All eyes turned to the mounted soldier with the green-crested helmet. Ulek caught his breath when he recognized Falcon Mattos. His face was bruised and swollen—from fighting the now-beheaded man, Ulek realized. He gaped in horrified awe at the man who had killed his own soldier and then impaled his head on a pike for all to see.

"This bully attacked a younger boy. I'm taking him to his father," the villager said, jerking on Derk's tunic.

"Boys fight," Mattos snapped. "Let them go. We don't have time to stop for every childish argument and—" His eyes fell on Ulek, who'd staggered to his feet. "Ulek?" Then he turned to look more closely at Derk. "*You* again. I told you what would happen if you caused more trouble." He jumped from the saddle and unsheathed his sword.

Ulek froze, expecting the bloodthirsty soldier to run Derk through.

Instead, Mattos grabbed the scruff of Derk's neck and began striking his backside with the flat of his sword.

The boy howled and struggled to get away.

Finally, Mattos released Derk, who hurried off, followed by his two friends.

"It'll be worse the next time!" Mattos shouted after them.

The red-bearded Galeedan who'd rescued Ulek rejoined the column with his family.

Ulek stood motionless as Mattos approached him. Had anyone else spanked his attacker with a sword, Ulek would have unabashedly enjoyed it. Because Mattos had done it, he'd been struck dumb. At first, the soldier represented safety. Now, Mattos was the man responsible for the head rotting on a pike not far away.

"Where's Kiri?"

Ulek swallowed, unable to find his voice.

"Where's Kiri?" Mattos asked again, dropping down on one knee. "Why isn't she with you?"

"Sh-She's traveling on her own," Ulek stammered.

Mattos's eyes widened. Then he scowled. "Why? I thought you were traveling together."

"Not anymore."

"So, you're both alone now. What happened?"

Ulek shrugged.

Mattos sighed as he rose to his feet. He stared at Ulek, as if he wanted to say more. "She shouldn't have left you," he muttered as he turned away.

Chapter 14

MATTOS

Crickets calling for mates filled the warm night. When Mattos had been a child, he'd asked his father about the noise. They had been staying at their country estate, and the next day his father had caught a cricket to show him, explaining the process. That memory now struck Mattos as surreal. It seemed impossible he had ever been that innocent. Three days ago, he'd killed and beheaded a young man he used to command.

Some of his soldiers talked, and occasionally a laugh rang throughout the camp, but most slept. Mattos sat alone outside his tent, using the dim light of his campfire to write an account of what had happened with Ozias and list the army property retrieved from the body. Even during a desperate retreat, the Sandamedan Army kept conscientious records.

Sparks flew over the crackling wood as Lucen stepped into the light. His eyes lingered on the heap of weapons and armor before he circled the fire. "Thought you'd like some company," he said, sitting beside Mattos.

"I don't want to talk about it," Mattos replied, his head still bent over the parchment. The last few days had been full of horror and guilt over Ozias's death. During his training, Mattos had been ordered to slaughter pigs to learn what it felt like to force steel through flesh and hear agonized screams. Yet nothing could have prepared him for choking a man and watching the life fade from his eyes.

"That's fine." Lucen leaned back on his elbows to gaze up at the stars. The two men had been silent some time when Lucen finally said, "Cylin gives thanks to Esnin for your safe return."

"Your wife is kind to think of me."

"I have some writing of my own I've been working on," Lucen said. "A letter to my parents." When Mattos looked up from his parchment, Lucen continued. "We all know why Ozias ran. The chances of us reaching Ishtia before the Charpans … My will is safe in Ishtia, and Cylin will get money from the army if something happens to me, but my parents— They were furious I married a Galeedan girl. Cylin won't be destitute, but she's lost her home. She's going to need a family to look after her." He paused, staring into the fire. When Mattos didn't respond, he continued. "If it comes down to a battle, she'll reach Ishtia. The company can hold off the horde for a time. She has a horse, she'll make it," he said, his voice firm, as if trying to convince himself. "I've told her to go to the military's widow house. She can live there, and they'll see to it she gets what's owed her, but I don't want that life for her. A family like mine could do so much for her."

"You think they won't take her in?"

"They refused to come to the wedding and haven't responded to my letters since then," Lucen said. "They think she's an ignorant barbarian. Why would they take her in?"

"Because you would be *dead,*" Mattos replied. "It's easy to be angry with a living son. But when the widow of their youngest child shows up at their door, would they turn her away? She'd be all that's left of you. Do you really think they'd dishonor your memory like that? Even if they didn't want to take her in, everyone would know she was their son's widow, Galeedan or not. The social pressure alone would make them look after her. And that's without grandchildren. If she reached Ishtia carrying your child, think of the power she'd have over them."

"She isn't," Lucen said, his voice hard. "We aren't all—" His abrupt silence left the unsaid words dangling between them.

"We aren't all as fertile as Marenda and I were?" Mattos lifted the metal pen from the parchment. "No, but fertility only counts when the mother and baby survive the labor."

"My friend, I am sorry." Lucen's voice sounded hoarse.

"Don't be," Mattos said with a dismissive gesture. "You're worried about your wife's safety and the quality of her life should anything happen to you. At least you love her. I never loved my wife the way I should have."

"I know you grieved for her—and your son."

Mattos closed his eyes. He could still feel the tiny babe, wrapped in a blanket, in his hands.

"Stillborn," the midwife had said. "Too early."

He'd held his son only for a moment before handing him back.

"Of course," Mattos said. "A man would be heartless not to." He sighed. "I never told you about Layna. After what happened to Marenda, I didn't think I should. A lot of rich men wanted Layna for a mistress, but she chose me. My mother wept when I told her I wanted to marry a servant girl. My father told me that, as his firstborn and only son, I needed to marry a girl from a good family to secure our standing. He said having his son marry the daughter of a poor fisherman would ruin all he had done for us and destroy my sisters' chances of making good matches. He said women like Layna tried to trap rich men's sons. I'm not from the senatorial class like you. You can marry a Galeedan without losing your position. I'm the son of a common fabric merchant, no matter how rich. The truth is my family did need me to make a good match. I needed to think of my little sisters. I did my duty to my family and told Layna I couldn't marry her." Mattos paused, staring into the fire. As often as he'd thought of Layna, he'd never told anyone this story.

Lucen sat silent and motionless.

After clearing his throat, Mattos continued. "She wed a blacksmith soon after, and my parents arranged my own marriage. They did their best to find a woman they thought I'd like, instead of choosing the first girl from a good family whose parents would agree to the match. Marenda was pretty and good-natured. I didn't love her. I even resented her a little. Duty to my family made me abandon the woman I loved and become a cold husband to a woman who deserved better. Marenda tried to be a good wife and would have been a good mother. But she knew I loved someone else. She left her home, friends, and family to live in an army fort in a foreign land with a husband who didn't want to be married to her. Even news of the babe didn't bring us closer. I didn't realize how lonely and stressed she must have been. I can't help but think that if I'd treated her better, if she'd been happier, she might not have gone into labor so early."

Lucen's eyes were wide. "I'm sorry."

Mattos shrugged. "It's not all bad. I hear Layna has two children now, and that her husband treats her well. A blacksmith's wife doesn't have to work as a servant. With the connection to Marenda's family, my sisters should marry well. If I die, they'll inherit my parents' land and my father's ships someday. It'll make them even more eligible as brides." Mattos met his friend's eyes. "Don't worry about Cylin. Her husband was brave enough to defy his family and marry the woman he loved. I think your parents will honor that."

Chapter 15

KIRI

The column had entered the Tarven Mountains, where the wind shrieked like angry spirits. All day, dresses and hair had billowed in an unrelenting dance. Now in the darkness, gusts attacked tents, snapping loose flaps, and pounding on the sides. Several tents even blew over.

Kiri huddled wide-eyed under her blanket, unnerved by the wind's humanlike cries. In the Forest lands, the soothing sound of rustling leaves accompanied windy nights. Never had she experienced such rage and violence from nature. She wondered how Ulek faired, and if a family had taken him in. Maybe if he sat with her, these strange forces of nature—in an equally strange land—wouldn't frighten her so. She hadn't realized how comforting his presence had been until they'd parted ways.

A gust of wind brought another piercing scream, followed by what sounded like muffled cries. How could the weather make such sounds? Surely lost spirits wandered the camp, unable to make their journey to the spirit world. Nearby, a horse neighed. Had the wind carried that sound too, or was the horse as frightened as Kiri? Another gust brought the sound of men shouting. What she heard next was unmistakable—someone running past her—a flesh-and-blood person.

Kiri jumped to her feet, throwing aside her blanket. Someone or something had attacked the camp. She didn't know what danger she faced, but she needed to slip out of the camp and hide. Keeping close to the ground, she crept away from the tents and wagons. A dappled gray horse reared up, its pale coat shining in the moonlight. Swords clanged in the distance; even the wind couldn't drown out that sound. A few people ran about while families gathered in confusion.

Kiri clutched her knife. If anyone attacked her, she'd have to strike quickly.

Mounted men rode into view. Kiri sucked in her breath as she recognized the riders who'd taken her and Ulek captive. People fled, screaming in terror. The riders pursued them, drew back their bows, and—

Kiri bit back a cry as a rider buried an arrow in a woman's back. When the woman fell, her children threw themselves on her, crying and screaming.

"Sprits of the forest, save me," Kiri choked. She broke into a cold sweat as her heart raced. The anguish of seeing innocents killed by cruel men once again overwhelmed her. She collapsed, shaking. *I must get up.* Kiri squeezed her eyes shut. *Breathe.* She still held the knife. She ran her thumb over the tree image burned into the leather—she knew it by touch. The tree, the symbol of her people. Her people had honored her by giving her this knife, this mission. *Move.* Kiri eased forward, crawling on her elbows, her stomach against the ground. She couldn't die now, before she had fulfilled her promise to her people.

The murderers rode on, shooting more arrows and cutting people down with their swords. More Charpans rode past, carrying supplies and leading two horses hitched to food wagons. Fighting sounds reverberated from elsewhere in the camp. Armored soldiers sprinted by, firing arrows at the fleeing riders.

Gradually, the sounds of battle became more distant. Only the unnatural howling of the wind remained. Somehow, Kiri had been spared. "Thank you," she whispered, lowering her head to the ground. The wind abruptly slackened, and a child's wail reached Kiri's ears. She rose, staring in the direction of the fallen mother. The violent winds returned as Kiri headed toward the woman. Her dress swirled around her, tugging at her legs.

Peering through the crowd that gathered around the body, Kiri saw that someone had broken off the end of the arrow and rolled the woman onto her back. She lay with her eyes closed and her yellow braid tossed over her throat. The front of the arrow protruded from her chest. She must have been struck in the heart and died almost instantly. All three of the children gathered around her looked to be under six. One girl sobbed so hard she started coughing.

Unsure of the proper death rituals, or how non-Forest people grieved, Kiri hung back. A Forest person would have leaned into the woman's ear and sung the song of farewell while her spirit lingered in her body. When the body became cold, they knew the spirit had left. Surely the woman's spirit still kept the body warm. Why did no one say goodbye?

The sight of the grief-stricken and now motherless children became too much. Kiri walked forward and knelt at the woman's side. She had been killed by evil men and died in terror like so many of the Mar Dun villagers. In this, Kiri felt kinship to her. It didn't matter what people she belonged to; her spirit deserved a proper goodbye. Kiri pressed her hand to the woman's chest and bent her mouth close to her ear. She felt warmth; the spirit still lingered. For a moment, Kiri hesitated, fearful the Galeedans would recognize the sound of Forest words. She decided to take the risk; they would probably think she sang in the Wanderer language. She began the song.

Go well on your journey
You have been loved
You will be missed
Do not worry about the world of the living
We give you permission to go

The children had stopped their wailing when Kiri began to sing and now stared silently at her, their faces wet with tears.

The song complete, Kiri sat back on her heels and looked up at the Galeedans who gaped at her.

Chapter 16

MATTOS

Mattos jerked awake, unsure of what had roused him. Outside, the wind howled and beat at his tent—nothing he shouldn't have been able to sleep through. *Another nightmare*, he thought as he rolled onto his side and pulled his blanket over his shoulders. He'd had them since the day he killed Ozias. Then, what sounded like a man's shout cut through the wind's shrieks. Mattos sat up. Another cry sounded in the distance. Tossing aside his blanket, Mattos leaped to his feet. He grabbed his sword and boots, not bothering with his armor.

He stumbled out of his tent, still pulling on his boots. The wind prevented the sentries from maintaining fires. Luckily, moonlight illuminated the camp. Most of his men emerged from their tents in confusion as well. Mattos mounted Nica after untying her reins from the tether pole. He rode bareback toward the direction of the shouts. As he rode through the camp of soldiers scrambling for weapons, he called, "Don't fire. It's Falcon Mattos." He didn't want to meet his end because one of his own soldiers didn't recognize him without armor in the darkness.

The familiar clanging of steel meeting steel reached his ears, but this was no training exercise. Had the mountain bandits truly dared to attack a company of Sandamedan soldiers? When Mattos came within sight of the food wagons, he saw his sentries, Ladius and Anundi, exchanging sword blows with two mounted men. He rode straight for them. As he neared the fight, he noticed the attackers' short beards and small, elegant horses. Charpans. The horde had caught up with them. A level of fear and rage he'd never felt surged through him.

The larger of the Charpans had forced Ladius back against one of the food wagons. Pinned, without the ability to even step backward, Ladius took the defense. He held his sword high and parried the Charpan's blows.

The Charpan must have heard the impact of Nica's hooves on the ground. Just before Mattos reached the fight, the Charpan twisted in his saddle and deflected Mattos's thrust. Freed from the attack, Ladius hurried to aid Anundi.

The Charpan sneered when the tip of his sword cut Mattos's right forearm. Mattos's senses heightened. His men's cries became clearer, and he took in his opponent's minutest details. He noticed the Charpan's crooked nose, sweat glistening on his face, and a tiny scar that cut through his left eyebrow.

His own blood ran down his arm. From the corner of his eye, he saw Ladius and Anundi pull the other Charpan from his horse. Many of his armed soldiers hurried to them.

The Charpan swiped at Mattos's head, and he just managed to repel the blade. The Charpan tried to cut and hack instead of stab; his sword was too long to stab in such close combat. Mattos intensified his attack, focusing on speed rather than power. He kept his onslaught high. The Charpan met the assault with fierce strength. The hilt of Mattos's sword quivered in his hands each time the enemy's blade struck his own. At a moment when the Charpan raised his heavy sword high, Mattos leaned forward with all the speed he could muster and plunged his sword into the Charpan's gut.

Grunting, the Charpan dropped his weapon. He clutched his wound as he glared at Mattos with pained eyes. Mattos met those eyes before stabbing the Charpan in the chest. This time, he fell from his horse.

As soon as the Charpan hit the ground, soldiers encircled Mattos and his two sentries. The Charpan Ladius and Anundi had been fighting lay on the ground, dead. Ladius panted over the body as he held his hand over a shoulder wound. Anundi held the reins of the Charpan's horses. The fresh soldiers looked about, seeing no enemy left to attack.

Mattos dismounted. The entire column should have been overrun with bloodthirsty riders. Instead, there was only fear, confusion, and the shrieking wind. Mattos realized it must have been the band of Charpans Ulek and Kiri had warned the column about. The horde had not reached them. "Search the camp, see if there are others. Alert the other camps and report back to me," he ordered. Most of the soldiers hurried away. "Someone see to Ladius," he added, although two men already moved toward him.

When the remaining men got a good look at Mattos, their eyes widened. "Sir, are you all right?" asked Mekindu.

"It's only a cut," Mattos said. When he glanced down at his wound, he realized blood spattered his chest and right arm. "It's not mine."

The wounded Charpan gasped, and Mattos crouched beside him. The man's eyes showed pain and anger as he coughed up blood. He glared at Mattos, as if unwilling to admit defeat or fear.

"Water," Mattos ordered. A few moments later, someone pressed a waterskin into his hand. When Mattos held the waterskin near the Charpan's mouth, he refused to drink. He had already started on his way to the city of the dead, or the sky world the Charpans believed in. He coughed up more blood, finally holding his mouth open. Mattos poured water into the Charpan's mouth, though he couldn't drink much before coughing again. Some of the hatred left the Charpan's eyes, to be replaced with fear and more pain. Only a few days ago, Mattos had killed Ozias, watching the life disappear from his eyes as he choked the breath out of him. Now he had killed a man in battle. When the dying man parted his lips again, Mattos gave him more water. He stayed like that until the Charpan finally succumbed to his wounds.

The man dead, Mattos rose to his feet. To his surprise, Diakiris stood beside him.

"They're gone," Diakiris said, "but it's cost us. Some are dead, many more are wounded."

"Who is dead?" Mattos asked in alarm.

"You didn't lose any men," Diakiris replied, "but I did." His eyes moved over the food carts, the dead Charpans, the Charpans' captured horses, and Ladius being stitched up by the company's physician, Omeldar. He turned back to Mattos. "It was the scouts sent ahead by the main force—about two dozen. At least *your* unit killed some. I've sent Lucen's men after the rest. When Omeldar is finished with Ladius, he'll see to you. I want you with me when I report to the Hawk."

Chapter 17

MATTOS

"How is it that a band of fewer than thirty Charpans got past our sentries, killed ten of our men, wounded others, and stole food from under our noses!" Hawk Thais flung his helmet to the ground. "If the Sandamedan Empire's army is going to let itself be butchered and raided by a few Charpan scouts, then we might as well throw down our arms and armor and *run* to Ishtia. We might get there faster without all that weight."

Thais paced back and forth, eyes bulging, a vein standing out on his forehead. His neck tendons strained against his skin, as if trying to break free. Mattos thought he looked like a wild dog, ready to tear out someone's throat. "We have five thousand Charpan riders chasing us. Five thousand! Yet you let a handful of them overtake this camp like a bunch of unarmed women. I never thought I'd live to see such incompetence and shame."

No one dared speak. All the officers stood around the Hawk's tent, where they had been ordered at dawn. Soldiers dug graves nearby.

The Galeedan camp stirred; most people probably hadn't slept after the attack. The wind had slackened, as if spent from the previous night's efforts. People milled about in shock and grief.

The Charpan band had been clever. They'd waited for a particularly windy night to drown out the sound of their approach. Creeping between army camps, they'd entered the main camp undetected. Once there, they'd attacked the soldiers from the very camp they guarded—the last place they had expected. With surprise and horses in their favor, the Charpans had targeted the sentries guarding food carts. The attackers had kept the soldiers occupied while other Charpans hitched horses to the food wagons and drove them away. They'd shot and cut down all in their path. Ten soldiers, five Galeedan men, three women, and two children were dead. Fourteen soldiers and nine Galeedans had been wounded. Four food carts, along with the horses that usually pulled those carts, had been taken.

Falcon Oistin, the only other wounded officer, carried his bandaged right arm in a sling. The arrowhead had pierced his upper arm, missing the bone. It had been easy to break the arrow and free it from Oistin's flesh. The physician had then cleaned, stitched, and bound the arm. Sweat trickled down Oistin's now sallow face. He shifted his weight from foot to foot, swaying slightly.

"How did we only kill two of them?" Thais asked.

Mattos stood near the front of the officers, his face still discolored from Ozias's punches. His right forearm bore stitches from the deep cut the Charpan had given him. He risked a glance at Diakiris, whose face revealed nothing. Four of Elmaturis's men had died last night. As Elmaturis's harrier, Diakiris shared the grief and shame.

"Not only have we disgraced ourselves and the soldiers who fell," Thais went on, "but we've lost most of our food without any chance of getting more. We don't have time to hunt or fish. My scouts informed me last evening that the Charpans are closer than we anticipated. Let me remind you that they aren't following our trail because defeating this company will make a difference in the war—it won't. They're following us because blood and battle are sport to them. The western riders want to instill fear in the empire's people when they hear of our gruesome deaths. If we continue at this pace, they'll overtake us. That means we have to double our pace while *starving*!" Thais hissed an oath through his teeth as he kicked his helmet out of his way.

Mattos realized Thais's screaming and pacing wasn't anger, but desperation. He decided Thais didn't look like a mad dog so much as a cornered wolf.

"We're down to one small meal a day for everyone. There'll be less time to cook and camp. Galeedans who fall behind will be left behind." Thais took a breath before continuing. "Your sentries will stop sleeping at their posts and do what they are supposed to. This wouldn't have happened if they'd paid attention to their surroundings. Considering how easy it was to steal from us, the Charpans might be back for more. I've sent scouts to follow their trail, but we all know how hard it is to track in these mountains. We've never been able to find the mountain bandits, so I doubt we'll find Charpans." Thais fixed his eyes on Mattos. "At least some of us reacted as imperial soldiers should."

Mattos fought the urge to lower his eyes. Diakiris had praised Mattos and his sentries for killing two bandits. This was probably due as much to Diakiris's desire to offset the mistakes of his cohort as to genuine pride. It was better for all of them to have heroes as well as failures from the attack.

"You and your men have honored us, Falcon," Thais said. "Once we reach Ishtia, you and your sentries will be publicly commended. Perhaps by Eagle Isandor himself."

"Thank you, Hawk," Mattos replied.

While some officers gazed at Mattos with newfound respect, several, including Elmaturis, glared. To have a fabric merchant's son command the men who killed a Charpan and kill one himself while they, men of the senatorial class, had killed none added to their disgrace.

Thais retrieved his helmet from the ground. He stared at it as if he didn't understand why it had been there before placing it on his head. "Once we bury our men and those Galeedans who fell, we are moving." Not bothering to dismiss them, he turned to walk away.

As soon as Thais turned his back, Oistin fell to his knees. When another officer grabbed his good arm to help him up, he vomited on the other man's boots. Mattos hurried to Oistin's side, where a few other men now crouched. The officer who'd originally tried to help Oistin lowered him to the ground, where he continued to vomit in violent spasms.

Thais strode to the gathered men. "What's wrong with you, Oistin?" he said, his eyes alarmed.

Mattos freed Oistin's arm from the sling and tore away the bandages, exposing black and swollen flesh. The wound oozed. "Poison," Mattos said. "The arrows were poisoned."

Chapter 18

ULEK

The wounded lay close to where Hawk Thais presided over the mass funeral. Most moaned between dry heaves, their stomachs emptied some time ago. The two children who suffered poisoned arrow wounds shrieked in agony. Ulek prayed to the goddess Esnin, the most merciful of the gods, to send the white ships for the children. They were doomed anyway, and he couldn't bear their screams much longer.

Ulek hadn't felt the arrow graze his leg. He'd focused all his attention on escape. Only after the attack did he notice a tear in his trousers, just above the boot. Pulling up his left pant leg revealed a small scratch covered in tiny beads of blood. At the time, he could only marvel at how close he'd come to being seriously wounded by a Charpan arrow. He'd even wished the cut had been deeper so he would have a scar to show off to other boys. Then the cut began to sting and secrete black ooze. By the time the stars disappeared from the sky, his leg had swollen, and a cold pain seized his heart.

Nearby, soldiers plunged shovels into the earth. They had started digging graves at the morning's first light, pausing only when the scouts returned. News the scouts had lost the Charpans' trail had spread quickly through the column. Ulek wondered if the soldiers would dig enough graves for the wounded or only enough for those already dead. The villager who'd carried Ulek to lie among the poisoned had promised him they wouldn't all die. "Boys your age have survived snake bites before, and the soldiers say the Charpans probably diluted the venom to make more of the poison. It was only a scratch, right?" As much as his head had spun, Ulek hadn't missed the man's placating tone or the doubt in his eyes. He'd allowed himself to hope when he'd seen the soldiers building litters and preparing carts to carry those too sick to walk. Then the soldiers had borne away their injured comrades, leaving the villagers lying on the ground. They would be left behind.

Ulek realized he would die. Even if he survived the poison, he would be too weak to catch up with the column. He had no food or water and no one to look after him. Some would stay behind to care for and eventually bury their relatives, but they wouldn't care for Ulek. He didn't expect kindness. Since his father's death, Kiri had been the only person to show concern for him, and she'd abandoned him.

Ulek thought of his mother resting alone at the top of the hill near his farm. Her husband rotted in the cottage, and soon her only child would rot in the Tarven Mountains. They belonged together on the hill overlooking the farm and the Elkin Forest, with wildflowers growing over them. Even the comfort of knowing they would be reunited in the Hills of Idenya couldn't banish the pain of their remains being separated for eternity.

Tears filled Ulek's eyes. He didn't want to die. He wanted to swim in the river, farm his own land, hunt in the forest, and sleep under the stars. He wanted to own a horse someday and gallop it over the hills. He wanted to raise a large family and live to be an old man. Now he'd never even have a dog.

I want to go home.

The sudden urge to be home overwhelmed him. Ulek envisioned his straw bed and brown homespun blankets. Somehow, if he could reach his own bed in the cottage he'd been born in, dying wouldn't be so terrible. He might even see Wildflower and Snowflake. Ulek rolled onto his stomach and raised to his hands and knees. His bare left foot pressed into the grass; he'd been forced to remove his boot when his leg began to swell. The world spun as he staggered to his feet. *I'll just keep walking till I get there. It's not so far.*

With each step, white-hot pain shot through his leg, but Ulek focused on going home. He stumbled through the prostrate crowd, not noticing he'd stepped on a woman's hand until she cried out. The ground was strangely unstable, as if it undulated under his feet. A few paces later, the ground surged up. Just before it struck him, Ulek felt arms seize him.

"Ulek!"

When Ulek opened his eyes, he lay on the ground again. A girl with large black eyes and a horrid scar running down her face called his name in a hoarse voice. "Ulek. What poison was it?"

Ulek focused on the girl. "Kiri?"

"The poison. Tell me the plant they used."

She made no sense. He needed to go home, and she asked him about plants. "Help me up, Kiri. I need to hurry." When he tried to rise, she pressed her hand against his chest.

"Ulek, what did the Charpans use? What did they put on the arrows?"

Ulek's head started to clear. "Why are you here, Kiri?"

"What did the Charpans use on the arrows?" she asked, her expression fierce.

Ulek finally understood. "Snakes. The soldiers say they used snake venom."

Kiri's eyebrows drew together. "What kind of snakes?" she asked in a hushed voice.

"I don't know. They were probably Charpan snakes." He closed his eyes as Kiri jerked up his pant leg to look at his wound, her silence more foreboding than any gasp of horror. Ulek cried. "Please, Kiri, help me stand. I need to get home." Kiri slipped her arms under him and pulled him to her chest. He pressed his face into the crook of her neck and let his tears spill onto her dress.

Kiri rocked back and forth as she murmured in a guttural language.

Despite Ulek's anger at Kiri for leaving him, her presence comforted him. No one had held him like that since before his mother had died. He let Kiri hold him until pain, sickness, and exhaustion pulled him into darkness.

Chapter 19

KIRI

Kiri stared in dismay at the meager amount of food the young soldier dumped into her bowl. When she looked up with an expectant expression, the soldier waved his hand to shoo her away. "Move along. That's all you get."

"I need more for someone else," Kiri said. "A boy."

"Then he can get it himself."

"He's sick."

"You think you're the first person to try that?" The soldier scoffed as he continued to hand out food to people in line. Without looking at Kiri, he said, "If the boy's too sick to walk, then he's too sick to come with us. If he wants to be fed, he'll have to walk over here himself."

Kiri opened her mouth to argue, but the set of the man's jaw told her it was useless. She walked off, studying the food wagons as she went. Now that soldiers guarded them so closely, it would be too difficult to steal from them. She could steal food from villagers too careless to guard their belongings, but that would be easier to do at night. She couldn't wait that long.

Just before the funeral had begun, two soldiers had come from the mountains and spoken to their leader. News that the Charpan trail had been lost spread quickly through the column. The food everyone depended on would not be recovered.

Her decision to pursue the Charpans had been an easy one. Kiri wanted to reach Ishtia before the horde did as much as anyone. She could run ahead of the column and fish in the river, but she didn't know the way. The mountains were too dangerous to travel alone, and she feared the fierce mountain winds and the open spaces that provided nowhere to hide. Much as she hated to admit it, she needed the column's protection to reach Ishtia. Another raid would be disastrous for the column. The Charpan band needed to be dealt with before they attacked again. Besides, if the column quickened its pace, it would need the stolen food.

But her main reason was Ulek. He lay in agony, possibly dying, and she was to blame. She'd killed his father—his last living relative and protector. She'd abandoned him once they'd reached the column, insisting he attach himself to a Galeedan family. He had tried to tell her no one would want him, yet she hadn't listened, focusing instead on her need to be rid of him. She'd been sent to kill Orrik, Kordrick, and Isandor to avenge Forest deaths and to protect her people from further bloodshed. Yet her actions had resulted in an innocent boy being poisoned. What kind of person did that make her? Did her single-minded desire to kill these men make her like them?

The Charpan band would have an antidote in case they accidentally poisoned themselves. Only a fool would handle poison without having an antidote. The scouts had lost the trail, but they were not Forest. Kiri would not lose the trail.

She'd find the Charpans, return to the column, and then lead the soldiers to where the Charpans hid. Once the Charpans were conquered, she'd find the antidote and bring it to Ulek. He would have to survive the first days by his own strength, but he wouldn't be healed. Without proper medicine, an injury infected with snake venom could fester for years.

People hurriedly packed belongings and doused fires as the morning sun rose higher over the horizon. The column would be moving soon. Kiri wrapped her rations in a cloth and placed it and the bowl into her sack. She wandered through the camp, growing desperate. She would need food, and lots of it, to go after the Charpans. She didn't have time to hunt or fish herself. She searched for Mekindu. He'd been friendly toward her, and might give her extra rations, but Kiri saw no sign of him. She knew only one other soldier.

Kiri quickened her pace, studying the soldiers in crested helmets. Finally, her gaze fell on a man with a heavily bruised face. "Mattos!" She ran toward him. He'd admitted to killing one of his own people, but she didn't have time to be wary of him. Although he'd killed a deserter, he might spare food to help an innocent child.

Mattos raised his eyebrows when he glanced up from where he adjusted his horse's saddle. "Kiri."

"I need food," Kiri burst out.

"You know where to get food," Mattos replied, sounding irritated. He continued to adjust the straps.

The horse turned her enormous head toward Kiri and sniffed, her gray nostrils expanding. Then she turned away, as if losing interest.

"I need some for Ulek," Kiri said. "He's sick."

Mattos paused, then turned to face Kiri. "Was Ulek wounded by an arrow last night?"

Kiri nodded.

"How bad?"

"A cut to his leg. It's swollen now."

"He doesn't need food," Mattos said. "He wouldn't be able to keep it down anyway."

"He'll need it when he catches up with the column," Kiri insisted.

"Are you staying behind with him?"

"Yes."

Undoing the clasp under his chin, Mattos removed his helmet. His purple bruises had faded. "We lost four food wagons last night. We all want more rations. I'm hungry, my men are hungry, but we need to make what we have last until we reach Ishtia."

Rage filled Kiri's spirit. The Galeedans who'd been poisoned were being left to die. "Ulek will live, and he needs food. *I need it!*"

Mattos's face darkened. "Kiri, the Charpans are close, much closer than people realize." He spoke in a low tone to avoid being overheard. "We can't slow down, and we can't spare food for people who might not survive anyway. I don't think we'll reach Ishtia in time. You and Ulek warned us about the Charpan band already here, so now I'm warning you about what we're facing."

The revelation about the Charpan horde only strengthened Kiri's resolve. She needed to find the band that had attacked last night and get back to Ulek as quickly as possible. "You have to give me food."

Mattos sighed. “I already told you I can’t do that.”

Kiri stared, unblinking, into Mattos’s eyes. “But you will. We warned you about the Charpan band. The army knew they were out there, and now people are dead because the army didn’t properly guard against them.”

Grumbling in Sandamedan, the soldier reached into his saddlebag and withdrew a handful of nuts and dried figs, which he placed in Kiri’s outstretched hands. “If you tell anyone it came from me, I’ll say you stole it.”

“I need meat.”

“By Odern, woman!” Mattos reached again into his saddlebag and tossed Kiri a large piece of dried meat.

Chapter 20

KIRI

Those who remained with the injured villagers watched the column fade into the distance. As the din of the column abated, they heard only the sounds of mountain winds and pitiful moans. The two injured children had ceased thrashing and squealing and now lay still, whimpering. One mother tried in vain to get her child to drink. The other child's mother sat with her knees drawn up to her chest, weeping silently. A feeble old man lay next to his sick, gray-haired wife, his arm thrown over her as if they slept. Every time she moaned, he whispered something in her ear. Several of the wounded had no one to care for them. One young woman lay breathing raggedly, her yellow hair matted with vomit. A muscular man tossed about during screaming fits. None came to his aid.

Whoever had laid Ulek among the sick had been kind enough to cover him with his father's coat. Kiri tucked her blanket under Ulek's head, trying to make him as comfortable as possible. She had delayed going after the Charpans until the column was out of sight, lest the soldiers tried to stop her. Now the time had come. Before the column had started, she'd stolen a waterskin from a soldier foolish enough not to guard his belongings. Now she pressed the full waterskin into Ulek's hand, knowing the delirious boy wouldn't respond. She needed the food for herself. As Mattos had said, Ulek wouldn't be able to keep it down anyway.

No one took notice when Kiri rose and walked toward the empty food wagons abandoned on the riverbank. Hoof and footprints from the fled Charpans overlapped each other on the muddy bank.

Realizing the Charpans had escaped across the river, Kiri removed her clothes. When she glanced over her shoulder at the villagers, she saw with relief that they were too far away to see her clearly. She didn't have to worry about them noticing her Forest tattoos.

After she stuffed her clothes into her sack, she tied the sack to the top of her head using leather strips. The low current didn't look strong, but she'd have to swim much of the way. She sucked in her breath as she stepped into the cold water. Loose rocks shifted under her feet, causing her to stumble. When the water reached her waist, Kiri gritted her teeth to keep them from chattering. Droplets splashed her face as water rose to her shoulders. Taking a deep breath, she lunged forward and began swimming. She couldn't swim as well as she could run, but she could manage the calm river.

Finally, Kiri's feet touched rocks. Staggering from the river, she collapsed, gasping, on the grass. Her sack slipped from her head. The wind on her wet body kept her from resting for long. Shivering, she reached into her sack for her Wanderer clothes and paused. Alone, she had no need for pretense. She pulled out the green Forest tunic and trousers she'd kept hidden since Orrik's death. She pressed her face into them, trying to catch the scent of home. Instead, they smelled sour from being packed away so long. After binding her breasts with the cloth she wore for running, she donned her Forest clothes. Her high-necked tunic extended to her hips, and the sleeves reached her knuckles. Forest clothing had to cover as much skin as possible to protect the wearer from shrubbery and insects and be tight enough not to catch on twigs or thorns. She pulled her hair back with a leather strip the way she did back home. Before slipping on her soft Forest shoes, she touched the doe tattoo on her left foot and the hare tattoo on her right. They were the same robin's-egg blue. The doe leaped, her graceful neck stretched forward, while the hare stood tense, prepared to run. Kiri had earned those markings in her thirteenth year, when she'd won her village's spring race. The spirits of the deer and the hare would give her strength now. Kiri raised her arms over head and arched her back in a gratifying stretch.

Obvious hoofprints marked the river mud—a Galeedan child could have found them. Kiri paused where the mud gave way to grass. She crouched low and turned her head sideways, determining the grass's natural height.

The indentations made by the Charpans' horses were easy to find. Kiri lay on her stomach to study the print closest to her. The shadows cast by the low sun displayed its depth. She traced her finger along the true print, her eyes searching for every sign of disruption in the grass and soil. Despite being bound by grass roots, some soil had been kicked up. They had been galloping. Kiri found the other prints made by the same horse. Then she circled around the prints made by the first horse, looking for those made by the others. Her circle became wider and wider until she had found the prints of forty horses.

Four of those horses had had metal nailed to their hooves and must have been stolen from the soldiers. Fourteen horses had left prints with tiny ridges of dirt near the front left or front right of the hoofprint. This indicated the horses' heads hadn't been perfectly straight but had been inclined slightly to the left or right. Kiri guessed these riderless horses had carried the stolen food and been led by their reins.

Mixed with the horses' tracks were two sets of footprints made by men wearing heavier boots than those who had trampled the bank. Kiri realized the prints must have belonged to the scouts sent to track the Charpans. The footprints followed the trail northeast, deeper into the mountains. She sighed. At least they weren't completely blind, although at some point they had lost the trail.

Kiri walked to the river for a drink and to fill her waterskin. Having found the track's pattern and direction, she would be able to follow it at a quick pace. She returned the waterskin to her sack, threw the sack over her shoulder, and began jogging along the trail. She focused on reading and following the tracks. There was neither past nor future, only the present task. Only the trail. Only the run.

Despite the increasing winds, it was exhilarating to run and track once more. Away from the soldiers' rules and the

Galeedans' unfriendly stares, she felt like a Forest woman again—free. She hadn't realized how hiding her identity had worn on her until this respite. She didn't have to lie, struggle to communicate, or walk with her eyes lowered. Now, far from all those people, she didn't feel so lonely.

As the sun rose higher, the grass gave way to dirt and rock. The mountains ahead had far less vegetation than those the column had been traveling. It hadn't taken Kiri long to notice the trail led to a mountain almost bare of life. Only the most stubborn grass patches and yellow wildflowers survived on its surface. Its peak dominated the horizon, looking down on the surrounding grass-covered mountains. Having lived all her life in a dense forest, Kiri couldn't judge distance the way non-Forest people could, but the mountain's base seemed to stretch out far. The gradual incline would make for easy climbing.

Kiri paused at the last visible track near the mountain's foot. The tracks appeared to stop on the hard surface. Knowing the trail's pattern and where the next tracks should be, Kiri lowered herself to the ground, careful to keep the spot she focused on between her and the sun's rays. She lay on her stomach with her right cheek pressed against the rock. Those pursued might not leave indentations on hard surfaces, but they disturbed the grit. No matter the surface, tracks never disappeared. Animals and people were of the Earth, just like children were of their parents. A sire could not deny a child who bore his eyes or nose; somehow the shared blood revealed itself. In the same way, the Earth could not deny her children. When the Earth's creatures walked on her surface, they left a mark behind. Always, there was a track.

As Kiri searched with the severe angle of ant eyes, a hoofprint revealed itself. It appeared almost shiny against the dull rock. Beyond it, more hoofprints appeared. Kiri continued to hug the ground, studying the tiny bits of grit the hoof had disturbed.

When she got to her feet, the hoofprints disappeared. She continued, keeping close to the ground and occasionally using her ant eyes to ensure she followed the trail. The Charpans had ridden around the base of the wide mountain and into a small valley. The terrain transformed from smooth stone into loose rocks and then grassy mountains in the distance. As she stalked the trail, Kiri spotted more footprints left by the army scouts. They had ceased tracking and had wandered about in circles. They must have lost the trail when they reached the rock and continued, hoping to find it again on a softer surface. Kiri found the spot where they must have admitted defeat. From looking at their tracks, she could tell they had stood side by side by the stone valley. From there, she could determine they had turned around and jogged back the way they'd come. As she traced her finger over their footprints, Kiri sensed the anger and frustration the scouts must have felt when they realized they had failed. Tracks were not only imprints of foot, paw, or hoof, but also of the emotions the animal or human had the moment they made the track. From reading their tracks, Kiri had learned the scouts were graceful and meticulous. They'd been frustrated by their failure.

For the first time, she saw the imperial soldiers as vulnerable, capable of fear, shame, and despair. She rubbed her hand over the stone, erasing the footprints. She didn't want to feel compassion for the soldiers.

Chapter 21

KIRI

Smoke and the scent of cooked rabbit wafted up the mountain Kiri climbed. Her heart pounded in anticipation; they camped close by. She moved carefully, wary of revealing her presence. There had been no sign the Charpans feared being followed or discovered, but Kiri wasn't taking chances. When she'd first seen smoke and realized the trail led to a valley, she'd changed direction and climbed up the mountain overlooking the valley rather than entering it at the mountain's base. Even before climbing up, she'd sat hidden, letting the sun cross the sky as she waited for any movement on the mountainside to indicate the presence of guards.

When Kiri decided she had climbed high enough to look down on the valley without being seen, she moved sideways toward the smoke. She hadn't gone far when the Charpans came into view. Two dozen men lounged by a large cook fire, their rough laughter resonating over the camp. One man relieved himself a short distance from the others while another inspected a horse's hoof. The horses hadn't been corralled or restrained in any way. They stayed close by, eating grass and wandering aimlessly in their small herd. The large Sandamedan horses stood with their new companions, showing little concern over their change in ownership. The food stolen from the column was piled not too far from the fire.

Kiri almost laughed at the Charpans' impudence. They'd attacked soldiers with far greater numbers last night, and yet they lazed in an indefensible valley without a lookout to ensure they hadn't been followed.

They have no fear, Kiri thought. Anger surged through her as she thought of Ulek, the whimpering children, and the old man lying next to his dying mate. During war, the Forest people dipped their own arrowheads in hemlock sap, but they only shot those arrows at enemy warriors, never children or those who didn't fight.

Moving sideways again, Kiri crept away from her view of the camp. When she reached a position she was sure the Charpans couldn't see even if they looked up, she moved down the mountain in a combination of walking, sliding, and climbing. She soon stood at the mountain base.

The low sun would set soon. Kiri determined she could reach the column by midday if she traveled all night and paced herself. She'd left markers along her path so she could find her way back, and the stars would guide her. She knew she could do it; she was the best long-distance runner in several villages. She stretched her legs before taking off at a jog.

Chapter 22

MATTOS

Word had traveled up the column that Oistin and five other soldiers wounded by Charpan arrows weren't expected to survive the day. The fierce mountain winds were unusually absent, allowing the moans and cries of the dying men to carry farther. Mattos gazed up the column, shielding his eyes from the sun. Not long ago, a soldier heading toward the front of the column had run past. Mattos feared he'd been sent to inform Thais of another death. He wondered who else Odern had called to the city of the dead. Falcon Oistin had ostracized Mattos for being from the merchant class as all the officers save Lucen did, but he'd never been cruel like Elmaturis. Oistin's wife and three-year-old son traveled in the column. Another officer's family cared for the boy while the wife—her red-rimmed eyes betraying the knowledge she would soon be a widow—walked beside the cart carrying her husband. The woman and boy would only be allowed the briefest of goodbyes before burying Oistin. The column no longer had time for proper funerals.

Two lead riders turned and cantered down the column. As they drew closer, Mattos recognized Hawk Thais's and Osprey Beldos's tall crests. To his surprise, they reined in their horses when they drew level with him.

"Come with us, Falcon," Thais ordered. "There's something I want you to see."

As Mattos urged Nica to take her place beside Thais's stallion, Thais asked, "The Wanderer girl traveled in your section of the column, didn't she?"

Mattos blinked. "Yes, she and the boy, Ulek. He was wounded by a Charpan arrow and left behind with the others. Kiri stayed to look after him."

"Kiri, yes, that's the girl's name," Thais muttered. "She caught up with us, and from what I've been told, has an interesting story to tell."

"The boy?" Mattos asked, fearing he already knew the answer.

"He's not with her—must have died soon after we left. I'm going to speak to her now, and since you know her, I want you to accompany me."

"Yes, Hawk," Mattos said. "But I don't know her well. I've only spoken with her a few times."

"That's more than anyone else in this company can say. You know how Galeedans mistrust and fear Wanderers." Thais shifted in his saddle to look directly at Mattos. "Tell me, does she seek attention?"

"Not at all," Mattos replied, taken aback. "Except for the boy, she's kept to herself. Hawk, if I may, what is this about?"

Beldos leaned forward to glare at Mattos from the Hawk's other side. "You're here to follow orders, not ask questions."

Beldos hailed from an old, senatorial family and resented the practice of allowing men from the merchant class to buy their officer postings. As the only commoner among the officers in the company, Mattos had learned to avoid Thais's second-in-command. As a superior officer, he could antagonize Mattos in ways Elmaturis couldn't.

When they reached the end of the column, they found several soldiers, including one of the company's scouts, gathered around Kiri. At the sound of the horses' approach, she turned to face them. She panted, and tiny beads of sweat glistened her flushed skin.

The three riders dismounted and walked toward the group. "Kiri," Thais began, "I hear you've seen the Charpans."

"I found them," she answered, pride in her voice.

"How?" Thais asked.

"I tracked them and found their camp."

Beldos crossed his arms. "You followed their tracks to their camp? Where is this camp?"

Kiri pointed to a distant mountain. "In a valley behind that mountain."

Mattos gaped at her. She hadn't wanted the meat for Ulek. She'd needed it for herself so she could track the Charpans and run back to the column. Had she really found them? And why? Who was this woman?

"We sent our best scouts after the Charpans, and they lost the trail," Beldos said in Sandamedan. "How could this girl find them when they couldn't? She would have had to track and find the Charpans, then run back to us all within a day and a half. She's lying."

"She told the truth when she warned us about the Charpan band," Mattos broke in.

Beldos continued as if Mattos hadn't spoken. "Wanderers never travel alone, and their women don't talk to outsiders. But this one appears from the hills with only a twelve-year-old Galeedan boy for a companion and tells us a story about running away from a cruel husband and being captured by Charpans. Those Charpans killed imperial soldiers, yet a girl and boy escape from them without a scratch?" He snorted.

"That boy's father fought in the Forest lands as an imperial soldier," Mattos said. "You think *he* was lying?"

"I think you should keep your opinions to yourself," Beldos said in a growl. "Unless, of course, you think a Falcon who's never seen a real battle knows more about military matters than an Osprey who was leading men to war when you were still suckling your mother's tit."

During this exchange in a language she couldn't understand, Kiri had stood motionless, her dark eyes flitting back and forth between the men. She stepped forward and pointed again to the distant mountain. "We have to go. We're losing time."

"The only way this girl knows where the Charpans are, is if she knew where the camp was all along," Beldos snapped. "She's one of them. She'll lead us into an ambush."

Mattos studied Kiri. Beldos's logic was sound; they knew nothing about this strange young woman, and she couldn't have been lucky enough to just stumble upon the Charpan camp. And yet … "She's shown concern for Ulek. And the Charpans don't need to lead us into an ambush. They've proven they're not afraid to raid us at night."

Kiri raised her chin and narrowed her eyes at the men. "Speak the common language."

"How dare you give us orders," Beldos said, his nostrils flaring. He moved toward Kiri with a raised arm.

As Kiri sprang backward, Mattos leaped in front of her, taking the backhand on his own neck.

"Get out of my way!" Beldos shouted.

"Beldos, enough!" Thais stood with fists clenched at his sides. "It doesn't help us to beat the woman who may know where the Charpans are."

Beldos scowled but didn't respond.

His neck stinging, Mattos took deep breaths to curb his rage. He could have grabbed Beldos's arm instead of jumping in front of Kiri, but that would have resulted in his arrest for insubordination.

The girl crouched a few paces away, watching Beldos with what appeared to be a mixture of fear, outrage, and bewilderment.

"It's all right," Thais called out. "I apologize for Osprey Beldos. We won't harm you."

Kiri rose but stayed put. She stared at the men with wary eyes.

Thais adopted a soothing tone. "You said you found the Charpans' tracks. How did you find them?"

The girl gave Beldos a wide berth as she strode back the way Mattos, Beldos, and Thais had just ridden, then crouched low to the ground. Without looking up, she gestured for the men to follow.

When the soldiers surrounded her, Kiri pointed at the grass.

Mattos saw nothing unusual.

"It's a track," she said, pointing from the grass to the horses and back.

The scout approached and lowered to Kiri's side to study the patch of grass she'd pointed out. After a moment, he said, "This is a fresh horse track."

Kiri continued to follow the trail backward, pointing out each track to the scout.

Eventually, the scout rose and faced the other soldiers. "She's a true tracker, Hawk."

"So, a Wanderer girl can track better than imperial scouts," Thais mused. "Why would nomadic craftsmen and merchants have the need for such a skill?"

Kiri didn't give an answer, but Thais didn't seem to expect one.

"She *is* a Charpan," Beldos burst out in Sandamedan. "This proves it. Wanderers don't know how to track."

"Wanderers are known for being mysterious," Mattos argued. "It's possible they have knowledge they don't share with outsiders." She'd lied to him about staying behind with Ulek, but she'd told the truth when she and Ulek had warned them about the Charpans. Something told him she spoke the truth now.

"I've heard enough," Thais said. Lowering himself to one knee, he beckoned Kiri.

She approached slowly, her eyes cautious.

When the Wanderer girl stood before him, Thais grasped her left wrist and stared into her face. "Why did you go after the Charpans?"

Kiri met his eyes without blinking. She swallowed, then spoke. "I want to live and go to Ishtia. I want medicine for Ulek."

Thais held Kiri's gaze a few more moments before dropping her wrist and sighing. "Who are you really?" he murmured in Sandamedan, as if to himself.

"What if she *is* one of them, Hawk?" Mattos asked in Sandamedan. "We outnumber them, and we need the food they stole. Does it matter why she leads us to the Charpans, so long as she does it? It's not an ambush if we expect it."

"The Charpans are mounted," Beldos said.

"As we will be," Mattos replied. "Officers and most of their relatives have horses. Even some Galeedans have mounts. We can probably manage fifty horses. Fifty mounted soldiers are more than enough to defeat two dozen Charpans."

Thais said nothing as he rose to his feet. He gazed at the distant mountain Kiri had pointed out, his expression contemplative. Finally, he said, "We won't be able to wait for you. We have to keep the column moving. But there's still time for you to fight a battle and catch up. You would have to leave immediately."

"But, Hawk—" Beldos began.

Thais held up a hand to silence him. "I want you to lead the attack, Falcon Mattos."

Chapter 23

MATTOS

The violent mountain winds barraged the horses' and riders' faces. Mattos kept his eyes narrowed to slits, tears slipping from the corners. Soon they'd reach the mountains covered in rock and dirt instead of grass. Then the wind would blast them with dust.

The fifty horses Mattos had requested had been provided. He hadn't been as lucky when he'd insisted on taking his own men on the attack. The riders had been hand-picked from every unit in the company, so Mattos commanded a hodgepodge of soldiers unaccustomed to taking orders from him or training together. Because Thais had wanted the best riders to go, Galeedans from landowning families and Sarpaskans made up the party—the two groups most likely to know how to ride. Mattos only knew a few of the men he led: his Owl, Mekindu; his Sparrow, Ladius; his soldier, Kordrick; Omeldor, his cohort's physician; a Sarpaskan soldier under Lucen; and two of Elmaturis's Galeedan soldiers. The others he knew only by name and face.

One other officer had been sent with the riders: Falcon Darius, Beldos's nephew. Because Darius, like his uncle, despised merchant class officers, Mattos avoided him when he could. The young man had been presented with his crested helmet only three months ago and had, through his family's influence, been placed in his uncle's company. Darius had volunteered to lead the attack, but Thais had been adamant that Mattos would lead. Beldos had intervened so that Darius had at least been allowed to go.

Thais had respected Mattos's wish that the party be made up of volunteers. The men seemed excited about the attack, calling to each other and laughing as they rode. After so much fear and tedium, they would finally face an enemy. They weren't running from this enemy, either; they were the aggressors, riding to a battle *they* had chosen. Though Mattos couldn't blame them for their zeal, laughing while stalking an enemy wasn't the behavior of an imperial soldier. He ordered them silent.

After beheading Ozias and killing one of the bandits, Mattos had fast gained a reputation as a dispassionate killer. While this earned him respect from the men and even some of the officers, it made him uneasy. Part of him felt pride at being known as a killer—what imperial soldiers aimed to be—while another part balked at the label. He'd always hoped that when he returned to his home city of Valdern, he would have earned the reputation of a brave man and a good leader. But did he want to go home with the distinction of being an accomplished killer? He didn't feel like he'd done anything worthy of praise. Even with Ozias, once engaged in the fight, he'd only been trying to preserve his life.

Mattos glanced at Kiri, who had succumbed to sleep soon after they'd started their journey. She sagged against Mekindu, her head lolling on his arm as he held the reins. Her exhaustion lent credit to her story, as if she really had tracked the bandits and hadn't had a chance to sleep for a day and a half. The farther they traveled, the more her deeds confounded him. She said she'd found and followed the Charpan trail alone on foot. Then she'd managed to run back to the column by midday a day after she'd left. To do so, she would've had to run through the night—an impressive athletic feat. If she were telling the truth, how did a girl fleeing a violent husband have the temerity and strength to do what she had done? If she were lying, then how did she have the fortitude and composure to walk among enemies who would kill her if they discovered her secret? Whoever she was, the woman had pluck.

Chapter 24

KIRI

Kiri awoke to Mekindu shaking her. Her body protested as she sat up and opened her eyes. She hadn't gotten the full rest she needed, and fatigue weighed on her more heavily now than before. When she took in her surroundings, she realized they already gathered at the foot of the mountain she'd pointed out, though the sun had far to travel before dusk. So, this was why non-Forest people chose riding horses over running. She lifted one leg over the horse's neck to jump down.

"Wait. I'll help you," Mekindu said.

Ignoring him, Kiri slid off the horse and landed with a grunt. She walked toward Mattos, who dismounted at her approach.

"What now?" Mattos asked, grimacing against the swirling dust. Fading bruises covered half his face.

Kiri's black hair whipped about. "Go around," she replied. "It's in a valley behind another mountain." She coughed when the wind blew dust in her mouth.

"How much farther?"

"Less than half a day's run."

"But how far is it?" Mattos asked again. "How many leagues?"

"Less than half a day's run," Kiri repeated in exasperation.

Mattos studied her a moment before sighing. "I see. Which way now?"

The others remained in their saddles as Kiri led Mattos around the base of the mountain to the same place she had stood the day before. She recognized the rocky terrain and the mountains covered in vegetation in the distance. She pointed. "In the valley behind that one."

Mattos squinted. "That's not far. Are there any places where they might keep guards? Will they be able to see us coming this way?"

"There weren't guards before. They didn't see me."

Mattos turned to stare at Kiri with an expression she couldn't read. She found much of what this non-Forest man did incomprehensible. He allowed her to guide him and his soldiers to the Charpans, yet he questioned her every time she gave instructions. He had protected her from the older soldier who'd tried to hit her, but he'd done it by taking the blow instead of grabbing the man's arm or punching him. Kiri had seen the rage in his eyes after being struck, but he hadn't retaliated. At home, such an insult would have resulted in a fight. Kiri had learned a soldier's helmet signified rank in a complicated hierarchy. The old soldier probably held a position higher than Mattos, though in a Forest village, even an elder couldn't strike someone without fear of being hit back. Perhaps Mattos had been afraid to challenge the other man. But why send a coward to lead an attack?

Mattos sighed and turned back to the distant mountains. "How did you track the bandits over rock?"

Kiri grinned. "I'm good."

"We'll find out," Mattos replied, giving a wry smile. Kiri noticed faint lines extending from his hazel eyes.

They walked back to the others, helped by the wind pushing their backs.

Instead of ordering everyone to continue, Mattos sent two riders ahead. The others dismounted and began to talk among themselves.

Kiri walked back to Mekindu, who stood patting Snow, the mighty white horse they'd ridden. "What is Mattos doing?" she asked.

Mekindu glanced at his Falcon, who drank from his waterskin. "What do you mean?"

"We stopped. We need to go after the Charpans," Kiri insisted.

"The Falcon sent riders ahead to make sure the Charpans don't have guards looking out for us."

"There are no guards. I *told* him."

Mekindu chuckled. "Perhaps he wants to make sure. Why are you so eager for battle?"

Kiri didn't answer. Mattos's refusal to trust her judgment would cost them time, but she could do nothing about it. Perhaps there would be time to return to sleep. She turned her attention to Snow, who stood closer to her than any horse had before. Since being captured by the Charpan band, she'd been on a few horses, but she hadn't had the chance to carefully study one. Snow's lashes curled over his large black eyes, and stray whiskers stuck out around his nose and mouth. Kiri patted the beast's forehead and slid her fingers down his long face to the soft gray area around his nose. Snow didn't seem to mind. Instead, he lowered his head to the grass and ate as if she weren't there. When Kiri stroked his neck, he continued to ignore her. She laughed, amazed that such a magnificent creature could be so harmless.

"I suppose he's quite different from those shaggy ponies that pull your wagons," Mekindu said, continuing to run his hand over the horse's white coat.

Kiri nodded, too entranced to speak.

"That's a fine animal," a deep voice behind them said.

"He is indeed," Mekindu answered. "He belongs to Falcon Elmaturis's new bride—a wedding present. Few in the empire are lucky enough to ever ride a stallion like him."

Soldiers rarely spoke the common language, even around Kiri. Most weren't considerate enough to use a language she understood. Curious about this polite soldier, Kiri looked over her shoulder and met the bright green eyes of the man who'd killed Wren.

Kiri stopped breathing. With her heart pounding in her ears, she turned back to face Snow. Except for the trembling of her entire body, she couldn't move. She'd only needed the brief glance to recognize him. The face of the man standing over Wren had been burned into her memory. Those eyes were unforgettable. Even after traveling with thousands of Galeedans and Sandamedans, she hadn't seen another pair of eyes that shade of green. Kordrick was Wren's killer. Had he recognized her? Surely not. Kiri had changed into her Wanderer clothes before catching up with the column.

Mekindu and Kordrick continued their conversation, their voices sounding a long way off.

Keeping her face averted from Kordrick, Kiri willed herself to turn aside and walk. With agonizing slowness, she put distance between Kordrick and herself. She didn't look back, afraid he would be watching. *A soldier. He's still a soldier. How could I be so stupid?* She'd spent all her time in the column looking for a Galeedan farmer while avoiding soldiers. She'd thought that, like Orrik, Kordrick had left the army and returned home. How little she knew of the empire's military and culture.

As she cast furtive glances at the gawking men, Kiri realized just how much attention she'd drawn to herself by tracking the Charpans and leading the soldiers to them. She'd known she was different from Galeedan and Sandamedan women, but she hadn't fully appreciated the extent of those differences until now. No Galeedan or Sandamedan could track as she could, and no Galeedan or Sandamedan woman would dare try. She recalled how the soldiers had reacted with anger and disbelief when she'd told them she'd found the Charpans. Kiri traced a finger along her scar. She'd come so close to revealing herself. If her behavior hadn't been so odd, Kordrick might have ignored her when he spoke to Mekindu, instead of looking right at her. Her carelessness had drawn his notice.

Loose pebbles crunched under Kiri's feet as she walked around the mountain base to the spot she had led Mattos. Finally alone, she sank to the ground. Kordrick hadn't followed. Kiri took deep, calming breaths. New complications marred any relief she might have felt over having finally found the man she sought. How would she kill him now? It would have been simple to kill a villager in his sleep. There would have been no way to determine who had done it, and the soldiers, preoccupied with outrunning the Charpans, would have moved the column on with little pause. Killing a soldier would be a different matter; most of them slept three or four to a tent where any struggle or cry would wake the others. They wouldn't take the death of one of their own as lightly as they would a farmer's death. Kiri buried her face in her knees. She needed to think of some way to kill Kordrick, and soon.

Chapter 25

MATTOS

In his perch overlooking the enemy's lair, Mattos almost laughed in relief. Not only had the Charpan band not been waiting to ambush the soldiers, they hadn't even posted guards—they had no fear of being followed. The band had made camp in a narrow valley low enough to avoid the fierce winds. Unlike the surrounding terrain, grass and wildflowers covered the valley and shrubs grew along the stream, trickling down the mountainside. The four imperial steeds wandered among the short Charpan horses, their front legs hobbled so they could only manage a slow walk. The grain and hard bread stolen from the food wagons sat untouched in a heap, though the wine sacks were nowhere to be seen. The men lounged around a cook fire, eating, talking, and cleaning weapons. By the look of the skins drying in the sun and the scent drifting up the mountain, they were enjoying rabbit meat.

"So, Kiri isn't a Charpan spy after all," Mattos murmured in Sandamedan. "She really did track the Charpans and run all night to let us know."

Crouching beside his commander, Mekindu chuckled. "She's proven to be more useful than any of us so far. Maybe we should let her join the attack."

Kiri, who sat a short distance from them, cut her eyes at Mattos after hearing her name.

"I count twenty-six," Mattos said, squinting, "but I think your eyes are sharper than mine, Mekindu."

"There are twenty-six of them," Mekindu confirmed.

"That matches the range Kiri and Ulek gave, and our guess after they attacked us," Mattos said. "This time, we'll have surprise in our favor."

Mattos and Mekindu crawled backward from their lookout point before standing.

"Stay here, Kiri," Mattos said. "You'll be safe."

Mekindu grinned. "You may be the first person to see imperial soldiers in battle without a reason to fear us."

Kiri's eyes widened, then narrowed as she clutched handfuls of her dress. "I won't look," she whispered. Rage—or maybe terror, he couldn't tell—flashed in her eyes.

The strength of her reaction surprised Mattos. Maybe the thought of the impending battle unnerved her. "That's probably wise," he replied. "There's no need for you to watch men die."

The two men walked and slid down to the mountain base, where the rest of the soldiers waited.

Darius scowled, his small eyes almost disappearing under his black brows, as Mattos and Mekindu approached. He'd been offended at being left behind while Mekindu, a mere Owl, had been permitted to accompany Mattos to the lookout point. "We should discuss plans for the attack," he said as Mattos mounted Nica.

"Nothing to discuss," Mattos grunted. "It's an ambush, not a complicated battle."

"Do you mean to go to battle with Charpans without a plan?" Darius said.

"The plan is to attack and kill them," Mattos said. He didn't have the time or the patience to deal with Darius's posturing.

Darius rode closer so his mount and Nica stood next to each other, facing opposite directions. His thin lips were drawn tight with anger. "Perhaps you've forgotten my family, and the fact that the Osprey is my uncle. I think it's in your best interest—"

"I think *you've* forgotten Hawk Thais put me in charge of this attack," Mattos said, "and it's in *my* best interest to get on with it." He spurred Nica forward. He wouldn't let Darius waste more time by trying to establish authority.

Mattos swept his eyes over his men, who had been trained to be a deadly force with sword, shield, and spear, so long as they were on foot. Those present could ride, but most had not been trained for battle on horseback. They were about to be tested. Fear gripped him. They had superior numbers and the advantage of surprise, but the Charpans were known to be fierce, merciless warriors. Only a fool would think no imperial soldiers would be killed or grievously wounded. Mattos cleared his throat and addressed his soldiers. "The Charpans are sitting around a campfire right now and aren't expecting an attack. They thought they could raid us, kill innocent children, steal our food, and then ride away without fear of being followed. Today, they will learn their mistake. There are only twenty-six of them, and the camp isn't far.

Once we charge the valley, we'll be on top of them in less time than it takes to piss. If we're lucky, we'll engage them before most reach their horses. Don't kill all of them. The Hawk wants prisoners."

Mattos had decided to leave his shield behind, in favor of bringing both his spear and bow. He'd slung a quiver of arrows over his back. As he put on his helmet, he called out, "May Odern guide us." His heart pounding in anticipation, Mattos raised his arm in a forward motion to signal his men to follow.

The soldiers burst into the valley at a gallop. A Charpan leaped to his feet, crying out a warning. Tossing food aside, the startled men grabbed their weapons and sprinted for their horses.

As they closed in on the camp, Mattos cried, "Soldiers of the empire, attack!" The men broke their silence, erupting in murderous shouts. The horses' hooves struck the ground in a steady tempo, clashing with the din of clinking armor, screams, and battle cries.

A lean Charpan armed with bow and arrows grabbed at a roan's neck. Mattos threw his spear just as the Charpan flung his leg over the roan's bare back. The spear caught him between his shoulder blades and thrust him against the horse's neck. He clung to the mane a moment before falling to the ground, where an imperial horse and rider trampled him.

Another Charpan sprinted toward a horse, his long brown cloak flying behind him. Mattos shot an arrow at him before he even reached a horse. Uttering choked screams, the Charpan fell to his knees and wrapped his hands around the arrow protruding from his throat. Blood oozed between his fingers.

Spears flew, some embedding in Charpan bodies, others landing in the ground. Both sides mixed, forming a heaving mass of violence and screams. Almost half the Charpans had reached horses and rode bareback as they fought, their bodies moving with their mounts as one. A broad-shouldered Owl astride a black stallion charged a Charpan on foot. As the horse and rider bore down on him, the young Charpan fell to his knees, drew back his sword, and sliced through the horse's front legs. Screaming in agony, the animal collapsed on his side, the whites of his eyes showing. As the Owl struggled to free his right leg from under the flailing stallion, the Charpan sprang on him, thrusting his blood-soaked sword into his throat.

As he reached into his quiver, Mattos spotted a kneeling Charpan dipping an arrow into a gold vial attached to his belt. An image of Oistin vomiting as he lay helpless on the ground flashed through Mattos's mind just as the Charpan pointed the arrow at him. Mattos let go of the arrow between his fingers; he'd never be able to nock and aim it in time. He slammed his heels into Nica's flanks and charged, reaching for his shield. When his hand closed around empty air, he recalled with a sickening pang that he'd left his shield behind. He ducked just as the Charpan loosed the arrow, almost crying out in relief when he felt it glance off his right shoulder guard.

Instead of fleeing or drawing another arrow, the powerfully built Charpan unsheathed his sword and charged.

Mattos drew his own sword just in time to block his foe's swing.

Blood and bits of flesh already stained the Charpan's yellow tunic. Grabbing Mattos's left vambrace, he yanked with remarkable strength, nearly pulling Mattos from his saddle.

Mattos struck repeatedly at his attacker, but the man parried each blow, all the while maintaining his tug on the vambrace. Mattos felt himself slipping from the saddle.

A soldier rode past, his mount bumping against Nica and knocking her sideways into the man at her side. Suddenly free, Mattos jerked his left arm back as he raised his right to strike again, but his assailant had disappeared. He must have fled to avoid being trampled.

Mattos spun Nica around and gazed out over the camp. Having spent their spears and arrows, the soldiers fought with swords and shields. Bodies littered the ground, arrows and spears jutting from their flesh like porcupine quills. The wounded moaned and writhed. One young Charpan gripped the shaft of a spear buried deep in his stomach. He threw his head back and wailed as he tried to pull it out with bloody hands. A soldier knelt nearby, a bloody stump where his right hand should have been. He stared at it in bewilderment, as if he didn't understand what had happened.

The heaviest fighting was near the still-burning campfire. Ladius and Kordrick rode amid the fray, cutting down the Charpans who tried to pull them from their horses. Mattos spurred Nica toward them.

As Mattos reached the fight, a young Charpan with an arrow in his leg threw down his sword as two soldiers on foot bore down on him. One of the soldiers, still caught up in taking lives, cried out and lifted his sword. Mattos reached down and grabbed his arm. "No, stop!"

The soldier blinked and stared at Mattos as if he didn't know him.

Mattos yelled the soldier's name as he shook him. "Wake up! Don't kill them all."

Recognition entered the soldier's eyes. He nodded when Mattos released his arm, then turned to take the prisoner.

As Mattos straightened, something crashed into him, knocking the air from his lungs. His left foot twisted in the stirrup before he hit the ground with something heavy on top of him. He gulped for air. When his vision cleared, he stared into the face of a Charpan sitting on his chest. Under his beard, the man's lips twisted into a snarl, revealing crooked teeth. One eye blazed with fury while one eyelid sank into an empty socket.

Mattos tried unsuccessfully to free his arms from under the Charpan's legs. He struggled to speak and order Nica to strike his attacker with her hooves, but he still gasped for breath and couldn't find his voice.

The one-eyed man lifted his sword over his head with both hands, the point aimed at Mattos's throat.

Mattos studied the sword with detached fascination. *So, this is the weapon that's going to kill me.* The blade was longer than Sandamedan swords, wide at the hilt and gradually narrowing to the tip. A braid-like design had been hammered into the steel from the hilt to the midpoint.

The Charpan brought the sword down.

Squeezing his eyes shut, Mattos braced for the cold steel, but instead felt warm liquid splash his face and neck. He opened his eyes to see an imperial sword buried deep into the Charpan's neck, his head almost severed. Kordrick stood behind the man, gripping his hair in one hand and the sword in the other. The blade that had come so close to killing Mattos fell from the Charpan's lifeless fingers and cut Mattos's neck before he jerked his head aside.

Hands pawed at Mattos and lifted him to his feet.

"Are you all right, Falcon?" a soldier asked.

"Yes, thank you," Mattos gasped. When he looked around, he saw soldiers taking prisoners. His attacker lay on the ground, now a corpse.

They had won.

Kordrick wiped his sword on the dead man's clothes.

"Kordrick," Mattos said, striding toward him, "are you the soldier I owe my life to?"

"I'm the one who killed him," Kordrick answered, gesturing to the body.

"I thank you for it," Mattos said, putting his hand on Kordrick's shoulder. With his other hand, he fingered the fresh cut on his throat. The realization of how close he'd come to being one of the bodies strewn on the ground struck him, and he shook with relief. He removed his hand from Kordrick's shoulder so the younger man wouldn't feel his trembling.

"Falcon," Kordrick began, "may I go after the Charpan horses? We don't want to lose them."

"I doubt they'll go far," Mattos replied. "They may already be mingling with our horses, but you're right to think of them. Take two men with you and bring them back."

"No—please, Falcon. I can bring them back myself."

Mattos hesitated. It would be difficult for a foot soldier to bring back so many horses, but then Kordrick had proven to be a good horseman. Mattos also didn't want to deny anything to the man who had just saved his life. Maybe he needed to be alone after the battle. "Very well, go alone if you want."

"Thank you," Kordrick replied. He mounted his horse and rode off.

After a soldier brought Nica to Mattos, he climbed onto her back and rode about the field of battle. Men carried their fallen companions to the edge of the camp, where they lay side by side. Others tended the wounded. Four prisoners had been taken; the rest of the enemies were dead or near it. Soldiers walked about, finishing off horses and Charpans beyond help. Others threw themselves on the food left over from the interrupted meal. They searched the grass, stuffing whatever bits they found into their mouths. Some drank from the wine sacks. A few soldiers leaned against each other, laughing in relieved hysteria.

"Leave the wine!" Mattos shouted. "Get back to your duties."

An approaching rider caught Mattos's attention. "Mekindu!" Relief overwhelmed him at seeing his Owl alive. "Where—"

"Falcon Darius," Mekindu burst out. "He's badly wounded. We need a physician."

Chapter 26

KIRI

The promise not to watch the battle had been a lie. When the soldiers charged into the valley, Kiri climbed to the lookout point to gaze down into the camp. This was not like the attack on Mar Dun. The Charpans had stolen food from families who needed it—worse, they'd killed unarmed people. They deserved to be attacked.

The camp was close enough to follow the attackers' movements. Mekindu, easy to identify by his mount, threw his spear into one of the Charpans running toward him. Kiri recalled how Mekindu had coaxed her onto his horse earlier that day and joked with her before she'd fallen asleep. A shudder ran down her spine.

Kiri fixed her eyes on the Charpans' swords and arrows, trying to will them into Kordrick's flesh. If he died in battle, she could take credit for his death because she'd led him to this fight. If he were wounded, she could offer to help bandage wounds and poison the bandage she used for Kordrick. The soldiers wouldn't suspect her when he sickened and died, not after she'd led them to the Charpans. She only needed a cut to his skin.

Kiri backed away from the lookout point. Watching would not kill Kordrick. She'd seen enough to know the imperial soldiers would win. Drawing her legs to her chest, she wrapped her arms around them to wait for the killing to stop.

When the mountain winds picked up, almost blocking out the screams, Kiri sighed in relief and buried her head in her knees. She was still exhausted from running all night and welcomed the opportunity to rest free from battle cries. Her breathing became even, and time seemed to slow as she entered a state between sleep and wakefulness.

"Kiri!"

She opened her eyes. How long had she been sitting there?

"Kiri?"

She lifted her head to find Kordrick standing bareheaded before her. Blood spattered his hands, armor, and face. His green eyes blazed above a strange smile. He looked exactly like he had in Mar Dun fourteen months ago.

Kiri jumped to her feet.

"I didn't mean to startle you," Kordrick said, still wearing that peculiar smile. "Don't be afraid. The battle's over. The Falcon wants you to join us."

"We're leaving now?" Kiri asked, backing away.

"Yes," Kordrick replied. "We should hurry." He started to back down the mountain. When Kiri didn't follow, he gestured her to join him.

As much as she loathed the thought of being near Kordrick, he would be suspicious if she refused to accompany him. She grabbed her pack and came toward him.

Kordrick waited for Kiri to reach him before he resumed walking. Once they were side by side, he spoke cheerfully, turning his blood-spattered face to smile at her. "Some soldiers are wounded and a few were killed, but it could have been much worse. We must offer thanks to Odern we didn't lose more. It's a horrible thing to lose a man who has fought beside you. Did you know I once fought the Forest people?"

"No," Kiri answered, almost choking on the word.

"They're vicious cowards," Kordrick said. "They won't fight in the open. They prefer to attack a man when his back is turned, or when he's asleep. We lost many men to those tree rats—men who were my friends." His eyes hardened as his smile faded. "It's worse when a man survives war and an enemy like that, only to be murdered in his bed like Orrik." Kordrick came to an abrupt halt. "Orrik and I fought the Forest people together. Did you know him?"

"No," Kiri whispered.

"But you heard what happened to him," Kordrick insisted. "Everyone's heard the story. His throat was cut in his bed. Everyone blames the Charpans we just slaughtered, but I say only a tree rat would kill a man in his sleep."

Kiri met Kordrick's eyes. She refused to cower before him. Did he know or did he only suspect? Was he trying to get her to say something to give herself away?

Kordrick leaned down so close Kiri felt his hot breath on her face. The stench of his sweat overwhelmed her.

"Tell me, Kiri," Kordrick drawled, "how did you manage to track the bandits when our own scouts couldn't do it? Where does a Wanderer girl learn such a skill?"

He knows. But how? If she ran now, she'd reveal herself to the entire column and lose her chance to kill Kordrick and Isandor. Even if she managed to hide from the soldiers and make her way home, she'd return to her people having failed them. Kiri didn't answer. Instead, she resumed walking, suppressing a shudder as she turned her back on Kordrick. She had to get away from him before he tricked her into revealing herself. Her time had run out. She needed to kill him as soon as she could—tonight or the next morning.

"Wait," Kordrick called as he ran after her.

Kiri turned just as Kordrick grabbed her pack with a blood-stained hand.

"This must be heavy. Let me carry it for you," he said as he pulled it from her shoulder.

"No," Kiri protested, grabbing the straps.

Kordrick easily tore the pack from her grip. "I'm curious," he said as he untied the leather strips that held the pack closed, "what does a Wanderer girl need to carry around with her all the time?"

Kiri lunged for the pack just as Kordrick turned it upside down. As her fingers closed around the pack, her Forest shirt and trousers fell at Kordrick's feet.

For the briefest of moments, Kordrick stood still, his eyes fixed on the Forest clothing.

Kiri took off like a doe, her only thought to escape him. Rough hands caught her hair, yanking her off her feet. Kiri screamed in pain, instant tears forming in her eyes. She hit the ground as Kordrick ripped the scarf from her head.

Kordrick entwined his fingers in the hair near Kiri's scalp. "By Odern, it *is* you," he growled as he jerked her head back to stare into her face. His green eyes blazed with palpable hate over his bared teeth. "When I first saw you, I thought my mind was playing tricks on me—that the memories of those days lost in the Forest lands were driving me crazy. But I remember the village girl who killed Imus. I saw him cut your face before he died. I told myself you were just another scar-faced woman around the right age. I actually believed you were a Wanderer—and then you tracked the Charpans." With his last words, he gave Kiri's hair a vicious tug.

Kiri grasped Kordrick's hands, trying to ease the pull on her scalp, to no avail. He outmatched her in size and strength.

"Most of these men have never fought the Forest people, but I know how you tree rats can track. You sniff out men like hounds," Kordrick growled. "Now that I have your clothes as proof of what you are ..." He jerked Kiri up so she stood facing him, her hands still wrapped around his wrists. Kordrick laughed as he brought his face near hers. "You thought you could walk among imperial soldiers, eat our food, and discover our weaknesses? We'll teach you the wrath of Odern. We'll cut you to pieces." He grasped Kiri's right ear, twisting as if trying to pull it off.

Shrieking in agony, Kiri slammed her fist into Kordrick's nose. She felt bone crack as blood sprayed her hand.

"You little tree whore!" Kordrick screamed as he stumbled backward, his hands covering his broken nose. "I'll smash your face in."

Kiri didn't get far before the soldier tackled her, hitting her with such force they rolled down the mountain. Her dress rose to her hips, exposing her legs to rocks and hard earth.

Kordrick grunted each time he hit the ground, but he didn't relinquish his hold. When they sprawled at the mountain base, he still gripped Kiri's arm.

Sky and Earth spun, making it impossible to tell up from down. Kiri rolled onto her stomach, unsure if she lay motionless or still tumbled. Her arm jerked, then she lay on her back with Kordrick's bloody face looming over her. Something hard struck her cheekbone, sending the world spinning again as light burst behind her eyes. Kiri groaned, dimly aware of Kordrick placing one knee on her shoulder. Somewhere on the wind, a voice whispered, *"He'll kill you too."* Kiri's eyes flew open. "No!" she screamed in the Forest language. In the vulnerable moment before Kordrick could place his other knee on her opposite shoulder, she twisted violently, throwing him off balance. He slipped off her shoulder, then grabbed her leg as she crawled away from him. Kiri hit and kicked in a wild frenzy.

When her foot smashed into something firm, Kiri broke free. She struggled to her feet and ran, her head still reeling from Kordrick's punch. Only when she realized she heard no sound of pursuit did she dare look back. When she did, she froze, staring at Kordrick in bewildered fascination.

He attempted to crawl, choking between whistling breaths. His green eyes bulged as his face turned pink beneath the blood and dirt. He fell to his side, clawing at his throat as if invisible hands strangled him.

Kiri approached, still wary.

Kordrick's eyes showed rage and hatred, but also panic and fear. He made no move to attack or flee, instead struggling for air that wouldn't come.

She'd crushed his air passage. It would have been difficult to do on purpose, yet she had done it unintentionally. Kiri fell to her knees, whispering words of thanks to her protective spirits even as the enemy before her fought for his life.

The soldier made one last attempt to reach his prey, crawling on his elbows toward her, teeth bared. Kiri stood. When Kordrick's fingers wrapped around her ankle, she kicked his hand away. Kordrick took a few strangled half-breaths before he dropped his head to the ground, unconscious. He lay on his stomach with his head turned to the side, blood from his broken nose trickling onto the hard earth. Sweat traveled down his face, leaving uneven streaks through the blood and mucus. A thin layer of dirt covered his armor and hair.

Pebbles crunched under her as Kiri knelt beside one of the men who had shattered her idyllic life. She pressed two shaking fingers against his throat where the lifeblood pulsed. There was the faintest throb—he still lived. Gritting her teeth, Kiri pinched Kordrick's nose shut and covered his mouth. It didn't take long; he only shuddered twice before his lifeblood stopped flowing. She sat beside the body in a horrified daze, memories of the attack on Mar Dun mingling with the shock of what had just happened.

A bird's cry brought Kiri back to herself. She didn't have time to linger. Once the soldiers found Kordrick's body, they'd be after her. She tugged at the cord around his neck until his leather pouch came free. As she lifted the pouch, she ran her fingers along the shapes burned into the leather. His name. She'd use it to prove she'd killed him. Kiri jumped to her feet, noticing for the first time the cuts and scratches mottling her legs. Her dirt-covered dress was ripped in three places, while her normally smooth hair fell in a tangled mess down her back. The left side of her face had begun to swell, making it hard to open her eye.

Kiri climbed the mountain toward the emptied contents of her pack. She'd have to travel to Ishtia on her own, outrunning both the imperial soldiers and the Charpans. She knew only to head north. It would have to do.

When she reached her Forest clothing, waterskin, and knife, Kiri thrust them into her pack, along with Kordrick's pouch. She reached inside to make sure Orrik's ring and the dried meat were still there. How long before the soldiers came looking for her and Kordrick? They couldn't track across the rocky terrain, but if they spotted her, she'd be caught—she couldn't outrun the horses.

As she shouldered her pack, an image of Ulek's delirious face appeared before her eyes. Had the boy lived? Even if he had, he had little chance of catching up with the column in his weakened state. She shook her head against the thought. She couldn't help him now. She half ran, half slid down the mountain. When she reached her scarf, she snatched it up, realizing with sudden clarity how close she'd been to death once Kordrick had ripped it from her head. The memories of Mar Dun, facing the man who'd killed Wren, her narrow escape from death, and the horror of killing a man with her bare hands became overwhelming. Something broke in Kiri, something she'd kept buried, something she'd been fighting since joining the column. Violent sobs burst from her lips, nearly doubling her over as hot tears spilled down her cheeks. Now that her weakness had fought its way to the surface, she could do nothing to suppress it. She wailed without restraint as she continued her descent, giving over to grief, fear, and despair.

At the mountain's base, Kiri turned east, away from the river and the column's path. She kept her gaze on the distant mountains to avoid looking at the corpse as she passed. Still crying, she broke into a sprint, as if she could outrun her horrors as well as the imperial soldiers.

Since joining the column, she'd realized how foolish her original plan to travel all the way to Ishtia alone had been. She didn't know these mountains, didn't know where to find food or water. Now she had no choice but to travel alone. She hadn't realized she'd have to travel farther than any Forest person ever had to reach Ishtia. No Forest person had been to a Sandamedan city; they knew only that Sandameda lay to the north. Her people had prepared her for so little of what she would face. They hadn't told her what it would feel like to kill a man in his bed, live in constant fear of discovery, or lie to people who befriended and trusted her. It had seemed so simple: kill Orrik and Kordrick, then find and kill Isandor. Each step also brought death closer to Ulek. He wouldn't survive if no one went back for him, but she wouldn't survive if she *did* go back. A dead woman would be no help to the boy.

Then an idea came to her. She paused, looking over her shoulder. Perhaps she could save Ulek and rejoin the column.

Chapter 27

MATTOS

Vultures already flew over the valley, their languid circling sending the message of death to all who saw them. A few were bold enough to land on the carcasses littering the ground despite the living moving about. Soldiers drove the scavengers from their fallen mounts and comrades, only to see them alight on another body close by. Then the chase would begin again, the persistent birds never retreating far. Only when the black wings settled on a Charpan were they left alone to pick at the dead flesh.

"Are these accursed birds starving?" Mattos muttered. "Can't they wait until the meat rots?" He'd always hated vultures. From a distance, the long black wingspan looked sinister, even mighty. Up close, the creatures were hideous and pathetic-looking with their bald, red-skinned heads.

His Owl rode beside him, his eyes fixed on his destination. Mattos wanted to ask about Darius, but they galloped, making conversation difficult.

At the end of the Charpan encampment, four battle-weary soldiers gathered around a fifth, who lay moaning on the ground. Upon reaching the group, Mattos and Mekindu dismounted, hurrying to the prone figure.

"Falcon Mattos," a bare-headed soldier said, rising. "I tried to get to him. I swear by Odern. But he was too far, and I couldn't—"

"Of course not," Mattos said, not to reassure the man, but to quiet him.

The wounded officer turned his brown eyes toward Mattos without seeing him. They rolled back into his head before resuming their blind wandering. Dried blood covered the right side of his face from a wound hidden by his helmet, which had been cloven on the right side by what could only have been a Charpan ax.

"Why didn't you remove his helmet?" Mattos asked, leaning toward Darius.

"It wouldn't come off," answered one of the kneeling soldiers, "and we were afraid to force it without Omeldor."

Mattos stared at Darius's blank eyes, bloody face, and ruined helmet. "This man needs a priest, not a physician."

Behind him, the bare-headed man murmured, "Odern called his name."

"How did this happen?" Mattos said, dread spreading into his gut. *The Osprey's nephew.*

"A Charpan on foot attacked him," answered the young, bare-headed man. "Falcon Darius knocked the Charpan to the ground, then he jumped from his horse to finish him off. A mounted Charpan with an ax rode up and—"

"He *jumped*—" Mattos cut himself off. Officers didn't insult or criticize other officers in front of common soldiers.

"Mekindu." Mattos turned to his Owl. "Have these men make a litter for Falcon Darius. I'll send you Omeldor."

Mattos rode toward the opposite end of the valley, close to the mountain they'd hidden behind, where he had seen men gathering the dead. The dead wouldn't be kept far from the wounded, and if Omeldor still lived, he would be with the wounded. Once Mattos reached the edge of the valley, it didn't take him long to find Omeldor, who hovered over the most grievously wounded soldiers, aided by four men.

Two of the wounded men lay motionless, their bandages soaked with blood. One didn't look conscious while another coughed up blood, his eyes fixed on a creeping vulture. A soldier drove the bird off, but it didn't fly far.

The man who'd lost a hand screamed and wept unabashedly as Omeldor tied a tourniquet around his wrist. Two soldiers held the man down as Omeldor bandaged the stump. "This will have to be cauterized," Omeldor said dispassionately, as if he had been talking about a mosquito bite. At forty-three, only seven years away from forced retirement, he was among the oldest common soldiers in the company. His hairline had started to recede, and lines extended from his hooked nose to the corners of his mouth. He gave a curt nod as Mattos approached. "Falcon."

"Falcon Darius is wounded. An ax to his helmet."

Omeldor rose. "Is he . . . coherent?"

"No, but he's awake."

Omeldor searched Mattos's face, then nodded, as if he'd seen in Mattos's eyes what he didn't want to say. He knelt beside his leather roll containing bandages, jars, and copper instruments. Removing some bandages and two small jars, he handed them to one of the men assisting him. "Honey and vinegar. There are plenty here who will need it." As he tucked his leather roll under his arm, he inclined his head toward the now one-handed man who cradled his stump and moaned as he rocked back and forth. “Give that man some wine.”

A company wine sack recaptured from the Charpans lay near the wounded soldiers. The wine was the Hawk’s property, and not to be commandeered by common soldiers, no matter the use. Mattos pretended he didn’t hear Omeldor’s command.

The dun-colored mare Omeldor had ridden into battle grazed nearby. As they walked toward her, Omeldor asked, “You don’t think he’ll live?”

“No, but I’m not a physician,” Mattos answered.

“It doesn’t take a physician to recognize a dying man,” Omeldor replied, slipping his leather roll into the saddlebag and mounting his horse. “Soldiers who often see battle learn quickly how to tell if a wounded man has been called by Odern.”

In reply, Mattos pointed in the direction where Darius lay. “That way. At the other end of the valley. There are several men with him.”

As Omeldor rode away, Mattos turned to look at the field of battle. Soldiers stood or sat about in groups. Some talked about the battle as they cleaned blood and human remains from their weapons. Others gathered around the dead and wounded, their eyes somber. Because they had been pulled from different units, they weren’t a bonded group, but in a company of 318 men living in close quarters, most knew each other.

Five dead soldiers lay side by side, hands folded over their chests, eyes closed. Their weapons, armor, and coin purses had already been removed. Wearing only tunics, trousers, and boots, they no longer resembled imperial soldiers.

Five. He'd lost five and had little hope for Darius and two of the badly wounded men. The man who'd lost a hand could no longer serve in the army. If the column reached Ishtia before the Charpans did, he would be discharged upon arrival. Mattos would have to explain all this to Diakiris, Beldos, and Thais. He'd have to look into Beldos's eyes and explain how his brother's son had died.

Someone had made the mistake of gathering the prisoners close to the dead soldiers, within sight of mourning comrades. Eight men surrounded the wounded prisoners, jeering and poking them with swords. Instead of cowering before their tormentors, they cursed and spat. Despite his bindings and an arrow protruding from his shoulder, one prisoner lunged at a man who taunted him, landing flat on his face. The soldiers guffawed. A broad-shouldered man tugged at his trousers and began to piss, aiming his stream dangerously close to where the prisoners sat.

"Stop this!" Mattos yelled, storming over.

Startled, the men sprang back. They had obviously been too preoccupied with their sport to notice Mattos. The urinating man splashed his own boots before he managed to pull his trousers back up.

"The Hawk wants these men for questioning," Mattos shouted. "How can he question them if they're dead or too injured to speak? Haven't you had enough blood?"

One man spoke up: "They killed Nevtu."

"Yes," Mattos replied. "And we killed plenty of their friends." He pointed at two men. "You two, see to the prisoners' injuries. It will be your heads if these men worsen."

The two men glanced at each other before crouching by the prisoners. They weren't physicians, but all imperial soldiers knew how to stitch and bandage wounds. The other six men moved away without further complaint. Mattos had, after all, beheaded one of his own men for desertion.

With the fear and excitement of battle wearing off, exhaustion overcame Mattos. He wandered over to the dead soldiers. Having heard his outburst, those who lingered gave him space.

Blood covered the bodies in varying amounts. An Owl, the one Mattos had seen die, had almost had his head severed. An arrow protruded from the eye socket of a Sparrow. The three other bodies concerned Mattos the most, for each had what looked like arrow wounds in his chest. Mattos couldn't suppress his shudder. He'd feared the Charpans' poison-tipped arrows, but he hadn't known they could pierce armor. He wondered how far the Charpans could be from their targets and still pierce armor. Despite their superior numbers, Mattos realized that without the element of surprise, the battle could have gone the other way. The unsuspecting Charpans had been under attack before they'd had a chance to string their bows, reach their horses, or grab their weapons. There was still the chance that those with arrow wounds had been poisoned, but it seemed most of the Charpans, in the desperate fight for their lives, hadn't had time to dip them in the poison vials. If the Charpans had already been mounted, with strung bows and quivers of fifty arrows on their backs …

Mattos walked between the bodies, removing the coin purses all imperial soldiers wore around their necks. A Falcon's duty was to look at the faces of the men who'd died under him. Each purse had had the owner's name burned into the leather in the event of death. A soldier's weapons and armor belonged to his unit, but the money he earned belonged to his family.

Glancing up, Mattos saw Ladius watching him. "So, you went into battle without Nuendos," Mattos said. "He must not have liked that." He spoke matter-of-factly. Everyone in the company knew Ladius and Nuendos shared the love between equals, but none cared so long as they had wives and provided their families and empire with legitimate children. Both men had fulfilled these expectations.

Ladius shrugged. "He's not as good a rider as I am. The Hawk wouldn't send him."

"Did these men have children?" Mattos asked.

"All five," Ladius replied. "Young Borus has a son he never met. His wife was going to join him when the babe was older. I suppose he was grateful they're safe in Ishtia and not being chased by the Charpan horde."

"Like your family?"

Ladius met Mattos's eyes. "Like my family."

Just as Mattos rose, he noticed an indigo figure sprinting toward him. It could only be one person.

Following Mattos's gaze, Ladius said, "Our little tracker. She should have stayed where you left her and avoided this ugliness."

"She's a strange one," Mattos said. As he turned away, a feminine wail reached his ears. He spun back toward Kiri, now close enough for him to make out details. She wept even as she called out to him, her dirty clothes in disarray.

Chapter 28

MATTOS

Mattos hurried to Kiri, followed closely by Ladius.

"Kordrick!" the woman sobbed. "Kordrick is dead."

Grasping Kiri's shoulders, Mattos bent down so they were face-to-face. A purple bruise covered her left cheekbone, and blood dripped from the corner of her mouth. "Kiri, what happened?"

"Charpans came."

Mattos glanced over his shoulder at Ladius's grim face before turning back to the woman before him. "Kiri, the Charpans are dead."

"No!" Kiri sniffled as she wiped the tears from her cheeks. "They came, they attacked me. They attacked Kordrick. I ran. I saw … I saw them kill Kordrick."

"You're sure?" Mattos demanded, his voice rising. "You saw Kordrick die?"

Wide-eyed, Kiri nodded.

"How many were there?"

Kiri squirmed as Mattos's fingers dug into her shoulders. "Two."

None stood between the three of them and the mountain. If the Charpans had tried to pursue Kiri, they must have turned back when they'd seen the soldiers.

"Where are they now?" Mattos asked, trying to control the alarm in his voice.

"I don't know, I ran."

"The poor girl is hysterical," Ladius said.

"I can see that," Mattos snapped. He took a deep breath and offered his hand. "Kiri, come with us."

Kordrick's body lay at the foot of the mountain near where the soldiers had hidden before the attack. Mattos studied their surroundings, searching for other Charpan stragglers. Only the mountain loomed over them, the rocky terrain, and distant peaks. Not far away, Kordrick's horse wandered at a slow pace. An enemy would have nowhere to hide. Even Kiri had calmed down, as if she understood she had nothing to fear. He reached his arm back to help her down.

After a brief hesitation, Kiri slipped her arms from around his waist and, hanging on to his arm, slid off Nica's back.

Jumping down after her, Mattos strode toward the body, where Ladius already crouched. Kordrick, covered in blood, lay facedown in the dirt, his helmet nowhere in sight. His nose had been broken, yet there were no obvious death wounds—no bloody gashes or arrows protruding from his body.

Bile rose in Mattos's throat. If it hadn't been for Kordrick, he would be a corpse on the field of battle. Against his better judgment, he had allowed Kordrick to go alone after the escaped horses, and now Kordrick traveled to the city of the dead.

"This is what killed him, Falcon," Ladius said, pointing to Kordrick's throat. "He suffocated."

Crouching beside Ladius, Mattos saw that Kordrick's throat had been crushed. There was no blood; it had been done with a blunt object. "Did they *beat* him to death?" Mattos said. It didn't make sense for armed soldiers not to use their weapons. Kordrick's sword lay on the ground not far from the body. Why hadn't the Charpans killed him with their own weapons? Perhaps they hadn't drawn their weapons when they'd gone after Kiri, a small, unarmed woman. Kordrick could have taken them by surprise, but even then …

"Kiri," Mattos called.

The Wanderer girl came forward, averting her eyes from the body.

"Tell me exactly what happened," Mattos said, staring up at her.

Kiri's eyebrows drew together. "I told you. Two Charpans came. They attacked me and Kordrick."

"Yes, but how?" Mattos pressed.

Kiri glanced down at the body, then back at him. For the first time since he'd known her, Mattos saw fear in her eyes. "I don't know," Kiri burst out in a shrill voice. "I ran."

"You said you saw the Charpans kill him," Mattos said, getting to his feet. "You said you saw Kordrick die."

Tears filled Kiri's already red-rimmed eyes. "I don't know," she said, backing away. "I didn't see … I didn't see everything."

When Mattos took an angry step toward her, Kiri stumbled backward, her eyes widening. “I don’t know,” she repeated, starting to cry again. “I ran. I *ran.*”

Mattos glared at her. She’d never shown fear or weakness until today. This was the girl who’d run away from a cruel husband and then escaped the very Charpans they had just killed. The girl who had tracked the Charpans and run through the night to tell the Hawk. The girl who had ordered imperial officers to speak the common language so she could understand them. Now she wept simply because he’d asked her a few questions.

“Falcon,” Ladius said, rising as he gestured to Kiri’s marred face. “Look at her. Those Charpans attacked her, and then she saw them kill a man. She’s not a trained soldier. It might not be clear to her.”

Mattos glanced back at Kiri, who sobbed, her face buried in her hands. He had just experienced his first true battle, and nearly been killed himself. The battle rage still surged in him, and Kiri had faced death as well. Ladius’s words held reason. Mattos started to turn away from Kiri when he glimpsed her peeking at him from between her fingers. She feared him, feared the questions he asked her—but why? He knew Kiri wouldn’t tell them exactly what had happened any time soon. Part of him wanted her to track the two Charpans who had killed Kordrick—they couldn’t have gotten far—but he surmised Kiri would refuse and probably become hysterical again.

Mattos bent to retrieve Kordrick’s coin purse. When he couldn’t find the cord, he slipped his fingers under the breastplate. Nothing. “By Odern, they robbed him,” Mattos muttered in disgust. He rose with a sigh. There were other matters to attend to: burying their dead, rounding up the herd, catching up with the column, and delivering the prisoners to Thais. Mattos would have to explain to Thais how he had lost five men—it would probably be eight by the time they reached the column—in the battle. Then there was Darius. Mattos had to try to get him to the column before he died. Whatever secrets Kiri had, he would have to learn them later.

"Ladius, get Kordrick's horse," Mattos commanded. "We need to take the body back. We don't have time to linger here."

Chapter 29

ULEK

The clouds traveled faster than Ulek had ever seen them move. Their shapes twisted and morphed; one moment he gazed at a herd of white horses, and the next he saw women in long gowns dancing across the sky. They looked so beautiful; fluffy white clouds against the blue sky.

I'm dead. I'm in the Hills of Idenya. He turned his head, hoping for a glimpse of Esnin—or his mother. Instead, he saw only the other Galeedans who'd been struck by poison arrows. The man who had screamed and cried now lay silent and still. The old man wept over his wife's body. The blond-haired young woman lay close by, her breathing shallow. There was no sign of the children or their mothers, then Ulek noticed two mounds close together. The mothers must have dug shallow graves for their children, covered them in dirt, and left to rejoin the column.

Still alive, Ulek thought, squeezing his eyes shut. His lower leg burned. He wished Kiri had stayed with him and held him as she had before. *Please, Esnin, take me.* It couldn't be long now.

Something foul-tasting coated his dry tongue. Ulek tried to swallow, feeling only his tongue scrape against the roof of his mouth. "Water," he rasped. No one brought him any. Esnin still had not heard his prayers. The clouds sped by.

His world had shrunk to one need, one word. Water. Ulek wondered if he would die of thirst or poison. The sound of grass rustling caught his attention. He turned his head to see the blond-haired young woman crawling toward him on her elbows. Ulek stared, unable to even feel curious. As he watched her drag herself closer, his own fingers twitched, touching what felt like leather. He held something in his right hand. With great effort, he raised his head to look. A waterskin. He could have wept with relief. As he used all his strength to lift the waterskin and remove the cap, it occurred to Ulek that drinking would only prolong his suffering, but he couldn't stop. The water must have been there two days, yet when he put it to his mouth, it tasted fresh and cold. It spilled over his parched lips, dribbling down his chin.

A growl-like moan escaped the woman's lips. She continued to crawl toward Ulek, her eyes fixed on the waterskin with fierce determination.

Ulek had a sudden urge to hold it out to her and an equally powerful one to keep it away at all costs. In the end, he did neither. The effort of lifting the waterskin to his mouth had drained all his strength. He closed his eyes.

Something pounded against the earth. A horse whinnied not far away. Had the white ships finally come for him, or had he survived only to be killed by the horde? With his ear pressed against the ground, he heard approaching footsteps. The orange light behind his eyelids turned black, and he knew someone bent over him, blocking out the sun.

"He's alive! Ulek is alive!"

At the sound of Kiri's voice, Ulek's eyes flitted open. At first, she was only a dark shadow against the sky, then details emerged: the curve of her cheek, a bruise, the scar running down her face, her large joyful eyes. She turned away to call to someone, her words sounding muffled and far away. Then liquid fire poured over his injury. Ulek screamed, trying to rise.

A hand pushed him down. "Be still," Kiri said. "It's medicine."

Ulek writhed in pain as his injury burned.

Then his head and shoulders were being lifted, and he found himself sitting upright with Kiri's arm supporting him.

Soldiers climbed off their horses to let them trot toward the river to drink.

"Ulek," Kiri said, "the Charpans are dead. The soldiers killed them."

Ulek gazed at his surroundings, his mind fuzzy. He could see and hear everything around him, but it held no meaning.

"Drink," Kiri commanded, pressing the waterskin to his lips. Ulek obeyed, though there wasn't much left.

When Kiri lowered the waterskin, Ulek saw Falcon Mattos, with yellow remnants of bruises on his face, crouching before him.

"So, you survived," the soldier said, flashing his white teeth. "You're a strong one. Do you think you can ride on your own?"

The world spun as Ulek tried to shake his head, and Kiri answered for him. "No."

"Didn't think so," the Falcon said, getting to his feet. As he turned away, he stopped and spun back to Kiri. "That's a soldier's waterskin. Where did you get it?"

"I took it. Ulek needed it."

Falcon Mattos passed a hand over his eyes. "Kiri, if you hadn't just led us to the Charpans . . ." He shook his head as he walked away.

Realization cut through the fog in Ulek's head. He'd survived the poison; he would live. Kiri and some soldiers had brought medicine and horses to carry the survivors back to the column. They hadn't been left for dead after all. Then the meaning of the Falcon's words struck him: *If you hadn't just led us to the Charpans.* And Kiri had said something about Charpans being dead. "They're dead?" he rasped.

"The Charpans are dead," Kiri repeated, her voice soothing.

Ulek's heart beat faster. The men who had murdered his father, kidnapped Kiri and him, attacked the column, and nearly killed him were dead. "I'm glad," he said. "I hate them and I'm glad they're dead." From the corner of his eye, he saw Kiri flinch.

The soldiers moved about in a hurry. After refilling their waterskins and watering their horses, they remounted. Owl Mekindu lifted the blond woman onto a small Charpan horse. She sagged in the saddle, barely able to hold herself up. As he watched her, Ulek wondered if she had managed to drink from his waterskin. The horse took a few steps, causing the woman to slide sideways. Owl Mekindu caught her as she fell. Instead of putting her back on the horse, he carried her to his own white stallion, placed her in front of the saddle, and climbed on behind her.

Ulek grunted as Kiri forced his boot on. Now that the swelling had gone down, it fit. When a soldier lifted Ulek off the ground, the world spun again. The ground passed under him with alarming speed while Kiri's indigo dress danced in the periphery. Once the soldier placed Ulek on a horse, he clung to the animal's mane, afraid he'd be sick. He stared down at Kiri, who handed him his blanket and his father's coat. She'd abandoned him, left him to travel on his own without the protection of family or friends. Why was she with him now? Perhaps she felt guilty that he'd almost died after she'd insisted they part ways.

As the soldier who'd carried Ulek climbed on the horse with him and took the reins, Falcon Mattos rode up to them. "Come, Kiri," he said, holding his hand out to her.

"I'll ride with—"

"Mekindu has someone else riding with him," he said, cutting her off. "Come now, or you'll ride on your own."

Kiri hurriedly grasped his hand. As he began to lift her, she pulled back, pointing at a nearby figure. "The old man."

Gazing in the direction she pointed, Ulek saw the old man sitting near his wife's body. He no longer wept, only sat staring into the distance.

"He wants to stay with his wife," the Falcon said.

"He'll die," Kiri said, wrenching her hand away.

"If the old man wants to stay, I'll let him stay," Mattos snapped. "It's his decision and his responsibility." He held his hand out to Kiri again. "Come *now*."

With a last glance at the old man, Kiri took the Falcon's hand and allowed him to pull her up behind him.

As the group rode off, Ulek turned to look at the old man who'd been left to die, wondering how long it would be before the white ships came for him.

Chapter 30

MATTOS

The four bound prisoners leaned against each other, showing neither insolence nor fear. When they'd been captured, they'd been angry and defiant. Now their eyes conveyed only indifference, as if they had accepted death and found everything leading up to it boring. Watching them, Mattos wondered if he could be so stoic if, after seeing almost all his companions die, he'd been wounded and captured, facing almost certain execution.

Two of the men were young, with fuzz instead of beards. One had deep lines stretched across his forehead and gray hair extending from his temples. The fourth had a lean face, with a neatly trimmed beard and intelligent eyes that flicked about, seeming to miss nothing. Mattos recognized him as the Charpan who'd only been taken prisoner after being knocked unconscious while fighting off three soldiers. All four of them wore bloody bandages. Omeldor himself had eventually seen to their wounds.

Hawk Thais stared at them with solemn anger, his mouth a straight line. Osprey Beldos stood beside him, his eyes fixed on the prisoners the way a predator fixed its eyes on prey. Falcon Darius had not made it to the column. Instead, he'd been presented to his uncle as a blanket-wrapped body, his armor and coin purse already removed. Beldos's grief had been terrible, and now his rage was more so.

Beldos's aides and the three Harriers in the company were also present. As the only Falcon in the group, Mattos stood close to Harrier Diakiris. The column trudged past, every face turned toward the prisoners and the men surrounding them. Some villagers even stopped when they came abreast of the group and had to be hurried along by soldiers who couldn't hide their own curiosity.

"Why were you here?" Thais asked in Charpan.

The lean-faced man responded, "To observe you. To report what you did."

"How did you cross the border without our knowledge?"

The lean-faced man's lips twitched as if Thais had said something amusing. "The Galeedan border is very long."

Like all rich or high-born children, Mattos had learned to speak Charpan at a young age. Rich Sandamedans didn't bother to learn the languages of their own provinces, but Charpa was a civilization with roads, cities, libraries, and a standing army worthy of their interest. A man couldn't call himself educated if he couldn't speak the language of his civilized neighbors. Yet this western Charpan had an accent very different from the one Mattos had learned to master. His words were rough, his voice guttural.

"And why did you attack us?" Thais asked.

"To slow you down so our tengish can overtake you."

"And what does your *tengish*"—Thais sneered at the Charpan word for horde—"plan to do?"

The Charpan cocked his head to the side. "Why do you ask questions when you know the answers? The tengish plans to kill you. If you did not already know this, you would not be running away."

Thais's nostrils flared as he stepped forward. "What does your tengish plan to do *after* we are dead?"

Without hesitation, the Charpan replied, "Take Ishtia."

The soldiers joined in Thais's laughter.

"That's impossible," Thais said.

The prisoner shrugged.

"Let me put some steel through his flesh," Beldos growled in Sandamedan. "Then he'll tell us what the horde is after."

Sneering at Beldos, the prisoner said in perfect Sandamedan, "Secrets and lies are for women. We say what we will do, and then we do it. Ask what you want to know. We will tell you."

Hearing their language on the prisoner's lips, the soldiers exchanged astonished glances.

The Charpan smiled. "Did you think us westerners were nothing but sheep herders?"

Thais recovered first. "You were educated in the East?"

Inclining his head, the Charpan answered, "I spent five years in the city of Zurpesh, but what is taught in the East can be brought to the West. There are many western Charpans who have never been to Zurpesh who know its teachings."

"Who are you?"

"I am called Elgust, son of Amelger of the Moon clan. May Sky God smile on our meeting, Hawk Thais of Sandameda."

His smile reached his eyes, as if he truly found the situation humorous.

"If secrets and lies are for women, then poison is the weapon of cowards," Thais spat. "You attacked the column with poison arrows and then fled instead of facing us."

"You outnumbered us," Elgust replied matter-of-factly.

"We still outnumbered you when we attacked your camp," Thais said, his voice smug.

For the first time, respect shone in Elgust's eyes. "Yes. We did not think you would find us." He glanced at Mattos. "It's a foolish warrior who underestimates his enemy."

"Enough of this," Beldos said. "Where are the others?"

Elgust turned his piercing gaze on Beldos. "The tengish will be here very soon."

Beldos drew his sword and strode toward the prisoners until he stood looming over them. "How many of you are there hiding in the mountains? Where else do you have bands?"

"There are no other bands," Elgust answered, blinking in surprise.

Beldos pointed a finger at Mattos. "This man claims two of your men killed one of his soldiers after the battle and escaped. There are two you've forgotten. How many more are you not mentioning?"

Elgust turned to Mattos, his gaze appraising. "I saw the bodies. I counted. There were originally twenty-eight of us. After we attacked you, there were twenty-six. Now there are only four. There are no others."

An image of Kordrick's body flashed before Mattos's eyes. Then he recalled Kordrick's face right after he'd saved his life.

As a mere Falcon, he was expected to keep his mouth shut, but he couldn't hold back. "Then who killed my soldier? He was alive and well after the battle. Not long after I found him with his throat crushed."

"Falcon …" Thais warned.

Even with Beldos standing over him with a drawn sword, Elgust didn't take his eyes off Mattos. "Do your men not fight? Perhaps he had a quarrel over which horses he could claim."

"Imperial soldiers do not murder each other," Beldos spat. "We are part of a disciplined army, not barbarians who spend their time raiding each other's sheep and horses. The captured horses belong to the company, to the Hawk." He leaned in close so that his nose almost touched Elgust's. "Who killed Falcon Darius? Who killed my nephew?"

"One of my men—of course."

Beldos pressed his blade against Elgust's throat. Blood trickled from where the point met skin. "Who was it?" he said between closed teeth.

During the questioning, the three other prisoners had been silent, their expressions guarded. They gave no indication they understood the Sandamedan words. Even with the blade pressed against their leader's throat, they showed no alarm. Only the tiniest flicker in their eyes revealed they had noticed.

His voice even, Elgust answered, "I don't know who it was."

"Beldos," Thais began, "this is not why—"

He drew back his arm, his sword aimed at Elgust's throat.

"Beldos!" Thais shouted, his voice sharp.

With his eyes never leaving Elgust, Beldos lowered his sword.

Thais ran forward and, grabbing Beldos by the shoulder, spun him around. None heard what Thais hissed in Beldos's face.

The murmuring that had risen among the officers died as Beldos sheathed his sword and stormed away.

Thais turned back to Elgust. "Where are the other Charpans? How many bands are here already?"

Elgust returned Thais's stare when he answered, "A rider of the tengish speaks only truth. Except for these three, my men are dead. If any had survived, they would have rescued us before we reached you. There is only the tengish coming."

Thais pointed at Mattos. "A woman saw two Charpans attack his soldier after the battle was over. What do you say to that?"

Once again, Elgust turned an appraising gaze on Mattos. "You brought a woman to battle? A woman?" A bitter smile spread across his face. "Secrets and lies."

Chapter 31

KIRI

"Kiri, what are you doing?" Ulek asked in alarm as he leaned forward to get a better view of his companion.

"It's nothing," Kiri replied, placing the point of her knife against her big toe. She flashed the boy a smile to reassure him. She'd removed her left boot and laid it across her foot to hide her leaping doe tattoo. The soles of her feet, calloused from years of running long distances, were almost immune to blisters. Not so with the skin under her toenails. Her run to find the Charpans and bring news of their whereabouts to the soldiers had taken its toll. The skin under her big toenail had turned deep purple while some of the blister puffed out past the nail. Gritting her teeth, Kiri slipped the tip of the blade under the nail and pressed it into the blister. Immediately, blood gushed from her toe.

"That's disgusting!" Ulek said, the look of fascination on his face belying his words.

Unconcerned, Kiri wiped her knife against the grass before slipping her boot on. In a few days, she'd be able to pull the nail off. Though she'd lost several toenails during her many years of running, they'd never failed to grow back.

"Did running all night cause that?" Ulek asked.

Kiri nodded as she sheathed her knife and returned it to her pack.

The sun had disappeared below the horizon, its rays still illuminating the pink-hued sky. Instead of the usual mountain winds, only a mild breeze disrupted the warm evening. Having just stopped for the night, people hurried about starting fires, putting up tents, and getting their evening meals from the soldiers. Since recovering the stolen food, the column had returned to its original rations.

A large gray dog with a white patch around one eye wandered close to them. Kiri tensed when it stopped, its gaze fixed on them.

When Ulek smiled at it, holding out his hand, the dog gave a slight wag of its tail. "Here," Ulek called. A low whine sounded from its throat.

"Get away!" Kiri yelled, charging.

The dog took off, casting a backward glance over its shoulder.

"You didn't have to chase it off," Ulek said, disappointment in his voice. "It wouldn't have hurt us."

Kiri turned to stare at him. How could he know the dog wouldn't have harmed them? One could never know an animal's intentions.

"I always wanted a dog," Ulek said. "My father promised me one, once we found a family with puppies to sell, but . . ."

"I'll get food," Kiri said, anxious to change the subject. The soldiers had gone back to allowing people to get rations for those not in line.

When she bent to gather their bowls, she saw Ulek push aside his bandages to peek at his injured leg. Most of the swelling had gone down, and the wound had finally dried up and started to close. The surviving Charpans had refused to give the antidote's whereabouts, but the soldiers' healer had found it when searching their possessions.

"Kiri?"

She turned her attention back to Ulek. "Yes?"

"Are you going to stay with me now?"

With a sigh, Kiri crouched beside him. She had asked herself that same question since finding the boy alive. When he'd told her no Galeedan family would take him in, she hadn't believed him. He was healthy, intelligent, and good-natured. Someday, he'd be a strong young man who could hunt for and protect his family. A Forest family would have seen the value in such a child, yet the Galeedans had left him to die. He would have if, on the way back to the column, Kiri hadn't convinced Mattos to stop where the poisoned Galeedans had been left. Now, with his father gone, no one else would protect or care for Ulek. She had no choice. "Yes, I'll stay with you."

His gray eyes narrowing, Ulek said, "You left me once before. You wanted to be on your own."

"I was wrong."

"Yes, you were," Ulek snapped. "We escaped the Charpans together. You were there when I saw my father. We warned the soldiers together." He stopped, waiting for her to respond. When Kiri didn't say anything, he continued, "You shouldn't travel alone."

"Not alone," Kiri agreed.

Sighing, Ulek leaned back on his elbows as if finished. When Kiri stood back up, he asked, "After we get to Ishtia, how will you find your birth clan?"

"I'll find them," Kiri replied, hoping he wouldn't ask more questions about the Wanderers. The less she said about the Wanderer people, the less likely she was to be caught in a lie. "I'll get us food." She started toward the rations line, hardly noticing the pain in her toe.

"I'll come with you," Ulek said. Brushing off Kiri's protestations, he stood and headed for the line. Despite his painful wound, he walked with only a slight limp.

As they made their way through the camp, Kiri felt eyes lingering on her. A few times, she met the stares of villagers who hurriedly looked away. A man walking past stopped in his tracks when he noticed her. As she ducked her head, Kiri saw him give her a respectful nod from the corner of her eye. *The Wanderer girl who tracked the Charpans.* Kiri kept her head lowered, uncomfortable with the attention.

They hadn't been standing in line long when people began to run past. Shouts could be heard in the distance.

"What's happening?" Ulek asked a red-haired boy who hurried by.

Without pausing, the boy called over his shoulder, "Come see! The soldiers are going to execute the prisoners!"

Chapter 32

KIRI

Before Kiri could stop him, Ulek took off in the direction the boy had gone. She chased after him, elbowing her way through the crowd. It didn't take long to reach their destination. A short distance from the encampment, the four prisoners knelt before the old soldier known as Hawk Thais, their hands bound behind them. Four soldiers with drawn swords stood close to their leader, while the rest formed neat rows farther back. The villagers gathered as close as they dared. Angry muttering swept through the crowd. Some hissed and yelled insults at the doomed men. The prisoners ignored the taunts, betraying no fear. Their long shadows stretched toward the people who had come to witness their death.

Spotting Ulek near the front of the crowd, Kiri made her way to him. When she placed her hand on his shoulder, he turned toward her.

"The one in red is their leader," he said. "I remember him."

Kiri regarded the red-clad prisoner who knelt between the others, his eyes scanning the crowd. The combination of darkness and fear had prevented her from studying the men who'd captured her and Ulek, yet with his lean features and prominent nose, the prisoner in red had a face not easily forgotten. She remembered the last time she had seen him, eating with his men while she and Ulek sat bound in the grass. He said something that made the other prisoners laugh. Kiri gripped Ulek's shoulder tighter. Who were these men who laughed in the face of death? Kiri tugged on Ulek's arm. "Come. Don't look."

The boy jerked away from her. "I want to watch. You should too. They captured us, they killed innocent people. I heard those poisoned children screaming before they died. The horde is driving us from our homes, and if they catch us, they'll kill us all."

The vehemence in Ulek's voice unnerved Kiri. He spoke truth, yet she feared he had another reason for wanting to see the prisoners executed. He believed they had killed his father.

The rage inside him was really for her. He just didn't know it.

"Ulek, you are too young."

"I'm a man now," Ulek replied, his expression indignant. "Don't tell me I'm too young." Spinning on his heel, he limped along the front of the crowd.

Kiri could only stare after him. In all the time they'd spent together, even when they'd found his father's body, he hadn't been like this. Something touched his spirit that hadn't been there before, something that wanted to feed off the prisoners' deaths. It would do him no good. Watching someone die, even someone responsible for one's suffering, would not ease that suffering. Kiri knew that all too well.

Hawk Thais, who until then had seemed to be waiting for some unseen signal, stepped closer to the prisoners. The crowd fell silent. To the Galeedans' frustration, he spoke in Sandamedan, addressing his soldiers. Confused and angry murmurs broke out. A few Galeedan women, who must have been married to soldiers, translated for their neighbors. It didn't help Kiri; no one translated his words into the common language.

The prisoner in red gazed at the crowd with an air of boredom until his eyes fell on Kiri. The bored expression transformed into a mixture of surprise and speculation. He cocked his head as a slow grin spread across his face.

Kiri stood frozen, unable to look away.

Still grinning, the prisoner nodded, as if mocking her. Then he spoke to Thais, interrupting him.

Thais spun around, his face tight with anger.

Leaning forward in urgency, the prisoner spoke rapidly.

Finally, Thais turned toward the crowd. When his eyes met Kiri's, he gestured for her to come forward.

Necks craned all around her as people tried to determine who had been beckoned. Kiri looked at her feet, pretending to think he had meant someone else.

"Kiri!"

She lifted her head. Thais gestured again, his meaning unmistakable. People stared as they backed away from her.

There was nowhere to hide, and nothing to do but obey. Kiri walked toward Thais, the weight of many eyes on her back.

When she stood before him, Thais said, "There's no need to fear these men. They've been bound and can't hurt you.

Elgust"—he indicated the prisoner in red—"has promised to tell us something important about the horde in exchange for a chance to speak with you." He nodded toward the prisoner, as if giving him permission to speak.

"So, your name is Kiri." Elgust's deep voice sounded amused. "May Sky God smile on our meeting again. Much has changed since we last saw each other."

"Get on with it," Thais commanded.

"Are you the one who led the soldiers to us?" Elgust asked.

Kiri glanced at Thais, who nodded. "Yes," she said.

"Then you are responsible for the deaths of my men." When Kiri didn't answer, Elgust said, "So, imperial soldiers depend on women to find their enemies for them. A wonder they don't have women fight their battles as well."

"This man is simply trying to delay his death," Thais said. "Kiri, you may return—"

"Are you the woman who saw two Charpans attack a soldier after the battle?"

"Yes," Kiri managed to whisper. She tried not to flinch as Elgust's eyes traveled over her face, lingering on her scar and the bruise Kordrick had given her. It felt as if he could see into her spirit, as if he knew what had caused her bruise just by looking at it.

"What did those Charpans look like?"

Kiri's hands shook. As she looked into Elgust's eyes, the realization hit her. *He knows.* Eastern Charpa shared more of a border with the Forest lands than Galeed did. There had never been border disputes with Charpa the way there had been with Galeed, and southern villages often traded with Charpan merchants. Wanderers originally came from Charpa.

A Charpan would know more about the Forest people and Wanderers than Galeedans, Sandamedans, or Sarpaskans. Of course he could tell the difference. He hated her for leading the soldiers to his camp. He planned to reveal her so she would be executed too.

Then, in a voice so low she almost missed it, Elgust whispered, "Forest."

Tears sprang to Kiri's eyes. She would die when her people had only been partly avenged. The empire wouldn't know she'd killed Orrik and Kordrick, and therefore, would not be afraid to attack Forest villages again. She had failed her people.

"What did you say?" Thais growled.

Through Kiri's tears, Elgust's face became a blurry mask. At least it spared her from meeting his knowing gaze.

"A Charpan blessing," Elgust said. "I wished Kiri luck."

Kiri blinked, causing the tears to roll down her cheeks.

"Is there nothing else you want to say to her?" Thais asked. "She didn't answer your question."

"No," Elgust said, staring at Kiri. "No, that is all."

"Very well. Kiri, you may go."

Kiri walked backward, wiping her tears, certain Elgust would declare the truth at any moment.

His attention back on Elgust, Thais said something in Sandamedan.

Elgust rose slowly to his feet, his reply too low to hear.

Heart pounding, Kiri turned her back on the prisoners. She knew she walked only because the crowd grew closer. Someone called her name, waving at her. Ulek. She headed for him. It seemed to take a long time to travel the short distance.

When she reached him, Ulek grasped her arm without a trace of his recent anger. "What did he say?" He leaned in closer. "Are you crying?"

Kiri could only shake her head.

"Hear me!" cried a voice in the common language.

All eyes focused on Elgust, who stood tall, his face alight with triumph. His voice rang out, clear and powerful, over the gathering. "The tengish is three days behind you! You will never reach Ishtia in time! You are all going to die!"

Alarmed cries burst from the crowd.

Thais yelled something at the four executioners, who sprang forward.

As the soldiers raised their swords, Kiri threw her arms around Ulek, pressing his face into her shoulder.

"Let me go!" Ulek cried, struggling to free himself.

"Don't look." Kiri clung to him with all her might. If he watched the prisoners die, he would remember it for the rest of his life. He would see the blood and torn flesh and understand no difference existed between a person and a deer butchered for food. Many knew this, but only those who saw people die by sword and arrow truly understood it. It would change this friendly, kindhearted boy into something else.

Though he squirmed and twisted about, Ulek didn't strike her, and Kiri managed to hold on to him.

The sound of metal hacking into flesh sent a jolt of horror through Kiri's veins. She glanced over her shoulder to make sure it was over. Four headless bodies lay in the grass, spewing blood. The executioners held the heads aloft to the sound of cheers from soldiers and Galeedans alike. She maintained her hold on Ulek—she didn't want him to see any of this.

No one paid any mind to the boy and Wanderer girl struggling in the crowd. Then Kiri noticed one crested helmet turn toward her and met the questioning eyes of the man wearing it. As everyone around them cried out in fear or cheered in bloodlust, Mattos and Kiri stared at each other across the distance.

Chapter 33

MATTOS

The full moon cast its light on the Sandamedan women as they gathered the few belongings they could take with them, their movements hurried and their voices hushed. Children who fussed or asked questions were quickly silenced. The horses snorted and stomped, sensing something amiss. Already mounted on her brown mare, Hawk Thais's wife rode among the officers' families, offering comfort through her calm presence.

Not far off, most Galeedans slept, exhausted from the day's journey. Some, however, stood about, watching the proceedings with bitter eyes. The time had come to send the civilians with horses ahead of the column. Officers and their families had started the journey with horses. Because some of those horses had become lame along the way, all officers were giving up their mounts to ensure their families and the families of other officers reached Ishtia before the horde. The horses captured from the Charpans had also been given to soldiers' families.

"You behave yourself," Mattos said as he ran his hand over Nica's blaze. She nuzzled him in response. Then she rubbed her head so hard against his chest he couldn't tell if she scratched an itch or wanted affection. "Ah, be gone with you," Mattos said, pushing her away. He feared he might weep if he prolonged the goodbye.

"Thank you, Mattos," a Harrier said as he took Nica's reins. "My wife will take her to your family as soon as they reach Ishtia."

"I'm glad I can help," Mattos replied. "She's a good horse. She'll serve your family well." He watched as the Harrier led her to a woman holding the hands of two small children. It was a relief knowing Nica would be sent to his parents instead of becoming a Charpan's property.

"This will cause resentment among the men," Mattos warned as he came to stand beside Harrier Diakiris.

"Common soldiers are always resentful," Diakiris replied. "It's what they do about it that concerns us."

Looking over his shoulder, Mattos said, "Some Galeedans are watching."

"So let them. There is no wrongdoing here. So far, we've made those with horses keep pace with the column. Now we're letting them go on without us. With the horde so close, who are we to stop them?"

"Those with horses are officers' wives and children," Mattos said. "The Galeedans will say the officers cared only about protecting their own families—"

"Most had horses all along, even before we left the garrison. Now that we're close to the governor's country estate and the main road, they want to go on to Ishtia without us. Should the officers force their families to stay and face the horde because it would make the Galeedans and the common soldiers feel better?"

"If there is no wrongdoing, then why are they leaving like thieves in the middle of the night?"

Diakiris gave Mattos a wry smile. "What purpose would it serve to force the column to witness an escape they can't have? There is no fault in letting our families go ahead of us, but, as you said, this will cause resentment."

Osprey Beldos walked past them. Spotting Mattos, he halted, his somber expression transforming into one of anger. Since being presented with his nephew's body, he'd treated Mattos as if he were to blame for Darius's death. "What are you doing here, Falcon? You have no wife or children. Are you here to gloat over people's misery?"

"I see no reason for Falcon Mattos not to be here, Osprey," Diakiris said dryly.

"And I see no reason for him *to* be here," Beldos snapped. "These men are saying goodbye to their wives and children, possibly for the last time. His wife is dead. As an officer without anyone to say goodbye to, he should be with his men."

"Is that an order?" Diakiris asked, shooting Mattos a warning glance.

Beldos glared at Mattos with narrowed eyes, then snorted in disgust. "Let him stay if he wants to witness what he doesn't have," he said before continuing on his way.

"Stay away from that man," Diakiris warned. Then he strode off to where his plump wife, Ria, and their three children waited for him atop their horses.

Nearby, Elmaturis's wife, Alanna, stood with her family. There were many of them present, having accompanied her to the garrison for her wedding. She was barely a bride, and soon would be a widow.

As he watched the farewells taking place around him, Mattos recalled the time he and Layna had secretly met to watch the sun rise over the ocean. Except for the distant fishermen readying their boats, they'd had the beach to themselves. They sat together in the cool sand as the sky gradually turned pink, obscuring the dimming stars. Then the sun appeared over the horizon, casting a golden path on the water. Fishermen claimed Veara, beautiful water women who floated on sea-foam and rode dolphins, danced upon that path every morning.

Layna stood, her normally pinned-up black hair whipping about her face in the breeze. "I want to swim." She began to pull her gown over her head.

"Someone will see," Mattos cried as he leaped to his feet. He stood close to her, trying to shield her from imagined eyes.

"They're too far away." Layna laughed, indicating the fishermen.

"Too far away to notice a naked woman? I don't think so."

"They won't notice if you don't make me stand here." Free of her gown, Layna dashed into the water, letting it reach her breasts before diving into a wave.

Slightly irritated, Mattos shed his own clothes and went in after her, intent on bringing her back. He was a strong swimmer, but Layna, a fisherman's daughter, had been swimming since she'd been walking. She stroked past the waves into calmer water with graceful ease.

When Mattos reached her, Layna floated on her back, laughing. His irritation dissipated. He couldn't resist her during her carefree, playful moods. They were what had drawn him to her in the first place. The sun caressed Layna's wet, naked body with orange rays. "Let's go to shallower water," Mattos urged.

As soon as Mattos felt sand under his feet, with the water up to his neck, he turned, waiting for Layna. Once she came within reach, he pulled her close, letting her feel his excitement. She kissed his nose before extricating herself and swimming away.

When they decided to come ashore, Mattos insisted Layna wait in the water while he dressed and then brought her gown to her. They held hands as they walked along the sand together.

Fishermen's children appeared on the beach, carrying rakes and buckets for clamming. Some of them, recognizing Layna, called to her. She waved back, tugging on Mattos's hand. "Want to help them?" she asked with a grin. She and the children showed him how to wade into the ocean and rake the sand under his feet to find the hard-shelled creatures. As a rich man's son, Mattos had never gone clamming and had only fished for pleasure, not out of necessity. He found it oddly soothing; as he concentrated only on the task at hand, he forgot about all other cares.

Too soon, Layna had kissed Mattos before saying, "My mother will wonder where I am, and you need to get back." She had turned and raced away, her still-damp hair flying behind her.

As he stood watching the officers' wives prepare to flee the horde, Mattos realized the happiest moments of his life had been spent with Layna that morning on the beach. He wished he'd known it at the time so he could have savored it instead of taking it for granted. Now he watched his companions kiss their wives and children goodbye, knowing they'd never see them again. He was twenty-three years old, and he would die in a matter of days.

It hadn't been long after the morning at the beach that Mattos had stood beside the spice stall in the bazaar, their usual meeting place, and told Layna he couldn't marry her. She had stood stone-faced, her black eyes wide, as he explained that his grandfather and father had worked too hard becoming rich for him to repay their efforts by marrying a fisherman's daughter. His family needed him to marry a well-born girl to secure good marriages for his sisters. He would inherit his father's ships and had money to attract a bride from a good family. But his two sisters, who wouldn't inherit as much, needed a well-connected relative to attract rich husbands. It all depended on him.

Tears filled Layna's eyes, but she didn't let them fall. Once she realized she couldn't change his mind, she turned wordlessly and disappeared into the crowd. Mattos called after her, but she'd been swallowed up by the people milling about.

Every time he walked in the streets or visited the bazaar, he looked for her. Then, two months after telling her they couldn't marry, Mattos saw Layna heading toward the fishermen's section of the bazaar, a basket of small bluefish balanced on her hip. This time when he called to her, she waited, ready to face him.

His heart pounded as he approached. When he finally stood before her, he said, "It's good to see you." He spoke shyly, afraid she might disappear again.

Her eyes cold, Layna nodded. Even with strands of loose hair falling in her face and beads of sweat gathered on her upper lip, she looked as lovely as ever. Her sleeveless green dress couldn't hide her curves. Her face was flushed and her eyes bright from the exercise of carrying the heavy basket.

"My father bought me a posting in the army. I'll be leaving for Galeed soon."

Layna shrugged, as if it made no difference to her.

"Have you been well?" Mattos asked.

"I am to wed Ortid, the blacksmith."

It took a few moments to understand that she would soon belong to another man. "B-But … " he stammered, "only two months ago we …"

"Some men are not willing to offer marriage, and some are. Ortid is a good man, a better man than some I've known," she said, her eyes filled with meaning.

"How many men *have* you known?" Mattos spat. "Does the blacksmith know you aren't a maiden, that you'll sneak out of your family's home to lie with a man?"

Layna set the basket at her feet and stepped closer to Mattos, her fists clenched at her sides. The scent of fish clung to her, filling his nostrils. "You think Ortid is a fool for still wanting me after I've been with you? You either never loved me, or you were too much of a coward to fight for me. Ortid knows all about you, and he thinks *you* are the fool." With that, she lifted her basket, turned, and continued to the fish market, her back straight despite the heavy load.

When Mattos returned home from the garrison to marry, he would see Layna one last time. The day before he and his new wife left for southern Galeed, Mattos took Marenda and his sisters to the beach.

Delighted with their brother's soft-spoken bride, the girls invited Marenda to join them in collecting seashells. The three of them waded in the ocean up to their thighs, their soaked dresses clinging to their legs as they deposited worthy shells in a pile on dry sand.

Having no desire to join in the game, Mattos wandered along the water line, occasionally jumping aside to avoid a wave that came in farther than expected. The air smelled of salt, wet sand, and cooked food from the nearby fishing village. Gulls flew overhead, their high-pitched cries never ceasing. Some walked about with impunity, paying almost no mind to the humans who came near them.

The fair weather drew a crowd to the beach that day. Fishwives went about their business chattering and washing clothes.

The docks stood at the far end of the beach where the land jutted out in a small peninsula. Here, merchants, sailors, and dock men bustled about, intent on their work.

The man caught Mattos's attention first. He stood at least a head above everyone else with the kind of muscles that could only be earned with daily hard work. His short beard accentuated high cheekbones. Then Mattos saw the woman standing at the man's side. Her lavender gown draped flatteringly over her curves, and strands of her wavy black hair had come loose from the bun atop her head. As she turned, Mattos caught a glimpse of her flawless profile. Layna. His mouth went dry.

The man slipped his arm around Layna's waist, pulled her close, and kissed the top of her head. Then she lifted her face so her husband could kiss her lips. He did so with a tenderness that belied his obvious strength.

Mattos's stomach twisted in knots. She looked so happy.

As if she could feel his eyes on her, Layna turned and looked directly at Mattos. Neither friendliness nor anger showed in her eyes, only the indifference one might have for a stranger. She had whispered in her husband's ear, who, after a glance at Mattos, had led her farther down the beach.

The appearance of Lucen and his wife, Cylin, jolted Mattos from his memories. Lucen held Edar's reins with one hand and gripped his wife's arm with the other. Cylin sobbed quietly as her husband led her toward the Sandamedan women. Several adult Galeedans who must have been Cylin's relatives followed close behind.

Lucen urgently spoke Galeedan to his wife, who only shook her head in response.

Though Mattos rarely spoke the rough Galeedan tongue, he understood it well.

"I won't go," Cylin said. "Everyone I care about is here."

"You have to," Lucen insisted. "You heard what that Charpan said. You have to leave."

Cylin jerked her arm from her husband's grasp, her red braid swinging as she did so. "No!" she cried, running into the arms of the woman who must have been her mother.

Lucen caught sight of his friend. "Mattos, help me," he called out, desperation in his voice.

Mattos hurried to Lucen's side.

Cylin's mother had already led her to Edar while the rest of the family followed. "Listen to your husband," the woman urged. "His kin will take you in."

"They hate me for being Galeedan!" Cylin burst out. "They think we're barbarians because we don't build cities or have a written language. Lucen won't say it, but I know."

From the corner of his eye, Mattos saw Alanna, now mounted on her white stallion, staring in their direction.

"Just help me get her on the horse," Lucen said to Mattos, his face haggard.

"It won't do any good," Mattos replied. "What's to stop her from turning Edar around and riding back here? You need to convince her to leave."

"Then help me convince her!" Lucen snapped.

Cylin's mother stepped beside Lucen, her arm still around her daughter. "Take her."

As Lucen grabbed his wife's elbow, she tightened her arms around her mother. "No!"

"My daughter," the older woman murmured, placing a hand on either side of Cylin's face, "you have a chance to go ahead with the Sandamedan women. The rest of us will follow you."

Fresh tears spilled down Cylin's face. "We should all travel together."

Grabbing his wife by the waist, Lucen lifted her onto the horse. He withdrew a slip of parchment from under his vambrace and handed it to her. "When you reach Ishtia, give this to my parents."

Everyone fell silent, knowing the letter contained a son's request that his parents take care of his widow.

Cylin twisted in the saddle and would have slid off the horse if Lucen hadn't held her on. "I want to stay with my family," she pleaded.

The anger and bitterness that had been building in Mattos's gut spread to his chest. Thousands of people desperate to live were going to die. Cylin, however, didn't want her chance at life. Had he married Layna, she wouldn't have been so foolish. She would have understood. She would have kissed him goodbye and gone with the other officers' wives. "Let her stay," he said, his voice harsh.

"What?" Lucen asked, dumbfounded. Even Cylin looked startled.

"Let her stay. Why should she be forced to run? Why leave her loved ones to accompany a group of women who have never accepted her, travel to a city she's never seen, all to throw herself at the mercy of people who were outraged their son married her?"

"Mattos," Lucen said, a warning in his eyes and voice.

Mattos looked straight at his friend's wife, who returned his stare with wide eyes. "She has a right to stay. If she wants to die, let her. She might not even be killed. She's young and pretty. If she survives the initial slaughter, I'm sure the Charpans will want to keep her alive. If she's lucky, one of them will claim her as the spoils of war and refuse to share her with other men. Life as a Charpan slave might not be so bad."

Cylin had gone still, her expression frozen into one of shock. Her gaze had turned inward, as if she saw the events Mattos described.

Lucen and Cylin's family gaped at him.

"The choice," he continued, "should be hers."

Lucen stepped toward Mattos as if to strike him.

"I will go."

Everyone turned to Cylin, who said more firmly, "I will go."

In the silence that followed, Alanna rode up to the group. Reaching across the short distance between them, she placed her hand on Cylin's shoulder. She fixed her dark eyes on Lucen, but she spoke the common language. "I will look after her, I swear it."

Cylin peered at the woman beside her. Alanna was a newcomer to the garrison, having arrived only to be told she had to leave a few days later. She hadn't had a chance to truly get to know her husband, let alone find a place among the officers' wives.

With tears sliding down her face, Cylin submitted to her family's goodbyes. She didn't resist when Alanna grabbed Edar's reins and led her to the Sandamedans.

"She'll be fine," Mattos murmured.

"I hope her next husband deserves her," Lucen replied.

Chapter 34

KIRI

After Elgust's chilling announcement the previous day, the column had continued on. Those unable to keep up with the increased pace had been left to fall behind.

Due to Ulek's weakened state, he and Kiri found themselves among the stragglers. Kiri kept Ulek's arm draped over her shoulders so he could lean on her. As they came within view of the encampment, Kiri noticed a mighty dwelling on the hilltop. It stretched as long as twenty horses standing in a line, the highest point as tall as four men. The sloping roof had been fashioned with overlapping red stones, each smooth and flat. The walls, bright in the sun's dying rays, appeared to have been crafted entirely with white clay. Kiri gaped in wonder. Nothing that size could be made from clay, yet there it stood. "Cybelon," she murmured.

"Cybelon?" Ulek replied, his breathing slightly labored. "No, Cybelon is a town on the border of Galeed and Sandameda. This is just the governor's country estate. He has a home near the garrison, but he spends most of his time here, closer to Ishtia. He and his household already left for Ishtia. They're probably there by now." With their destination in sight, Ulek walked faster.

At last, Kiri and Ulek wandered into camp. Most Galeedans had wrapped themselves in blankets and collapsed on the ground without bothering to pitch tents. Families huddled together, their haggard faces revealing fear and exhaustion. Babies wailed in indignation, their mothers having given up cleaning them every time they soiled themselves. The few sheep and goats that had made it this far had to be prodded onward with sticks and leather belts before they were allowed to rest beside their owners. Only the most beloved dogs were still cared for by their families. The rest wandered about, staring at people with mournful eyes or fighting each other for scraps.

After Ulek sank to the ground with a grateful sigh, Kiri went to procure their rations.

As Kiri waited in line, she saw Mekindu walk past, assisting a young woman. Kiri recognized her as the only person besides Ulek to survive the Charpans' poison. Kiri would have greeted Mekindu if she hadn't noticed how he and the woman leaned toward each other. They wouldn't want to be bothered.

The woman's square face bore large blue eyes and a prominent nose. Her yellow hair had been matted with vomit the last time Kiri had seen her. Now it fell over her shoulders in two clean braids. Mekindu gazed at her with the respectful shyness of a man looking for more than a night mate. Even surrounded by frightened people and hunted by the horde, the pair exchanged irrepressible smiles.

In Kiri's village—or any Forest village—people often said both the urge to love and the urge to mate were stronger than the fear of death. Perhaps non-Forest people were the same, even if they pretended otherwise.

In the Forest, mating was simple. At night, people gathered around the central fire to share food and listen to the village's best singers and storytellers. If drummers could be compelled to play, there would be dancing as well. Children fell asleep in the arms of chatting relatives. The old dozed where they sat, everyone pretending not to notice. During these gatherings, people often wandered off together, with no one paying any mind. Life mates were more obvious. Instead of wandering into the forest, they would head toward their sleeping place, their arms wrapped around each other.

Kiri had had two night mates in her life—a modest number for a woman of twenty. The first had been a great hunter six years older than she. A strong, handsome man, Lido had enjoyed the attention of many women and had ignored Kiri's obvious interest in him. He'd treated her like a child, offering only polite smiles at her attempts to gain his notice. One night in her sixteenth year, while she knelt by the fire braiding hair with her friends, Kiri decided she'd had enough of his dismissals. Rising to her feet, she headed to where Lido sat tearing into a hunk of venison. Instead of walking past him into the forest, she stopped before him, willing him to look up at her. He must have seen the determination and desire burning inside her, for when Kiri continued into the forest, he followed. The next day, he went back to treating her with courteous disinterest.

The second night mate had been Wren. Kiri wasn't foolish enough to think she'd loved him as a mate. They'd only spent a few days together as mates, but they'd been friends since childhood. That was its own type of love. Since his death, Kiri hadn't wanted any man. Yet, as she watched how Mekindu smiled at the woman, she felt hollow. Not only would she never know the joy of having a life mate, but she would never again take a night mate. She hadn't considered that when she'd left the forest, knowing she almost certainly traveled to her death. Now the thought of never holding another man left her cold. Even after all that had happened in Mar Dun, losing Wren, and killing Orrik and Kordrick, blood still flowed through her veins.

Kiri tore her gaze away from Mekindu and his companion just as the young soldier giving out rations slopped gruel into her bowl, which was more than most received. Kiri shot a questioning glance at the soldier, who returned her look with a warm smile.

"Good day, little Kiri."

"You know me?"

His smile transformed into a grin, revealing crooked teeth. "*Everyone* knows who you are."

Kiri made her way back to Ulek with a bowed head. She didn't want the soldiers to notice her or know her name. Her plan had been to blend into the crowd, not have every soldier and Galeedan learn her name. Her decision to track the Charpans and Elgust's very public desire to speak with her before his execution had brought her to this.

Ulek accepted his bowl gratefully, digging with gusto into the food Kiri found tasteless. Between bites, he said, "The horses are gone."

At first, Kiri didn't understand. She had just walked past the horses used to carry food. However, at second glance, she saw that the rest of the horses were indeed missing.

"The horde will catch us," Ulek continued, his tone bitter. "That's why the officers sent their families on to Ishtia. We won't make it, but if they ride fast, they will. The Charpans will also have to stop to fight the soldiers and kill us all. That will give the officers' families some time."

A quick survey of the camp confirmed Ulek's words. The Sandamedan women, who usually stood out with their bare arms and dark hair piled high on their heads, were nowhere to be seen—including their children.

Kiri didn't answer, for she couldn't deny the truth of his words.

Stars twinkled overhead—the same stars that shone over the Forest lands. Kiri gazed at the endless sky—the one thing she preferred about Galeed. Back home, one had to climb to the top of the tallest tree or find a meadow to truly see the sky. Here it was ever present, magnificent in its size and shifting colors. The stars seemed closer here, as though the trees back home somehow pushed them farther away.

What should she do? There had been truth in Elgust's voice when he'd said the horde would be upon them in three days. Now they only had two days left. She could sneak away from the camp, steal food as she'd done before, and run ahead of the column. She could leave tonight, outrun the slaughter, and reach Ishtia on her own. The moon shone brightly, as if urging her to go, promising to light her way. Perhaps she would still be able to kill Isandor and fulfill the will of her people.

Beside her, Ulek slept wrapped in his father's coat, exhausted from walking all day on an injured leg. She couldn't take him with her; even when he returned to full strength, he wouldn't be able to keep up. She had promised not to leave him again, but she had also made a promise to her people. They depended on her to send a message to the empire. Kiri glanced at Ulek's sleeping form. Perhaps they could hide together in the mountains, wait for the bloodshed to be over, and then continue. But how long would it take the horde to return home? Perhaps they wouldn't be satisfied by killing everyone in the column. Maybe they'd ride for Ishtia and camp outside the great city walls she'd heard so much about. If this happened, Kiri and Ulek would be trapped in the mountains for months, maybe even years, before they could safely travel north.

Restless, Kiri got to her feet and crept between the sleeping forms, waking no one. In the forest, children learned to move soundlessly almost as soon as they learned to walk. The night kept silent and still, as if even the mountain winds had been cowed by the mounted warriors fast approaching.

Ulek had explained that only a Sandamedan could be governor of Galeed and that the house had been built in the Sandamedan style. Understanding the building might help her understand the Sandamedans. As she placed her hands against a wall, she caught her breath. Instead of clay, she felt rough stone. Had the Sandamedans carved the entire thing out of a giant boulder? She ran her hands along the wall in fascination. Whatever substance made up the house, the Sandamedans had created it. Kiri walked on.

As she rounded a corner, the sound of trickling water caught her ear. She followed it to a break in the wall where a low wooden gate stood ajar. The scent of flowers emanated from beyond the gate. It swung open as Kiri pushed, and she found herself in a large area full of flowers and shrubs, surrounded by high walls. In the center stood an intricate stone carving of what appeared to be a fish leaping from a shallow pool. The fish, unlike any Kiri had ever seen, had fins shaped like a bird's wings and a long, snakelike body. A continuous stream of water gushed from the fish's open mouth into the very pool from which it appeared to leap.

Kiri approached and held a hand under the water pouring from the fish's mouth, letting it flow over her skin. Where did the water come from, and what kept the pool from overflowing? Removing her hand from the water, she traced her fingers over the fish's scales, each of them perfectly detailed. Kiri had seen many carvings in her life, stone and wood, but she'd never seen anything like this. She had a sudden longing to be back in her village just so she could tell everyone about the stone fish with water flowing from its mouth.

In a state of wonder, Kiri explored the area. The flowers gave off the sweetest fragrance she'd ever smelled. The shrubs were oddly shaped, as if trimmed by human hands. As she stepped around a tall bush, Kiri found herself staring up at a soldier with a raised sword, his skin and armor glistening like snow in the moonlight.

Her scream caught in her throat. As breath returned to her lungs, she realized the soldier couldn't be real. No living human had such white skin. She reached out a hand and grasped the sword, feeling cold stone—a carving. Unlike the fish, he'd been made from a type of stone she'd never seen. Turning in a slow circle, she saw nine other white carvings standing against the walls, equidistant from each other.

Kiri walked along the walls, examining them. There were five men and five women. Each appeared to be in their prime: strong, healthy, and beautiful. Three of the women wore their hair piled atop their heads in the Sandamedan style. When Kiri stepped before one of the women with loose hair, she paused in surprise. The naked woman held a blanket just above her breasts, her back arched and her chest thrust forward. The way she stood with one leg bent caused the blanket to fall to the side, exposing the perfect curve of one hip and the outside of her thigh. Her head tilted to the left, an inviting smile on her face. Everything about her said, *Mate with me.* Kiri stepped away from her, feeling as if she had intruded on a private moment.

Forest people rarely depicted humans in their carvings or rock paintings, preferring animals. When they *did* carve or paint humans, they never gave them faces. Yet these ten Sandamedan carvings were so perfectly detailed they looked as if they could wake up and walk about at any moment.

Despite the great beauty that surrounded her, Kiri's spirit filled with a sense of foreboding. If the Sandamedans could create like this, then what powers of destruction would they also have?

Chapter 35

MATTOS

Even lying on a soft bed with the sweet aroma of flowers drifting through the open window, Mattos couldn't sleep. He couldn't remember the last time he'd been alone like this. As an officer with his own quarters, Mattos had had some privacy, but at night, he'd hear voices in adjoining rooms. He normally would have welcomed solitude, but now it left him at the mercy of his thoughts without the distracting presence of others.

Sitting up, Mattos swung his legs over the edge of the bed. He'd removed everything but his trousers when he'd readied for sleep. Now he pulled on his tunic and shoved his feet in his boots. He felt vulnerable without the familiar weight of his weapons and armor. He had worn them for so long they had become part of him.

Hawk Thais had commandeered the governor's abandoned house for the officers' use. The room Mattos had chosen appeared to belong to one of the governor's daughters. A mosaic of a purple and silver butterfly decorated the floor, and the walls had been painted lavender. It reminded him of his sisters' rooms back home. He opened the shutters of the large window to find the courtyard. Tossing one leg over the sill, Mattos stepped into the courtyard's garden.

If there had been a place to seek out company at this hour, he would have done it. Instead, he wandered through the garden, the statues of the Sandamedan gods his only companions. The brilliant full moon illuminated the glittering Sarpaskan marble they'd been carved from. Sculpted by Lentavus himself, they'd been brought to Galeed to awe those who visited the governor.

He paused before the statue of Imari standing in a provocative pose. Lentavus had captured the unmistakable invitation in her eyes. He wondered if the renowned artist had sculpted her from his imagination, or if he'd had a beautiful woman in his studio gazing at him with that expression, only a sheet to hide her nakedness. It would have been a grievous insult to the gods to interrupt the creation of a goddess's statue to embrace the very woman who posed in her place. Perhaps Lentavus had instead poured all his lust and longing into his work.

Mattos's mother and sisters had many sculptures of Imari on the altar dedicated to her. Artists depicted her as a maiden, a temptress, a woman with child, a matron, and a crone. At thirteen, Mattos had sneaked a sculpture of Imari as a temptress to his room and taken a hand to himself. He'd never been pious, but after joining the army, he'd sometimes wondered if Imari had ever told Odern, her husband, how he'd dishonored her. Looking at her smile, Mattos had the feeling she'd kept his secret. Men never prayed to the goddess of women. All the same, he tapped his forehead in gratitude.

After circling the garden, Mattos noticed a bench half-hidden by a tall bush. As he sat on it, he heard the courtyard's gate creak open. He straightened, thinking another restless officer had wandered into the courtyard. Then he noticed the small figure wore a short dress. Kiri. The house and the courtyard were off limits to everyone except officers. She should have been sleeping outside with the Galeedans, but the Wanderer girl openly disregarded rules.

Kiri always seemed self-contained and sure of herself. Now she appeared dumbfounded by her surroundings. With parted lips and eyes full of wonder, she stuck her hand in the water flowing from the stone fish's mouth. She acted as if she'd never seen a fountain before, but that couldn't be. Though the Wanderers' nomadic lifestyle prevented them from building anything of permanence, it allowed them the freedom to travel to distant lands and view the wonders made by other men. Having no allegiance to any country, most clans traveled along trade routes from city to city. If Kiri had never been to Ishtia, then she certainly would have been to Zurpesh and seen public fountains there. She walked around the courtyard, studying the statues of the gods.

Mattos rose. Walking toward her, he said, "Magnificent, aren't they?"

Kiri spun around, alarm etched on her face.

"It's all right," Mattos said, holding up his hands. "It's Falcon Mattos."

As he stepped into the light, Kiri visibly relaxed. "What do you want?" she asked.

"I should ask you that question. You aren't allowed to be here. The house is only for officers."

Without hesitation, Kiri replied, "I'll leave," and turned to go.

"Wait."

Kiri paused, looking over her shoulder.

"I grew up in a house like this," Mattos blurted out to keep her from leaving. She was all that stood between him and solitary reflection.

Kiri's eyes widened. "You lived in a house like *this*?"

"I live in a garrison. But my family's home is similar to this one."

"In Ishtia?"

"I'm no Ishtian," Mattos answered, smiling. "I grew up in Valdern. My sisters and I used to look for seashells on the beach. If we sat in the courtyard on quiet nights, we could hear the waves crashing ..." He paused, gazing into the distance. Though mountains surrounded them, part of him listened for the sound of waves crashing against the shore.

Mattos sat on a nearby bench with a heavy sigh. He leaned forward, resting his elbows on his knees. "The legions are dead, Kiri. They're all dead."

The Wanderer girl stared at him, uncomprehending. She seemed so foreign with her short dress, her accent, and her strange ways. Yet didn't her very foreignness make her the perfect person to talk to? She'd pass no judgments—at least none most Sandamedans would care about.

"The legions on the beaches of Charpa," Mattos went on. "There were two thousand men trapped there after our ships were destroyed. Any other force that small would have been killed months ago, but these men were imperial soldiers and they held off the Charpan Army for over a year. It's a testament to their courage that they lasted that long." He shook his head. "Eagle Isandor oversees the army, not the navy. He's been fighting the Forest people, trying to forge a land route to Charpa. If the emperor had given Isandor the reinforcements when he asked for them … if the legions on the beach had held on longer …"

Kiri's gaze had an intensity that hadn't been there before. She came to sit next to Mattos, her eyes never leaving his face.

"It won't be much longer," Mattos continued. "Before, the emperor focused on reaching Charpa by sea. He'll still send more ships, but now with what's happened, he's given Isandor the reinforcements he asked for. He'll burn all the trees in the Forest lands if he has to. He'll get to Charpa on foot, but it's too late for the men who were stranded there."

"How do you know this?" Kiri asked, her voice hoarse.

"The governor thought we might come this way. He hid a message in a place where he knew the Hawk would find it."

"When will this happen?"

"It's probably already happening. The Eagle is in the Forest lands now. I've heard the Forest people are hard to kill, but Isandor will find a way." He sighed. "We won't live to see it, though." Mattos wouldn't have dared say this to any of the Galeedans they escorted, but Kiri was unlike anyone he knew. Instead of crying or showing panic, she remained still, her expression stoic.

"Isandor is in the Forest lands?" she asked.

"Yes."

She laughed then, a harsh, bitter sound that jolted Mattos from his contemplative mood. "We won't reach Ishtia?" she finally said.

"No, we won't. We might, *might* reach Cybelon, but it isn't a defensible city. It isn't even a city. It's just a border town. Its walls are made of wood. We'll arrive in a day or so if we aren't overtaken first. The Hawk sent a messenger to the Eagle requesting help, but it won't do any good. The Eagle is too far away to reach us in time."

Getting to her feet, Kiri paced back and forth.

Mattos studied her in the moonlight. She had the eyes of a doe: large and black and framed by long lashes with a slight curl. Her full lips were well shaped, and her skin appeared soft and smooth. Her thick hair fell to her waist, as black and shiny as a raven's wing. Rich Sandamedan women would pay a hefty price for a wig made from such hair. She was small-boned and slender, but even her dress folds couldn't hide the sway of her hips.

Mattos hadn't been alone with a woman in over two years, and the effect of Kiri's presence caught him off guard. Of course, he had noticed her litheness; he was alive, after all. But her scar and loose clothing had kept him from looking closely at her. Now, with the intimacy of being alone with her under the stars, he fully appreciated her beauty.

"You sent Sandamedan women and children to Ishtia," Kiri said, still pacing.

"The officers' wives and children, yes. They have horses. If they ride hard, they'll make it."

"Do you have a wife and children with them?"

Shaking his head, Mattos stared at the tiles under his feet. "My wife died two years ago in childbirth. She and the baby. Unless my mother can bear another son, and she hasn't born a child in fifteen years, my father's line will die with me." When he looked up, he saw Kiri staring at him with something akin to pity. She looked away when their eyes met.

"You don't care about other soldiers' wives and children?"

"Of course we care. But the common soldiers and most Galeedans can't afford horses. If everyone had a horse, outrunning the horde wouldn't be a problem."

"Why do you not go?"

"What?"

"Officers have horses. Why are you still here?"

Mattos gaped at her. "By the gods, woman, what do you think I am? You think I would forsake my vows? Abandon *my men*? I am no coward."

Kiri shrugged, seemingly oblivious to his reaction. "If you go, you'll live. The Galeedans and other soldiers will die. If you and the other officers stay, you'll die, and the Galeedans and other soldiers will still die."

"We gave our horses to officers' families. To run would be worse than death."

"The soldier you killed didn't think so."

The woman's audacity rendered him speechless. None save Lucen had dared mention Ozias to his face, and Lucen knew better than to ever do it again. Even his superior officers had refrained from saying that name in his presence. Yet, instead of appearing confrontational, Kiri's demeanor seemed ingenuous. She had simply been stating a fact.

"Kiri," he said, trying to keep his voice level, "do not ever mention that man again. I killed him because he broke his vows and abandoned his brothers and those he'd sworn to protect. Odern demanded his death."

"Odern?"

"Odern, the god of war," Mattos said, gesturing toward Odern's statue.

The Wanderer girl walked past him to stand before the marble god holding his sword aloft, ready for battle. "You worship a god of war?"

"All soldiers of the empire do."

The disgust on Kiri's usually stoic face was unmistakable.

"It's not just death and battle," Mattos said, affronted by her expression. "Odern is the god of the warrior ethos, of honor, duty, sacrifice, and brotherhood. You wouldn't understand."

"I know what war is," Kiri said quietly, her eyes fixed on the statue.

"What would your people know of war? The Wanderers have never fought one."

Kiri remained silent so long, Mattos thought she wouldn't respond. Then she turned to him. "I think people who have the wisdom to choose travel and trade over death and conquest know something about war."

Mattos sighed. He resisted the temptation to point out that the Wanderers' distaste for war was due, in part, to their inability to win one. She'd know that already, and he didn't want to offend her. "You think Sandamedans are cruel for conquering other people?"

"Perhaps you should ask a Galeedan or Sarpaskan."

"In all your travels, did you not learn the story of these lands?" Mattos burst out in exasperation. "Neither the Galeedans nor the Sarpaskans are from these shores. The Galeedans sailed here in black ships with their axes and

Great Hounds. They raped and pillaged and drove the Sandamedans living here north. A few hundred years of farming has softened them, but when they arrived, they were fierce warriors who wore bear skins and painted themselves with the blood of their enemies."

"The Galeedans stole lands from the Forest people," Kiri murmured.

"My people grew stronger while they grew complacent," Mattos continued. "We took our lands back, but we didn't kill them or drive them out. We made them citizens. We let them keep their ways and their religion and serve in the army. We don't rape their women, we marry them. Sandamedan and Sarpaskan soldiers are sacrificing their *lives* to protect Galeedan villagers. Is that cruelty?"

"And the Sarpaskans?" Kiri asked.

"Sailed here from Teletmoora. They didn't rape or pillage as far as I know, but they forced the Yayida inward from the coast. We took nothing from them that they didn't take from the Yayida."

"What about Charpa?" Kiri said. "They stole nothing from you. They didn't start this war. What right does the empire have to attack them? And if you win, who will be next? How many more people have to die before the empire is satisfied?"

How many times had he asked himself those questions? Mattos exhaled. "Only the emperor knows."

"That can't be true," Kiri said. "If your people decided to stop fighting, the emperor would have to end the war. If he didn't, your people would refuse to follow him and choose a new emperor."

"It's not that simple."

"I think it is." Kiri headed for the gate.

"Where are you going?" Mattos called after her.

Kiri paused at the gate just long enough to call back, "To Ulek. I'm going back to Ulek."

Chapter 36

ULEK

Ulek shifted in the grass, trying to get away from whatever tickled his nose. The previous day's journey had exhausted him. He didn't want to wake up and start the process over again. Villagers nearby stirred and ate their morning meals. Once again, something soft tickled his nose. When he reached up to brush it from his face, his hand landed on something solid and furry. Suddenly alert, Ulek propped up onto his elbow and came face-to-face with a gray dog lying at his side.

As soon as the dog saw Ulek's open eyes, it stood on its long legs. It looked almost as big as Ulek, with a long snout and bushy tail. A white patch splashed across its chest and another encircled its right eye. One ear stood erect while the tip of the other flopped down. Most intriguing were the dog's mismatched eyes, one brown and one blue. It was the same dog Kiri had chased off the day of the Charpan prisoners' executions.

Unsure what the animal would do, Ulek held still as they stared at each other. Then, after expelling his breath, he murmured, "Hello."

The dog licked his face with its oversize tongue, its tail wagging wildly.

"Stop," Ulek half commanded, half laughed as he pushed it away. He sat up, wiping the slobber off his face.

The dog remained, its eyes fixed on him, its tail still wagging. Its ungainly long legs and disproportionally large paws suggested it still had growing to do.

For the first time since his father's murder, excitement coursed through him. Ulek had always wanted a dog, and now, after so much grief and fear, one had found him. Many dogs followed the column. This one must have been abandoned like so many others when food had become scarce and terror had enveloped everyone.

"You're mine, aren't you?" Ulek murmured, reaching out and stroking the soft fur. A quick look told him the dog was male. "I'll call you Brense. It's a good name for a dog."

A sharp cry interrupted the moment, causing Brense to jump backward.

Kiri stood with her eyes fixed on Brense, her clothes still rumpled from the night's sleep. Around them, most Galeedans still slept wrapped in their blankets. Kiri seized her pack and swung it back and forth as she approached the dog. "Go! Go!"

Brense danced backward, his ears flat against his head.

"Kiri, no!" Struggling to his feet, Ulek grabbed her arm. "Stop, you'll hurt him."

"The dog must go," Kiri said, her expression hard.

"No!" Ulek yelled. "He's my dog. I'm going to keep him."

Kiri gaped at Ulek. "No dog!"

"I'm keeping him," Ulek insisted. He crouched, holding out his hand. "Don't be afraid, boy. Come back."

Brense crept forward, his body low to the ground, his eyes on Kiri.

"No dog," Kiri repeated.

Something inside Ulek snapped. He rose to face Kiri. There had been times he'd argued with her or shown frustration the way one might show frustration toward an elder sister, but he'd never allowed himself true anger. Now he didn't hold back. "He's my dog. Mine! First, I lost my mother, and then my father was murdered in his bed. I have no kin left, and now I'm running away from my home because a horde of Charpans wants to kill me. This dog could have lain down next to anyone, but he chose *me*, and I'm keeping him. You can't stop me!" He knelt in the grass and held his arms out to Brense, who continued to creep forward.

When Ulek glanced over his shoulder, he saw Kiri standing with her back to him, her arms limp at her sides.

Encouraged by his attacker's turned back, Brense came forward to lick Ulek's hands, his tail wagging again.

"I think he's part Great Hound," Ulek said as he scratched behind his new friend's ears.

Kiri didn't respond.

"My people brought them with us when we came to these shores," Ulek continued. "We used them in battle. They had their own armor and were given warriors' burials. When the Sandamedans conquered us, they took our best Great Hounds and killed the rest, even the puppies. They're forbidden to us."

Ulek paused. Kiri still stood with her back turned, but he knew she listened.

"A Sandamedan soldier might kill him if they suspect he's part Great Hound. Especially if he has no one to protect him. Who'd make a fuss over a stray dog?"

"What did they do with the dogs they took?" Kiri asked without turning around.

Still petting Brense, Ulek looked over his shoulder at Kiri. "Nobody knows. We aren't even supposed to ask about them. The Sandamedans won't talk about it. It makes no difference for Brense, though. The Sandamedan soldiers might kill him if we don't keep him close to us."

Slowly, Kiri turned around. Instead of the anger Ulek had expected, she looked sad, with downcast eyes and slumped shoulders. "I'll get our food," she said.

Ulek sighed in relief. He had won.

Chapter 37

KIRI

"Cybelon!" Ulek gasped. "We made it to Cybelon."

As the high walls came into view, relief swept over Kiri. The non-Forest people had cut down tall trees, transported them to this place, and stood them up around the village. However they'd done it, it had obviously been a huge undertaking. The walls rose as high as four men, and the tops had been sharpened so each tree looked like a giant spear. Mattos had said the town was indefensible, but surely this place could offer some protection.

Surrounding the walls were fields where non-Forest people grew plants from turned dirt. Kiri had seen growing fields before, but never of such size. These stretched far into the distance in neat brown rows, and long yellow grass rippled like water in the breeze. The entire village must have toiled all day in those fields. Now the fields stood abandoned except for the strange wood and straw figures that had been erected amid the plants. Some had what looked like human eyes and mouths painted on what must have been their heads. They were nothing like the beautiful carvings Kiri had seen the night before. She shuddered, wondering if the people of Cybelon worshiped such creatures.

Trotting beside them, Brense whined, as if he shared Kiri's thoughts. The negative attention the dog might attract, as well as the danger he posed as a large predator, concerned her. But there was no dissuading Ulek from keeping him. Luckily, the soldiers didn't seem to notice him, and he'd shown no aggression.

"That's right, boy," Ulek said. "We made it."

Kiri wondered what they had made it to. She'd been in danger from the moment she'd left the forest, but she hadn't felt helpless until now. She'd *chosen* to leave her home in order to kill three men. She'd chosen to join the column and then she'd chosen to track the Charpans and lead the soldiers to them. She'd even chosen to be Ulek's companion. She'd had control over her fate throughout her journey.

Once she entered Cybelon's gate, however, she'd lose all control. Her fate would depend on the horde, the imperial soldiers, and the high walls of Cybelon.

The sting of regret and failure assailed her. Kiri had promised to kill Isandor. Yet as she fled to Cybelon, Isandor fought in the Forest lands and the Charpan horde rode between them. Confident of her abilities as she was, Kiri doubted she could slip past the entire horde if she tried to go home. She'd lost her chance to kill Isandor. She could only hope one of her people would succeed where she had failed. It wouldn't be easy; Mattos had spoken as if Isandor was a great warrior.

Kiri squared her shoulders as Cybelon's walls drew nearer. If she could not keep her promise to kill Isandor, she could at least keep her promise to stay with Ulek. When she'd left her village, she'd known there was little chance of return. It made no difference whether she died in Cybelon or Ishtia.

As Kiri, Ulek, and Brense passed through the wooden gates, Kiri looked around in amazement. In the Forest lands, most villages contained one hundred to 150 people. Cybelon must have contained hundreds of people. As Kiri wondered how the villagers had managed to remember every name and face, it occurred to her they might not all know each other. Straw-roofed homes stood next to each other along wide dirt roads. Some of the houses appeared to be made of the same substance as the governor's estate, while others had been built with stones piled on top of each other.

Nearby, the yellow-haired woman Kiri had begun to think of as Mekindu's life mate fell to her knees and kissed the ground. The people of the column milled about in the center of the village. Some appeared relieved while others gazed about fearfully, as if the horde already surrounded them. Everyone looked exhausted.

No one emerged from the houses to welcome the newcomers. Cybelon was abandoned.

After finding a stone house that offered some shade, Kiri and Ulek sat next to it and leaned against the wall. Brense curled up beside them, panting quietly. Ulek rested his head on Kiri's shoulder.

Imperial soldiers hurried about, rounding up Galeedan men and leading them through the gates they had just entered. Kiri spotted Mattos exiting a house across a dirt road with some of his soldiers. He surprised her when, after catching sight of them, he hurried over. He had never sought her out before. Mattos crouched before them, saying, "So you finally made it. I was looking for the both of you. How is that leg?"

"It's much better," Ulek replied. "But it still hurts when I walk for too long."

"You're young and strong. You just need some time off your feet," Mattos said.

It hadn't been until the previous night, when she'd seen him without his armor and crested helmet, that Kiri had realized how young Mattos was—probably only a few years older than she. Without the presence of the other soldiers, there had been vulnerability in his eyes. After learning he'd lost his wife and child, she felt she understood him better. Among the non-Forest people, men raised the children they sired, not the children their sisters bore. Not only had this man lost his life mate, which was devastating enough, but he had lost a child he would have loved and provided for. He hadn't mentioned a new wife or other children, and probably didn't have them. No wonder he usually acted so stern. Tragedy and grief marked his life.

Reaching under the armor he wore on his chest, Mattos pulled out a piece of bread. "I found this in one of the houses." After picking off a few green spots, he divided it in two and gave one piece to Kiri and the other to Ulek.

Kiri ate the bread, moved by the unexpected kindness.

Ulek took a bite out of his piece before tossing the rest to Brense, who caught it in midair.

Kiri scowled. In the Forest, tossing away a gift of food or giving it to an animal would have been a grave slight.

Mattos didn't seem to mind. "That dog looks part Great Hound."

"He isn't," Ulek said, his voice sharp. "Look at his spots, and his blue eye. He's just big."

"Ah, of course," Mattos said, giving Kiri a sly smile. "I have to go," he said as he rose. "You should find a house to stay in, one in the center of town." He gestured to the stone house he'd just exited. "Go there. It's already been searched. No one will bother you."

"When will—" Ulek cleared his throat. "When will …"

"Tonight," Mattos answered without looking at them. "The horde should reach us some time tonight." He turned, then stopped. Looking over his shoulder, he said, "Kiri, walk with me."

Kiri stood and joined Mattos.

After they had gone a few paces, Mattos said, "You won't run ahead to Ishtia?"

"Ulek would not be able to keep up."

"You can't save him," Mattos said.

"I can't *leave* him," Kiri replied.

Mattos studied her. "You would give up the chance to save yourself for a Galeedan boy you haven't known long? Why?"

Kiri looked away. "I am … responsible … for him."

"I understand responsibility," Mattos said. "I've made vows to Odern and my empire. I have a duty to my country, my commanders, my men, and my family. But what duty does a cast-out Wanderer have to an orphaned Galeedan boy?"

I killed his father.

This time, Kiri met his gaze. "The duty of doing what is right."

Mattos studied her a long time, his eyes solemn. "Kiri, you don't know what it'll be like when the town falls, and it *will* fall. If the Charpans spare your lives, they'll take you as slaves. And there will be nothing you can do to protect that boy. You're right. He wouldn't make it to Ishtia, not with that leg, but *you* might."

"I know what it will be like," Kiri said, almost in a whisper. "I know, and I won't leave him."

Mattos sighed. "May we all match your courage when the tengish comes."

"You have courage. I've seen it."

They stood gazing at each other as people bustled around them. Mattos looked like he wanted to say more. He cleared his throat but said nothing.

Kiri suspected the reason he lingered. War, and its accompanying horrors, would descend on them soon. Mattos probably wanted some gentleness, some human kindness before it came.

Finally, he nodded at her before rejoining his soldiers.

Chapter 38

MATTOS

Trying not to breathe in the stench, Mattos helped drape an untanned animal skin over the town wall. The vinegar they'd found while searching the houses had to be saved for injuries, so instead of dousing the skins with vinegar, they'd urinated on them. The animal skins, which had come from the tannery a short ride from the town, were their best defense against flaming arrows. Mattos sent a silent prayer of thanks to Livius, the god of industry, that Cybelon had originally built up around a tannery and not another trade.

Cybelon had been teeming with people going about their daily chores the last time Mattos had been there. Most had worked in the fields while bakers, blacksmiths, butchers, and apothecaries plied their trades inside the walls. Women gathering at the two wells had spoken with friends as they collected water. The competing scents of bread and herbs had mingled in the air as the sound of a hammer striking metal rang throughout the town.

Now the town seemed lifeless, even with thousands of Galeedans gathered inside. There were no friendly greetings, no laughter, no smell of baking bread wafting down the dirt roads. Only terror and impending death.

Mattos leaned over the wall to see how the Galeedan men who had been pressed into digging a ditch around the walls had fared. His fingers tightened on the sharpened wood when he saw what little progress they'd made. When he'd first passed through the gates, he and his men had been commanded to search the houses for shovels, wine, vinegar, sulfur, resin, honey, blankets, cloth for bandages, and anything that could be used as a weapon. The Cybelonians hadn't left many tools behind, and several of the ditch diggers were forced to use their bare hands. Of those who didn't have to dig with their hands, most had been supplied with the short shovels all common soldiers carried with them. Some of the men worked farther out, digging small holes meant to break the Charpan horses' legs.

Cybelon didn't have the defenses of a garrison. Its walls had been built to keep out bandits, not a mounted army. Even the platform Mattos stood on wasn't sturdy or wide enough to support fighting men. If the Charpans tried to scale the walls, they'd probably fall to the ground once they did. Of course, they wouldn't try to scale the walls. They'd do their best to set the town ablaze or bash the gates in.

The sun began its descent. The horde would be upon them soon. Cold fear coursed through his veins, and Mattos tried to comfort himself with the thought that he faced certain death. If he could accept that, there would be no need for fear, only the desire to die well.

Hope was dangerous. He tried to crush it by reminding himself that although the Hawk's aides had been sent to

Ishtia to request help, they would receive none. Ishtia would never send the city guard to assist them. There weren't enough soldiers to make a difference for Cybelon, and those men would be needed when the horde attacked Ishtia. If Mattos commanded the city guard, he would make the same decision. Isandor and the western army were already deep in the Forest lands. Even if Isandor turned them around immediately, they would never reach Cybelon in time.

"Dust," a soldier beside him muttered.

Mattos glanced at him, unsure he had heard him correctly.

"Dust," the man repeated, pointing this time.

Following his gaze, Mattos saw the faint cloud of dust in the distance. Never had he seen dust over the fertile soil and lush grass of Galeed. It rose above the horizon like the shadow of death.

Chapter 39

KIRI

Water sloshed out of the bucket, spilling onto Kiri's boots. Her arms and shoulders ached as she emptied the bucket's contents onto the straw roof beneath her.

"I think that's enough," Ulek called down to the Galeedan man who had taken charge of making sure they properly drenched the roof. Soon after Kiri and Ulek had claimed the house Mattos had suggested to them, a Galeedan family had entered and taken over the lower floor. It turned out to be the family of the boy, Derk, who'd thrown a rock at Kiri when she'd first joined the column. He and Ulek had glared at each other when the family had first entered the house. Ulek told her later he and the boy had gotten into a fight, and Mattos had beaten Derk with his sword for starting it.

The yellow-bearded father had soon begun to order everyone about as they prepared the house for the attack. The mother, who carried her baby in a sling, and her daughter had taken multiple trips to the well to fetch water. As the two smallest capable of the job, Kiri and Ulek had been chosen to stand on the roof and dump water onto the straw. The father and Derk had tugged ropes slung over a beam to get buckets to them. Brense paced before the house, occasionally barking at Kiri and Ulek.

The father hurried inside. A moment later, he climbed through the upper window and pulled himself onto the roof. "You're right, Ulek," he said, hands on his hips as he admired their work.

The father and Kiri climbed from the roof to the window and into the upper floor.

As Ulek struggled to follow them, Kiri reached out to help him. "I can do it myself," he said. Still, when he let go of the roof, he allowed her to grab his hand and pull him inside.

Kiri and Ulek followed the man outside to where the mother and children waited. Derk, three or four years older than Ulek, undid the rope knots that had been tied around the buckets' handles. The girl, who looked about seven, stood near her mother and fussed over the baby.

Kiri hadn't come close to the babies she'd seen during the journey. Now curiosity overtook her. She approached the mother, who eyed her with suspicion.

The baby stared at Kiri with a solemn expression in its blue eyes. A pale tuft of fine hair stuck up from the middle of its head. The intelligent way the baby regarded her appealed to Kiri. Smiling, she reached for it.

Grasping her finger with one of its pink-hued fists, the baby pulled her hand to its mouth.

Kiri laughed as the hard gums closed on her finger.

"It's time to feed him," the mother said as she lifted the baby from the sling and headed for the house.

As the Galeedan family reentered the house, Kiri stared after them, her finger still damp from the baby's mouth. Perhaps it *had* been time to feed him, but the Galeedan woman obviously hadn't wanted Kiri near her son. Even after traveling with Galeedans who had mistrusted her since she'd joined the column, the rejection stung. She would have liked to have held the baby, even if just for a moment.

"We still need drinking water," Ulek said, interrupting her thoughts as he stepped beside her. "We won't be able to get it once the Charpans attack."

"I'll go," Kiri said.

Ulek nodded without offering to go with her.

Getting water must be a woman's job, Kiri thought. Non-Forest people had responsibilities only for women and others only for men.

"Take Brense with you," Ulek said.

"No, he can stay here."

"Please, Kiri. He wants to explore the town, and he'll protect you."

Kiri glanced at Brense, who wagged his tail as he gazed up at her. She wondered how Ulek could know what the dog wanted, and what he thought she needed protection from as she fetched water.

"Fine," Kiri said, too tired to argue. She picked up a bucket and headed for the well as Ulek walked toward the house. Brense followed him until Ulek turned and pointed at Kiri. "No, go with her." After a brief hesitation, the dog loped after Kiri.

Kiri studied Brense as he trotted beside her. What an unnatural creature, to prefer the company of humans to his own kind. The Forest people didn't tame or keep animals. Until she'd joined the column, she'd never been close to a dog, never known an animal that didn't fear humans. Even the horse she and Ulek had ridden to escape the Charpans had seemed strange for allowing them to climb onto its back.

Because Kiri and Ulek had chosen a house in the center of town, she didn't have to walk far to reach the well. Several women gathered water, and Kiri waited her turn. When she could finally approach, she peered into the dark hole, surprised by its depth. Why couldn't non-Forest people build their homes near rivers and fetch their water there? Why dig these deep holes? After traveling with the column so long, Kiri knew nothing the non-Forest people did made sense. They spent all day in the fields coaxing plants from the soil, when everyone knew plants grew without human help. They dug holes in the ground for water when the earth provided plenty of water in lakes, streams, and rivers. They fed and tended large animals for meat when it was easier to hunt. They built huge houses made of strange materials when a simple wood hut would suffice. They'd forgotten how to track, listen to the forest, and survive in the wild. She'd never imagined people would work so hard to do the unnecessary.

After filling her bucket and starting back, Kiri noticed Mekindu's mate struggling with a bucket, her blue dress wet down the side.

When the woman looked over her shoulder and saw Kiri and Brense, she stopped. She waited until they were abreast of her, then said, "You're Kiri."

"Yes," Kiri replied, surprised the woman addressed her.

The woman smiled, pushing her yellow braid over her shoulder. "I'm Anwyn."

An offer of friendship. Besides Ulek, no Galeedans, not even the family staying in the same house, had given Kiri their names. She returned the other woman's smile.

"Mekindu says you ran away from your husband," Anwyn said. "Is that true?"

"Yes."

Anwyn started talking as if she'd been holding the words back a long time. "I ran from my husband too." She released a shaky breath. "There were times I regretted leaving. I found work washing clothes in the town near the garrison, and I had enough to eat, but it wasn't a good life. The women wouldn't talk to me. I had no husband, but I wasn't a maiden or a widow, so the men thought I was ... available." She gave Kiri a searching look. "Are you ever sorry you ran?"

Pretending to be non-Forest had been far more difficult than Kiri ever imagined, yet as she gazed into Anwyn's earnest face, she felt a level of guilt she'd never experienced. She'd endured horror and loss, but this Galeedan woman had been regularly beaten by the man who should have loved her, and then been badly treated by her own people. "I'm not sorry," Kiri whispered.

"Really?" Anwyn's expression brightened as if Kiri had told her the horde had turned around. "You think it was worth it?"

Worth it? Was Anwyn so lonely she thought she might be happier living with someone who beat her? Kiri thought of how, like Ulek, Anwyn had been abandoned with those who'd been struck by poisoned arrows, with no one staying behind to care for her. Yes, she probably was that lonely. Kiri could only smile in response.

"It feels so good to talk about this with another woman," Anwyn said. "Even now, with the horde coming."

Kiri couldn't meet her eyes.

"Mekindu said you were nice." Anwyn gave Kiri a sidelong glance. "Some people … some people don't like me and Mekindu being friends because my husband is still alive."

"I don't care," Kiri replied, her tone gentle.

Anwyn's eyes filled with gratitude. They walked together in companionable silence until Anwyn said, "That's a good dog—stays right with you. What's his name?"

"He's called Brense. He belongs to Ulek."

At the sound of his name, Brense pricked up his ears.

"The boy you're traveling with?" Anwyn asked. "I heard the Charpans murdered his father."

Kiri flinched. Justified killing occurred in battle, self-defense, or in defense of others. A murderer killed in rage or cold cruelty. They did it for selfish reasons. "Yes," she said stiffly.

"The poor boy," Anwyn murmured. "Life is hard without kin. It's good of you to take care of him."

Kiri found her mouth too dry to answer.

"Would you like to walk with me to where I am staying?" Anwyn asked.

Kiri nodded.

"It's close to the gate," Anwyn said. "I had trouble finding a place, but an old woman made her family take me in."

As they neared the gate, the houses gradually grew smaller and less sturdy-looking. They had only one level, and none had been built with stone or the claylike substance. Instead, they were made of thin slabs of wood. They seemed insubstantial and ugly, as if no pride had been taken in building them. The sound of men shouting orders and preparing for the attack grew closer.

Finally, Anwyn inclined her head toward one of the small wood houses on the edge of town. "This one." The windows hadn't been closed, and the door, which hung crookedly in the entrance, looked like a child could kick it in.

Kiri knew it wouldn't matter in the end, but it disheartened her to discover one of the few non-Forest people who had shown her kindness stayed in a defenseless home so near the gate.

With a sigh of relief, Anwyn set her bucket on the ground near the door. "Thank you for walking with me," she said, brushing a strand of hair from her face as she stood up. Before Kiri could say goodbye, Anwyn asked, "Since we're so close to the gate, do you want to see what the soldiers are doing?"

At first, Kiri hesitated. Part of her feared seeing the readying for battle. Then she noticed the hopeful expression in Anwyn's wide blue eyes and realized she wanted to prolong their time together. As she placed her own bucket beside Anwyn's, Kiri said, "Yes, let's see."

It didn't take long to reach the village wall. Soldiers and Galeedan men gathered supplies and reinforced the gates. Some were still dumping water over dwellings. They paid no mind to Kiri and Anwyn, or to Brense, who sat beside them. Then a tall man extricated himself from the group around the gate and headed toward them. Mekindu.

Beads of sweat traveled down Mekindu's dust-covered face. He gazed at Anwyn the way an exhausted man might gaze upon sleeping furs. "Little Kiri," he said, smiling, as he reached them. Then he turned his attention to Anwyn. "You found a place then?" he asked, lowering his head toward her.

"Yes," Anwyn replied. "Not far from here." She started to say something else when an angry shout startled all three of them.

"Mekindu, what are you—" The advancing soldier with the green-crested helmet broke off his words when his eyes fell on Kiri. It was Mattos.

"Falcon, I . . ." Mekindu began. Before he could stay more, Brense charged Mattos, barking ferociously, his fur standing on end.

The dog stopped a few paces from Mattos as if an invisible barrier existed between them. He continued to bark, his lips curled up to reveal glistening fangs.

Kiri stood frozen. She'd tried to warn Ulek about the dog.

A fierce expression appeared in Mattos's eyes as his hand moved toward the sword hanging from his hip. Then he paused and seemed to relax. He crouched with his right hand extended and murmured in Sandamedan, his tone soothing.

Still barking, Brense danced around the crouching soldier, never coming close enough to touch him. Twice he darted toward the outstretched hand, then sprang backward at the last moment. Finally, he paused long enough to sniff Mattos's fingers before retreating. He stopped barking, and he approached to sniff the hand again. His tail gave the slightest wag.

Mattos waited until Brense licked his hand before rising. He turned angry eyes on Kiri. "Why didn't you call him off?" he demanded.

"I was afraid," Kiri answered. Did he really think she had control over that animal?

"Afraid?" Mattos said. "You're the one he was protecting. You're lucky I didn't kill him."

He's protecting me? Kiri stared at Brense, who came to sit at her side. Would a dog really protect a human? She hadn't been in danger, but with the way Mattos had yelled and strode toward them, an animal could easily have mistaken him for a threat.

"Why are you talking to women while your men work?" Mattos asked, turning his attention on Mekindu.

Mekindu spoke stiffly. "Anwyn was wounded by a Charpan arrow. You remember her? I inquired about her injury."

"Help her to where she's taken shelter. Then get back to work." Without waiting for a reply, Mattos turned to Kiri. "You and your dog should go back to your shelter. We can already see the dust kicked up by Charpan horses."

"Kiri, are you coming?" Anwyn asked.

"You go," Kiri replied, waving her and Mekindu on. She knew they'd want to speak alone.

The pair moved away with Anwyn leaning on Mekindu's arm.

Kiri waited for Mattos to return to his duties. Instead, he stayed.

"You should go, Kiri." Now that Brense had settled down, Mattos no longer appeared angry. He seemed calm, even weary.

She had no reason to stay, yet Kiri didn't want to return to the home she shared with Ulek and the Galeedan family. When the soldiers had attacked Mar Dun, no one had seen them coming. Kiri had been laughing at a joke Wren had told her as they shared a meal, and then people had been dying around her. She could still feel the horrid shock of that moment. When the band of Charpans had ridden into the camps, firing their poison arrows, she'd been huddled in a blanket trying to sleep. Each time, she'd been taken unawares, without a chance to face the enemy before they attacked. She couldn't let it happen again. "I want to see the Charpans."

Mattos's eyes widened. "What?"

"I want to see the Charpans," she repeated firmly.

"There's nothing to see but dust."

"I want to see the dust," Kiri said, meeting Mattos's gaze. She willed herself not to blink first.

"I can't let you on the wall," Mattos said. "Go back to Ulek."

Her eyes burned, but Kiri still refused to blink. She lifted her chin. "I tracked the Charpans. I led soldiers to the Charpans. Now I will see Charpan dust."

This time, Mattos had no response. He stared at Kiri, his lips pressed together. Then he looked toward the wall. "So you did," he said thoughtfully. "I suppose we owe you. Very well, if you want to see the horde coming to kill us, follow me."

Men cast surprised glances at Kiri as she climbed onto the platform. She walked to the section of wall above the gate, trying not to breathe in the stench of urine. The top of the wall extended an arm's length over her head, but if she stood on her toes, she could see between two sharpened points. Clouds of dust rose over the horizon, extending far from east to west. Even the column hadn't kicked up this kind of dust. The Charpans had to be as numerous as the trees in a forest. She stood transfixed, unable to look away. The sun began its descent, and the horde would be upon them before it rose again.

As the dust clouds grew larger, Kiri became aware of Mattos at her side. It seemed strange that he stood there, considering he'd scolded Mekindu for talking to women instead of working.

Mattos spoke as he gazed at the approaching dust. He started so quickly Kiri didn't catch his first words.

"—but I've been to Teletmoora. I was supposed to take over my father's fabric business one day, so I had to learn." He glanced at Kiri. "Have you ever been there?"

Kiri hesitated. Would the Wanderers have visited Teletmoora? Questions about Wanderers made her nervous. Giving the wrong answer could betray her. If she said no, it might seem suspicious, but if she said yes, he might want to discuss details. "No," she replied.

"I suppose not," Mattos said. He continued speaking, barely pausing long enough to breathe. "It's strange how your people spend their lives traveling from city to city, yet you don't cross the sea. Teletmoora is a lot like Sarpaska. My father does most of his business in Teletmoora because they have the best red dyes. When I was old enough, he took me with him on one of his trips. We stayed with Achi, the merchant my father has traded with for years. Achi dined at our house many times, but I'd never seen a Teletmooran woman until I went there. They wear *powdered gold* in their hair."

It was clear from the way he spoke that Mattos considered this remarkable. Kiri widened her eyes to appear impressed, though his focus on something so mundane confused her. A murderous horde would be upon them soon, and he, a soldier of rank, talked about how women decorated their hair.

Turning toward her, Mattos said, "My father's rich, Kiri, and a fabric merchant's family will always be well dressed. But I sat at Achi's table, with his wife and daughters sitting there covered in jewels and gold dust. I'd never seen that kind of wealth. Can you imagine having so much gold you could grind it up and wear it in your hair every day? Achi took me to the Scholars' Library and the Temple of the Sun. They weren't as large or well made as our own libraries or temples in Sandameda, but they were magnificent and more detailed. So ornate. There were jewels in the walls. It's remarkable they weren't stolen."

Mattos gave a deep sigh. "Now we have the horde riding toward us because the emperor wants Charpa's gold. Maybe he'll declare war on Teletmoora next. Many believe it's the gods' will for the Sandamedan Empire to conquer the world. If the emperor is willing to attack Charpa for its wealth, how could he resist Teletmoora? Maybe after we've killed enough people, my mother and sisters can wear gold powder in their hair too."

The bitterness of his last words struck Kiri with the force of a physical blow. The man beside her considered the war folly. If the decision had been up to him, his people would never have invaded Charpa. It had never occurred to Kiri that Mattos would fight in a war when he thought no good would come of it. Mattos loved his city, his empire, and his gods. He wore his armor and crested helmet with pride. He belonged to his people as much as Kiri belonged to hers. Yet he fought in a war he didn't believe would benefit his people. It made no sense. Of course, elders had to be heeded when they shared their wisdom. One had to put aside private desires for the sake of one's people; no village would survive long without sacrifice for the common good. But Mattos had revealed a level of obedience she'd never encountered.

Compassion swept over Kiri as she contemplated the meaning of this. She had chosen certain death to save her people, but Mattos had gone to war simply because his people asked him to. It felt strange to have such thoughts. Here she stood, disliked and mistrusted in a foreign land, waiting for the arrival of men who wanted to kill her, burdened with the knowledge she would fail her people, and she felt respect and sorrow for an imperial soldier. It was more than that, though. Despite Mattos killing his own soldier and wearing the same armor as those who attacked her people, she liked him. The realization, one she never thought possible, startled her. Kiri studied Mattos's face as he gazed at the horizon. His eyes were full of resignation. Perhaps, after losing his wife and baby, a part of him longed for death. Either way, they would both be in the spirit world soon—she with her people, and he with his.

Mattos's thoughts must have been of the afterlife as well, because he asked, "What gods do your people believe in?"

This question Kiri didn't fear answering. She didn't have to worry about revealing her ignorance about the Wanderer people because no one knew what gods or spirits they worshiped—a secret they kept from all outsiders. Even the Forest people who traded with them often were forbidden from witnessing their rituals. Kiri could give any answer, and Mattos would accept it. She decided to answer truthfully, as a Forest person. Imperial soldiers didn't know what the Forest people believed, either.

"There are no gods. Only life and death."

Mattos turned to stare at her with an incredulous expression. "You don't believe in the soul? In life after death?"

"The spirit world is after death."

"But you said …"

Kiri sighed in exasperation. What nonsense to think her people had no afterlife because they had no gods. Holding up an open palm, she said, "Living world." Then she held up her other palm. "Spirit world. Life and death. See?"

His eyebrows drew together. "You don't pray to anyone?"

"We pray to spirits."

Raising his eyebrows, Mattos said, "Your people worship spirits?"

Kiri sighed. "We don't worship anyone. We can't see sprits until we die and enter their world. Some protect us, some are indifferent, and some are dangerous. We pray to the protective spirits and the spirits of our dead. Life and death."

"Life and death."

Brense barked from where he sat by the ladder. The time had come to leave. Ulek would be worried, and Kiri still had to retrieve her bucket from where she'd left it by Anwyn's door. "I must go," she said.

Mattos turned back to the horizon and the rising dust. "Today is a good day for prayer."

Reaching out, Kiri squeezed Mattos's hand to comfort him. "The spirit world is a good place."

As Kiri loosened her grip, Mattos held her hand fast. She stared up at him in bewilderment, but he wouldn't look at her. The feel of Mattos's warm and calloused hand unexpectedly reassured Kiri, as if he had taken on some of her burden. She curled her fingers around his. Mattos ran his thumb over her knuckles. Neither spoke as they gazed into the distance. Only when Kiri gave a faint tug did Mattos relinquish her hand.

Chapter 40

KIRI

Confusion. Screams. Fear. *The Charpans are already here. How did I not hear them coming?* There were Sandamedan words. Not the rough and guttural Charpan words that sounded like a low growl, or the smooth words of the common language that flowed into each other like water. Not the harsh Galeedan words that could only be made with the tongue pressed against the roof of the mouth or behind the front teeth. One couldn't mistake the Sandamedan language. They used words as cold, sharp, and precise as their weapons.

Kiri knew the pain and terror well; once experienced, one didn't forget it. She no longer had control over herself. She could no more choose to scream than she could will herself not to. No, the sounds she made had been ripped out of her, as if an evil spirit had reached down her throat and torn her voice from her body, releasing every shriek, wail, and scream she'd ever been capable of making.

The world spun as Kiri looked to the side. Her face had been sliced open. Yes, she remembered now. She blinked, trying to focus. An imperial soldier stood nearby, his armor covered in blood. She had never seen him before, never heard of him, yet she recognized him as Orrik, a Galeedan who had a farm just beyond the forest. She had no way to know this, yet she knew it with certainty. A younger soldier with green eyes stood beside him. Kordrick. *I'm not supposed to know this, not yet.* Time had become jumbled, so that the past and present occurred together. She squeezed her eyes shut, trying to make everything clear.

When she opened her eyes, she saw she lay curled up on the ground, her hair stiff with blood. Bodies of people she knew, had spoken with a short time ago, littered the ground. Wren lay among them.

The soldiers sat nearby, eating the venison that had been cooking when they'd attacked. Orrik turned his gray eyes on her. *Just like Ulek's eyes.* Then Ulek stood next to his father, gazing at her with the same eyes.

Ulek had never been there before.

Kiri froze. She wore her Forest clothing.

Ulek didn't react. Instead, he just stared at her with a peaceful expression, as if he didn't understand the significance of her clothing, as if he found nothing strange about her bloody face.

Struggling to her feet, Kiri stood before him: dirty, exhausted, and covered in dried blood. "I am Forest."

Ulek only blinked.

This had never happened before.

"I am Forest!" she screamed.

Still, Ulek did not react.

The men surrounding them disappeared. When Kiri glanced around, she saw she and Ulek stood in his home, with his father's body lying on the bed where they had found him the morning after they'd escaped the Charpans. No longer covered in blood, Kiri stood dressed in the finery she wore to ceremonies. The tunic fell almost to her knees. Unlike the usual greens and browns meant to make the wearer blend into the forest, the garments had been dyed a brownish red. Blue beads obtained through trade with the Wanderers decorated the sleeves in graceful, leaflike designs. The leather shoes, also dyed red, were covered in the same designs from toe to heel. Kiri's oiled hair had been divided into three parts, with one thick braid falling down her back and two smaller braids framing her face.

This had happened before, but it was all wrong now. Kiri should have been disguised as a Wanderer, not clad in her best Forest clothing.

Sniffling, Ulek wiped tears from his eyes. "My father," he said in the Forest language. When had he learned her language?

"I killed him," Kiri replied.

"No, Kiri," Ulek said, shaking his head. "The Charpans killed him."

"*I* did it," Kiri insisted. "I entered your house in the night and put a knife in his throat while you slept in the next room. That's how the Charpans captured me. I was close to your house because I had just killed your father. He was already dead when the Charpans came here."

"It was the Charpans," Ulek said with conviction.

Rage exploded in Kiri's chest. Why wouldn't he hear her? "I am Forest!" she screamed. "I killed your father. Look at me and know what I am!"

The world shook.

"Kiri!"

A dog barked in the distance.

"Kiri, wake up!"

Ulek's face loomed over her, his gray eyes wide with concern. Brense stood nearby, barking.

"I killed him," Kiri whispered.

"You're speaking the Wanderer language. I can't understand you."

Kiri took in her surroundings. She lay in a soft bed in the upper level of the house Mattos had told them to stay in. When she and Ulek had climbed into the bed, she'd believed it impossible to sleep with the horde so close. Yet, somehow, she *had* fallen asleep, and the horrible dream that had come to her many times before had visited her again.

"You had a bad dream," Ulek said. "You were shouting in the Wanderer language."

"I'm sorry I woke you," Kiri murmured, rubbing her eyes.

"Brense, hush!"

At Ulek's command, the dog whined and lay on the floor, his head resting between his paws.

There were murmurs from the family that had taken over the lower floor. Brense must have woken them.

Turning back to Kiri, Ulek said, "It's all right. I'm sure you're not the only one with bad dreams." After a few moments of silence, he whispered, "The horde isn't here yet. We'd know if it was."

"Yes."

With a weary sigh, Ulek lay back down, his head resting on Kiri's shoulder. In a surprisingly short amount of time, his breath against her neck became even. Kiri lay on her back, trying to calm her heart.

Something landed on the end of the bed, causing one corner to dip. Brense.

"Bad dog. Off the bed," Kiri whispered, trying not to wake Ulek.

Brense walked up the bed until his whiskers brushed her forehead as he sniffed her hair.

"Off."

The dog licked her face.

Kiri laid her hand against Brense's shoulder, ready to shove him off the bed. As her fingers sank into the soft fur, she hesitated. She stroked him the way she'd seen Ulek and Mattos do. Brense nuzzled her hand. Sighing in defeat, Kiri closed her eyes. "You can stay," she whispered.

Brense pressed himself against her as he lay down.

Just as Kiri drifted into sleep, men began shouting in the distance.

Chapter 41

MATTOS

The narrow platform rocked under Mattos's feet as his men shifted their weight. He grabbed one of the sharpened tree trunks to steady himself, hoping the platform wouldn't collapse. Osprey Beldos had ordered Mattos's unit to man the walls above the gate. With the Charpans about to attack, he could do little to punish Mattos for his nephew's death, but he could ensure Mattos and his men were given the most dangerous assignment. Three other Falcon units manned Cybelon's other three walls. The men gripped their swords and shields, ready—even anxious—for battle.

The horde appeared as a mass of shadowy figures in the dim moonlight. If it hadn't been for the clinking of metal or the snorts of many horses, Mattos might have thought the dark shapes were mere tricks of the eye. Occasionally, a horse screamed as it broke its leg in one of the holes dug for that purpose. Instead of charging Cybelon, screaming in bloodlust, the Charpan riders had surrounded the town without uttering a single cry.

They're playing with us, Mattos thought. The anticipation of battle could be worse than the battle itself, and the Charpans were drawing out the wait. Mattos felt his unit's tension. They were like a bow drawn too long.

A speck of light appeared in the distance. Then another. The horde continued to light torches and arrows until the fields surrounding Cybelon reflected the starry sky. There were five thousand of them—five thousand Charpan riders against three hundred soldiers and a few hundred untrained, unarmed Galeedan men.

The fire illuminated the horses and riders, allowing Mattos to study those closest to him. Beneath helmets that covered only the top half of the head, they wore red fabric that fell to their shoulders. Their bulky tunics were jewel-toned reds, oranges, golds, greens, and blues, their leather boots and trousers brown or black. Boiled leather served as their armor. Swords half the length of a man and double-bladed axes hung from their belts. Each rider had a full quiver slung over his back, a second full quiver hanging from the saddle, and a bow resting across his knees. They carried no shields, focusing on speed rather than protection. There were no crested helmets, unusual armor, or regalia to identify the leaders. Any one of the riders could have been the high chief. The horses had been splattered with red paint, giving them the appearance of having been bathed in blood. Or maybe it really was blood.

The horde let out a battle cry in one voice. It started out low before rising into an undulating shriek that must have carried for leagues. A foul smell wafted along the wall. One of the men had shit himself. The Galeedan men on the ground shifted and murmured until the Osprey barked a command to be silent.

Mattos resisted the urge to scream back at the horde, knowing the yells of his men would seem pathetic compared to the mighty horde war cry. The complete hopelessness of their situation finally sank in. He threw back his head and laughed in despair and defiance. A laugh that said, *We are all going to die here. There is* nothing *we can do to prevent it.* But it also said, *Well then, let's get on with it.* To his surprise, his men laughed too, the sound of their deep voices heartening.

Hawk Thais stood with the rest of the company in the courtyard before the gate. Behind him were about one hundred Galeedans. The rest of the Galeedans had been sent to guard the other three walls. Thais lifted his sword over his head, giving the signal to fire.

"Fire!" Mattos cried, grabbing an arrow from his quiver. He sensed his men's relief as they drew their bows. The wait was over.

Charpans fell from their saddles as wounded horses screamed. The horrid battle cry ceased as abruptly as it had begun.

Mattos smiled in grim satisfaction when his arrow found the eye of the man he'd been aiming at.

The soldiers on the ground loosed a volley of arrows into the sky, which easily found purchase among the mass of flesh, man and horse, gathered outside the town.

A low-pitched horn blared in the distance. At the sound, the nearby riders surged toward the gate, which had no ditch before it, and hacked at the wood with swords and axes. A wall of flaming arrows rose above the town, casting its defenders in orange light before raining down at them.

Mattos felt the impact of each arrow that hit his shield. One managed to pierce the leather and wood, the iron point coming close to his head. Another arrow struck the platform a finger's width from his left foot. All around him men screamed as the whistling projectiles rained over them.

They could do nothing but crouch beneath their shields under the continuous barrage. No sooner had the last arrow of one volley struck the ground before another volley of flaming arrows lit the night. From the corner of his eye, Mattos saw the Galeedan men—who had only makeshift shields they'd pieced together from materials ripped from houses—run for shelter. To his surprise, Hawk Thais ordered the soldiers to let them go. Many of the Galeedans didn't reach the houses. They lay screaming in agony as still more arrows pierced their flesh. Two men caught on fire. With the arrows protruding from their bodies, they were unable to roll enough to put out the flames.

I don't want to die cowering on my knees, Mattos thought as he rose and peered over the wall under the cover of his shield. Though they were almost upon their enemy, not a single Charpan arrow fell among their own horses or riders. Mattos sucked in his breath in reluctant admiration. Sandamedan archers could never have achieved such precision.

As long as a clear path to the gate remained, the Charpan riders seemed unwilling to risk their horses in the ditches. The riders swarmed before the gate, attacking with weapons and their own weight. The untanned hides hadn't failed the town. The walls and gates hadn't caught fire, but they were starting to give under the onslaught. Chunks of wood littered the ground.

"Take the shield of the man to your right and hold it over him," Mattos shouted. "Let him fire the arrows on the men along the walls." He grabbed the shoulder of the man who crouched beside him. "On your feet!" he commanded.

The order passed down the line. His men rose as arrows continued to rain down on them.

"Aim for the men at the gate," Mattos called.

Most of the arrows caught in the Charpans' thick armor, though some pierced the leather. Others hit exposed faces and necks. A few struck the unarmored horses. Where men and horses fell, others took their places. Riders close to the wall retaliated with their own arrows. One soldier fell from the platform after being hit just above the collarbone. Balen, who'd been so careful to shield Anundi, who stood to his right, was struck under his left arm. Anundi managed to keep him from falling. Then Jefton went down.

Pain gripped Mattos's stomach as he witnessed his men being slaughtered. Their efforts were futile, yet what else could they do except keep going or give up?

"Mattos!"

Mattos looked over his shoulder to see Harrier Diakiris shouting up at him, his shield held over his head. "Get down from there. All soldiers are needed at the gate."

An arrow grazed his boot as Mattos called, "To the gate! To the gate! Off the platform!"

The soldier closest to the ladder climbed down, struggling to hold his shield aloft. The line moved slowly. The rickety ladder had been built to hold one man at a time, not several heavily armed soldiers at once. Anundi almost fell as he struggled down the ladder while carrying Balen on his shoulder.

As Mekindu started down, an arrow pierced his right thigh. He screamed as he grasped at his wound.

"Mekindu!" Mattos cried, grabbing his Owl's wrist to keep him from falling.

"I'm all right, Falcon," Mekindu panted, beads of sweat glistening on his forehead. "It's a clean wound—went straight through."

Mekindu reached the ground with the arrow still protruding from his thigh. Mattos saw with horror that the tip of the shaft still burned.

When all his men were off the platform, Mattos began to climb down. Twice his foot found open air where there should have been a rung. When he was close enough to the ground, he slid the rest of the way down.

Men ran about putting out small fires. Others carried the screaming wounded to shelter. Mattos managed to gather his unit in formation near the gate. Balen had been carried to one of the shelters for the wounded. Orston wept over Evendos, who had fallen to his death. Mekindu broke off the arrowhead and removed the shaft from his leg with shaking hands. Then he tied cloth around the wound to stop the bleeding.

As he broke off the arrow that had pierced his shield, Mattos hoped the Charpans had been so focused on lighting their arrows that they hadn't bothered to poison them. Besides, the poison worked too slowly to make a difference in this battle. The flaming arrows had killed and injured many, but drenching roofs with water had prevented the town from catching fire.

The entire company, save those who'd already been killed or injured, crouched under their shields before the gate.

Only Thais and his aides stood, the aides desperate to shield their leader.

Soldiers tugged ropes attached to pulleys rigged up on either side of the gate. Ropes that had lain upon the ground before the gate rose until they were pulled taut at a height taller than a man.

Then Mattos understood. They were going to open the gate. The Hawk must have anticipated the horde's innumerable arrows might render them helpless. As soon as riders entered the town, the volleys would cease. Even the bloodthirsty western Charpans wouldn't risk hitting their own men. The Hawk hadn't wanted a ditch before the gate for this reason. The Charpans' greater numbers could be controlled if they entered the town through one narrow opening.

"Open the gate!" Thais cried, drawing his sword. "I want a barricade of their bodies."

As the gate creaked open, three quick bursts sounded from a nearby horn. The arrows stopped falling. Then the riders charged, screaming into the town.

The first riders rode straight into the ropes, which hit them across their chests, unseating them. Soldiers sprang on them before they hit the ground. The riderless horses galloped down the narrow roads, seemingly unaware of the missing weight.

More Charpans poured into the town. Several more hit the ropes, while those behind them avoided the trap. A horse and rider leaped over the rope, moving together as if one creature. The horse's head extended forward, its legs drawn up, while the rider leaned forward as well, one hand upon his mount's shoulder and the other brandishing an ax. They landed as gracefully as if they had only cleared a low fence. More horses and riders followed.

A Charpan took off a soldier's head with one swipe of his broad sword. The head rolled between the feet of the soldier's companions, who were forced to kick it aside as they tried to keep their own heads.

Mattos had barely registered these events before a rider was upon him. He had just enough time to block the sword with his shield, which vibrated at the impact. With his own sword, Mattos lashed at the saddle belt, cutting through the belt as well as the horse's flesh.

The horse screamed as the saddle slid off its back. Leaping off his mount, the rider landed on his feet. He forced Mattos backward, attacking with vicious strength.

The Charpan's blade hit his shield with such force that Mattos feared the shield might crack. He didn't have a chance to use his own smaller sword. He could only defend himself, keeping his shield lowered just enough to see his opponent's movements. Mattos stumbled back a few more steps. The Charpan grabbed the pommel of his sword with his left hand as well, and now, each blow doubled in power.

A mixture of ferocity and triumph shone in the Charpan's eyes, as if sure of his victory.

Mattos gritted his teeth. The Charpan didn't seem to know shields could be weapons too. When his enemy held his sword over his head for another strike, Mattos lunged, driving his shield into the Charpan's chest and face.

The impact knocked the Charpan backward, and blood spurted from his nose and mouth. Still, he hadn't dropped the sword.

Sweet Imari and all the gods, Mattos thought before charging again.

The Charpan brought his sword down as the shield crashed into him.

Now on the offensive, Mattos exposed his right side as he struck at his opponent's left wrist with his sword.

The Charpan cried out as the blade cut into bone. The armor sewn into his tunic and his thick leather gloves kept the wrist from being severed. His left arm fell limply to his side. After taking two backward steps, he ran at Mattos, sword held high.

By Odern, does he feel no pain? Mattos had felt his sword hit bone. The Charpan's wrist had to be broken and sliced open, yet the man fought with a smashed nose and broken wrist as if they were mere scratches.

When the blade next hit his shield, Mattos ran forward, trying to knock the Charpan over. It became a shoving match, with each man straining against the other. Mattos's boots dug into the ground as he pushed his shoulder into his shield—something he must have done a thousand times in training exercises. Two rows of soldiers would line up across from each other shield to shield. Then they'd push, grunting and sweating until one line forced the other backward. Whichever line backed into the rope placed behind it lost. It took all Mattos's strength to get the other man to budge. With agonizing slowness, Mattos gained ground.

The Charpan abruptly tumbled backward. Mattos almost fell on top of him. When he looked over his shield, he saw the Charpan had tripped over a body. Before his enemy could get back on his feet, Mattos slammed the edge of his shield into the man's stomach. Then, with the wind forced from the Charpan's lungs, Mattos used his shield to knock the sword from his grip. Mattos dropped his shield and fell upon his disarmed enemy, plunging his sword into his throat.

Mattos rolled onto his back. A stinging pain flared just above his knee. Looking down, he saw blood oozing from a cut in his trousers. When he glanced at the corpse next to him, he saw a bloody dagger in its right hand. The Charpan had fought to the last, taking up a dagger when he'd lost his sword.

Since the moment the Charpan had attacked him, Mattos's world had shrunk to the deadly combat between them. Now he looked around, taking in the battle. The riders had been pushed back to the gate. Soldiers swarmed around them, forcing them farther back.

Retrieving his shield, Mattos limped toward his men. He had only just reached them when he realized the fighting had ceased. There, blocking the gate, lay a pile of horse and Charpan corpses, just like the Hawk wanted.

The soldiers stood in awe of the massive pile. They had kept the mighty horde from taking Cybelon.

At least for now.

Chapter 42

KIRI

The distant screams of man and horse blended into one continuous roar. Kiri and Ulek sat on the edge of the bed, saying nothing, while Brense whined as he paced by the window. The dim candle cast his shadow, five times his size, onto the wall. The baby on the lower level began to cry, and the muted sound of his mother comforting him drifted up to them. Thunder rolled in the distance. A storm approached.

Kiri dug her nails into her palms, trying not to remember how babies and children had wailed the last time she'd been in a village under attack. If she hadn't experienced the attack on Mar Dun, it would have been incomprehensible that the riders would kill children and babies. Even now, she had hope the Galeedan baby would survive if they hid him during the fighting. Maybe a rider, battle rage spent, would find him and spare him. Maybe one of the riders would have a sister or wife desperate for a child. *No.* Kiri pushed the thought away. The imperial soldiers who had attacked Mar Dun had killed without mercy or discrimination, and the Charpan riders would do the same. The Charpan who had known her to be Forest had promised this.

"There's a shovel under the bed," Ulek said, interrupting Kiri's thoughts. "I found it in one of the houses the soldiers hadn't searched and hid it from them. I can use it as a weapon if the Charpans make it this far."

With her mouth too dry to speak, Kiri didn't respond. The boy's hopeful courage only made the moment more painful.

When she didn't answer, Ulek reached for her hand. "Don't be afraid. I'll protect you."

Kiri turned to face him. Ulek had lived twelve years—long enough to understand their situation. She studied the gray eyes so much like his father's. Every time she looked at him, a part of her looked at the man who had slaughtered innocent people. Sometimes she found it hard to meet his gaze.

Now, as she studied Ulek's face, his reassuring smile didn't reach his eyes. He acted brave for her sake, just as an adult would act brave so as not to frighten a child. She didn't know whether to laugh or cry. How had someone like Orrik sired and raised such a boy? Kiri squeezed Ulek's hand. She didn't regret killing Orrik, yet the guilt of lying about who she was and what she had done clawed her insides.

A nearby whinny startled them both.

Brense growled.

Ulek ran to the window, cracked open the section of wood the Galeedans called shutters, and peeked outside. After a moment, he said, "It's just a horse. Must have lost his rider."

Hurrying to his side, Kiri looked over his shoulder. The

riderless horse continued its charge deeper into the village, carrying a horrifying message. The gates had been breached. The horde was inside the village.

Kiri pulled the shutter closed and tugged Ulek to the center of the room. How long did they have? She gripped the straps of her pack. Somehow it made her feel a little less vulnerable, as if her Forest possessions carried the strength of her people.

Footsteps sounded outside the room. Then the little girl and the Galeedan woman, carrying her baby, burst through the door. The woman said something to Ulek, her eyes panicked.

Ulek translated. "Her husband sent them upstairs. He and Derk are guarding the door." He drew a shaky breath. "I should be down there with them. Derk is only three years older than me."

"No," Kiri said, grabbing Ulek's shoulder. "You should protect us here."

Ulek hesitated, then nodded.

The Galeedan woman sat on the edge of the bed, facing the door, and lowered the baby to her lap. The little girl curled up beside them.

Arms crossed, Kiri glared at the woman's back, not bothering to hide her resentment. This woman hadn't wanted Kiri to touch her baby, yet she thought nothing of invading her space and occupying her bed. Even the realization that, under the circumstances, she was being ridiculous didn't dampen Kiri's irritation. If she was going to die tonight, she didn't want to spend it with someone who disliked her.

When Ulek returned to the bed and sat down, Kiri

followed.

Brense continued to growl at the window.

The Galeedan woman sniffled, obviously trying to hide her crying from her daughter. Kiri returned to digging her nails into her palms. Of course the woman wept. Her mate and son guarded the lower level, ready to die fighting the Charpans. Once they were killed, her daughter and baby son would have only an unarmed, untrained woman, a boy of twelve armed with a shovel, and a small Forest warrior armed only with a knife in her boot to defend them.

Kiri squeezed her eyes shut, concentrating on her breathing and heartbeat to block out all sound and fearful thoughts. She gradually fell into a kind of trance, where she could feel her spirit. *Spirits of Mar Dun,* she prayed silently, *I killed Orrik and Kordrick. Please forgive me, for I cannot kill Isandor. I traveled far into the north to find him, only to discover he is in Forest lands. Please give someone else the courage and strength to kill him. Please watch over our people. I will be with you soon.*

A woman's nearby scream startled Kiri from her trance. She blinked as she returned to the world around her. She didn't know how much time had passed. The scream had been close. More screams filled the night before they all abruptly stopped. Ulek went rigid beside her.

Brense charged the window, barking.

Thunder rolled, louder than before.

The little girl said something in a frightened voice as she

clasped her mother.

More screams, closer this time. Then the guttural shouts of Charpan men.

Diving to the floor, Ulek reached under the bed for the shovel.

A crash brought Kiri to her feet. It had been so close. It had to be—

A cry of rage, fear, and pain sounded from the lower level. The Charpans were inside the house.

Kiri ran for the door. From the corner of her eye, she saw Ulek heft the shovel in the air and the Galeedan woman drag her children under the bed. Kiri drew the knife from her boot. She'd abandoned Wren to aid Meadow and her children. Knowing she'd saved them was her only comfort when painful memories of the attack overwhelmed her. She'd fight to her last breath protecting these children.

Kiri hurried down the stairs toward the sound of battle. She reached the bottom in time to see a giant Charpan in a blood-red tunic raise his sword over his head with both hands. With blood pouring down his face from a gash in his forehead, the Galeedan father lunged at him, grasping the Charpan's sword with his hands overtop the Charpan's. The two men fought for control of the weapon while a second Charpan, too young to have a full beard, used an ax to hack at the chair Derk used to defend himself.

Kiri slunk into the room, keeping to the shadows. Two flickering candles provided the only light. She might be able to approach the Charpans without them seeing her. She took another step toward the Charpan wrestling for the sword when he looked up, his eyes fixed on something behind her.

"Get out of the way!" Ulek shouted as he shoved Kiri aside.

Kiri slammed into the wall as Ulek ran at the Charpan with his shovel raised high.

The younger Charpan abandoned his attack on Derk to defend his companion. His ax caught Ulek's shovel just before it struck the face of the Charpan in red, sending the shovel flying across the room. After kicking Ulek aside, he brought his sword down on the Galeedan father's collarbone.

The Galeedan man collapsed on the ground, screaming, until the older Charpan plunged the sword they'd been fighting over into his chest.

Derk let out the kind of cry Kiri had only heard in Mar Dun. He charged his father's killer with the hacked-up chair, a half-wail, half-battle yell escaping his lips. With one swipe, the younger Charpan knocked the chair from the boy's grasp and cut a bloody line across his chest.

Derk fell back with his hands over his wound.

It all happened in the time it took for Kiri to crouch beside Ulek, where he lay clutching his stomach. Now that the Galeedan man and boy were down, she couldn't attack the Charpans with only a knife. She cast frantic eyes across the room, searching for the shovel, when she spotted a Charpan bow and arrow lying on the floor.

As the Charpans stalked Derk, who crawled backward on his elbows, Kiri dove across the room, snatched up the bow, and nocked the arrow.

The older Charpan raised his sword above Derk, the tip pointing downward.

"Charpans!" Kiri yelled.

The men turned toward her as Kiri, on one knee, pulled the drawstring. The bow wouldn't draw. Kiri's heart pounded faster. She pulled with all her strength, the drawstring digging into her fingers, yet she could only draw the bow the length of a hand. Forest people made their own bows and arrows. The stronger the maker, the more strength one needed to draw the bow. Everyone knew that, but Kiri had never encountered a bow crafted like this before. She gritted her teeth. Despite her small size, she'd long ago developed the skill and muscle strength needed to pull a bow. Harder. She had to pull harder.

Slow smiles formed on the Charpans' faces. They laughed as they lowered their weapons. The older one sheathed his sword. Then, reaching over his shoulders with both hands, he lifted his own bow and arrow. He nocked the arrow and drew the bow, laughing the entire time.

The blood coursing through Kiri's veins went hot. They mocked her even as they prepared to kill her. Kiri let the bow and arrow clatter to the ground as she stood; she wouldn't die on her knees. With her hands balled in fists at her sides, she stared back at the man aiming the arrow at her. In her periphery, she saw Derk crawling to his father's body and Ulek struggling to his hands and knees.

"No!" Ulek cried. His voice sounded far away.

The Charpan's eyes hardened as his laughter ceased.

Kiri held her breath, waiting for the arrow.

A shadow flew between Kiri and the arrow aimed at her. The Charpan screamed before falling to the ground with the shadow on top of him.

When Kiri saw the blood gushing from the Charpan's torn-out throat, she shifted her attention to the dark shape hovering over him. It wasn't a shadow, but a snarling creature standing on the man's chest. Its fangs glistened in the candlelight. When the animal turned its bloody face toward her, Kiri drew a sharp breath. It was Brense. *Part Great Hound.*

When Brense had attacked, the younger Charpan had stood dumbfounded. Now, lifting his ax, he charged the dog.

Brense spun around, his teeth bared at his attacker. He lunged just as the Charpan swung his ax down at him. The snarls transformed into a high-pitched cry. Brense landed in a corner, where he lay whimpering.

When Ulek screamed, the Charpan turned toward him, advancing with his bloody ax.

Ulek. In one movement, Kiri dropped to the ground and seized the bow and arrow. Rolling onto her back, she stuck her legs in the air and laid the bow sideways across her feet, with her soles pressing against the wood. She nocked the arrow, grasped the drawstring with both hands, then scooted so she could aim the tip at the Charpan. She pushed with her legs and pulled with her arms, her entire body straining toward one goal.

Ulek managed to grab the shovel just in time to block the ax. A loud clang sounded as the shovel broke in two, the metal part slamming into the opposite wall. Ulek stumbled and fell.

Blood dripped from Kiri's fingers as the drawstring cut into her flesh and tears slid from the corners of her eyes.

Sprits, please. The drawstring began to give.

Harsh, angry words spilled from the Charpan's lips as he placed one boot on Ulek's chest.

The boy clawed at the boot, trying to squirm free.

Every muscle in Kiri's body quivered with effort. A strangled noise tore itself from her throat.

At the sound, the Charpan looked over his shoulder at her, his eyes widening when he saw the arrow pointed straight at him. With every bit of strength left in her, Kiri threw back her head, drew the bow farther, and loosed the arrow.

Chapter 43

ULEK

Matron Calla kept her lips pressed in a thin line as her needle pierced Brense's skin. Ulek stroked the dog's fur, trying to comfort him. When Matron Calla had first started to stitch him up, Brense had flinched and whimpered. Now he lay still, too exhausted to struggle.

Derk half moaned, half sobbed from where he lay in the corner. Ulek didn't know if he cried from pain or grief. Ulek couldn't look directly at him. The other boy's loss reminded him of his own father's violent death. The matron's behavior mystified Ulek. He'd expected her to collapse in tears when she'd seen her husband's body. Instead, she'd retrieved her sewing kit, gone straight to Derk's side, and cleaned and stitched his wound. When she'd finished, she'd gone to Brense and attended to him as carefully as she'd attended to her son. She'd done all of this with hard eyes and a stony expression. She never stopped moving, as if a pause or moment's rest would undo her.

Kiri had tossed a blanket over Eldorn's body and then dragged the Charpan corpses outside after removing their weapons. Now she sat next to Daneen, who held her baby brother in her arms. Kiri began a song of strange words and unknown meaning, her voice clear and pretty.

Brense gave a sudden yelp, and Ulek pressed his forehead close to the dog's ear. "It's all right, boy. You're a good dog. You saved Kiri." *And Kiri saved us.*

Glancing up at Matron Calla, Ulek asked, "Will he live?"

The woman didn't answer, her eyes filled with intense concentration.

Ulek wondered if she'd even heard him. He ran his fingers through the now sticky fur close to Brense's wound. The bloody gash ran along his left side, ending above his back leg. It wasn't as deep as an ax blow could have been. It must have glanced off him when he'd leaped into the air.

The distant rumbling had grown louder. Then a flash of lightning lit the night sky as if it were day. A crash of thunder followed, so loud it startled Kiri and Daneen.

Matron Calla sat back on her heels with a distant look in her eyes. "It will be a blinding storm," she said, speaking for the first time since she'd seen her husband's body. "I've felt it in the air all day, just like the night Daneen was born."

Thunder rolled so loudly it seemed the house shook. Ulek could remember two blinding storms and had learned why they were called "blinding." The animals had had to be safely shut away in the barn, and Ulek's family had huddled together in their cottage. When he'd peeked outside, he'd seen nothing but a wall of water. The thatched roof had leaked in several places, and the next day's repairs had been made to the barn and the cottage. Ulek's mother had said the gods cleansed the earth during such storms. Ulek looked to where Derk lay, then shifted his eyes to the blanket-covered body. If the earth had ever needed cleansing, now was the time.

Chapter 44

KIRI

He almost died. Kiri ran into the now muddy road before collapsing onto her hands and knees. *He almost died in front of me. We* all *almost died.* She sank lower, letting her forearms touch the ground, and rested her head on her hands. She'd almost witnessed another massacre—seen more children die. They were not her people, and Ulek was Orrik's son, yet somehow that didn't matter. When the Charpan had stood over Ulek with his ax raised, her horror had been equal to what she'd felt when Mar Dun had been attacked. Something stirred inside her, something she needed to fight.

Kiri took a deep breath, taking in her surroundings. She'd never known rain like this. The dense forest sheltered her people from most showers. If children wanted to play in the rain, they had to do it in a meadow or clearing. Even the storms she'd experienced since joining the column hadn't prepared her for the wall of water pounding her. She kept her head lowered so she could breathe. Surely, if she turned her face to the sky, she'd drown.

She saw no moon, no fires, no Charpans, soldiers, or Galeedans. There was only darkness, the mud that sucked at her fingers, the rain beating down on her and the sound of the deluge striking the ground. Perhaps she had died and now knelt on the path to the spirit world. But she hadn't. She had never felt life flow through her with such strength. Her heart slammed as the rain pounded her. Some of the rain striking the back of her head traced paths along her face before converging and falling in droplets from the tip of her nose. She breathed in the mingled scents of mud, her own wet skin, and doused fires. And everywhere the roar of water attacked the earth.

Spirits didn't have beating hearts. Spirits didn't feel, hear, or smell as she did. *I am alive.* The stirring began again, stronger this time. Kiri gritted her teeth against it, not knowing what she fought. She only knew she needed to fight it.

Then the struggle ended—so quickly that Kiri only had time to cry out in defeat. The determined numbness that had enveloped her since her people chose her to carry out their will shattered. She tried to hold on to it, tried to keep herself closed off and ready for death. Kiri rose to her knees, her hands clawing at the scarf wrapped around her head. After so long, her spirit could no longer deny its own gentleness. And now, with death so near, everything that had protected her and prepared her for death abandoned her. Kiri doubled over, gasping for breath. Then she collapsed in complete surrender. "I want them to live," she whispered. "*I* want to live."

Kiri didn't know how long she lay in the rain and mud before she stood and walked. She gave no thought to where she headed, yet her feet moved with purpose. She had no fear of stumbling or losing her way in the darkness. She could find her way by feeling the ground. She walked blindly amid the downpour, open and vulnerable for the first time in over fourteen months.

Flickering orange lights appeared behind the rain. As she came closer, Kiri recognized them as torches. How did they stay lit? Then she heard the cries and groans of men in pain. She must have wandered close to the gate, where the fighting had been hardest, and where they kept the wounded. The torches must be under the platform she had walked on earlier that day. Had it been the same day? It felt like there had been many sunsets since she had stood with Mattos and seen the dust kicked up by innumerable horses. The Charpans were gone. Had the fierce warriors been frightened off by rain? She approached one of the torches, its dancing flames all she could see through the sheets of rain. She stood, uncertain, as she awoke from her dreamlike state. Then she heard a familiar voice call, "Kiri?"

Chapter 45

MATTOS

The soldiers barely had time to gaze upon the pile of corpses when, with the loudest clap of thunder Mattos had ever heard, the sky released pounding rain. It was the kind of rain that rendered one almost blind, making everything outside of arm's reach a blur of water. Without command or discussion, the soldiers moved toward the area under the platform.

Mattos quickly located his men where they leaned against each other, exhausted and grieving. The timing of the rain couldn't be ignored. Someone said something about the will of Odern. Another man muttered, "I guess their Sky God wasn't so happy with their flaming arrows."

Owl Alistes came to stand at Mattos's side. "We took Mekindu to the shacks for the wounded." He jerked his chin toward Anundi, who leaned against the wall with red-rimmed eyes. "Balen died before Anundi could get him to the shacks. And Jefton—"

"I know," Mattos said, cutting him off. "I saw." He took a deep breath. "Send someone to see about Mekindu. I'll find out what's happening."

The senior officers had made the gatehouse adjacent to the gates their war room. Mattos made his way there. He found Lucen, Elmaturis, and a few other Falcons gathered by the doorway straining to hear the Hawk's and Osprey's words.

To his surprise, Elmaturis nodded when he approached. Dried blood caked his face from a fresh gash across his cheekbone. He bore none of the arrogance and enmity he'd always shown. "Mattos. Barsis and Alentor are dead."

Falcons Barsis and Alentor were only a year or two older than Mattos. They hadn't been his friends, but Barsis had always been cordial and Alentor had expressed empathy when Marenda and the babe had died. Mattos nodded gravely, too weary to respond.

Soldiers carried the wounded through the mud and rain to nearby shacks. Those not seriously injured sat under the platform tending to each other. Several bandaged or stitched up cuts. One of Lucen's Owls knelt across from a Sparrow, whose now crooked nose bled. The Owl slipped a bronze instrument up his patient's nostril and lifted the bone as he pressed down on the outside of the nose. Satisfied, he stuffed strips of leather up the younger man's nostrils. "Now hold your nose in place as long as you can," he commanded.

Finally, Harrier Diakiris exited the gatehouse, his expression grim but determined. He gathered his Falcons around him. "The timing of the rain bodes well for us. We don't think the Charpans will attack again until their priests decide what this means."

"Their arrows?" Lucen asked.

"Stay under shelter in case they fire a volley," Diakiris replied. "I suggest we use this time to see to our wounded and rest. We don't know when we'll get another chance."

Mattos made his way through the throng of exhausted soldiers to his own men. He relayed Diakiris's orders to Alistes and learned Mekindu was conscious and being tended to. Then he found a place where he could sit and lean against a beam.

He didn't know how long the reprieve would last, but Mattos planned to make the most of the time he had. Reaching into his boot, he withdrew the small leather kit all soldiers carried. He opened the kit, lifted an already threaded needle, and stitched the cut above his knee. With the battle energy still coursing through his veins, he barely felt the pain. He finished and tucked his leather kit back inside his boot. Then he leaned his head against the beam, trying not to think of the men he'd lost.

Someone stepped close to the torch nearest him. At first, he thought a soldier sought shelter. Then the flame illuminated a small figure in a dress. Only one woman would dare come this close to the gates.

"Kiri?" he called.

The figure stepped under the platform, the light revealing a face with large eyes and a scar running down the left cheek. Water dripped from her clothes, which clung to her body like a second skin. Mattos didn't ask why she had come or order her to safety. She did what she wanted, and in truth, safety didn't exist in Cybelon.

"Come sit with me," Mattos said wearily as he rested his head against the beam and closed his eyes. He heard her settle beside him.

"The Charpans are gone," Kiri whispered.

"No," Mattos answered without opening his eyes. "They've stopped the attack for now, but they're still here. The Charpans love fighting more than they fear their Sky God. Their leaders will say Sky God sent the rain as a blessing, or that maybe he put out the fires because he wanted them to have a challenge worthy of them. Maybe they'll say Sky God is displeased with them because they didn't offer enough prayers before the battle. Then they'll sacrifice some horses to appease him and attack us again. It makes no difference. It's only a matter of time."

"We will still die?" Kiri asked.

This time, Mattos opened his eyes and turned to meet her gaze. "Yes."

Kiri showed no fear or alarm. Only grief flashed in her eyes. She passed a hand over her mouth as she murmured something in the Wanderer language.

Mattos didn't attempt to comfort her. What could he say? Instead, he chipped at the dried blood on his right vambrace with his thumbnail. It made little difference, and when he saw that blood also covered his hands, he laughed bitterly. Of everything he'd hoped to accomplish in his life, he'd only achieved one thing—one skill he'd be remembered for. "I've killed men," he said, still laughing. "I'm a killer."

Staring at him with a strange intensity, Kiri reached out to touch one of his bloody hands. "I am a killer also," she murmured.

Mattos turned toward her, giving her his full attention. "You killed a Charpan?" he asked in disbelief. He'd seen Charpans ride into the town but hadn't thought they'd make it to the center where he'd told Kiri and Ulek to hide. How could this small woman kill an armed rider?

"I killed a Charpan," Kiri said matter-of-factly. Then her eyes took on a faraway look. "I've killed before," she whispered, a tremor in her voice.

"Who?" Mattos breathed.

"The man who did this," Kiri replied, running her finger down her scar. "The men who killed innocent people."

"I thought your husband gave you that scar."

Kiri met his eyes but said nothing.

Everyone assumed the cruel husband Kiri claimed to be running from had cut her face after finding her with another man. It explained why she'd been alone, when Wanderers never traveled alone. A phrase Mattos had heard countless times since joining the army came to him: "A dead man has many secrets; a dying man has none." Kiri spoke the truth. They faced death, and she felt the need to reveal her true self, as so many had done before her, so that someone would know her before her life ended.

"How many?'

Kiri held up three fingers.

Sweet Imari. "Who were they?"

"Evil men," Kiri said.

Mattos waited for her to elaborate, but she said nothing more. She'd said the men had killed innocents. Someone close to her? He wondered if the men had been bandits. Considering the distances Wanderers traveled, they could have been anyone. With her small frame, Kiri didn't look capable of defending herself, let alone killing anyone. Yet, she moved with agile grace and had proven herself an athlete and skilled tracker. Studying her, Mattos suspected she was stronger than she looked.

"I'm sorry for your suffering," Mattos said.

She didn't respond.

"And now here we are, two killers waiting to be killed." He laughed again. "We won't have to wait long."

Kiri stood and stared into the rain, which still fell in buckets. Then she turned, her hand outstretched. "Come."

"Come where?"

Instead of answering, Kiri grabbed his arm and tugged.

Mattos rose and allowed Kiri to pull him two steps before he realized she meant to leave the protection of the platform. He halted. "Kiri, it's raining."

She glanced over her shoulder with a wry smile that seemed to say, *Really? I didn't notice.* Then she tugged his arm again.

"Wait." Mattos pulled free and walked toward where Alistes sat. "Don't get up," he commanded as his Owl started to rise. "I need to leave the platform. Blow your horn if I'm needed or if there are any changes."

Mattos headed back to Kiri, pausing long enough to grab the closest torch and hold his shield over it. Then he allowed Kiri to pull him by his elbow into the deluge. He didn't know how she managed to navigate her way in the rain with only a faint light. He could only trust she knew where she was headed and follow, trudging through the ankle-deep mud. He could have stayed under the platform, but that would have meant sitting by himself within earshot of the wounded as they screamed and groaned.

They hadn't gone far when Kiri stopped, the rain no longer pounding them. Mattos lowered his shield to find they stood beneath the overhang of a small wooden structure. When he examined the shelter, he realized it was a shack on the outskirts of town, where the poorest villagers would have lived. He had to duck to keep his helmet's crest from catching on the thatch overhang. No light or sound escaped through the numerous cracks in the walls. None had sought refuge here; it might have protected one from wind or rain, but not an attack.

Kiri pushed at the rickety door to no avail. The corner had become stuck.

"No one's here," Mattos said, laying a hand on her shoulder to stop her. He had thought she'd meant to show him something or bring him to someone in need of help. If she only wanted a place out of the rain, they would have been better off staying under the platform.

Kiri glanced up, the torchlight reflecting in her black eyes. Water droplets slid from the hair plastered to her face, down her neck, into the hollow of her throat. She stared at him with a calm, determined expression, and Mattos grasped what she wanted.

After easing Kiri out of the way, Mattos slammed his shoulder into the door and stumbled into the shack. The light flickered across the small area, revealing a table near the clay chimney and sleeping furs thrown over straw in the corner. A leather hide would have separated the sleeping area from the rest of the home, but it had been torn down to cover the town walls.

Without a word, Kiri stepped inside and began to rearrange the sleeping furs.

Mattos pushed the door closed until the corner again became stuck, then he placed the torch in the chimney. When he turned to Kiri, she sat on the furs, watching him with eyes as inscrutable as a wild animal's. He stepped toward her.

"Wait!" Kiri's hand shot up, her expression alarmed.

Mattos froze. Had he misunderstood?

"Your armor …"

Of course. He'd been a fool to approach her with such intentions while in blood-splattered armor. He began to remove it.

Kiri's expression softened into one of calm.

An invisible line stretched between them, and if Mattos crossed it, he would be abandoning a way of life. He was an officer in the army of the Sandamedan Empire, only son of a wealthy fabric merchant, and educated with the sons of the senatorial class. She was an illiterate foreign girl, scarred, alone—a killer. To lie with her would be an insult to his station and upbringing. Some men might have argued they only gave in to a base weakness, that she meant no more than those who sold themselves at bathhouses. But Kiri meant more than that.

At last, Mattos shed his muddy boots and stood up wearing only his tunic and trousers. "Kiri?"

She still didn't smile, but she held out her hand in invitation.

Chapter 46

KIRI

The rain had slackened only a little when Kiri sat up, drawing her clothes to her. She didn't want to leave the warmth provided by the furs and Mattos, but she knew better than to cling to the reprieve they'd found. Better to relinquish life's fleeting moments of grace than to clutch at them, only to see them slip through one's fingers. Besides, she couldn't linger. Ulek needed her and would worry if she didn't return soon. As she reached for her dress, Mattos murmured, "I should have given you Nica."

She glanced over her shoulder. "Nica?"

"My horse," he said, still lying among the furs. "I should have given her to you and Ulek. You would have made it to Ishtia. Instead, I gave her to another officer's family." Mattos faced Kiri, but the torch gave little light, so his eyes were cast in shadow.

Kiri shrugged. "Another woman and child won't be killed by Charpans. You still saved lives."

"But I gave her to an officer's family without hesitation. I didn't even consider giving her to you."

"It's nothing," Kiri said, careful to keep her tattoos hidden as she tugged on her dress. Even in the dim light, she'd been vigilant about staying under the furs.

"I didn't consider it because I thought an officer's wife and child were worth more than … more than you."

Mattos spoke as if he confessed something shameful, yet Kiri saw no shame. He was Sandamedan, Ulek was Galeedan, and everyone believed her to be a Wanderer. She understood why a soldier would prefer to save his own kind, perhaps even a woman and child he knew.

"We should go," Kiri said.

Mattos slipped his hand to Kiri's waist, pulling her back down to him. She allowed herself a moment to close her eyes and rest her head against his chest. His strong, steady heartbeat pounded in her ear. His body's warmth enticed her to stay longer, to forget the world outside. They'd found a place of comfort amid fear, suffering, and death. She'd heard elders speak of moments of peace during painful and challenging times but had never experienced one until now.

Though she didn't understand all the Sandamedan Army's rules, Kiri knew Mattos should not have left his men. Young men could usually be counted on to break rules in order to mate, but their time had ended. He had responsibilities, and she had Ulek. Besides, the storm would not keep the Charpans away forever—Mattos had said so himself.

Kiri sat up again. "We should go."

"Yes," Mattos agreed, reaching for his clothes.

Kiri waited for him by the door. When he stepped beside her wearing his full armor, Mattos placed a hand on her shoulder and bent to kiss her. "Don't come back to the gate," he said as he opened the door.

Without responding, Kiri sprinted into the heavy rain. She let her body, which seemed to have a knowledge all its own, take her back to the house where Ulek waited.

The rain did not pound her as heavily as it had before. Kiri turned her face up to it, feeling every drop as they splashed against her skin. She experienced her surroundings in a way she hadn't in many months. She felt as alive as ever. She wanted to cry and laugh at the same time, but mostly she wanted to keep living.

The house where she'd been staying appeared before her, and Kiri pushed open the door. She found everyone where she'd left them. The dead Galeedan man lay where he had fallen, the blanket Kiri had used to cover him now stained with blood. The wounded Galeedan boy lay on the floor, his head in his mother's lap. The little girl cradled her baby brother while Ulek sat in the corner stroking Brense's fur. With her spirit whole again, it felt like an entire day had passed since she'd stumbled out of the house, but to the others, very little time must have passed.

When Ulek met her gaze, exclaiming "Kiri," her eyes filled with tears. Now, when she could feel everything, she couldn't deny it. She, avenger of her people, loved the son of one of the men who had murdered Forest people.

Chapter 47

MATTOS

Mattos took two steps in the rain before he realized he'd forgotten the torch. He continued without hesitation. It hadn't been much help, allowing him only to see the wall of water before him. Kiri hadn't led him far from the gate, and he headed in its direction. The near blindness and deafness brought on by the downpour afforded him a surreal isolation. Death and suffering seemed far away. For now, there was only darkness, the roar of water, and the lingering memory of Kiri's touch. He wished he and Kiri could have stayed in that shack, where they'd found ephemeral refuge from death, cruelty, and memories neither wanted to face.

In the moments they'd spoken under the platform, and when they'd lain together in the shack, he'd revealed his true self to her. It felt good to be seen. And he'd sensed her true self also—her trauma, grit, and the sorrow she tried so hard to hide.

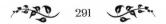

The torches beneath the gate soon appeared like a row of lighthouses leading him to shore. He stepped under the platform to find Alistes still sitting, in the same place Mattos had left him.

"No word, Falcon," Alistes said.

Mattos nodded. He hadn't been gone long and didn't appear to have been missed. He headed to the shacks for the wounded. He heard the groans even through the pounding rain. When he reached the open doorway of the closest shack, the smell halted him in his steps. Blood, sweat, wine, urine, and shit had all mingled into a stench unlike anything he had encountered. He took one more deep breath of the clean air outside before ducking through the entrance.

Two torches illuminated the men who lay on the dirt floor. Some groaned while others labored for breath. Two were unnaturally quiet. One of Elmaturis's soldiers crouched by a prone figure, offering him water. When he saw Mattos, he rose. "Falcon."

"Carry on," Mattos said, backing out through the doorway.

He found Mekindu in the third shack. His Owl lay bareheaded against the wall, his teeth gritted against the pain. A bloody bandage encircled his right leg just above the knee. Someone had placed a dirty cloth under his head in what must have been an attempt to offer comfort.

"You'll have quite a scar to show off," Mattos said, crouching.

Mekindu grimaced. "It's good of you to come see me, Falcon." Sweat beaded along his forehead and upper lip. "Balen?"

"Odern called his name."

Mekindu's gaze turned inward as he took two deep breaths. "It's letting up," he murmured.

At first, Mattos thought Mekindu spoke nonsense. Then he realized the rain had started to abate. He studied the bloody bandage, remembering how Oistin's injury had turned black. It was still too soon to know if the Charpans had used poisoned arrows.

"Omeldor bandaged it himself." Mekindu grunted, following his gaze. "He says it's clean." He took a deep breath, eyes closed, then struggled to stand. "I was just resting," he said. "I'm ready to fight."

"No, Mekindu. You're injured and—"

"Please, Falcon," Mekindu interjected. "I know the odds, and I'd rather die fighting than be killed by a Charpan while lying here."

Mattos couldn't argue. He'd make the same decision. He grabbed Mekindu's hand and hauled him to his feet before tugging the other man's arm around his neck. They walked slowly toward the gate with Mekindu leaning on Mattos. When they reached their unit, Orston hurried forward to take Mattos's place.

"I'll return soon," Mattos said. Then he went in search of Harrier Diakiris to learn their orders.

The cloth that covered the lower half of Mattos's face couldn't block the acrid stench of sulfur. Diakiris had tasked him and his men with preparing their most gruesome weapons—weapons so cruel they were only used in defense. Mattos crouched with those who ground up sulfur. Some of the men tossed handfuls of sawdust into sacks. Resin and sulfur would be added to the sacks, which would then be soaked with oil. Once soldiers lit these sacks on fire, they would hurl them down on the invading Charpans. Clay bowls had been carried up to the platform to be used as firepits. Mattos had always considered these sorts of weapons cowardly; far better to face a man blade to blade. But not now. Not when a few hundred soldiers protecting innocents faced a horde five thousand strong. He doubted they had enough incendiaries to make much difference anyway. Few in Cybelon had been able to afford oil, so they hadn't found much of it. The soldiers had ransacked wine merchants' stores in search of the sulfur they used to keep wine from turning to vinegar. They'd had little luck and had only found enough supplies to give a few Charpans an agonizing death.

Intent on his work, Mattos gave a start when he realized a man crouched beside him. He turned to his unexpected companion. It was Elmaturis.

"It's not right the way the Osprey gives you the most dangerous or dirty tasks," Elmaturis said, as if continuing a conversation. "It's not your fault Darius died. There's always risk of death in battle, and from what I hear, Darius got himself killed."

Too taken aback to respond, Mattos set the grinding stone aside. In the time he and Elmaturis had been stationed together, Elmaturis had spoken to him only out of necessity or to make snide comments. He'd certainly never heard Elmaturis speak ill of a member of his own class.

Elmaturis kept his eyes on the ground. "I think you're a brave man, a good officer. I just thought you should know that." Then he stood and walked away, not waiting for a response.

Mattos could only stare after him.

Stars shone even as the black sky faded to deep blue. Dawn would be upon them soon. From beyond the wall, the Charpans, who had been eerily quiet during the storm, began calling to each other. Several men froze when they heard the guttural shouts. The shouting grew louder before transforming into a chant that sounded like the entire horde picked it up.

Mattos had learned to speak Charpan as a boy, and though the western dialect differed from the eastern dialect he'd been taught, he could still make out the words.

Sky God, we live to praise you
Our lifeblood flows with your rain
We breathe your wind
Let us honor you with victory
Behold our offering

Soldiers crowded the wall, trying to peer through tiny holes and niches created in the battle. One or two Owls ordered their men back to work, but most didn't bother. They'd finished their work, and none of the officers showed concern about the rush to see what the Charpans did. Mattos pushed his way to the platform's ladder, the jostling men giving way when they saw his crested helmet. When he climbed onto the platform, he joined the archers who stared over the wall. The Charpans stood just out of firing range, the lightening sky and torches illuminating the tangled mass of man and beast. Three figures stood apart from the horde, their backs to the wall. The chant grew louder as a man came forward, leading a stallion that tossed its head as if in impatience. It was small, like all Charpan horses, but perfectly formed with a black coat that had an almost blue sheen.

One of the three waiting figures accepted the horse's reins before drawing a dagger. The stallion threw back its head and whinnied, as if sensing the man's intent. The sky rapidly grew lighter as more stars disappeared. A pink and orange glow appeared along the horizon.

Common soldiers couldn't speak Charpan, so Mattos translated the chant for the men gathered around him. "They're sacrificing a horse," he explained.

The chant had reached the apex of its volume. The Charpan with the dagger raised it above his head, enabling those nearby to see the blade. When he turned toward the brightening horizon, the entire horde followed his gaze, bearing an expression of anticipation. Only one Charpan did not stare into the distance. The man who had led the stallion to its killer stepped forward, pressing his face against its cheek. He stood there a moment, grasping a fistful of the horse's mane. His shoulders shook almost imperceptibly, as if he wept. As quickly as he had embraced his horse, the man stepped back and squared his shoulders, joining his companions in awaiting the dawn.

The horizon deepened to a rich orange with pink and yellow rays extending outward. Then it appeared: a golden slice of sun peeking over the earth. The Charpan with the dagger moved so fast Mattos didn't see the blade enter flesh. One moment the stallion tossed its head back in alarm, and the next it collapsed. The chanting stopped so abruptly that numerous soldiers close to Mattos startled.

Whatever beauty there had been in the morning's first light and the chanted prayer dissolved into barbaric cries and spilled blood. The magnificent stallion that had stood so proudly a short time ago was torn apart. Charpans fought for the chance to dip their hands in the horse's still-gushing blood and then press them against their tunics and faces. Mattos wondered if the man who had given his horse to be sacrificed joined in the fracas or if grief held him back.

As Mattos turned from the wall, he noticed that many of the archers gazed at him expectantly, as if waiting for him to explain further what the enemy did. "It won't be long now," he said as he walked back to the ladder. He had barely stepped off the bottom rung onto the courtyard when he heard the drums.

Chapter 48

MATTOS

It was not the rhythmic booming of before, but a wild, discordant sound. Mattos froze a moment before hurrying to his men, pushing his way through the soldiers rushing the last of the incendiaries onto the platform. Officers needlessly shouted commands. Their defensive positions had been determined and communicated to the soldiers earlier that night. The units adopted solid block formations, ultimately forming one large block in the courtyard facing the gates. There were not enough men to guard every wall without being spread too thin, so the Galeedans had finally been abandoned. If the Charpans scaled or broke through the other three walls, the people hiding in the town would have no one to defend them. When Mattos thought of Kiri facing an ax-wielding Charpan, he pushed the image from his mind. He could do nothing for her. Those kinds of thoughts could undo a soldier, and he needed his wits about him now.

In each unit, experienced soldiers stood in the front, with the youngest and most inexperienced second, and the oldest and most experienced in the back. Like all Falcons, Mattos stood at the back of his unit. This enabled him to watch his soldiers, assess the situation, and urge them to advance if need be. Mattos studied each of his men. All were covered in blood, sweat, and mud. Most had dark circles under their bloodshot eyes from lack of sleep. A stench beyond the usual smell of sweaty men emanated from them. To Mattos's surprise, none appeared afraid. They stood quietly, facing the gate with grim expressions. They were probably too exhausted for nerves. Perhaps they had become so accustomed to battle in one day's time that they were now going through the motions, without thought to the outcome. Or maybe they were resigned to the outcome.

Mattos wanted to address them, but what could he say? They were already prepared to die fighting, which is all he could ask of them. He couldn't think of any words that wouldn't make it sound as if he were just echoing the speeches of heroes in songs and poems. He could only stand silently with them.

Soon, Charpan war cries accompanied the wild drumming. A soldier on the platform gave a signal, and the Sandamedan archers let loose a volley. The Charpans sent their own volley. The soldiers clustered together, their shields forming a protective shell over each unit. Two short bursts sounded from the company's trumpets, and the men on the platform tossed the incendiaries onto the enemy. Mattos gritted his teeth against the resulting screams from men and horses. He'd seen what burning oil and resin could do to dead flesh but had never witnessed it thrown on a living creature, and he didn't wish to now. The incendiaries gone, the men on the platform hurried down the ladder to rejoin their units.

The gates fell away piece by piece as ax blades appeared where there had been sturdy wood only moments before. The wooden walls swayed under the onslaught of the entire horde. With a crack like thunder, the gates burst open. Charpan riders galloped into the town, only this time no rope made them falter. They rode around the pile of fallen riders and horses.

As soon as the riders entered the town, those still outside ceased firing their arrows for fear of hitting their own men. The imperial archers continued to fire theirs, but now they aimed at the riders who had already passed through the gates.

Within moments, Mattos's unit engaged in battle. He had the strange sensation he and his men had never stopped fighting the Charpans from their first onslaught, that everything that had happened in between—the rain, lying with Kiri, visiting Mekindu, preparing the incendiaries—had been a dream.

A screaming rider engulfed in flames galloped into the courtyard on a black stallion, soldiers and riders alike giving way before him. It seemed strange to Mattos that though the flames leaped high on the man, the horse seemed unharmed. Then he saw the burning rider sink an ax into a soldier's neck before seeking out another victim. The man burned, yet he showed no pain. He didn't even appear to be injured. When the rider next swung his ax, Mattos saw that orange flames licked at it like firewood. He sucked in his breath. Metal did not hold fire, and human flesh could not touch it without pain and injury, yet the burning rider with his horrifying weapon defied both of those facts. It felt like he studied the burning rider for a long time, when in truth Mattos could focus only a moment on him before he turned his attention back to his men, shouting at them to stand their ground.

Orston went down first. Then Alistes, who sank to his knees coughing up blood. Ladius died on his feet after a Charpan blade almost severed his head. Then Mattos lost track of who stood and who fell.

The walls near Mattos's unit swayed under the weight of Charpans trying to bring them down. Splinters of wood sprayed the ground as axes cut openings in the walls. The narrowness of the gates kept the riders from overwhelming the soldiers. Only so many riders could enter at a time, and the soldiers could fight them off before more entered. Once the walls came down, there'd be no holding the riders off.

As his companions sprang forward to meet the attack of three riders, Stavis, a young soldier in Mattos's unit, hung back, staring at the combat as if in a daze.

"Forward!" Mattos screamed. "Forward!"

Stavis didn't move.

A soldier who had been behind Stavis grabbed his shoulder and screamed in his face, yet Stavis didn't react. The man who had grabbed his shoulder spun to defend himself against a rider with a blood-spattered face.

Cursing, Mattos pushed past several of his men. When he reached Stavis, he struck his back with the flat of his sword. "Forward, forward!" Only then did the young man seem to awaken from his trance. He ran to aid the soldiers ahead of him.

A brown stallion screamed as a soldier's blade sliced into its right foreleg. The horse went down headfirst, throwing his rider forward. Mattos raised his sword just as the man slammed into him. They hit the ground hard, with Mattos on the bottom. When he tried to strike the rider, he found his sword arm was trapped between them. With alarm bordering on panic, Mattos jerked his body upward, freeing himself. Then Mattos realized his sword was buried in the rider's gut. The rider must have fallen onto it. Mattos pulled the blade free, staring at the dying rider with dumbfounded relief. He rose to his feet, still staring at the rider lying before him, when an inhuman cry sounded from close behind him. Mattos spun around and saw the burning rider, his flame-covered ax raised high, galloping straight for him.

Chapter 49

KIRI

The screams of dying men and horses and the clanging of metal against metal seemed louder this time. Kiri hugged her knees, breathing deeply to calm herself. She slipped her hand to her throat to feel the strength of her life pulse.

The day's first light slipped through the cracks in the boarded-up windows, and the illumination given off by the burning candles seemed weak in comparison. Kiri studied the Galeedans around her. The yellow-haired mother sat by her wounded son while her daughter tried to comfort the fussing baby. Not long before, the woman had spoken and Ulek had translated for Kiri, explaining that the wounded boy would live. The Galeedan father still lay on the floor where he had died, a blanket covering him. Ulek sat next to Brense with the weapons taken from the dead Charpans laid out before him. Whenever the dog whimpered, Ulek ran his fingers over his fur.

The baby's cries grew louder as he tried to squirm out of his sister's arms; she spoke soothingly to him to no avail. The little girl said something to her mother, but the woman gave no indication she'd heard.

Without thinking about her actions, Kiri walked across the room and lifted the baby from his sister's arms. Kiri balanced him on her hip to keep a secure hold on him. The little girl seemed relieved to have someone else take her brother. The Galeedan woman, who had refused to allow Kiri to even touch her son the day before, said nothing.

The baby stopped fussing and stared at Kiri with open curiosity. She'd known he would be soft and warm, but the glittering intelligence in his blue eyes caught her off guard. He seemed to look deep inside her, as if he could hear and understand her thoughts. In that moment, as she grasped the power of his young spirit, the thought of seeing his light extinguished with cruelty and bloodshed became unbearable. It occurred to her then that she didn't have to witness his death or the deaths of Ulek and the other Galeedans. She had merely to go outside and open her wrists with her knife. She would die anyway, but she didn't have to allow vicious men to determine how. What good could come of her enduring another slaughter? Surely it would be better to die by her will than someone else's.

Kiri had barely entertained the thought before she shook her head against it. Her spirit had its own light, and it was not her place to choose when it would travel to the spirit world. She pressed her face against the baby's head and inhaled his scent. If she let the blood flow from her wrists, she would be abandoning this child, Ulek, and the rest of the Galeedan family. She recalled Mattos's words the night she had gazed at the figures carved in stone. *To run would be worse than death.* She lowered the now-quiet baby into his sister's lap and straightened to meet Ulek's gaze. She couldn't abandon these people by taking her own life, but she could die defending them.

Still meeting Ulek's eyes, Kiri crossed the room and crouched before the weapons he had laid out before him. They had two axes, two bows, forty-three arrows, and a sword as long as her body. One ax would have been light to the Charpans, a weapon they could hold with one hand. Kiri lifted the smaller ax, the only weapon she could wield, and stood.

"Kiri, what are you doing?"

She didn't answer Ulek. He would try to stop her. She strode out the door, slamming it behind her. The mud reached her ankles and sucked at her feet with every step. The place appeared deserted. The Charpans had not made it into the town, and the Galeedans still hid in their houses, yet the sound of fighting reverberated. The ax grew heavier with every step, the handle digging into her palms.

Though the screams of dying men sounded from every direction, Kiri could discern where it was loudest. She ran, passing the well where she had gathered water only one day before, with the mud splashing her legs and dress. She ran down a row of houses, turned a corner, and found the battle.

The Charpans had pushed and cut their way through one of the walls. An opening large enough for five men walking abreast now existed. Riders burst through the opening as if being born into the world with the sole purpose of blood and violence. The soldiers met them with their own violence, and the result was death. They fell into each other as if they longed to die in battle. No one ran. No one held back.

Kiri froze, remembering the last time she'd seen imperial soldiers in the act of killing. She'd seen them the day she'd led them to the Charpans who had stolen their food, but then she'd been far away and hadn't watched for long. No, the last time she'd truly seen imperial soldiers in the act of killing, she'd been in Mar Dun. Only then they hadn't been fighting Charpans; they'd been fighting her people. They'd been fighting *her*. The thought of fighting beside them shook her resolve. She closed her eyes, thinking of Ulek and the baby she'd held. She could do this. Kiri opened her eyes and studied the imperial soldiers. There weren't many left. Their bodies littered the ground alongside riders and horses. Most still fought at the gate, while smaller groups fought at the openings the Charpans had made. A soldier with a green crested helmet came into view, and Kiri recognized Mattos without seeing his face. A memory of his scent came to her, then he disappeared in the battle. Kiri lifted her ax and ran toward the spot where she'd seen him.

A desperate cry cut through the screams and clanging metal. "Stop! Wait!"

Kiri spun around to see Ulek running toward her, carrying a Charpan blade he could barely lift.

With a shriek of rage and horror, Kiri ran back to him. She didn't stop when they reached each other. Instead, she grasped his tunic at the neck and hauled him to the side of a house and the illusion of protection it offered. "Why did you come?" she half yelled, half sobbed.

"I came to fight with you." Ulek panted. "I couldn't let you go alone."

"No! Go back. You—" Kiri froze. Where could he go? The house had already failed to protect them once. Kiri knew now the Charpans would not spare children. Before she knew what she did, Kiri pulled Ulek to her, clasping him so hard it must have been difficult for him to breathe.

Ulek returned her embrace, and they stood there holding each other, still clinging to their weapons with one hand, while nearby men struggled to kill each other. Tears gathered in Kiri's eyes as she buried her head where Ulek's neck and shoulder met. It didn't matter where the boy hid. The Charpans would find and kill him before the day's end. The most she could do was to keep Ulek close to her so he wouldn't die alone. She brushed aside the curls that fell past his brows, gazing into Ulek's gray eyes. They were so much like his father's. Nothing would ever change what his father had done to her people, or what she had done to his father. It would always be between them, yet at this moment, it didn't matter. Kiri placed her hand on Ulek's shoulder. "Ulek, my brother," she whispered, "we will go to the spirit world together."

Chapter 50

MATTOS

The giant black silhouette rode toward Mattos. Orange flames leaped over the empty darkness where the rider's face should have been. The blazing ax hit Mattos's shield with such force he almost dropped to his knees.

Before Mattos could recover, the ax slammed into his shield again, sending painful vibrations through the handle. It was the most powerful blow he had ever received. He dropped to one knee before stumbling back to his feet, just in time to block another ax swing. The stench of burning leather filled his nostrils as he gasped for breath. Mattos looked up, smoke stinging his eyes as he did, to see the ax coming straight at him. He jerked his shield up to stop the blade.

The strength of the blow forced Mattos backward, the deep mud making it even more difficult to hold his ground. Then the same inhuman cry he'd heard the creature utter before sounded again. In a kind of frantic desperation, Mattos dropped the shield, grabbed the rider's forearm, and pulled with strength born of fear and rage.

The creature still leaned off his mount at a vulnerable angle, and Mattos managed to pull him so that only one leg remained atop the horse. Then Mattos felt the burning pain in his palm. Tears streamed down his face as he continued his attempt to haul his opponent down. In the moment before pain forced him to let go, he saw his enemy fall from the horse. The riderless stallion galloped into the melee, its black coat gleaming with bloody handprints.

Unharmed, the flame-engulfed creature rose to his full height. He stood almost a head taller than Mattos, with unbelievably broad shoulders. He still held the burning ax in his massive right hand but bore no shield, as if injury were impossible.

The sound that emanated from the creature made the hairs on the back of Mattos's neck stand on end. The laugh sounded almost human, yet it reverberated unnaturally.

Mattos gripped his sword even as he knew it could not protect him. The short Sandamedan swords were meant for precise stabbing, not for withstanding the onslaught of a flaming battle-ax. His discarded shield lay several paces away, too far for retrieval. All of this went through Mattos's mind in the time it took to blink. He kept his blistering left hand in a loose fist.

The creature grasped the ax with both massive hands as it charged.

Mattos ducked and jumped aside to avoid the ax's swings. Despite the creature's superior strength and size, Mattos dodged its attacks. He wondered if the creature had poor vision. Even as he kept his eyes on his attacker, Mattos became aware that far more Charpans surrounded them. From the periphery of his vision, he saw them riding past and knew they must have forced their way through another opening. Charpans and soldiers fought close by, but all avoided the burning creature.

A dying Charpan collapsed at his feet, and Mattos had to step on his chest to leap out of the way of the swinging ax. Then a riderless gray horse galloped between him and the creature and caught Mattos on the shoulder, knocking him on his back. Mattos didn't feel the impact of the horse or the ground. Rising to one knee, he saw a fallen soldier lying an arm's length away, the handle of his shield still clasped in his left hand.

The horse had knocked the creature aside as well, and it regained its footing as Mattos reached for the shield. All sounds were muffled; the shouts, horse screams, clanking metal, and Charpan drums all seemed far away. Distant horns Mattos hadn't noticed before blasted, incongruent with the wild drumming. Even so, he heard the distinct snap of a finger breaking as he tore the shield from the dead man.

He had just lifted the shield when the ax slammed into it. Still ducking under the shield, Mattos jabbed his sword into the creature's left calf, just above his boot.

The creature let out a half-pained, half-enraged roar with the same eerie vibrations Mattos had heard before. It wore thick leather trousers as all Charpans did, but the Sandamedan blade had cut through the leather and into what felt like flesh. Mattos stared at his red-soaked sword; the creature could bleed. Mattos got to his feet as his opponent stumbled backward. He was faster than the burning creature, and the leg wound might slow it more.

When the ax swung again, Mattos bent at the waist, letting it pass overhead, and drove his shield into his enemy's arm, forcing it into a deeper follow-through. Then he stabbed the creature's exposed side with all his strength. He felt give, but the sword couldn't pierce what lay under the leather. He looked directly at the creature's burning face. Smoke filled his nostrils and the flames danced dangerously close to his eyes. Despite the featureless black silhouette, Mattos had the sensation his enemy met his stare. *You injured me, but you can't beat me,* the gaze seemed to say. As if on instinct, Mattos lifted his sword from the creature's side and slammed the pommel where the nose should have been.

The head snapped back. Mattos heard something crack before the creature shoved him backward.

Having gained enough space to use his ax, the burning creature charged again, swinging wildly.

Mattos jumped aside, avoiding the ax swings, and slammed into the creature from the side. He attacked the face again, this time with his sword blade. The world shifted. He didn't realize they'd hit the ground until he moved to the side and found himself lying in mud.

Beside him, the creature started to rise, letting out a vibrating groan as it did.

Then Mattos pounced on the creature. Flames danced around him as he pummeled the burning blackness where the face should be. Somehow, he had lost his sword and now used his fist. Blood and burns formed on his knuckles, but the battle energy flowing through his veins kept him from feeling pain. At some point, the creature stopped moving. Even its ragged breathing ceased.

Mattos stared at the burning heap he sat upon, not knowing if he'd killed it. One could only kill a living thing, and if the creature had never truly lived, then it couldn't die.

He didn't have time to find out. A moment later, he had retrieved his sword and battled a different rider. When the man fell, clutching the gaping wound at his throat, Mattos scanned the battle for officers but saw no crested helmets. Chaos reigned. The Charpans surrounded them, and still more poured through the gates and the openings they'd cut through. Mattos screamed orders at the soldiers near him, more than half of them belonging to different units. He urged them into formation to create a unified defense.

He'd managed to organize about fifty soldiers into a square formation when he saw a flash of indigo in the corner of his eye. He spun in that direction and saw Kiri and Ulek, armed with an ax and sword, running toward the battle. As Mattos stood frozen, unable to accept what he saw, a Charpan on foot charged at them.

Kiri shoved Ulek out of the way, then dove under the Charpan's sword. She hit the ground hands first and rolled onto her feet, still clutching the ax.

Though they no longer ran to the battle, Kiri and Ulek were getting closer and Mattos realized he sprinted toward them. The Charpan turned on Kiri again. With a sickening lurch in his stomach, Mattos knew he wouldn't reach them in time.

When the Charpan attacked again, Kiri sprang backward. She lost her footing and collapsed into a sitting position in the mud. The Charpan raised his sword over her as Ulek ran toward them, struggling to lift his own sword above his waist.

Kiri scrambled to all fours and reached for the Charpan's lead leg, clutching his heel and driving her shoulder into the inside of his knee. At the same time, Ulek slammed into him.

The Charpan fell. It was all Kiri needed. In what appeared to be one fluid motion, she sprang to her feet and brought the ax down on her enemy's throat.

Mattos reached her just as the Charpan let out his death cry, the man's blood spattering his greaves.

"Kiri!"

Without responding, Kiri wiped the bloody ax on her fallen enemy's clothing.

Ulek stared at Mattos, still clasping the hilt of the Charpan sword he could barely lift.

"Kiri!" Mattos repeated, grasping her upper arm.

Finally, she turned her black eyes on him, her mouth set in a grim line.

"Kiri, Ulek, get out of here!" Mattos shouted. "Run!"

Recognition and an expression of calmness spread across Kiri's face. Speaking deliberately, she replied, "To run would be worse than death."

Mattos gaped at Kiri. She'd repeated the words he'd spoken that night in the garden. For a moment, he considered arguing with her. Then, tightening his grip on her arm, he said, "So be it," and hauled her toward the soldiers still standing. He called out to Ulek to follow, but the boy already ran after them.

Time slowed. Mattos no longer felt pain or exhaustion. He observed his body dispassionately as he ran. He killed two Charpans on the way back to his soldiers. Then he fought among them again, and Kiri and Ulek crouched at the center. His world shrank. Only Kiri, Ulek, and the surviving soldiers mattered.

Memories of voices came to Mattos: his family laughing on the beach while he and his sisters played, being tutored, Marenda crying in panic, "It's too early!" Layna's sighs as they lay together, then her voice, as clear as if she stood beside him, "Why won't you fight for me?" He almost turned to look. He realized without emotion that he hadn't just failed Layna and Marenda, but he'd failed himself. He could fight a battle, but he had lacked the courage to fight in life. Instead, he'd let it be decided for him.

His focus shifted, and the sound of the horns he'd heard before came to him. Louder now, and they seemed to battle the wild drumming. The Charpans had pulled back. Those inside the town retreated. The horns sounded again, and this time Mattos recognized them. That moment when all pain and exhaustion had ceased, he had died without realizing it. The horns he'd heard were the horns of Odern, and he fought in Odern's army now.

Mattos scanned the town. It appeared he was still in Cybelon—an illusion he had carried with him from life? One platform ladder stood in place. Mattos ran to it and climbed, mindful of the missing and broken rungs. The platform swayed under his weight. Much of the wall and the platform's support were missing now. Mattos grabbed the sharpened point of the wall and gazed out. Tens of thousands of imperial soldiers swarmed the tengish as more appeared on the horizon.

When the horns of Odern sounded again, tears slid down Mattos's face. Eagle Isandor had done the impossible. He had reached Cybelon, and he had brought his army with him.

Chapter 51

MATTOS

The Charpans had to retreat soon. The Sandamedan Army greatly outnumbered them, and drawn-out battles were not part of tengish battle tactics. A horde hit hard and fast, then rode off. It would play a game of attack and retreat for the purpose of exhausting and frustrating a larger enemy.

Mattos ordered the few uninjured survivors to tend to the wounded. With Omeldor dead, they could do little for the seriously injured. Mattos and a young soldier carried a man to the center of the courtyard and laid him down next to a man missing three fingers. Those who could be safely moved were placed side by side in the courtyard to make treatment easier for the army physicians when they arrived. The Hawk's body lay beside them, his eyes closed and his hands folded over his chest.

When Mattos straightened up, he caught sight of a familiar crested helmet. Hurrying to the man's side, he looked down into Lucen's empty stare. Blood covered the ground beneath Lucen's body. A quick inspection revealed a Charpan blade had cut deeply into the inside of his right leg, severing the major artery. An arrow protruded from his left leg, and he gripped his bloodstained sword.

"You fought till the end," Mattos said as he closed his friend's eyes. "Now you fight with Odern." He knew grief would soon replace the numbness he felt.

As Mattos walked away, his thoughts still on Lucen, he soon found himself almost on top of the burning creature he'd killed earlier. The flames had gone out, leaving only a faceless, black-clad figure. Mattos gazed in awe, half expecting the creature to come back to life. Crouching, he poked at what should have been the face but felt leather. Surprised, he grasped the top of the creature's head and tugged, pulling off a large hood that had covered the head.

A man, a regular man.

Mattos had beaten the Charpan to death. The dead man's broken and disfigured face would have been unrecognizable to those who'd known him: the nose smashed, a horrid gash where the sword had cut him. Mattos shuddered. He had done this to a living man.

A piece of carved wood stuck out from between his teeth. How had the man not been burned? As Mattos examined the hood, he realized burned leather made up the outer portion, and a rough woven fabric that hadn't been burned made up the inner. The hood had two small eye holes that must have been difficult to see out of.

"Falcon?"

Mattos had been so focused on the body and strange hood that he hadn't heard the man approach. When he looked up, he found himself staring at an Osprey he'd never seen before.

"Osprey," he said, rising to his feet and standing at attention. Beyond the Osprey's shoulder, he saw soldiers pouring through the gates. They had won.

The tall Osprey looked about thirty. His suntanned face wore an expression of bewilderment. "Your name, Falcon."

"Mattos, sir."

The Osprey studied Mattos for a moment, his dark eyes lingering on the blood. His own armor was relatively clean, with only dust marring his appearance. "Here," he said, removing his waterskin and holding it out to Mattos. "You look like you could use it."

Mattos silently thanked the gods when he tasted the water. If the man who had offered it hadn't been an Osprey, he might have drunk the whole thing. He handed it back, wiping his lips. "Thank you, sir. I am grateful. How are you here? We thought you were too far."

"We were already marching to your aid when we received your plea for help," the Osprey said. "The Eagle suspected you wouldn't reach the capital in time. He pulled us out of the Forest lands and marched us here. He wasn't going to risk a garrison and thousands of citizens being slaughtered."

"I'm grateful he didn't."

The Osprey studied the dead Charpan at their feet. "A burner," he said.

"I didn't realize he was human at first," Mattos said. "I thought he was a creature from the land of the dead. Then I killed him, but I wasn't sure he was truly dead."

The Osprey regarded Mattos with an expression of amazed respect. "You killed a burner? There aren't many soldiers who can say that." He glanced back at the Charpan. "They're meant to terrify their enemies. They wear fabric resistant to flame, then they put leather on top of it, cover their upper bodies and weapons with resin, and light themselves on fire. They have whistles"—he jerked his chin toward the carved wood between the Charpan's teeth—"to make inhuman sounds."

"If he wanted to terrify me, it worked," Mattos replied.

Before they could say anything else, five officers approached, the one in the middle wearing the three-crested helmet of an Eagle.

Mattos drew in his breath.

The Eagle strode forward until he stood in front of Mattos. Despite his average stature, the Eagle was an imposing figure. His hooded black eyes held a sharp intelligence.

"Falcon," the Eagle said, "is this all that's left of the company?"

"Yes, Eagle," Mattos replied.

Eagle Isandor scanned the courtyard as if looking for someone. "Where is the Hawk?"

"The Hawk is dead, sir."

The Eagle turned his sharp eyes back on Mattos. "Where is the highest-ranking officer?"

Mattos met the Eagle's gaze. "I am the only officer, sir."

Chapter 52

KIRI

The army swarmed around Cybelon's walls. Kiri didn't know a number high enough to describe them; she could only have said they were like ants in a colony. She'd never truly grasped the Charpans' numbers because she'd never seen the full horde. Looking at the imperial soldiers, she hadn't known so many people existed in the world, and these were only strong young men. There would be even more women, children, and older people back in their villages.

Ulek excitedly shifted on the platform beside her. "Look, Kiri! The Charpans won't come back now. The entire army is here."

Kiri barely heard him. She stared at the scene below them. Some Galeedans had gathered by the broken gates to cheer the soldiers who were able to enter. Others wept. Most, however, hurried about assisting the wounded. Dead soldiers and horses covered the ground, though there were no Charpan bodies. The Charpans had taken their dead with them when they'd retreated.

Blood had turned the mud red. Wounded men screamed as they were lifted from the ground. Severed limbs were left lying where they fell. Many of the buildings were burned with the doors dismantled to be used as shields.

The imperial soldiers outside the walls had begun to dig graves, put up tents, start fires, and organize their camp. Vultures landed near the dead. They were chased from dead soldiers but were left alone to feed on horses.

Lowering to sit, Kiri leaned against the wall and drew her knees to her chest. She was exhausted, filthy, and in shock that she still lived, yet her thoughts lingered on the western army. Her own people were like the wolf, strong and intelligent, but their survival depended on controlling their numbers. A she-wolf wouldn't breed if she couldn't feed her pups. Yet, the non-Forest people let their numbers grow so that they had to plant their food, raise animals, and invade other lands to keep from starving. *So many.* The imperial soldiers had prevented the slaughter of innocent people. Because of them, Ulek, the baby she'd held, and so many other Galeedans lived. They'd driven the Charpans away, and if the Charpans returned, the soldiers would fight them off again. Their might and numbers both comforted and horrified Kiri. They represented protection from the horde, but when they attacked the Forest people… It didn't matter that the soldiers didn't know the forest or have the heart of Forest warriors. There were too many of them. They were the salvation of the Galeedans and the doom of her people.

A firm hand on her shoulder brought Kiri back to the present. "That's him," Ulek whispered, awe in his voice. "That's Eagle Isandor."

The middle-aged man Ulek pointed to stood in the center of the courtyard surrounded by soldiers with crested helmets. Unlike any other soldier Kiri had seen, his own helmet bore three crests that fell to his shoulders. The armor covering his chest and stomach had been shaped to resemble a man's muscles. He wore a green cape that fastened at the shoulders with thick medallions, giving him a powerful, broad-shouldered appearance. His hooded eyes appeared like slits in his angular face. Deep grooves ran from his nose to the corners of his mouth, which he pressed into a grim line.

Even from where Kiri sat, she sensed an energy about him, as if he had a more powerful spirit than most. An involuntary shudder passed through her as she gazed down at the Eagle—the last man she had to kill. Unlike the other men she'd been commanded to kill, he hadn't been in Mar Dun, yet he frightened her the most. His very stance indicated a strength the others hadn't had. The protective spirits of Mar Dun had sent him to her so she could kill him. They had given this gift because the Forest people depended so much on his death. With their greater numbers, the imperial army wouldn't fear the Forest people. They needed to learn the Forest people could kill even their most protected leaders. Once they understood that, they would not be so quick to attack.

As three soldiers stepped away from the Eagle, Mattos came into view. Kiri's chest loosened. *He's alive.* Relief she didn't want to admit to surged through her. Unlike the Eagle and most of the soldiers he'd brought with him, Mattos was covered in blood and dirt. He'd removed his helmet, revealing a dirty and sweaty face.

It seemed the Eagle asked questions, and Mattos gave brief replies. It made no difference that their voices carried to the platform, for they spoke Sandamedan. Then the Eagle turned toward the platform and met her gaze. Without looking away, he spoke, and Mattos's answer included "Ulek" and "Kiri."

Kiri flinched when she heard her name.

The Eagle continued to stare, offering no greeting or acknowledgment. Then he nodded, as if to himself, and turned his back to her.

Chapter 53

KIRI

"Where are you going?"

Kiri turned at the sound of Ulek's voice, her hand on the door handle. "I'm going to see Anwyn."

Ulek didn't move from where he sat on the floor. After the Galeedan woman had stitched Brense up, she'd placed a blanket in the corner and laid him on it. Since the Charpans had been driven off, the dog had barely moved and Ulek refused to leave his side. He spent long stretches of time absently running his fingers though the gray fur, while Brense would beat his tail against the floor once or twice before letting it rest.

After a moment, Ulek nodded, his expression still solemn. "I'm glad she lived. Please give her my greetings."

Kiri slipped outside into the clear bright day. The ankle-deep mud had already begun to dry. Women chatted as they gathered water at the well, while their children chased each other in the village square. Some people seemed to walk with no purpose other than to enjoy being outside. They acted as if they hadn't almost died one day ago.

The path to the front courtyard soon grew crowded with villagers hurrying to and fro with tools and supplies. One large man carried a pile of wood that looked like it had once been the wall of a shack.

The sounds of men calling to each other grew louder, and Kiri stepped out into the courtyard. The town walls had been repaired. Debris covered the ground in a few places where shacks and small houses had once stood. She couldn't tell if the structures had burned down or if, having been already damaged, they'd been torn down for materials. The ground, which had once been packed flat, was now uneven. The bodies, severed limbs, armor, and weapons had been removed. The gates remained open, revealing the army camped outside. Soldiers entered and exited the town as they went about their business.

As she walked along the courtyard, Kiri noticed the tiny shack where she and Mattos had mated had been destroyed. Nothing remained but the clay fireplace covered in ash, bits of straw, and charred wood. Anwyn's shelter might have been destroyed too. Even if it hadn't, Kiri wouldn't have recognized it. She walked the perimeter, scanning the face of any woman with a long yellow braid.

After the Charpans had fled, Kiri and Ulek had been walking to the house they shared when Kiri caught sight of Anwyn tugging on the arms of passing soldiers. She'd been begging for news of Mekindu when she met Kiri's gaze. There had been a moment of acknowledgment between them—a relief the other had survived. Then Anwyn turned back to the soldiers, desperate for news, and Kiri and Ulek continued on their way, too exhausted to speak.

A woman's shout rang over the courtyard. "Kiri! Kiri, here!"

Anwyn hurried through the crowd, loose strands from her braid falling in her face. She grasped Kiri's hands. "I was so happy to see you and Ulek safe. A day ago, I thought we all would die, and now . . ." She gestured toward the army camp beyond the open gates.

"I'm happy too. I came to see you."

Anwyn's eyes lit up. "Walk with me," she said, giving a gentle tug before she released Kiri's hands.

As they fell into step, Anwyn asked, "Where will you go when we leave here?"

"To my birth clan."

After a few moments of silence, Anwyn said, "I'm going to Sarpaska to find Thulu the Revered. He believes everyone has worth. There are people who follow him, people he protects." She spoke in an urgent tone. "He doesn't turn anyone away." Anwyn stopped, seizing Kiri's arm. "You and Ulek could come with me."

Kiri could only stare at the other woman, unsure if she'd understood her.

"Our own people left Ulek and me to die," Anwyn continued. "Your husband cut your face, and your clan cast you out. Maybe your parents will convince your birth clan to take you in, but do you really want to live with people who will despise you? Thulu welcomes outcasts." Anwyn's blue eyes widened with sincerity.

Even after the cruelty she'd witnessed, and the suspicion with which the Galeedans regarded her, Kiri couldn't imagine any people casting out one of their own. Among the Forest people, only murder would warrant such a punishment. The way the Galeedans had treated Anwyn and Ulek seemed just as cruel. Kiri had never known loneliness, or the feeling of not belonging, but Anwyn and Ulek had. Anwyn's words contained hope. Kiri would not survive after she fulfilled the will of her people; she'd known that since she'd left the forest. But Ulek would live, and he would have no one to look after him or care for him. Perhaps Anwyn and this Thulu she spoke of …

"Is this place far? How will you get there?"

Anwyn's intense expression softened into a gentle smile, and she released Kiri's arm. "Mekindu will take me. He is too badly wounded to stay in the army, but he'll live. The army will pay him for his injury. Once he's well enough to travel, we'll leave. I would have gone to join Thulu on my own, but Mekindu said he would follow me wherever I go."

"I'm going to my birth clan," Kiri said, "but Ulek must go with you."

"The boy is attached to you," Anwyn said in surprise. "Would he go without you?"

"My birth clan won't accept a Galeedan. *You* take him," Kiri answered, her voice firm.

After studying Kiri's face a few moments, Anwyn nodded. "We will take him. I promise." Reaching out for Kiri's hand once more, she said, "I've never had many friends. I hope you change your mind and come with us."

Relief washed over Kiri as she headed back to the house Ulek had begun to refer to as "home." She'd wanted to see how Anwyn faired, and to find out if Mekindu lived, and in doing so, she'd found a solution to what would happen to Ulek after she passed into the spirit world. She could pass now in peace, with no worries about the living. Now killing Eagle Isandor was her only concern.

She'd slipped into the army camp last night in search of the Eagle's tent. In the center she'd found it, the tent much larger than the others, guarded by four soldiers. The light of several candles glowed through the fabric. The candles worried her. Kiri had found the tent in the deep of night, when everyone except guards should have been asleep. Yet the Eagle had been awake. If he had been awake last night, would he be awake most nights? It had been impossible not to hope that she might kill the Eagle and sneak out of the camp alive; she could move about unseen and knew how to kill in silence. But Kiri had pushed that hope away. If the Eagle made the slightest sound or gave any struggle, it would alert the guards. No, she shouldn't think of escape or returning home. She would focus on killing Isandor, nothing else.

A soldier stepped into her path, interrupting her thoughts. "Hello, Kiri," Mattos said. All traces of blood and dirt were gone. Bandages covered his knuckles. He seemed weary, but except for the dark circles under his eyes, he looked physically well.

"Hello," Kiri responded.

"I came to see you."

A bittersweet ache formed in the back of Kiri's throat. He'd sought her out. Kiri smiled. Surely a man who'd survived such a battle would be honored by his people and eventually find happiness. She hoped so.

When Kiri didn't respond, Mattos continued, "I spoke with Ulek. I'm sorry his dog was injured."

"Brense is strong, I think he'll live."

"Let me walk with you the rest of the way," Mattos said.

They walked in silence for a bit, and Kiri tried not to wonder what his opinion of her would be once she killed Isandor. He didn't hate her now, and only the present mattered. She had no future.

"I've been promoted to Harrier," Mattos said. "They think I'm a hero."

Kiri heard no trace of bragging in his voice; he sounded wry.

"This is a good thing," Kiri responded.

"It's because I'm the highest-ranking man in my company who didn't die." He gazed into the distance. "My friend Lucen, my superior officers, and most of my soldiers are dead. Most of the men I've lived with for three years are dead."

The force of Kiri's pain and empathy startled her.

They walked in silence until they reached the house. Not knowing if she should invite him inside or bid him goodbye, Kiri leaned against the wall.

Mattos did the same, gazing down at her. "May I visit you again?"

Kiri wondered if he wanted to mate with her again. It wasn't good to take the same night mate more than once, but people had been known to attempt it.

Mattos must have intuited her thoughts because he said, "I do want to lie with you again, Kiri. I'm a man after all.

But I also want to talk to someone who knows me, even if that's all you want. The other officers respect and like me because I'm one of the few company survivors, but they're still strangers."

Kiri hesitated only a moment. She would kill the Eagle tonight. She and Mattos would never see each other again, but right now she felt content knowing he desired her company. He ought to know she wanted his as well, even if, later, he didn't believe anything she told him. "Yes," she said, smiling. "Come tomorrow."

Chapter 54

KIRI

The candles had burned low, their light illuminating only Ulek's and Brense's silhouettes. Kiri gazed down at them, saying her silent goodbyes. Ulek had placed Brense on the bed, and now they slept curled against each other. Kiri ran her fingers over the fur of the dog that had saved their lives. She didn't touch Ulek for fear of waking him. "Goodbye," she mouthed in the Forest language. "May you travel safely to Sarpaska and find happiness there."

She slipped out of the room and crept down the stairs. When she reached the bottom level, she lowered her pack to the floor, crouched in front of it, and pulled out her Forest clothes. It had been so long since she'd worn them. Her eyes brimmed with tears as she traced the leaf embroidery along the neckline of her shirt. Kiri would fulfill the will of her people and spend the last moments of her life dressed as a Forest woman, not in disguise. She changed in the darkness, reveling in the feel of her own clothing, and bound her knife to her lower right leg using leather strips. She loosened the scarf she kept wrapped around her head, letting it fall to the floor. She plaited her hair in the Forest style, with one thick braid falling down her back, and two smaller braids framing her face. This was a style for celebrations and ceremonies, not for hunting or killing. But it seemed fitting to put extra care into her appearance on the last day she would draw breath. She traced her fingers along the scar running down her face. The area stung every time she recalled the sword cutting through her skin. She stuffed her Wanderer clothing into her pack. She tied a strip of leather around her lower leg and tucked the pouch that bore Kordrick's name under it. She'd long since buried the coins she'd found inside to avoid them clinking together. Finally, she grasped the braided cord she'd removed from Orrik's neck and tucked it under the leather strip as well. She left her pack in the corner. By the time anyone in the house woke up, she would already be dead.

As she opened the door, the full moon bathed her in soft light. Kiri closed her eyes as she took a deep breath. Then she closed the door and dashed into the night.

Kiri became a shadow, unseen and unheard. Due to the moonlight, she took a circuitous route to the army camp, avoiding the main road and people who might stand in their doorways or look out windows. She moved cautiously, listening for any sound of movement. She had to remain motionless as a man urinated in a narrow path between two houses. Behind one house, she found two people locked in an embrace as they mated standing against the wall. They gave no indication they saw her as she slipped past.

Moving through the town with such caution seemed to take a long time, but finally Kiri reached the army camp that lay beyond the open gates. As she approached, a minor commotion broke out near the front of the camp. Kiri froze, listening. It sounded like two men arguing. Then she heard other soldiers hurrying toward the argument. She knew she could easily slip past everyone, but tonight she would take no chances. She'd enter the camp from a different location.

Kiri put some distance between herself and the camp before running alongside it. She relished the run and the chance to feel wind in her hair again. She always felt free when she ran. When she'd covered enough ground, she stopped. She faced the camp, catching her breath. As if of its own volition, her body moved so she curled up with the palms of her hands and her forehead pressed to the ground. "Spirits, please." She tried to think of the right words, but only managed *please.* The protective spirits knew what she had to do, what was at stake. Nothing mattered now—not revenge, not her life—but protecting her people. She rose and headed for the camp.

Although she slipped past the guards with ease, she became more vigilant as she entered the camp. With only tents for shelter, the soldiers would be more likely to hear someone pass. Kiri moved between the tents as silently as she'd been trained to move between trees.

Because she hadn't found the Eagle's tent from this direction, it took some time to locate it. Just when she feared she'd gone too far, she found it, with a guard standing at each corner as expected. Relief washed over her when she saw no candle glow from the inside. The Eagle slept. The moonlight put her at a disadvantage, but one side of the tent was cast in complete shadow. Creeping to the tent next to the Eagle's, Kiri gazed at the two guards in her view. They didn't seem concerned about anyone trying to harm the Eagle. Judging by their stance and the way they shifted their weight from foot to foot, they were bored. With another tent so close by, they didn't glance in her direction, focusing outward instead.

With painstaking slowness, Kiri moved toward the Eagle's tent, her stomach close to the ground. Her entire being focused outward, hyperaware of her surroundings. The grass felt cool and damp. Men coughed and stirred in their sleep. The guard to her left scratched his nose. A man snored not too far away to her right. Little by little, she crossed the short distance.

When she reached the tent, she angled herself so she lay alongside it. She reached underneath and pushed up against the taut material, testing its give. It had enough. With her head pressed against the ground, she lifted the material and peeked inside.

Only darkness and silence—no snoring or even breathing. As her eyes adjusted, she made out a table and several chairs, but no bed. In one corner, a rack held the Eagle's armor upright. Hanging fabric divided the small area from the rest of the tent. Kiri pushed against the fabric, squeezed under it, and rolled to her feet.

She stood motionless, listening for any indication she'd been noticed. She heard nothing but the sounds of a camp at night and one guard clearing his throat.

Kiri kept her hand steady as she freed her knife from its sheath. She moved toward the thick fabric dividing the tent, pushing it aside. This room had a fur-covered bed in the corner. Kiri's pulse quickened as she gazed at the long shape under the furs.

As she stepped inside, she noticed a faint light she hadn't seen before. She spun to see a small candle flicker dimly on a table. The light grew brighter as a much larger candle was lit. The hand that had lit the candle reached a bit farther and lit a third candle, revealing a man lounging on a chair beside the table. He gently placed the wick on the table before turning to face Kiri. His hooded eyes stared with intensity. His expression was calm—friendly, even.

"Hello, Kiri," Eagle Isandor said. "I've been waiting for you."

Chapter 55

KIRI

Kiri gripped her knife, ready to spring on Isandor, when she saw three soldiers, weapons drawn, standing behind him. When Isandor had spoken, there had been the heart-pounding energy brought on by alarm. Now, as Kiri stared at the soldiers, something cold flowed through her veins, causing her to go numb. She couldn't move. She could barely feel the knife in her hand.

Isandor continued as if she had accepted an invitation to his tent and he had planned this meeting. "I didn't spend months fighting the Forest people without learning something about them. They don't meet their enemies in open battle. They attack when they can't be seen and then hide. They sneak about. A man doesn't become Eagle of the most powerful army the world has ever known by being stupid. I suspected what you were the moment I first saw you."

The three soldiers and Kiri didn't move as the Eagle spoke. They all stood transfixed, gripping their weapons.

"But I didn't know for sure," Isandor continued, "until my soldiers brought this young man to me."

The hooded eyes shifted to his left, and a figure Kiri hadn't noticed stepped into the light.

"Ulek," Kiri said, but she made no sound. Only her lips moved.

Ulek's eyes were red and swollen. His face appeared unnaturally white in the dim illumination. He looked at Kiri with a blank expression, as if he had never seen her before.

"I woke up," he said in a flat tone, "and you were gone and Brense was whining at the door. I went downstairs just as I heard the door shut. I looked out the window and saw a Forest woman running from the house. I thought it was a dream. Then I saw your pack. I went through it and I found your clothes. I found this." He held out his hand. The wooden ring she'd taken from Orrik rested in his palm in two pieces. It must have broken when Ulek had shoved her against the wall as he'd attacked the Charpan. When she'd grabbed the braided cord, she hadn't bothered to make sure the ring dangled from it. "My mother's ring. It was you. That's why the Charpans captured you the day my father died." His eyes blank, as if in shock, he said, "That's why you were so close to the house. You're the one who killed him."

The numbness settled over her chest. "Yes," Kiri said, her voice almost a whisper. "I killed him. He and other soldiers came to Mar Dun. They killed children, elders. They killed my friends. They did this." She pointed to her scar. "My people killed four. Then they sent me, and I killed Kordrick and Orrik. We killed them all."

Ulek's blank expression transformed into one of horror. He stepped back, staring at Kiri as if she were a vicious beast.

The Eagle said something in Sandamedan. Then the soldiers charged.

Chapter 56

KIRI

The cracks and tiny holes in the walls and roof let in the only light in the windowless room. Yellow beams pierced the darkness, traveling along the dirt floor as the sun moved through the sky. The chain connected to the metal cuff on Kiri's left ankle killed any hope of digging her way out. At first, she'd tried to slam the cuff against the stone wall, only to realize she'd break her ankle long before she broke the cuff.

After she'd been taken prisoner, Kiri had been dragged back to Cybelon and taken to a large house near the gate. Other chains hung from the walls, and Kiri guessed the house to be the place where the townspeople had kept rule breakers.

Once she accepted there was no escape, Kiri lay unmoving on the floor with no blanket or pillow. Three days had passed since she'd been captured with nothing for her to do but think of how she'd failed her people. Not only would the Sandamedans not fear the Forest people, but they would hate them more than ever. One torturous thought came to her repeatedly: *What if they retaliate*? Their leader's death would have caused fear, grief, and alarm. There would have been confusion and uncertainty before a new Eagle could have been chosen. Now they gathered at full strength, and because they'd driven off the Charpans and captured Kiri before she could harm Isandor, they would be confident of their abilities. They were also angry.

The two guards who brought her food and water once a day stared at her with a hatred she'd never faced. Even after all she had endured, it chilled her every time they entered the room. They'd made no move to harm her, but hostility came off them like steam.

On the second day, the taller guard had untied his trousers after putting the bowl of food on the ground. He'd urinated on the food and left with a sneer. Kiri hadn't minded not eating. With lying on the ground all day, she hadn't needed the energy and she'd had no appetite. As she'd sipped her water, she'd noticed her hands shaking. The guards frightened her more than she cared to admit.

When the door creaked open, Kiri sat up, placing her hands in her lap. The guards wouldn't let her stand when they came in, but she wouldn't lie on the ground as if beaten. She stared straight ahead, willing the guard to leave as soon as possible.

Instead of putting the food and water on the ground, he stood over her. Kiri's heart beat faster, but still she wouldn't give him the satisfaction of looking up at him.

"Kiri."

With a start, Kiri's gaze shot upward, meeting familiar hazel eyes.

Mattos stood with his helmet under his arm. His armor had been cleaned and polished since she'd last seen him. "Have they hurt you?" he asked.

Kiri shook her head.

Laying the bowl and cup on the ground, Mattos crouched before her. "Hungry?"

Kiri glanced at the food, still unsure what he wanted.

As if hearing her thoughts, Mattos said, "I'm not here to hurt you. If the Eagle were willing to let in men who wanted to kill you, the entire army would have been here already."

Kiri lifted the water to her lips, never taking her eyes from Mattos as she drank. "Why don't you hate me?" she asked, setting the cup down.

Mattos sat back with a sigh. "I'm not sure I don't, at least not a little bit. You killed one of my men. I should hate you. But I'm a reasonable person. The Eagle told me what you said, about what happened at Mar Dun."

When Kiri flinched, he smiled grimly. "I've never fought the Forest people, but even I've heard rumors of that village. Kordrick was one of my own men, though he refused to talk about it. I know imperial soldiers massacred a Forest village. I understand why you and your people want revenge. My people would have done the same, but they'd have sent an entire army, not one woman."

"One Forest woman was enough," Kiri said. "Many Forest people would have been seen and stopped. No one worried about one woman. Isandor would be dead if not for …" Her throat closed over the name. After swallowing, she said, "Ulek?"

"He's well. Mekindu plans to follow the Galeedan woman to Sarpaska to join that mystic. Ulek's going with them. You don't have to worry. Mekindu will look after him. Even his dog will live. He's well enough to travel with them."

Kiri nodded. Ulek might despise her, but at least he would be safe.

"He was looking for me," Mattos continued. "When he reached the camp, he told the guards he needed to speak with me. Of course, they refused him. Who'd believe a child who claimed to have seen a Forest woman running around at night so close to Ishtia? He made a lot of noise, so an Osprey came to see what caused all the commotion. Then Ulek said your name. The Osprey remembered how the Eagle had asked about you. He decided to take Ulek to see him. Once the Eagle heard what Ulek had to say, he knew you were coming for him. He's a smart man." Mattos shook his head. "Much smarter than I am. You tracked the Charpans when our own scouts couldn't. You can run like our best athletes. I saw you kill that Charpan. You admitted to killing men. Of course, you're a Forest woman. I was a fool not to see it."

He kept silent a few moments before he asked, "Why did you lie with me?"

Kiri blinked, trying to make sense of the question. Did the non-Forest people need a reason to mate? Did he think she'd done it as part of her plan? He'd already thought her a Wanderer. "A doe doesn't give a buck a reason," she finally said. "He doesn't ask for one."

Mattos sat back, eyes wide. "By Odern, you *are* a wild creature. You have no shame."

"Only the non-Forest think shame is a good thing."

Mattos swallowed. "Is that what it was? Two animals mating in the wild?"

The vulnerability beneath his stoic exterior tugged at Kiri's heart.

Something appeared to shatter in Mattos. His face crumpled as if he held back tears. He lowered his head, saying, "They're going to execute you."

Suppressing a shudder, Kiri asked, "How?"

Mattos lifted his head, his expression earnest. "It will be quick. Beheading is considered merciful. They say those who die that way don't suffer."

The image of the beheaded Charpans set Kiri's heart pounding. She recalled the Charpan who'd recognized her as Forest yet hadn't revealed her. She'd tracked him and his men and caused their capture and deaths. Had some part of him known she would meet the same end?

"When?"

"Tonight. After the sun has set."

Kiri closed her eyes. As the initial shock wore off, she felt … relieved. She hoped the spirits would forgive her for her failure.

"I considered not telling you," Mattos went on. "I didn't want you to have to count the hours until your death. But then I thought not knowing might be worse. Prisoners can be imaginative in the ways they might be tortured or killed. And someone would have to tell you eventually, or you'd see the sword and know. I wanted you to hear it from me."

Kiri opened her eyes to find Mattos staring at her.

"It would be treason for me to help you escape," he said, "and I'm no traitor. But it's not treason to beg for a woman's life, no matter what she's done or tried to do. I told Isandor how you tracked the Charpans and enabled us to retrieve the food they'd stolen. I told him how you've cared for Ulek. He wouldn't spare your life, but he promised your death would be merciful. In honor of how you helped the company and the Galeedans, he agreed to a private execution. Only Isandor, the executioner, and a few Hawks will be there."

When Kiri didn't react, Mattos grasped her hand. "It could have been much worse. Everyone wanted a public execution. You would have been screamed and jeered at by thousands. And if you'd been taken to Ishtia, you would have been marched through the streets in chains as a conquest. The entire city would have come to see the wild Forest girl humbled and executed. A year ago, *I* would have gone to see such a thing. I couldn't save your life, but I could make your death easier. I did fight for you, Kiri. As much as I could."

It struck Kiri then that this Sandamedan soldier cared for her the way a man cared for a woman he hoped to make his life mate.

She stared at their joined hands, afraid to look at Mattos's face. Cuts and scratches crisscrossed his hand, so much larger than her own. Bandages still covered his knuckles. They sat together, Kiri running a finger back and forth along his thumb for some time. Finally, Kiri looked up to meet Mattos's gaze. Seeing the grief in his eyes, she realized she felt the same about him. She'd come to love Orrik's son as a brother, but to care for an imperial soldier …

"Will you be there?" she asked.

"At your execution?" Mattos squeezed his eyes shut, his expression one of agony. Then he released a breath. Opening his eyes, he said, "I think the Eagle will allow it. I let Layna go, Marenda and our child were taken by the gods, and

I saw most of my men slaughtered by Charpans. I survived all that. So, yes, Kiri, if it will bring you any comfort, I will be there."

Kiri gripped his hand tighter. She couldn't hide her fear.

Mattos pulled her into an embrace as he whispered Sandamedan words.

Kiri buried her face in his neck as she'd done when they'd mated.

Someone banged on the door, calling out in Sandamedan.

"I have to go," Mattos said, extracting from the embrace. He stared down at her. "I will be there." Then he turned and walked out the door.

Chapter 57

KIRI

They came for her after dark. It wasn't the young men who'd been guarding her the past three days. These two soldiers looked older, with crested helmets and long capes. One of them freed her from the metal cuff, saying only, "Come."

Kiri walked between them through the town. Only three nights ago the moon had been full, and it still gave enough light that the soldiers didn't need torches. One of them kept a firm grip on her upper arm, as if fearing she would slip away in the darkness. Though the men said nothing, they didn't seem to regard her with the same hatred her guards had. Instead, they kept a kind of distance, as if an invisible wall separated them. Kiri tilted her head back, taking in the moon and stars. She hadn't realized the significance of what Mattos had done for her when she'd been chained in that tiny room. Now she understood he hadn't just spared her thousands of people screaming at her. He'd also seen to it that she would die under the stars on a peaceful night.

When they left the town, they walked past the army camp, heading into the hills. Kiri kept her gaze on the stars and took deliberate steps, mindful of the feel of the ground beneath her. Such sensations might not exist in the spirit world.

Three forms took shape in the darkness at the top of the hill Kiri and her guards ascended. As they drew closer, Kiri realized one of the forms was a horse. The other two were men, one tall, and the other shorter with a slight build. Then the details of their faces became apparent. Kiri recognized Isandor, but she'd never seen the tall soldier standing beside him. The hill leveled off at the top, providing them with a flat grassy area perfect for a ceremony. Kiri wondered if it had been carefully chosen ahead of time.

"Where is Mattos?" Kiri asked. The guard who'd been gripping her arm released her. It hadn't occurred to her that Mattos wouldn't keep his promise, or that the Eagle wouldn't let him come.

"He will be here," Isandor replied. "I've summoned him. Let us talk while we wait. Walk with me." When Kiri hesitated, he smiled. "Are you in a hurry to die?"

"I am ready to die," Kiri said, lifting her chin.

"No, you are too young. Even soldiers eager to fight and kill don't want to die. But I admire your courage. If your people didn't have courage, we wouldn't be speaking now. You would be dead already."

As he spoke, Kiri noticed the sword, longer and wider than the blades soldiers usually carried, hanging from the tall soldier's belt. Willing herself not to shudder, Kiri fell into step with the Eagle.

"Do you know why this war started?" Isandor asked, coming to a halt.

"No."

"The war started because the emperor is a greedy fool. Were I to say that in public, I'd be executed, but it's the truth. I'm an Eagle, not an emperor. I don't declare wars, I just win them, and my soldiers fight them. This war can't be won without a land route. The Sandamedan Army is the greatest in the world, but they fight on foot. They aren't sailors or horsemen, but the Charpans are. The emperor won't accept defeat. He would have the army destroy itself down to the last man on the Charpan beaches before he gave up. What should I do, girl? Let the emperor destroy my army? Or do I destroy your people for the sake of a land route? Those are my only choices."

Kiri didn't answer.

"Killing me would not have saved your people," Isandor said. "Another man would have taken my place. Your people could never withstand the full might and numbers of the Sandamedan Army. I will burn every tree down if I must. I still don't know how your people stop the fires, but I promise that for every fire put out, I'll start two more. In the end, after thousands of soldiers and Forest people are dead, I will win. You've seen my army. You know this now. But there is a way for both of us to save our people. Your people could let us travel through your lands. In return, no Forest people would be harmed or killed. No village would be destroyed. No food would be stolen."

"They will not agree."

"Not if you aren't there. But you, who have seen the might of the Sandamedan Army, can convince them."

Kiri looked at the soldier with the long sword in confusion.

"I will spare your life, Kiri," Isandor said, "if you agree to return to your people and tell them what you have seen here. Tell them they must let us through, or die."

Kiri shook her head. "Your people tried before. It was no good."

"A few hundred men tried before. The emperor was in a hurry, and the admiral was ambitious. They ordered ships built to carry soldiers to Charpa. The emperor didn't listen to me. But our navy has failed, and the emperor is listening to me now. All our efforts will be turned on your people. This will not be like before."

Kiri didn't answer. She didn't want to speak for the Eagle, even as she felt a desperate panic to warn her people. Isandor's tone, expression, and posture revealed he spoke the truth. She'd seen the army with her own eyes. They'd driven off the Charpans, even though the Charpans had horses and they did not. The Sandamedans were fierce warriors.

Seeing her hesitation, Isandor continued: "If your people were weak, I would not make this offer. We would march into your villages as we pleased, and your people would be wise to scatter. But your people understand the power of fear. The stories I've heard of your tactics are the stuff of nightmares. A soldier is a fool not to be afraid before battle, but the kind of terror your people create spreads like a disease. I can't have that in my army, so I'm willing to negotiate. Let that be a comfort to you."

Kiri turned to face south. To go home. To see her family again. To warn them. To live. How would they react? What would her people say when she admitted she'd bargained with him to save her own life instead of killing him? How could she face them and admit her failure, then urge them to give in—to let imperial soldiers walk through their lands? "I promised my people I would kill you, that I would give my life to do so."

Isandor's tone became imploring. "Orrik and Kordrick both served the empire. You murdered them, and I, the Eagle of the Sandamedan Empire's army, am letting you go. It's treason for me to set you free after murdering a soldier, but I'm doing it. I'm doing it for the love of my people and my army. I'm doing it to save lives. We would both be breaking promises to our people, but we would be doing it to save them. Executing you in the name of obeying the laws of my empire would mean losing my only chance to save soldiers' lives. Dying today to fulfill your promise would mean losing your only chance to save Forest lives. It's up to us, Kiri. What will we do?"

Kiri whirled around. "I did not murder! My elders told me to kill them just as you tell soldiers to kill Charpans. Do soldiers murder?"

Isandor raised his eyebrows. "Their deaths were acts of war? As I said, your people have questionable tactics."

If Kiri refused Isandor, she'd be executed but would keep her promise to her people. If she agreed, she would have to return home and admit that not only had she failed, but she'd promised to carry a message from the man she'd sworn to kill. When she thought of facing everyone, death seemed preferable. But if she didn't agree, then her people would have no warning. How could she make such a decision for her people without an elder to guide her? She had only her own judgment. "How can my people trust you?"

"I'll send a small group with gifts first," Isandor promised. "There wouldn't be enough of them to harm your people. They'd only be guests in your forest. An ambassador would lead them, and, if your people allowed it, they would live in your villages. The people sent would be highly valued by the empire, and they would be at the mercy of your people. Once the army arrives, they wouldn't do anything to endanger the lives of the ambassador or those who came with him. So long as your people let us through your lands, we would have no reason to harm you. Our war is with Charpa."

Isandor needed her. Kiri saw that now. And his need brought truth to his words. And if he spoke the truth, her people had to be warned. Drawing herself to her full height, Kiri looked Isandor in the eye. "I will go."

Relief passed over Isandor's face. "Thank you, Kiri," he said, his voice strong with emotion. "Thank you."

As Kiri stepped toward the waiting soldiers, she realized she shook uncontrollably. She had escaped death yet again.

A tall figure joined the soldiers, and Kiri recognized Mattos's gait. Still shaking, Kiri made her way to him.

Then someone much smaller stepped out from behind him.

Kiri froze as she and Ulek gazed at each other. Kiri's heart pounded in her ears. Neither of them spoke. Something wet touched her fingers. Glancing down, she saw Brense nuzzling her hand. As Mattos had said, he'd recovered well. She stroked the dog's head before he trotted back to Ulek.

"Who brought that boy here?" Isandor said, his voice furious.

"Please, Eagle," Mattos began. "These two have become attached. The boy is the reason Kiri was caught. This day will haunt him the rest of his life if they don't have a chance to speak."

Ulek stared at the long sword hanging from the soldier's belt. "Don't kill her," he said.

The world spun. Kiri sank to one knee to steady herself. Everyone's voice sounded far away.

"She killed your father. I thought you wanted her dead," Isandor said.

"I did at first. But now . . . Fal— Harrier Mattos told me she's a Forest soldier. She followed her orders. Her village was attacked. Bad things happened."

Tears slid down Kiri's face. She stared into Ulek's eyes, seeing his father's eyes. They gazed at each other before Kiri choked out, "Ulek." When he came to her, she pulled him into an embrace. At first, he tensed, and she wondered if he would pull away or hit her. Then he relaxed into her, almost knocking her over. As Kiri and Ulek held each other, Kiri noticed Mattos and Isandor speaking.

Mattos turned to stare at her, a look of surprised joy in his face.

One of the soldiers with a crested helmet brought the horse forward.

Isandor approached Kiri and Ulek. "There's plenty of food in the saddlebag, as well as Galeedan clothes. You won't pass as Galeedan, but it's better than dressing as a Forest woman. Travel the way you came, through the mountains, and you should avoid the Charpans. They haven't gone back to Charpa. They're licking their wounds until they can fight us again, but they aren't looking for a lone woman on a horse. I know the Forest people don't like horses, but this one's a gentle mare and you'll travel much faster with her."

Kiri rose and walked toward the horse. It had a dark brown coat, with a black mane and tail. When she placed a hand on its shoulder, it bent its head to sniff her. Kiri turned to look back at Ulek. She cared for Mattos, perhaps more than she wanted to admit, but he belonged to his people as much as she belonged to hers. His world was one of steel, stone carved into humans, war, and words on paper. But Ulek … "Come with me."

Ulek blinked. "What?"

"Come with me, to my people. Be my brother."

Ulek gaped at her. "I— you killed my father. I don't want you dead, but I can't …"

Kiri rushed to him, grabbing his upper arms. "Be my brother. You will have a family, a village. You will be loved."

"I can't just become a Forest boy."

"If you come, you'll see. We will teach you the Forest way. My brothers will be your brothers. My sister will be your sister. You'll have a place, a home."

Ulek looked at Mattos and Isandor, who appeared stunned. Whatever Mattos's reason for bringing Ulek, it hadn't been this.

Finally, Ulek turned back to Kiri, his face revealing his internal battle. Tears swam in his eyes. Then he spoke in a choking voice, "Yes."

They walked together to the horse. Kiri climbed on first, then helped Ulek up behind her.

As Mattos stepped up to the horse, he slipped his hand under Kiri's pant leg to grasp her bare ankle. He said nothing as they stared at each other.

"I'm happy you survived the battle, Mattos," Kiri said. "I wish you well. And thank you … for fighting for me."

Mattos cleared his throat, as if struggling for words. "From now until the day I die, I will think of you every time it rains."

"Goodbye, Harrier," Ulek said.

Kiri kicked the horse's sides as she had learned to do. Mattos's hand fell away as the horse began to trot. With a short bark, Brense took off after them.

Chapter 58

MATTOS

Mattos watched them go. How could the boy choose a culture, a way of life so different from everything he knew?

"By Odern, I didn't expect that," Isandor said. "But I suppose it's good the boy is with her. He can ride much better than she, and this is his country."

"His father killed her friends and loved ones, then she killed his father, and now she adopts him as a brother?" Mattos wondered aloud.

"Strange things happen in war," Isandor replied. "The rules we've been taught from birth shift." He gestured to the men standing nearby. "These men are loyal to me; they won't speak a word of tonight. I'll inform the emperor the Forest girl who tried to kill me is dead. Every single one of us would be executed if the emperor learned otherwise." Isandor cast a sideline glance at Mattos. "I don't think silence will be difficult for you since you so emphatically argued in favor of letting the girl live."

"I won't speak the truth of tonight until I look upon Odern's face," Mattos promised. He watched the horse and dog run into the distance. "What if her people don't listen?"

"They will listen," Isandor said. "She's the only Forest person to travel so far from their lands. She's seen and done things none of the others have ever dared to do. Her people sent her to us to die, but she lived to return to them riding an animal they fear. She will be a queen among her people."

"We will see."

"*You* will see when you go to the Forest lands, *ambassador*."

"Ambassador?" Mattos spun to face Isandor. "Eagle, you can't mean— I'm only a Harrier—a brand-new one."

Isandor chuckled. "You still don't understand. You're the hero of Cybelon. The entire army knows your name. Even now a messenger rides to Ishtia with news of how you held off the horde in Cybelon until the army arrived. You will be respected throughout the empire. You have a bond with Kiri and argued for her life. You were present when I freed her and gave her a horse to help her return home. That should gain you some goodwill among the Forest people."

"I didn't do anything the officers and soldiers who fell didn't do," Mattos said. "I was just one of the lucky few who survived."

"Heroes are often just the lucky few who survive."

"I can't be an ambassador," Mattos insisted. "I don't even speak their language."

"Nobody who isn't Forest does," Isandor replied, "and I hear you have a gift for languages. It shouldn't take you long to learn." His voice became firm. "You'll do it because the emperor will name you once I tell him you're the most qualified person. You'll do it because your empire needs you to do it. But mostly you'll do it because you want to. How else will you see her again?" The Eagle turned and started down the hill. "Join me for a drink, ambassador," he called out. "We have much to plan."

About the Author

J. H. Dahler is the author of *The Forest Girl*, her debut fantasy novel. After eighteen years as a librarian, she waved goodbye to spend more time with family and focus on writing her high fantasy series. Hiking and traveling are at the top of her to-do list, especially to ancient ruins and stunning landscapes, but she's also dedicated to the cozy life: curling up with a good book and snuggling her two dogs. Jodie lives outside of Baltimore, Maryland, with her son and husband.

Connect with the Author

www.jhdahler.com
tiktok.com/@jhdahlerauthor.com

Leave a Review

If you enjoyed *The Forest Girl*, will you consider leaving a review on your platform of choice? Reviews help indie authors get more readers like you.

Author Q and A:

1. Which character did you come up with first? Kiri, Mattos, Ulek? Someone else?

Kiri came to me fully formed before I thought of any other characters, world, or even a plot. I built the entire story around her.

2. How do you keep all the different nations and armies and characters straight in your head? Do you have an Excel sheet or table to keep track of everything?

I kept a simple Word document with every culture listed. At first, I had to refer to it, but once I got immersed in the story, it was easy to remember.

3. What was the hardest scene for you to write? Why?

The battle scenes were, by far, the hardest! I had to convey what was happening well enough so the reader could see it, include the POV character's thoughts and emotions, and avoid repetition and indeterminate pronouns. The last part is especially hard when two people of the same gender are fighting, and you don't know the name of one of them. This is something I never appreciated in others' writing until I attempted a fight scene myself. I've found the easiest scenes for me to write involve dialogue between two characters of different genders.

4. How long did it take you to write *The Forest Girl*?

As embarrassing as it is to admit, this book took me about fifteen years to write. Multiple times I put it aside to balance life, like having a baby, with my full-time job. I'm not one of those people who can get up at five to write, get their kids up and ready for school by eight, kick butt in a demanding career, and then cook, clean, check homework, and hit the gym in the evening. I admire them, but I don't have the energy to join their ranks. I like my sleep.

That being said, this was my first book, and I was learning as I went. I attended classes and read plenty of books on writing. I also spent considerable time researching ancient civilizations, battle tactics, tracking, etc. Most of the research never made it into the book, but that's how it goes. Once I started my second book, I was amazed at how much faster it went.

5. How do you come up with the names for your characters and settings? Especially ones like Ozias, Lentavus, and Diakiris?

This was a lot harder than I thought it would be. I'd think I'd made up a name, only to google it and find out it already existed. I learned that if it sounds like a name, especially if it's pretty, it already exists in the world or someone else's fantasy book. I became sensitive to using names that belonged to other cultures, or that had been used by other fantasy authors, but realized it was unavoidable. Humans have been putting sounds together to make names for a long time; everything has been taken. I thought I'd made up Kiri and used it a long time before I researched it. It turns out, it's a name in multiple cultures, and in Maori, it means "tree bark." I'd say that meaning is pretty serendipitous.

I wanted the names to fit the culture/language they belonged to. Ozias, Lentavus, and Diakiris are Sandamedan, and I wanted Sandamedan names to sound Greek or Latin.

6. **Kiri eventually decides to help her enemies live. She learns forgiveness. Was that always where you wanted to go with this novel, or did it just happen organically?**

I think Kiri's biggest realization at the end is related to Otto Ludwig's famous quote: "His highest ideal was at first to die gloriously for something; now his ideal is the supreme one: to live humbly for something." Kiri's plan was to go out in a blaze of glory and vengeance, but ultimately, she realizes the best way to protect her people is to return home and admit she failed. She'll also have to convince them to give in and let the Sandamedans in their lands. It's a humbling path, but one that will save tens of thousands of lives. I always knew Kiri would fail, but the ending happened organically.

7. **Mattos becomes a wise leader. What did you hope readers would learn from him?**

He has a strong sense of responsibility and a desire to fulfill his duties, which are admirable qualities, but he doesn't question the expectations and edicts of his family, his culture, his religion, or the army. He's managed to suppress his conscience at great personal cost. By the end of the story, Mattos has begun the journey of listening to his own moral compass. I hope readers who struggle with the same issues learn to listen to their consciences.

8. Did you model the Sandamedan Empire after any empires from history or from other novels?

I modeled the Sandamedan Empire loosely after the Roman Empire. I kept the skilled engineers, invention of cement, ethnically diverse legions, patriarchy, and desire for conquest. I also kept some social mores, like the focus on duty and desire for social status.

Made in the USA
Middletown, DE
08 November 2022

14325026R00222